A Crimson Splendour

A Crimson Splendour

Alfred Draper

PIATKUS

Apart from some obvious exceptions, the
characters in this book are entirely fictitious. No
such regiment as the Rocks exists.

Copyright © 1991 by Alfred Draper

First published in Great Britain in 1991 by
Judy Piatkus (Publishers) Ltd of
5 Windmill Street, London W1

**The moral right of the author
has been asserted**

*A catalogue record for this book is available
from the British Library*

ISBN 0 7499 0090 3

Phototypeset in 11/12pt Compugraphic Times by
Action Typesetting Limited, Gloucester
Printed and bound in Great Britain by
Butler & Tanner Ltd, Frome and London

It is courage, courage, courage, that raises
the blood of life to crimson splendour

– George Bernard Shaw,
Back to Methuselah

Chapter One

He paused for breath during his ascent of the steep staircase, worn smooth by the feet of countless pilgrims, which led to the platform supporting the pagoda that was the most revered shrine of Theravada Buddhism. The Shwe Dagon seemed to float high above the city of Rangoon as if aware of its hallowed status. The summit of its cupola was higher than the dome of St Paul's Cathedral, and the impression that it was suspended in space was enhanced by the fact that it was built on an eminence 168 feet above the most famous port in the Far East. The man-made hill was believed by the devout to be a deliberate attempt to put the pagoda as close as humanly possible to paradise, but the real reason for the extra elevation was more mundane: the ground on which the shrine stood had once been a stagnant swamp liable to heavy flooding. Like so many other things in life the myth was more attractive than reality.

It was a hot airless morning without the slightest puff of wind to set in motion the hundreds of gold and silver bells which normally tinkled a melodic accompaniment to the chanted prayers of the faithful.

The pagoda had been his first glimpse of Burma when he had sailed up the Rangoon River and seen it from the deck of the ship that had brought him from Calcutta. Then the burnished gold of the cupola, glinting like a beckoning star in the fierce noonday sun, had appeared to be transmitting celestial messages. And, like so many others, that first sighting had ensnared him and he had fallen in love with the country and its people. Since then he had visited the

1

pagoda many times. It was often the first call on a regular excursion which took him to the Royal Lake, through the teeming cosmopolitan streets, down to the non-stop bustle of the ship-crowded port.

Sergeant Harris was by choice a solitary man who preferred to spend his off-duty days perambulating the city, savouring its sights and smells, instead of swilling beer in the sergeants' mess. Although he was aware that some of his fellow senior NCOs regarded him as a 'rum sod' it did not worry him. What concerned him more was the knowledge that the rankers respected him for being extremely efficient, and very much concerned for their personal welfare. That was all that mattered to him. He knew too that some of the sergeants thought him a bit 'la-di-dah', with an accent that was somehow out of place among men who had had little formal education. They suspected he had some dark secret he was anxious to conceal, and there had been occasions when none too subtle attempts had been made to pump him about his past, even to the extent of suggesting that Harris was not his real name. One particularly inquisitive CSM had gone to the trouble of looking through his service record, but that he knew had revealed little other than that he had enlisted in the Regiment's home town seven years earlier, been rapidly promoted, and sent out to Burma as a replacement for a man who had died of cholera. But with the passing of time the questioning had ceased for the regular army was full of men who wanted to escape from something or other: maintenance arrears, the dole queue, bigamy, or sheer boredom, and if a man sought anonymity he was entitled to it. The army was overpopulated with Smiths, Joneses, Browns – and Harrises too for that matter.

Ironically in view of his deep affection for Burma, he hoped it would not be long before he saw the pagoda receding into the distance from the stern of a ship homeward bound for England. Although Burma, in soldiers' parlance, was a 'cushy number', it was no place for a regular when 'home' was in imminent danger of being overrun by the most efficient and ruthless military regime the world had ever witnessed. Since the outbreak of war against Hitler's Germany, Britain had suffered a series of calamitous defeats. Its

2

army had been miraculously evacuated from the beaches at Dunkirk, and there had been further humiliating evacuations from Norway, Greece and Crete. Now London and other major cities were being pounded to rubble as a prelude to the launching of Operation Sealion – the invasion of Britain. Standing by to repel the invaders was a poorly equipped army supported by the Home Guard, a civilian force armed with pikes, cudgels, sporting guns and antiquated firearms retrieved from museum vaults and the gun rooms of stately homes. Harris was plagued by a sense of guilt. That was where he should be, not in Burma where life continued in its hedonistic peacetime way. He had in fact been born in India, but it never occurred to him to think of England as anything but 'home'.

His frustration was further increased by the knowledge that everyone happily accepted that Burma was a military back-water, where knowledge of the war's progress depended on a good wireless set and the scant reports which appeared in the *Rangoon Gazette*. Quite recently Duff Cooper, Churchill's Minister of Information, in a fleeting visit had apologised to the small British army stationed there for missing out on the fighting, and Harris had felt like giving him a good kick up the arse. The politician had had no idea how much resentment his patronising remarks had aroused among men who had no wish to sit out the war performing ceremonials, taking part in manoeuvres which no one believed would ever be put to practical use, playing endless games of football and wasting their energy in fruitless tug-of-war competitions thousands of miles from the real thing. The dandified minister had added insult to injury by confidently predicting that the war would never reach the Far East. To which Harris's unspoken response had been: Then what the hell are we doing here?

Most of the garrison troops were long service regulars who had not seen Blighty for many years, but to whom King and Country was more than an empty slogan. It was an affront to their professional pride to know that the defence of both was being left to an army of conscripts and volunteers. They felt like boxers who had trained hard and long, only to be told they would not be allowed in the ring. And yet so great was the complacency in London that young officers posted to Burma to replace senior NCOs who had been commissioned and sent home to stiffen the new army that was being built up, had been advised to take mess kit and polo equipment, and make sure that they had an adequate supply of visiting cards, because the custom of 'dropping' them was rigidly adhered to, and anyone who failed to comply with etiquette would find themselves a social leper.

These thoughts passed through the sergeant's mind as he moved to the side of the covered staircase and removed the heavy 'coal scuttle' topee which was more likely to cause heatstroke than protect the wearer from sunstroke. Harris fanned himself with the rim. That was all it was good for. Every old sweat knew from experience that the antiquated headgear was one of the most useless items of the many issued by the army, but they also knew it was a disciplinary offence to be seen without it during the hours of daylight. He mopped his brow with a khaki handkerchief and conjectured with considerable pleasure how many pints of ice cold beer he would need to consume to replace the liquid he had sweated out. Five at least in his favourite bar near the YMCA, one of the few not out of bounds to BORs.

He replaced his helmet, adjusted the chin strap and resumed his climb. It was just as well, he mused, that Hitler's armies were too overstretched on too many fronts even to contemplate attacking this outpost of Empire, because the small military presence was woefully ill-equipped to resist the onslaught of a determined assault. His own battalion might have a surfeit of topees in the stores but it did not possess one tin helmet. There was also an acute shortage of automatic weapons; mortars, Bren-carriers and mechanised transport. As for the uniforms they wore it was as if someone had been asked to design the most inappropriate apparel for fighting in Burma where malaria and other tropical diseases were rampant, and any exposed skin was an open invitation to dinner for the countless insects which thrived on human blood. It consisted of an open neck shirt, heavily starched shorts which reached down to the knee caps, hosetops bearing the regimental colours, ankle puttees, heavy boots, and a pipe-clayed belt. The only thing to be said in favour of the

4

inelegant Bombay Bloomers was that they distinguished the men from the boys, for sun-tanned knees were the hallmark of long service − a point not lost on new arrivals who were cut down to size with the retort, 'Get some sun on your knees, lad.'

Harris found no consolation in the knowledge that the other two battalions of the British Army in Burma, the KOYLI up country, and the Glosters also in Rangoon, were no better off. He wondered what strings he could pull to wangle a posting back to the 2nd Battalion on duty on the South Coast of England. He had missed one opportunity when he had turned down the chance of a temporary commission because that might have meant a probe into his past, which did not bear scrutiny.

In appearance he was what some military writers described as the perfect infantryman: four inches short of six feet with an erectness that made him look taller, and a compact well-muscled physique capable of marching twenty miles in the dehydrating heat with a pack on his back that would have made many much bigger men wilt. His dark hair was cropped too short to be described in any fanciful way, and he disdained the moustache so favoured by many of his fellow sergeants. His features were strong and regular, and most women would have described him as good-looking, but for a scar which ran from the corner of his right eye down to the side of his mouth which no exposure to the sun had managed to conceal. As soon as he spoke it was obvious he had not come from the deprived background from which the army drew so many of its recruits. When he smiled, which was rarely, the scar gave him a slightly sardonic appearance, which was misleading for he was a man of quiet integrity. The army was the be all and end all of his existence, and like a tank or a rifle he was moulded for just one thing − fighting. The knowledge that he was not doing what he had dedicated his life to was gnawing away at his intestines like a maggot inside an outwardly perfect apple.

He was disturbed from his reverie by a half blind beggar who tugged at his shirt and intoned in a sing-song incantation words that he knew to mean, 'By your pity alone can I eat.' He dropped some small coins into the extended bowl thinking that Burma really was the land of waving palms, and cadging a commendable occupation there. The most respected members of the community were the hpoongyis, the shaven headed monks in their saffron robes who had to exist on what was given them. It seemed an anachronism to him that humility and the lack of worldly goods were so highly valued when the pagoda was covered from base to summit with pure gold, and had an unseen weather vane which was studded with thousands of diamonds, emeralds and rubies. It was even more remarkable to him that the gold-encased edifice had been erected over a relic chamber which was said to contain something as uninspiring as a hair or tooth, he could not remember which, of the great God Buddha himself. It was a contradiction which appealed to him. A bit like the army he served and worshipped; demanding all and giving little in return.

As he neared the top he was relentlessly accosted by vendors of gold leaf, for it was considered a privilege to add a personal contribution to the exterior of the shrine, together with sellers of tapers, incense, flowers, mirrors, beads and other trinkets. Around the praying platforms were grotesque gryphon-like statues with red, lolling tongues and rolling eyes, multi-coloured dragons and massive elephants kneeling in postures of mute supplication. But what impressed him most was the total lack of hushed reverence encountered in Christian churches. There were countless pretty girls wearing small black pill-box hats with a flower tucked behind one ear, a brightly coloured silk shirt and a white muslin jacket with a splendid shawl draped over one shoulder, their childlike faces caked with thanaka, casting flirtatious glances at the young men who passed. They were, he thought, among the most beautiful women in the world despite the huge white cheroots clamped between their teeth which had been stained by betel nut. They had the appearance of being breastless, but he knew from personal experience this was untrue; their bodies were every bit as voluptuous as the most nubile European woman's. But large breasts were considered unfeminine here and so they bound them, much as Chinese women did their feet.

He heard the sound of prayers coming from the tazoungs,

but decided not to venture inside because that meant removing his heavy boots, a tiresome business and also risky because army boots were much prized. He peered through the gloomy entrances, and in the light of the flickering tapers he could see the images of Buddha, once rather simple effigies but now encased in layer upon layer of gold leaf, each skin-thick investment carefully placed by those who sought to buy a one way ticket to heaven. From time to time a big bell tolled and he knew it had been struck by a pilgrim who had made a large donation and was anxious to make sure that his bid for nirvana – that state of total bliss to which all good Buddhists aspire – had not gone unnoticed. There was, he had discovered, a touch of pragmatism in the Burmese: they did not hide their spiritual light under a bushel. When they had made a biggish donation they struck one of the tongueless bells with a deer horn, just in case the Recording Angel had dozed off.

Harris's own religious beliefs were too nebulous for him to be cynical of the Buddhist. A man shrewd enough to buy his way to heaven was not to be despised or underestimated. As far as he was concerned church parade was just another part of army life; a duty which had to be fulfilled. As compulsory as PT or a short-arm inspection. But he could not deny the feeling of exhilaration when the battalion marched through the streets of Rangoon to the stirring music of the regimental march to attend divine service in the Cathedral, although he personally preferred the more 'family' nature of the service when it was held on the parade ground and the piled drums served as an altar with the colours resting against them in readiness for a blessing from the padre. Like most soldiers he did not have a great faith in the efficacy of prayer, being more conditioned to believe 'if it's got your name on it', which ensured you went towards the gunfire and not away from it. Nevertheless, he was prepared to hedge his bets and get down on his knees when it came to survival.

So how could he criticise the Buddhist who had acquired great wealth and wanted to show some physical proof of his goodness by building little sugar-white pagodas of sun-baked bricks so that he could be entitled to be called Phaya-Taga – one who had achieved great spiritual attainment. It was

7

certainly less arrogant than the expatriate Britons who had amassed great fortunes from a country they ruthlessly exploited while talking earnestly about the 'white man's burden' yet insisting on being addressed as Burra Sahib and Thakin.

Harris enjoyed these discussions with himself about the relative merits of the two religions because the army did not encourage any conversations of a controversial nature; any discussion of politics and religion was strictly taboo because they led to fisticuffs, which meant that talk in the barracks largely centred around women, booze and sport.

After an hour he had had enough of gold and incense and retraced his steps down the staircase and made his way to the Royal Lake where he stood admiring the youngsters engaging each other in aerial combat with their fighting kites before making his way towards the centre of the town. He lingered in the Chinese quarter where the carcasses of gleaming red ducks hung bill-down on long racks and dried fish carpeted the pavements, and the exotic aroma of freshly cooked food wafted from the stalls and barrows which were so numerous it was difficult to imagine how they all prospered. A pineapple man with a tray balanced precariously on his head clanged a bell with his free hand, touting for custom. There were men selling ice cream, lemonade and vermicelli, and girls with hair the colour of a crow's wing selling betel nut and cheroots which ranged in size from nearly a foot long to others no bigger than a cigarette. From there he went to the Indian quarter, reeking of spices and housing the work benches of the silversmiths, wood carvers and umbrella makers. He felt quite drab in his heavily starched khaki as he was jostled by women in blazing saris, Persians in elegant frock coats and Burmese men in gaily coloured longyis and short eye-dazzling jackets, a gaung-baung of silk wound round their heads. Disdaining any desire to emulate the peacock was a naked Coringhi with rings in his nose. Harris felt a little better for seeing him.

Old Burma hands, especially the 'jungle wallahs' — a term which loosely lumped together anyone who worked up country in timber, oil, tungsten or rubber — dismissed Rangoon as not being the *real* Burma. To see that you had to travel to the land of the Kachins, Karens, Shans and the giraffe-necked women of Loikam. There one encountered torrential rivers, dense forests of teak and rhododendrons abounding with game and birds, and a simplicity of life that was as near as one could get to an earthly paradise. It could well be true as far as Harris was concerned for he had never been further north than the barracks which were situated on the outskirts of the town like an old Locke hospital, because the army was not very popular and, although necessary, best kept at arm's length.

Harris was well aware that the primary reason for the presence of his battalion was what were known as Internal Security Duties, and Duties in Aid of the Civil Power, which meant they were no more than glorified policemen who could be called out to restore law and order when racial conflict broke out between the various communities. These were the most onerous duties which the regular soldier was called upon to perform, for they were fraught with disaster. Riots and insurrection could only be suppressed by the use of the *minimum* amount of force necessary to restore law and order, something which deliberately had never been clearly defined. What he did know from personal experience was that any action, no matter how successful, was usually considered excessive by the inevitable enquiry that followed any disturbance. This enabled the civil powers to adopt a Pontius Pilate attitude and deplore the over zealous conduct of the troops. A sledge hammer had always been used to crack a walnut.

As he strolled through the congested streets and observed Muslims who slaughtered cows mingling with Hindus who revered them as sacred and Burmans who did not seem to resent their presence in their land, he knew that the tolerance was only superficial and festering below the surface was a deep and intense hatred that at any time was likely to erupt into an orgy of violence. But there was no sign of it today; all was multi-racial harmony in which a live and let live atmosphere prevailed, and Harris with his soldier's inbuilt optimism was determined to enjoy his day off. One should never anticipate the next battle, just appreciate the lull.

He continued through streets which bore names such as

9

Dalhousie, in memory of the great Viceroy in the days when Burma was ruled from Delhi, and others which were simply numbered, American-style. Swaying tramcars with clanging bells vied with rickshaws hauled by panting coolies and slow moving carts drawn by slate-grey bullocks. Automobiles of all sizes and makes, from prestigious Rolls-Royces to clapped out bangers, hooted their horns, scattering the pedestrians like startled pigeons.

Architecturally the fusion of east and west was even more incongruous. There were two imposing cathedrals – one RC, the other C of E – numerous churches of every denomination, temples for Hindus, mosques for Muslims, synagogues for Jews, and places of worship for Armenians and Parsees. In some of the more squalid back streets there were timber hovels on which lines of washing fluttered like distress signals, while around the Lake and other salubrious areas were the homes of the better off Europeans, built in mock-Tudor style, which could have been transported brick by brick from a Surrey stockbroker belt. There were cinemas, hotels, gambling dens and fetid opium houses standing cheek by jowl with colonnaded Victorian edifices housing the Secretariat, Law Courts and other administrative departments, all solid reminders that although numerically outnumbered the British held the reins of Government. There were also the offices of the big companies such as Steel Brothers, the Bombay Burmah Trading Corporation, Jardine Matheson, Burmah Oil and Ellerman's; the seats of power of the 'box wallahs' who controlled much of the timber, rice, oil and mineral resources of the vastly rich country.

Over their chota pegs in their exclusive clubs the 'box wallahs' who did not give a damn for being considered the social inferiors of the elite civil servants or resentful at being named after the itinerant Indian door-to-door salesman who carried his wares in a suitcase, proudly boasted that they were the *real* rulers. What they did have in common with the 'government wallahs' was the firm conviction that it was only the white man's presence which enabled this pot-pourri of contrasting races and cultures to blend together like the instruments in a well-conducted orchestra. While courteous and paternalistic to those not fortunate enough to have a

10

white skin, they remained socially aloof and kept their clubs closed to Chinese, Indians, Burmese, and the unfortunate offspring of a casual coupling between white and brown.

They believed that everyone preferred it that way, especially the Burmese. On the surface the indigenous population, of whom there were 112,000 in Rangoon, appeared an indolent, often work-shy people, seemingly content with their lot and willing to be dominated by their benevolent masters, having no aspirations for complete self-government and extremely grateful for being allowed to have a partial say in the running of their own country. But the bland exterior cloaked a proud nationalism which was encouraged and fanned by the growing number of politically motivated priests. This had been reported by Army Intelligence, but the claims had been dismissed as alarmist and ill-founded. It was obvious to anyone with a pair of eyes that Burma was the showpiece of the Empire.

The Burmese were vastly outnumbered by the Indian community, mostly Tamils from Southern India who had been brought in to build the roads, docks, and railways, and remained to crew the paddle steamers, fill most of the labouring jobs, man the police force, drive the taxis, pull the rickshaws and remove the 'night soil' from the 'thunder boxes', jobs which the Burmese had no desire to take away. Even so, the Indians were hated and reviled by the Burmese largely because their ranks included the money lenders who had attained great wealth by the exorbitant rates of interest they charged, and who had become powerful landowners by buying out the more profligate Burmese who had the national weakness for reckless gambling. But what galled the indigenous people most was the undisguised contempt the Indians had for the country; they made no attempt to put down roots, preferring to send the money they made back to the homeland to which they aspired to return.

The Chinese kept very much to themselves, exercising their entrepreneural skills without causing too much offence. The smaller Japanese community were largely dentists, hairdressers and photographers. Many of the latter were spies who regularly reported on military activities and used their cameras to take pictures of vital installations which they sent

11

back to Tokyo. But nobody was aware of their nefarious activities because no one bothered to check. The idea that Japan constituted a menace was too far-fetched even to merit consideration. They had their hands full fighting the Chinese in Manchuria. Apart from that, they must know they were no match for the highly trained, well-disciplined British troops. It was common knowledge that the Japs were so short-sighted they could not hit a barn door from ten feet.

There were also some 20,000 Anglo-Burmans who filled many of the subordinate positions in government service and the bigger companies. They were hard working and more British than the British, but unlike their counterparts in India were not despised and subjected to derisory appelations such as 'cafe au lait' and 'chilli cracker'. Although what were known as 'companionable marriages' up-country were not officially encouraged, they were quite common and many of the European bachelors took Burmese mistresses, happy in the knowledge that such liaisons would not affect the girl's marriage prospects because Burmese men were extremely broad minded in such matters. Most of the European bachelors lived in communal accommodation known as 'chummeries', and it was said that the rear staircases had been worn as smooth as those leading to the Shwe Dagon by the feet of the girls who crept silently up them.

Sergeant Harris had no deep feelings about the careful social classifications though he was as much a victim of it as any native. BORs were treated as pariahs, coarse men who swore, drank too much, frequented whore houses and did not know how to conduct themselves in polite society. He had even known people move to another railway carriage when a soldier had entered. Yet for all their shortcomings they were a necessary evil. It was comforting to know that Tommy Atkins was at hand in the unlikely event of anyone lighting the fuse to the powder keg the pessimists harked on about. Harris hoped their optimism was justified and the heat had not caused partial amnesia, because no great period of time had elapsed since the Burmese had given vent to their hatred of the Indians. In 1938 a protest meeting at the Shwe Dagon pagoda had developed into an anti-Indian rampage. Shops were destroyed and looted, and several

12

Indians murdered. The police had been unable to cope and the army had been called out and forced to open fire on the rioters.

Harris did not suffer from a short memory. He could still vividly recall every minute of it. He had been leading a small foot patrol which he had ordered to open fire when they encountered a group of people about to set fire to an Indian they had doused with petrol. A priest who appeared to be some kind of ring leader had been killed by a bullet from a Lee Enfield and loud protests had been made to the Governor that a holy man who would not hurt a fly had been foully murdered. The inevitable inquiry followed and he had been immensely relieved when it was found that he had *not* used excessive force. But it had been touch and go and he had been forced to sweat blood. The memories had come flooding back as he had sat in the stuffy court room and had feared that history might repeat itself and the past catch up on him. But he had been absolved of any improper action and allowed to remain plain Sergeant Harris, a name he had adopted from the blind on a tobacconist's shop next to the recruiting office.

An hour and a half after leaving the pagoda he reached the waterfront and port area. His shirt was clinging to his back and the sweat was trickling down his bared arms. He sat on a bollard to ease his aching feet, a great believer in the soldier's maxim: 'Never stand when you can sit.' The Hlaing river, commonly called the Rangoon river, was so wide it was difficult to imagine the port was twenty one miles from the sea. The air was filled with the hiss of steam winches, the rattle of cables and the clatter of cranes as they bent their gantries like the beak of some prehistoric bird, deep into the holds of cargo ships tied up alongside. At anchor were even more ships, some waiting to come alongside, others being loaded with rice ferried out in great barges. Above the mechanical babble of the port the voices of the coolies raised in song could clearly be heard as they laboured near naked in the dungeon-dark holds.

Dwarfed by the cargo ships were the water taxis which scuttled across the river like insects on a pond, and the elegant laung-zats which sat long and low in the water and

13

were rowed by several men moving as rhythmically as a well drilled eight. Here too past and present mingled, for vying for trade with the steam and oil-powered vessels whose funnels crayoned the sky with black plumes of smoke were stately high-prowed junks and elegant sailing ships. The port was never silent and at night, under the blaze of arc lights, the loading and unloading continued, for here all the immense wealth of Burma eventually found its way.

Harris filled his pipe and listened to the cacophony of steel and steam that despite its clamour seemed to promote a sense of tranquility. He wished he could hail a water taxi and go out to one of the big liners and book a one-way passage home. He felt like a cavalry charger that had been prematurely put out to grass, and forced to scent the whiff of battle from a safe distance. He felt a slight rumbling in his stomach which reminded him it was time to eat. He rose and made his way along the Strand, passing the hotel which bore the same name and was renowned for its cuisine and insistence that diners must dress for dinner. But that was of only academic interest to him, the hotel being strictly out of bounds to other ranks. That did not worry him either as there was no shortage of places where one could eat excellent food at a reasonable price; in fact, one was spoilt for choice. He rather fancied going to the place where a Chinese girl would wait on him and crack sunflower seeds with her teeth before handing them to him. At the completion of his meal she would wipe his face with a heated and perfumed towel. Such luxuries were a delight after the rigours of army life. First, however, he would quench his thirst. The first one would not touch the sides.

As he idly contemplated the pleasures ahead, he was startled by the raucous hoot of a car horn which forced him to jump back on to the pavement. He had a momentary glimpse of a fire-engine red sports car, the hood down, being driven too fast for safety by a young woman wearing a topee that looked more fashionable than practical and was clearly worn as a status symbol. He muttered softly, 'You stupid bitch,' realising a raised voice was a waste of breath for the car had turned with a screech that left the smell of burning rubber into a road that led uptown.

14

Avril Carfax spotted him the moment he stepped off the pavement and automatically pressed down hard on the accelerator. Roads, she believed, were meant for motorists and she classified pedestrians into two groups — the quick and the dead. Not that she meant it literally; after all, she had tooted. She had also seen the white stripes on his rolled up shirt sleeves and recognised him as a Rock from his hose tops and the regimental flash on the puggaree wound round his topee. She had no idea why they were so called, and no interest whatsoever in finding out.

(At Blenheim on the left bank of the Danube the regiment, although hopelessly outnumbered, had stood firm against repeated assaults by the French after Marlborough's cavalry had failed in their first attempt to break the enemy lines. Their steadfastness had contributed significantly to the conclusive victory that followed and Marlborough, most impressed by their refusal to retreat, had remarked, 'They were as immovable as rocks,' and so Rocks they had been ever since.)

Avril's action had been instinctive. Although she had never met a soldier below the rank of captain, she had been encouraged to believe that 'pongos' were lecherous men of doubtful background and pedigree, and little more than uniformed servants. She would have been appalled if she had heard Harris's description of her; she considered herself a typical English girl in an alien land, a bit fun loving perhaps, but certainly not shallow and empty headed, and well aware that appearances mattered very much indeed. The British were the backbone of Burma, and therefore expected to act accordingly.

It had been drilled into her that nothing was more important than appearance, for on it depended the respect without which the British community could not survive. Appearance was really a euphemism for what the Chinese called 'face', but as the Chinese were ridiculed for attaching so much importance to it, another word had been found. Status was more appropriate, but that sounded far too pompous. Since childhood a litany of correct behaviour had been drummed into her in which something was either the 'done thing' or the 'not done thing'. Social survival depended on toeing the line and conforming.

If Avril had been back 'home' in this most perilous time in Britain's turbulent history she would no doubt have enlisted in one of the women's services, but as she was in Burma, remote from the conflict, she could do her 'bit' by displaying the stiff upper lip and carrying on as before, because any outward sign of concern would be misconstrued as defeatism. And so she played tennis, danced, sailed, watched cricket and polo, went to the races and changed her clothing at least three times a day. Every Saturday night she would gather round the piano at the club's regular singsongs and almost burst her lungs with choruses of 'There'll Always be an England' and 'There'll be Bluebirds Over the White Cliffs of Dover' — which she had never seen.

It did not strike her as at all incongruous, or even slightly ridiculous, and it certainly never crossed her mind that girls of the same age in England operating capstan lathes in munitions factories and struggling along on rationed food and clothing, might find her blatant patriotism somewhat hypocritical in view of her way of life.

If war had not been declared she might have developed into a less blinkered young woman, for she would have been sent to school in England where her outlook would have been broadened. Not perhaps to the extent that she would have flouted convention when she returned to Rangoon, but enough to have made her realise the world was not an oyster and she the pearl. But her father, with the perspicacity that marked his business deals, had seen Munich for the farce it was and decided she should be educated at a Rangoon High Anglican convent, which whilst not strong on academic achievement was not going to be bombed off the face of the earth. He saw it as no loss that while his daughter could wield a tennis raquet with masculine power and drive a car with a skill that would be applauded at Brooklands, it was doubtful if she could boil an egg, make a bed, or sew on a button. With servants so cheap and plentiful there was no need.

It was understandable, therefore, that Avril should have no qualms about her way of life; she had known no other. All that concerned her just now was to get home

16

to bathe and change, and be back at the club in time for the presentation of prizes by the new Governor, Sir Reginald Dorman-Smith, who had recently replaced that old stick-in-the-mud Sir Archibald Cochrane, a naval VC who did not know one end of a horse from the other. She had only seen Sir Reginald from a distance, but was struck by his good looks; he looked more like a film star than a politician. This time she would actually meet him for it had been an outstanding season for her. She had won the ladies singles final in straight sets, and the mixed doubles in partnership with Higham-Murray, a shining star in a galaxy of talented young civil servants, but alas happily married.

The Governor stood at the apex of Rangoon society, and with a bit of luck she might end up with an invitation to tea on the lawn of Government House. In Rangoon that was on a par with a garden party at Buckingham Palace, and would certainly put a few noses out of joint, especially among some of the older memsahibs who had been angling without success for the honour of treading the billiard-table smooth lawns which fringed the hideous edifice, and represented the pinnacle of social attainment.

It was at such functions that one could hope to meet the younger members of the ICS, 'the heaven born', who if they did not blot their copybooks were destined for high office and the ultimate accolade of a KCMG, referred to by jealous non-recipients as 'Kindly Call Me God'. They were recruited from the cream of England's two major universities and usually had a family background in keeping with their academic qualifications. They were the most eligible bachelors in a land where prospective husbands of the necessary calibre were thin on the ground, and it was her firm intention to net one, preferably sooner than later. She certainly had no intention of becoming attached to any of the young men who worked for the big companies, even though her father had risen from their ranks. Although they were jolly good fun, they drank too much gin and whisky and seldom let their minds rise above their fly buttons.

Marriage to a 'jungle wallah' was also out of the question; that amounted to little more than a living death. Not that she knew anything about Central or Upper Burma, or the

17

natives who populated those areas. She knew only Rangoon and Maymyo where she moved to in the hot weather.

Although she was only nineteen she viewed marriage as a matter of some urgency, because opportunities were rare and when they did come had to be grabbed, much as a bad service had to be punished. A chance missed was to be regretted.

She accepted that a price had to be paid for expensive dinners and dances and was quite happy to indulge in what she and her friends called 'heavy petting', but she was determined that when she walked up the aisle of the C of E Cathedral on the arm of her father she would be virgo intacta. When a young woman lost her maidenhead in Rangoon the news spread like a fire in a field of stubble, and one was apt to be written off as 'easy game' or 'shop soiled'.

Avril was by any standards a beautiful girl with strong, bronzed legs and arms, which she was aware were displayed to advantage by the short, sleeveless one-piece tennis dress. She wore her fair hair long and what was not covered by her topee had been bleached to a near white, but her face was as pale as Devon cream. Exposure to the sun was considered infra dig, not for health reasons but because too deep a tan could lead to a misunderstanding. There were far too many women around who tried to put their dusky complexion down to an incautious over exposure to sunlight to want to add to their number.

She drove quickly up the tree-lined drive that led to the large house that stood in its own spacious grounds on a ridge overlooking the Royal Lake. The garden was ablaze with tropical flowers and shrubs, for everything grew in wild profusion in the lush fertile soil: Golden Mohur, bougainvillaea, poinsettia, glorious canna lillies, hibiscus, and flowers that brought a touch of 'home'; zinneas, delphiniums of eye dazzling blue, marigolds the colour of butter, stocks, phlox and asters, all standing erect against a lush emerald background of weedless grass. Bent low over the beds and lawns were four malis who watered everything with reckless profligacy.

The house was large and rambling and had been built to the specific instructions of Alex Carfax. The exterior was based on a photograph of a large country house in Buckinghamshire he had seen for sale in a back number of *Country Life*. Tall Tudor chimneys poked skywards, although fires were never required in Rangoon, while large timber beams latticed the brickwork. The dictates of the climate where a cool breeze was an essential ingredient to comfort had forced him to make some out-of-character modifications: instead of the period windows in the original there were large rectangles shaded with bamboo blinds, and a wide veranda around three sides of the building. The rooms were large and high, with teak floors to withstand the ravaging ants which would devour anything soft. Much of the furniture, although antique in appearance, was also made of teak but rarely used; it was purely for appearance. The chairs in which one sat were made of rattan. Suspended from the ceilings were fans as large as a ship's propellors, which churned the sultry air, creating enough breeze to combat the humidity which otherwise coated books, shoes and clothing with mildew. Only at night when a wind came in off the sea was the place comfortable. Rather incongruously he had named it Balmoral.

Alex Carfax came down the broad front steps as Avril drew up, and he shouted to one of the houseboys to push the car under a canopy of bamboo canes. A young man wearing a white shirt, matching long trousers and a green cummerbund, appeared as if from nowhere, leaned inside and released the handbrake, then steered it from the outside as he manhandled it into the shade. He was not allowed to drive it.

Alex Carfax gave his daughter a perfunctory kiss on the cheek. 'Congratulations are in order, or so I hear, lass.' His voice still retained a strong Scottish burr, something he had never tried to eradicate; he was as proud of it as a veteran was of his campaign medals. He spoke slowly, giving a sense of gravity to the most trivial remarks. 'The secretary laddie phoned and said you'd romped off with the top prizes. Daddy's proud of his wee girl.' He put an arm round her shoulders and led her into the house where he shook a handbell, and when a uniformed servant appeared he ordered glasses and a jug of fresh iced lime juice. He slumped into a rattan chair, put his feet on the footrest, and lit a Havana cigar. The days when he had smoked cheroots had long since passed.

Avril sat facing her father. 'Is Mummy home? I thought she might like to attend the presentation. H.E. has consented to do it.'

'Wouldn't miss it for all the rice in Burma. Be back soon. Just popped down to Rowe's to order a few extras for Christmas, then she's off to the cold store to see about the turkey, a beef joint and a ham. Not far off now.'

Rowe's was the English departmental store, Rangoon's equivalent to London's Harrods, which sold virtually everything, and as the festive season approached shopping became something of a spree as people purchased items reminiscent of a Christmas at 'home', for the holiday was celebrated in a strictly traditional manner. Every house would have a Christmas tree festooned with multi-coloured baubles and miniature crackers and topped by a tinsel star. Despite the heat, dining tables would groan under the weight of food that provided an umbilical cord with 'home', and walls would be covered with cards of Santa driving a sled being hauled by reindeer, and robins perched on yule logs, and for a brief spell everyone would forget that snow never fell on Burma.

Normally Mrs Carfax did not do the shopping; it was considered too demanding a chore and was usually entrusted to the head boy, but Christmas was a religious occasion which served as an annual reminder to the Burmese and others that the English were not heathens.

As she sipped her cold drink, Avril asked, 'Are you coming, Daddy?'

'Sorry, I'd love to but I've a pretty important business appointment.' He nodded for added emphasis.

'On the golf course?' she said teasingly.

'As a matter of fact, yes.' Mr Carfax sounded solemn. 'But it's business with pleasure. The best possible combination. Take it from me, only fools say they don't mix the two. Nothing like getting someone relaxed to strike a hard bargain.' He winked. 'Let them win a few holes and they start making concessions.' He tapped the side of his

20

forehead. 'I'm a canny old Scot, remember, lass.' Canny was one of his favourite words; he saw it as extolling virtues that the Scots and no others possessed. Avril thought it vulgar, but had the good sense not to say so. She was aware that some of the business community thought him a bit on the sharp side.

Alex Carfax was in his middle forties and hastening towards unsightly corpulence. His paunch was beginning to sag over the belt which held up his white duck slacks and his cheeks bore the ruptured veins of the heavy drinker, which even the deep tan brought about by years in the tropics could not conceal. Like so many of his countrymen he had been forced to leave impoverished Scotland which offered little scope for an ambitious youngster, and had been attracted to Burma which was ripe for exploitation. He started in a lowly capacity with one of the major companies, but quickly displayed considerable entrepreneural skills which, coupled with a ruthless streak, made him an extremely wealthy man by the time he was thirty. Now he had a rice warehouse on the river front, a solid stake in the oil wells at Yenangyaung, and an interest in rubber. He also owned a flourishing import-export business largely confined to luxury goods. From the UK he imported whisky and gin and sporting equipment, and from Rangoon exported tin, silver, jade, rubies and other precious stones.

He was excessively proud of his background and loved to boast, as only a rich man can, that he came from crofter stock, and with a few drinks under his belt rhapsodised about the virtues of the land of his birth which he had not been able to leave quick enough and had no desire to ever set foot in again. He was perfectly happy where he was. He was a member at Mingaladon, the finest golf course in the Far East, belonged to several fashionable clubs including the Pegu, the oldest and most exclusive in Rangoon, and owned several horses which he raced at Kyaiksan.

Once a year he donned a kilt for Burns Night when it was 'open house' at Balmoral and he stood, skean-dhu in hand, over a steaming haggis to propose the toast to the 'Great Chiftain o' the Puddin'-race'. He poured tumbler-sized tots of malt whisky before attacking the haggis with such ferocity he could have been enacting the massacre of Glencoe, intoning in a Harry Lauder voice:

His knife see Rustic-labour dight,
An' cut you up wi' ready slight,
Trenching your gushing entrails bright
Like orie ditch;
And then, O what a glorious sight,
Warm, reekin', rich!

That was the extent of his nationalism, for he knew which side his bread was buttered. He had no urge to play golf on the hallowed, windswept links at St Andrew's when at Mingaladon he had the services of a caddie, and a fore caddie who would deftly remove his ball from the rough with a big toe as dexterous as a crab's claw. In Rangoon he had someone to remove and put on his shoes, and he was surrounded by employees and servants who addressed him as if he were a minor deity.

Avril said, 'Have you met the new Governor? You've never said so.'

'Aye. Over drinks at Government House where he gave a handful of the more important Burra Sahibs a wee pep talk about how important it was to export as much as we could because the dollars we earn are helping the war effort. Like teaching your grandmother to suck eggs! None of us needed reminding that we had to do our bit. Almost broke into song when he talked about Winnie's great relationship with Roosevelt. That didn't go down too well with us old Burma hands. That bugger in a wheelchair wants to ring down the curtain on the Empire. Help! The Yanks'll bleed us dry, like they did last time. Then, when the real fighting's over, they'll come in singing 'Over There', and claim the glory. Look at those young American flyers who spend their time in the Silver Grill. What're they called – The American Volunteer Group? Civilians in uniform paid a fortune to fight for Chiang Kai Shek, but not for us. Not that the Chinks have got much change out of them. Too busy drinking and womanising with the riff raff.'

Avril had seen them and thought them colourful young

22

men, shooting up the place with six guns, just like a Wild West film. But she did not want to argue with her father and provide him with an opportunity to mount one of his favourite hobby horses – his mistrust of America – she wanted to hear more about Sir Reginald.

'You can't blame him for banging the drum, Daddy. That's his job. But what's he really like?'

Carfax pondered. 'Smooth in an old school tie way, but knows bugger all about Burma. Whitehall has never thought that necessary in anyone they've sent here. Typical square peg. Got the right pedigree and that's all that matters to them. Harrow and Sandhurst, service in the First War. Then a career in politics ending up with him becoming Minister of Agriculture which he managed to cock-up. He assured us that Burma was well prepared to meet any aggression, which we all know is rubbish. Not that it matters, nothing is going to happen here. He's a good figurehead with his plumed helmet and all that twaddle. Like his memsahib more. Got a good eye for a horse.'

From that Avril gathered her father did not rate the new Governor too highly. He was, to use a phrase Carfax frequently employed, 'small beer'.

Her father glanced at his watch, grunted and hauled himself out of his chair. 'Time to change.'

He emerged five minutes later wearing shorts, tartan stockings, a flamboyant shirt and a white linen cap. 'The British don't deserve to win this war, lass. We control most of the rubber producing countries, yet somehow we've managed to create a shortage of golf balls. Wouldna credit it, would you? What they need in Downing Street are a few hard-headed Scots businessmen. Never mind, we'll muddle through.'

Avril walked to the front door and waved as he drove off in his bottle-green Rolls, then retraced her steps, leaving a wake of discarded clothing as she headed for the bathroom – a pair of canvas plimsolls, white ankle socks, her dress, panties and brassiere – calling out as she did so, 'Nellie!'

Nellie was her personal servant whose real name was Naw Ma Nyunt, but Avril found that too difficult to pronounce so she had rechristened her. She was a lively intelligent girl

23

who spoke some English having been educated at one of the American Baptist Missions. She appeared from the veranda where she had been sitting waiting to be summoned, moving with a feline grace to pick up the trail of discarded clothing. She had an almost doll-like face with a short nose, wide nostrils and high cheekbones. Her black hair, dressed with coconut oil, was neatly coiled and she had a hibiscus flower behind one ear. She wore the traditional longyi, a starched muslin ingyi, and a pair of red laquer sandals. Totally devoted to her mistress, it never occurred to her to question the manner in which she was treated. Avril acted like all memsahibs. In any case, Nellie was happy in her work. She had a hut in the servants' quarters, and the memsahib was always buying her new clothes so that she would look smart and giving her pretty but inexpensive trinkets to add to the many she loved to wear on her embroidered jacket.

In spite of the vast sums Mr Carfax had expended on Balmoral, the bathroom remained a primitive affair; modern plumbing was a rarity. A large zinc bath rested in a cement trough with raised edges, and set at an angle so that the water could drain away through a hole in the floor. A large earthenware chatti filled with water stood by the bath, with a dipper resting on the top. Avril stood naked by the bath eschewing the modesty she would have exercised in the presence of other Europeans at the swimming club, for it did not matter if a servant saw you naked. The parts of her body usually covered by a swim suit were an ivory white and her breasts were full and firm from rigorous exercise. She slid into the bath, saying, 'No hot water, Nellie, just cold.' A request which the maid was immensely relieved to hear; it saved her from the irksome task of carrying in the heavy kerosene tins in which water was heated over a wood fire. She filled the dipper and ladled it over her mistress like someone serving outsize helpings of soup, carefully avoiding her hair. 'Don't worry about wetting it,' said Avril irritably, 'you won't do any damage.'

She was proud of the fact that she never needed a perm or even a set. A brisk rub with a towel and one hundred strokes from a brush wielded by Nellie and it was at its best again. She visibly relaxed and felt her skin tingle, experiencing a vague sexual pleasure as the cold water poured over her shoulders, trickled down her body between her breasts, thighs, and the cleft between her rounded buttocks.

Avril was reluctant to step out of the bath; she knew that as soon as she did she would be pouring with sweat, and if she dressed too early would be forced to change yet again before attending the prize giving. She wondered how to occupy her time. The heat and humidity of Burma often made the task of taking the simplest decision most difficult. Despite her preoccupation with the heat she knew that when the monsoon, which lasted from May to late September, came round again she would be praying for the heat, because rain in Burma had to be experienced to be believed. The skies simply opened and the rain came down as if some heavenly dam had burst its banks. It would beat a tattoo on the roof of the house and veranda that made you want to scream.

'Tell me about your latest boyfriend, Nellie,' she said for want of something more important to discuss.

Nellie giggled and coyly lowered her head. The modesty was feigned because like so many Burmese girls she was an outrageous flirt. 'I have two now, because my number one lover wants to marry me and I do not want that. I do not want to live in a house on stilts with pigs inside. I like it more here.' She sounded quite haughty, and there was a sing-song intonation to her voice which tended to become a screech when she was excited, and the sudden change indicated she was about to reach that stage. Avril enjoyed goading her until that happened.

'I think I'll have a word with him and tell him I want to marry you off.'

Nellie shrieked her indignation. 'No, no. I would like to marry a British soldier. Oh yes, very much. Then one day I could go to England and see the King.'

Avril knew that some Burmese girls did marry British soldiers, but they were few and far between; the majority were only promised marriage. They found themselves high and dry when the man finished his tour of duty and sailed home in a troopship, but they never learned. In any case they usually ended up marrying one of their own kind, so no great harm was done.

25

As Nellie leaned over her to ladle more water, Avril sniffed in an exaggerated way. 'I'll tell you something, Nellie, you'll never hook a British soldier if you drench yourself in that awful sandalwood muck. If you want to smell nice you can use some old perfumes I've finished with. But take a tip from me and forget about soldiers. England isn't Burma, and girls here who do manage to marry a British man have a difficult time.'

She put her hands on the side of the bath and levered herself upright. Nellie stepped forward and enveloped her in a large white towel. As she briskly dried her mistress, she pressed her to elaborate on the problems that confronted Burmese girls in England, but Avril had already lost interest in the subject. She had suddenly thought of a way to bridge the time until the prize giving: she would write the long postponed letter to her Aunt Edith who lived in a place called Chelmsford, where it always seemed to be raining or snowing and never quite right for the garden.

Chapter Two

Privates Wagstaff, Fazackerley and Simmonds sat on top of a bed playing one of their interminable games of pontoon. They were naked apart from their service issue underpants. A day rarely passed without the dog-eared, well thumbed cards being produced, but their enthusiasm remained undiminished. The school had started when the battalion was based in Deolaly, a transit camp near Bombay that was such a depressing place it had given birth to the phrase 'doolally tap' which to the BORs meant 'bonkers', and pontoon had been the antidote against them going round the twist. That had been eleven endless years ago, for after a long stint which included Delhi, Meerut and the Khyber pass, they had been shipped to Burma where it seemed they would not see Blighty until the war was over.

The dormitory they sat in was long and lofty with big, wide, open windows in the sloping roof to provide the maximum ventilation. Big white-bladed fans rotated slowly above them, and the neatly folded mosquito nets above the cots hung down like giant crysalises. The dormitory was almost prison-like in its simplicity; rows of cots in regimented lines stood on each side of the spartan room, with every item of kit and equipment carefully laid out as if for an unexpected and surprise inspection. By the side of each bed, regulation distances apart, was a small locker containing the few personal possessions the average soldier had acquired over long years of service overseas. The lockers were absolutely sacrosanct, and it was more than a man's life was worth to display the slightest curiosity about their contents. The

27

carefully preserved letters and faded photographs were all they had to remind them that they were still individuals and not just names and numbers, and that a world existed outside the narrow confines of the army. Apart from those cherished possessions their lives were an open book. They ate together, bathed together, marched together and almost slept together, and they certainly drank together in the wet canteen where beer was cheap and plentiful.

It was a life of stupefying boredom in which more time was spent 'charpoy bashing' and staring blankly at the 'punkahs' than anything else, for heat dictated that everything had to be accomplished in the coolest part of the day. Nevertheless the life they led had its compensations. If they had the cash they could have their corns cut, nails manicured, and their washing done by the itinerant dhobi wallahs. They could even get someone to shave them. They were well fed and enjoyed a medical service seldom available to the working class back home. They were not called upon to think a lot, because the bugle regulated their lives. Its brassy quavering call woke them, told them when to eat and when to sleep. It even told them when the mail from home arrived; a rare event, for a letter took three weeks and a local newspaper, which kept them abreast with news of their home town, a month. There were many, however, who received neither.

Wagstaff studied his single card with great intensity before saying to Simmonds, who held the bank, 'Buy one.' He received another card and nodded, and waited for Fazackerley to be dealt his card. Fazackerley picked up his dentures, inserted them and said, 'Buy one.' He seemed content with what he had been dealt and said, 'Stick,' before removing his false teeth.

Wagstaff continued buying until he had five cards which he laid face downwards with a look of smug satisfaction.

Simmonds turned over his own cards and announced, 'Pay nineteens and over.'

Wagstaff, already reaching for the pile of rupees, said, 'Pay me. Five carder.'

Fazackerley, toothless, said with a great deal of gum and spittle, 'You jammy sod, Waggy.'

Wagstaff said, 'Put your choppers in for Christ's sake,

Zack. I can't understand a word you say; apart from that, I don't need no shower bath.'

Fazackerley inserted his teeth. 'If you weren't starkers, I'd swear you had those cards up your bloody sleeve.' Not that he really believed that Wagstaff needed sleeves, he was convinced that he had memorised every stain and crease on the back of each individual card and was able to tell what was on the underside, which was why he invariably won.

'You have all the fucking luck,' said Simmonds.

'Luck ain't got nothin' to do with it, Simmo.' He tapped the side of his head with a forefinger. 'To win at this 'ere caper you've got to 'ave it up 'ere. All you got is between your legs.'

Simmonds grinned, not in the least offended; it was acknowledged that he possessed the largest penis in the battalion, and anyone who disputed that had only to say, 'Give us a flash,' for him to produce physical proof.

They were three totally dissimilar yet inseparable men. They drank together, spent their days off together, covered for each other, stood shoulder to shoulder in brawls against all comers, and had even shared the same woman in a Rangoon side-street brothel where ladies from Japan, Paris and Russia had drifted like rudderless ships through professional careers marked by a steady decline in accommodation and clientele. But as Simmonds liked to remark, 'You don't look at the mantlepiece when you poke the fire.'

They might have given careful thought about dying for each other but there would have been no doubt about their decision, although such sentiments were never openly expressed, and they would have scoffed at anyone who even hinted that they were capable of such intense camaraderie.

The rest of the Company called them 'The Three Musketeers', to which they retorted, 'Naturally. All for one, one for all, and every man for himself.'

Sergeant Harris referred to them as 'Kipling's Three', but as they had no idea what he was talking about they viewed it as some kind of secret joke.

Only one thing meant more to them than each other and that was the Regiment. Asked to explain what it did mean to them they would have been unable to put their feelings into words. It was just about everything: mother, father, family. And it was not just confined to the men they knew; they also shared the past with the men who had died for it. It was too nebulous to express in words. Like being asked to define love, patriotism or loyalty. It was all those, and something more. The battle honours on the Colours were not mere place names, they were part of their heritage. When, and if, they were called upon in battle to fight to the last man and the proverbial last round, they would do so unthinkingly; any alternative was too dishonourable even to contemplate. In short, the Regiment was their whole being, and the reason for their continued existence. The loyalty was almost tribal in its intensity and incomprehensible to anyone outside its close knit unity. They would concede that there were other fine regiments they would fight back to back alongside, but they believed, without any arrogance, they were not in the same class as the Rocks.

Wagstaff was almost as proud of his Cockney heritage as he was of the Regiment, although he had never heard of it until he had walked into the recruiting office, lied about his age and accepted the King's shilling, and left it to somebody else to decide which regiment he should join. He had not been prompted by any military zeal, just a yearning desire to get away from the suffocating boredom of the oil shop his father owned in a squalid back street off the Elephant and Castle. When he left school at fourteen it had been automatically assumed that he would don a brown apron and help his father behind the counter. He had sold sawdust for cats to do their 'business' on, paraffin for heaters, canes for the backsides of recalcitrant children, candles, nails by the ounce, mousetraps, and bundles of kindling, and charged the batteries for old ladies whose sole company was the wireless set. He had stuck it for nine months before hanging his overall on a hook behind the door and going home to pack a small suitcase. He had written a 'Dear Mum and Dad' letter and not seen them since.

He took to the army like a duck to water. At Port Said during a seven days leave in which he was seldom sober, he had had his entire chest and back tatooed with a typical British hunting scene depicting pink-coated men on horses, scent-sniffing hounds and the brush of a fox disappearing up his backside. It was, he thought, the time when he became a real soldier. Over the years he had acquired the cunning of a fox, and an almost boyish charm that was so infectious he could have convinced all but the most sceptical of his innocence if found standing over a headless corpse with an axe in his hands. He was entitled to wear two good conduct chevrons, points uppermost, on his uniform, denoting he had served five years without a blemish on his record. In two years time he would be entitled to add a third chevron for he would have completed twelve years of what he called undetected crime.

Without any formal instruction he had acquired an uncanny aptitude for anything mechanical. When he lifted the bonnet of a vehicle he seemed able to sniff out the fault. The Transport Officer said it was a gift you either had or did not have. Some men had it with mules and horses; Wagstaff had it with the internal combustion engine. Yet he stubbornly resisted all efforts to persuade him to forsake footslogging for less arduous tasks in the workshop of the transport section. It would have meant deserting his 'oppos'.

If Simmonds had a Christian name, no one knew it. He was known to all his comrades as Simmo. He was a great shirehorse of a Yorkshireman whose torso was covered with tell-tale blue scars, the hallmark of the man who had spent long periods bent double hewing coal from a narrow seam. Like the beast he so resembled he was incredibly strong, yet amazingly gentle until roused, when he could develop into a raging bull. He was the oldest man in the battalion although no one was sure of his actual age. He was certainly entitled to wear five chevrons denoting twenty-one years service, but it was rumoured he had served much longer, re-enlisting when his time was up because, like an old lag who can't keep out of prison, he knew no other life but the army. It was also said that he had fought at the fag end of the First War, but he would neither confirm nor deny it. He had never wished for, or sought, promotion; he was a born follower who never questioned an order, and if told to walk over a cliff edge would have done so with arms swinging, head erect and shoulders square.

Fazackerley was one of a family of thirteen who were spawned in a Liverpool slum amid grinding poverty and mass unemployment. He had joined the army purely to survive and be guaranteed four square meals a day. He was still bean-pole thin, although he ate enough to satisfy three normal men. His hair was cropped close to his skull and his false teeth, which would have looked more at home in a horse's mouth, gave him an almost cadaverous appearance; he was a good soldier but a born skiver, and no great respecter of other people's property. His prodigious thirst was comparable to his appetite for food, and surprisingly considering his appearance, he was a renowned womaniser. He was not entitled to sport any good conduct chevrons because he had lost them all. Yet there was no finer marksman in the battalion, and no one could match him over a mile.

As the pile of rupees mounted in front of Wagstaff, the other two players decided that it was time to call it a day otherwise they would not be able to go to the wet canteen without a loan from Waggy, which always had strings attached.

'I've been finkin',' said Wagstaff. 'Wiv Christmas just aroun' the jolly 'orner we oughta give Sarn't 'arris a little present of some baccy.'

Simmo tossed his head back and rolled his eyes in exaggerated astonishment. 'You must be off your rocker, Waggy. You don't go giving sergeants bloody presents. Everyone'll think we fancy him or something. Next thing you'll be asking him to tuck you in at night.' The scorn in his voice was immense.

It was also affected, because one just couldn't be heard having a good word to say for a sergeant. Secretly, however, they had a deep respect for Harris who went out of his way to look after their interests, because officers were usually a bit remote and could not be approached directly. But they had only to go to Harris with some real or imaginary grievance and he would immediately take the matter up.

'Listen, Simmo. Christmas is supposed to be the time of goodwill to all men, and that includes sergeants. We'll be givin' each uvver somethin', but he won't even get the smell

32

of an oily rag. Ever know him get a letter? No. He don' do a lotta mixin' either. It ain't askin' a lot.'

Zack said, 'I'll chip in. Poor sod hasn't got anything, not even a first name – leastways if he has I've never heard it. We can make it clear we don't want any favours.'

'You can speak for yourself on that score,' said Simmonds.

'Leave it to me then,' said Wagstaff. 'I'll put a nice card wiv it.'

'I won't sign it,' said Simmonds stubbornly. 'I'll be anonymous. No name, no pack drill.'

'Don't you ever think about Sarn't 'arris, Simmo? You fink he was jilted or somefink? 'e don't let on much, do 'e? Makes a oyster bloody talkative.'

Fazackerley said, 'The army's full of odd bastards, Waggy. Men who are running away from something, or looking for something. Whatever it is, they're entitled to keep it to themselves. All that matters as far as we're concerned is that he's a bloody good NCO.'

Wagstaff glanced up at the cheap alarm clock that rested on the top of his locker. 'Time to tart up. The wet'll be open in a 'our's time. So let's do a juldi move.' He rattled the coins in his hand. 'First call's down to me.'

Sister Kitty Bradshaw strode briskly through the wards followed by half a dozen Anglo-Burmese nurses who waited anxiously and nervously for her to speak. It could be a word of praise or a sharp reprimand; all silently prayed that it would not be the latter, for the sharp end of Sister Bradshaw's tongue could reduce one to tears. Her evening rounds, prior to the senior surgeon's inspection, was a considerable ordeal because the Sister seemed to have eyes in the back of her head. She paused by one bed, straightened the temperature chart hanging at the foot, and uttered some words of comfort to the patient before striding purposefully to the next bed. 'Who is looking after this patient?' she snapped.

A nurse whispered, 'Me, Sister.'

'That mosquito net has been tied up in a most haphazard fashion. It won't do. Now put it right.'

33

The girl darted forward and resecured the net with trembling fingers.

Sister Bradshaw said, 'That's much better. Well done. Now see that it is always neat and tidy, even when it isn't in use.'

There was not a hair out of place, and her uniform, from the starched hat to her white shoes, was spotless, and no one, unless told, would have believed she had had little or no sleep for the past forty-eight hours. Apart from an acute shortage of fully trained European nurses the matron was absent up country attending a special meeting of senior medical personnel in Mandalay. She was dog tired but determined not to show the least sign of fatigue; a firm believer that the nursing staff's efficiency depended entirely on personal example.

She was a short plumpish woman in her middle thirties, with streaks of grey already visible in her auburn hair which was tied in a tight bun at the nape of her neck. She was utterly dedicated to her work, and her brusque manner concealed a great affection for the young nurses who worked under her, but she was acutely aware that a firm hand had to be evident otherwise the Anglo-Burmese girls would lapse into slap dash habits which seemed part of their nature.

Her father, who was a GP in Hertfordshire, had served in Burma during the First War and told her of the appalling sickness rate in the country and the great need for qualified nurses, and from the time she sat on his lap listening to his tales of the distant land she had never been in any doubt that nursing was her vocation and that it would be fulfilled in Burma. After four years at London's Middlesex Hospital she had applied for service in Rangoon, where she had been for fifteen years. Years that had passed so swiftly she found it hard to credit she had been away from home so long.

During the past forty-eight hours she had been run off her feet, supervising the birth of babies, treating serious burns cases, administering countless injections, and dealing with a multitude of cholera, malaria and dysentry cases. Although there was a separate ward for European patients she was happier when dealing with the natives who placed such blind trust in her, whereas some of the white patients seemed to view her as no more than a senior servant. They were quickly put in their place. If she was brusque at times with some of her junior staff and a trifle over firm with patients who wouldn't help themselves, she was positively abrasive with the Europeans, especially those who were patronising to her staff. She had no time whatsoever for people who worried about the colour of a person's skin. 'Blood,' she snapped, 'is always red.'

When her own rounds and the senior surgeon's were completed, she walked across the courtyard to the small detached bungalow which was her quarters. She kicked off her shoes and poured herself a stiff gin which she topped up with tonic and added a measure of quinine, then she stretched out on her bed. She looked at the watch pinned to her tunic and cursed inwardly. She was due to go to the Strand Hotel for a long standing dinner date, but she felt too tired to make the effort to dress for the occasion and wished the Europeans would not make such a point of dressing for dinner. She could enjoy good food without having to dress up to the nines. God, how the men seemed to love parading around as if the Strand was the Ritz in London.

She toyed with the idea of ringing the young man's chummerie and telling him she couldn't make it because she was needed in the theatre for an emergency operation, but decided that would be unkind. The young man had probably been looking foward to it all week. Miss Bradshaw had no illusions about her looks; she accepted that she was on the short side and did not cut a striking figure in a swim suit, but unattached women were not too plentiful in Rangoon and bachelors were quite proud to be seen escorting a white woman − even her. She leaned over and reached for the *Rangoon Gazette* on the bedside table. Apart from some brief and sketchy war news and air raid statistics from London, and the Weekly Health figures which disclosed one death from cholera and 24 new cases of smallpox, there was little of interest to her. The Scottish kirk had been broken into, an attempt had been made to abduct and seduce a widow, and concern was expressed over a cinema strike which called for a speedy solution. The letters page was largely taken up with correspondence as to whether dress regulations should be relaxed and shorts and open neck shirts permitted in offices, and a debate about proposed reforms in the horse racing and breeding policy. As far as Miss Bradshaw was concerned Rangoon was on another planet when it came to war.

She tossed aside the newspaper, finished her drink and went into the bathroom. Once I start eating and making a hole in a decent bottle of wine, she told herself, I'll forget how tired I am.

She might even summon up the energy to venture on to the dance floor, and if the young man was nice and attentive she might not need too much persuading to go back to his chummerie. All work and no play ... Apart from that, it would be pleasant to demonstrate to someone that she ws not a hidebound martinet but quite a warm person at heart. In the loneliness of her room, where she could let her hair down physically and metaphorically, she often regretted the need to maintain the image of the stern disciplinarian, but she had the consolation of knowing that her bark was worse than her bite.

Tomorrow, she reflected ruefully, she had to conduct another of those ghastly first aid lectures for the European wives: how to treat burns, how to tie a sling, identify various fractures, put on a splint and administer to any other injury that could be expected as the result of an air raid. It would be time consuming and rather pointless, because few of the women treated the lessons seriously, turning them into social occasions because they honestly believed they would never be called upon to attend any injured. Their complacency was quite depressing.

Alex Carfax teed up his ball at the last of the short par threes and hit a six iron which struck the slope to the right of the green and bounced down to within five feet of the flag. 'Learned my golf on the Scottish links,' he lied. 'A canny shot, you'll agree,' he said, with smug satisfaction.

His partner nodded in mute agreement. He wasn't enjoying the game because Carfax kept up a non-stop commentary about where he should hit the ball, how his head was coming up, and how at the end of his top swing he looked as if he

36

was playing a piccolo. He was surprised to find that he was three up, and had a nagging suspicion that he had been over generous in the terms he had agreed to over the sale of some surplus rice he had.

He hit his own tee shot to within inches of his opponent's and felt a resounding slap on his back which made him flinch. He hadn't been in Rangoon that long, and the sporty nature of his host was rather alien to him.

'Take a tip from me,' said Carfax, 'and get some of your surplus cash to Calcutta, Brown.'

Brown was almost relieved for he had expected another lesson: his grip was loose, his stance too open. 'You're worried that the war will reach here?' he asked anxiously.

'Not really, but when the powers that be start building air raid shelters and recruiting volunteers for fire brigade duties, I can't help feeling that it's better to be cautious than careless.' Carfax shrugged. 'What does it matter anyway? Interest rates are just as good in India.'

'I read only the other day,' said the perplexed Brown, 'that Churchill has sent the *Prince of Wales* and *Repulse*, two of our mightiest battle ships, to Singapore as a warning to the Japs of what they're in for if they try anything. They could be here in no time if Emperor Hiro, whatever his name is, does anything daft.'

Carfax put his hands on his hips and sounded aggrieved. 'Don't think I'm panicking, far from it; but I'm a firm believer in not putting all my eggs in one basket. Of course I don't think the Japs will attack us. Why on earth should they? Just look at it this way: would you invest all your capital in one company? Of course not. All I'm doing is playing the end against the middle.'

When they reached the green Carfax sank his putt. There was no need for him to throw away any more holes, he had accomplished his objective.

'You're three up and four to play,' he said, 'Fancy a sporting bet? I've fifty rupees that say we'll end up all square.'

Brown nodded without a great deal of conviction. 'You're on.' He had a nasty feeling he would be forking out money in the club house. He was right. Putts that earlier in the round Carfax had conceded as 'gimmies' now took on a different complexion. 'Can't give you that one,' he said, 'a real tricky one.'

At the seventeenth they were all square, and Carfax said, 'I'll be sporting about this, Brown. Double or quits?'

Brown nodded miserably. What had started out as an enjoyable round had suddenly soured. He realised Carfax was a bandit in spikes.

At the nineteenth hole he handed over one hundred rupees, and Carfax said, 'Tradition here is the loser buys the drinks.'

Brown thought that Carfax was a real shit and a man you did not play golf with again. If nothing else it had been a salutary lesson.

Avril had got no further than the date (December 7, 1941) and 'Dear Aunty Edith', and sat at her dressing table nibbling the tip of her pen wondering what on earth she could say that would be of the slightest interest.

Five minutes elapsed before she began writing in a firm schoolgirlish hand, thin up and thick down, just as she had been taught.

There really isn't a lot to say because life goes on very much the same as before. It's hard to imagine that our people, civilians and soldiers, airmen and sailors (she did not want to overlook anyone), are dying. The air raid casualties and the damage being done to London and other places are regularly printed in the *Gazette*, so we are kept abreast of things. Sometimes we feel quite out of it, but we do our bit. I have been busy knitting Balaclava helmets for the troops back home, and we hold lots of raffles to raise money for other comforts.

She cursed as a bead of sweat dropped off her forehead and landed on the paper, smudging the ink. She was about to crumple the page up and start afresh when it occurred to her that Aunty Edith might mistake the mark for a tear.

She wrote furiously for half an hour, filling four pages with news of her conquests on the tennis court and the looked forward to meeting with the Governor, the promised arrival of troop reinforcements, not really necessary but comforting, and the latest subject of considerable gossip, the fact that while Rangoon had no air raid shelters worth talking about, the Governor had had a deep one excavated in the grounds of Government House.

She imagined how pleased Aunty Edith would be to receive such a long chatty letter because life in England must be pretty gloomy, what with the black-out and traipsing out into the garden to take shelter in the Anderson.

She finished, 'All my love, Avril', then added a P.S: 'Sorry about the tear, but just thinking about you made me cry.'

She looked at her watch: she had timed it to perfection. Half an hour to dress and make her way to the club for the presentation of trophies. She selected a dress with considerable care and attention; a photograph of her with Sir Reginald was certain to appear in the *Gazette*.

Chapter Three

Sir Reginald Dorman-Smith was asleep under his mosquito net when he felt his shoulder being vigorously shaken. He opened his eyes and saw the shadowy figure of his Military Secretary standing upright by the side of his bed. He parted the net and picked up the bedside clock. It had to be something important to wake him at this ungodly hour; it was only 6.30 a.m.

'What is it?' he asked brusquely.

'Bad news, I'm afraid. The Japs have attacked the American fleet at Pearl Harbour. They've sunk a heck of a lot of ships and destroyed a large number of aircraft.'

Sir Reginald swung his feet out of bed, feeling to his surprise a sense of relief. America could not keep out of the war now. The day would go down in history as one of the most infamous in the not inconsiderable chronicle of man's treachery.

Anticipating that Britain would automatically declare war on Japan he said boldly, 'I'll broadcast to the country. Urge everyone to stand firm and fight to the end until the forces of evil and corruption are destroyed. I'll assure the people that Burma is prepared and ready to take the offensive. The army is at their action stations and the civil defence forces at the standby.' He felt the need to assert himself as the country's leader, although in his heart of hearts he knew the rousing words he was about to deliver were empty rhetoric: Burma was totally unprepared, and no doubt he would shoulder the blame for years of neglect, even though he had only been in the country for a few months and was still finding his feet. But he couldn't go on the air and tell the truth and absolve himself by saying that his repeated requests for more aircraft and troops had been ignored by Whitehall for too long. Neither could he announce that the rescue, demolition and debris clearing services existed only on paper, and the fire brigade and ambulance service were starved of vehicles, there were too few roof spotters and fire watchers, and what shelters there were offered little or no protection. Although he had done his hardest to remedy the situation there just had not been enough time. But he could not tell the people that. It would be disastrous for morale, something which was high on his list of priorities – so high in fact that he tended to become a bore he was so obsessed with it. In a vague way he thought that if there was enough of it victory was assured.

The one consolation, he thought, was that Pearl Harbour was a long way from Burma and Japan would have her hands full tackling the Americans and would therefore ignore Burma for quite a while, which would give him breathing space to get the country on a real war footing.

He dressed hurriedly but with care, aware that his appearance, to which he always paid meticulous attention, was even more vitally important. People would be looking for any outward sign of panic. He would also drive to the radio station in the Rolls; that would be good for morale.

As he drove through streets teeming with people who were blissfully unaware of the tragic events thousands of miles away because they did not possess a radio, he told himself that he could now concentrate on more important things than garden parties and other time consuming trivialities. Yesterday he had come very close to yawning in public. Presenting trophies at a tennis club was not his idea of high public office. Yet everyone thought he had nothing more urgent to attend to. The social scene might have a role to play in normal times, but times were no longer normal. Momentous events were in the offing, and they were what he was destined to control and the reason he had entered public life. His head was not for nodding his way round unsaddling enclosures but tackling immense problems with courage and coolness.

Alex Carfax, his wife and daughter, listened to His Excellency's broadcast as they were having breakfast. When the Governor had finished Carfax said, 'No need to panic. Churchill may have declared war on Japan – little else he could do in the circumstances – but it won't reach us. Even so it was a canny move on my part to transfer most of my funds to Calcutta. A wee bird whispered in my ear that the banks were doing it, and that was good enough for me. Better safe than sorry.'

'How can you be so sure they won't attack us?' asked Avril anxiously. 'The Yanks thought that, and look where it's got them.' Her voice expressed none of the confidence her father exuded.

'Simple, lassie. If Japan does try anything, she'll have to take a swipe at Singapore first, and they don't call it the Gibraltar of the Far East for nothing. It's impregnable. Any invasion would have to be from the sea, and the coastal guns are some of the biggest in the world. What's more those two mighty battleships are there. When the Japs have been seen off there, the *Repulse* and *Prince of Wales*, plus a lot of fighter planes, will come here quicker than you can say knife. Christ, the little yellow bastards will soon realise they've bitten off more than they can chew.'

Mrs Carfax said hesitantly, as if anticipating the answer, 'Alex, I think I would be happier if you could arrange for me to go to Maymyo or Mandalay. If, and it's only if, anything did happen I could fly from there to Calcutta with Avril.'

'What about Christmas? Do you think I'm going to hold open house without a hostess? Stop fretting, woman. Take my word for it, if there's the slightest danger I'll see to it you both get out. There'll be plenty of ships sailing for Calcutta. The one thing we mustn't do is panic. We must set an example to the natives. If they think we've got the wind up our kilts they'll be off and away like rats deserting a sinking ship.'

His reassuring words had their effect, and the earlier sense of pervasive gloom was quickly dispelled. Mrs Carfax began to talk with great animation about her plans for Christmas.

The inital sense of panic which gripped Rangoon with the news of Pearl Harbour vanished like snowflakes on a hot griddle, and life quickly resumed its normal routine when Japan did not appear at all interested in Burma. But the optimism was short lived. It faded with the news that Malaya had been invaded, not from the sea but from inland, and the much vaunted impregnability of Singapore was a myth: the big guns could only fire to seawards and offered no threat to the invading army. Forty-eight hours later even more catastrophic news emerged: the *Prince of Wales* and *Repulse* had been sunk by enemy aircraft with great loss of life, which meant the British naval presence in the Far East was virtually non-existent.

Again a deep gloom descended on the city, but as the days ticked by and Burma remained unmolested, a sense of complacency was restored and all thoughts of war were banished as everyone again concentrated on Christmas.

Chapter Four

An atmosphere of euphoria enveloped Rangoon like a comfortable blanket. It was Christmas Eve. The sun shone with brilliant intensity and the Europeans, busy doing their last minute shopping, paused to greet all and sundry with, 'Merry Christmas, in case I don't see you on the day.' People who had shunned each other in the club or on the race course, forgot their differences and went out of their way to be affable; the spirit of goodwill was as intoxicating and heady as brandy.

Even the native population was in a joyous celebratory mood, for when it came to the day Christ was born they forgot their own religious differences and wholeheartedly joined in the festivities; the mood was so infectious. Apart from that there was so much money being spent nearly everyone was certain to pick some of it up: the shopkeepers from the booming trade, and those in more menial jobs in over-generous tips which seemed part and parcel of the annual ritual in which backs were slapped instead of backsides kicked. The natives made the most of it, fully aware that things would return to normal as soon as the last notes of 'Auld Lang Syne' faded on the midnight air that heralded the beginning of a new, happy and prosperous New Year.

Then an unexpected sound was heard above the customary bustling clamour of Rangoon: the stomach churning wail of an air raid siren. But there was no sense of alarm. Everyone assumed it was a practice alert. Then their ears picked up another unaccustomed noise: the steady throb-throb-throb of aircraft engines. Eyes searched skywards, and overhead they saw formations of bombers escorted by fighters, flying in perfect formation, as if performing in some aerial display. The solitary anti-aircraft gun on Monkey Point boomed, and a cottonwool puff of shellfire appeared like a fleecy lamb well out of range of the tight and disciplined formations.

It was as if the gunfire was the starting pistol for an orgy of carnage and destruction. Dark plum-like objects were seen tumbling from the under-bellies of the bombers, swiftly followed by dense clusters of smaller incendiary bombs, so close together they resembled swarms of descending locusts.

Within seconds high explosive bombs were blasting cavernous holes in the more substantially built buildings, and completely flattening the less robust native premises which were mainly wooden, while the incendiaries started fires which quickly spread among the tinder-dry shops and dwellings so that entire areas became blazing infernos. There were not enough fire engines to bring the blazes under control, and the frustrations of the firemen were worsened by a shortage of hoses and scarcity of water.

Then anti-personnel bombs were dropped which cut swathes through the natives who, not knowing any better, stood gazing in bewildered curiosity at the bombers. Many of the wiser Europeans headed for the slit trenches which had been dug on the sides of some of the roads. Others went to the newly constructed shelters, blissfully unaware that the cement had not yet dried and they were inviting entombment.

The bombers turned and made another leisurely run over the city, again concentrating on the native areas and the harbour, choked with ships sitting on the water and alongside the quays, as vulnerable as fish in the proverbial barrel.

Then other smaller aircraft appeared in the sky, darting like hornets among the closely packed bombers. Two dark shapes which expanded into massive mushrooms descended with deceptive slowness, and as they neared the ground two figures were clearly visible dangling from the parachutes' harness like marionettes.

Within minutes the streets were littered with the charred skeletons of trams, buses, bullock carts, cars, rickshaws and lorries. In the barbed-wire encircled compounds housing the Lease-Lend equipment destined for China, enough transport and equipment to satisfy the entire needs of the impoverished British army went up in great gouts of flame and smoke as petrol tanks ignited and ammunition caught fire and exploded with ear-shattering crumps.

Several enemy bombers tumbled from the sky, trailing red and yellow comet tails of fire and smoke, and the more knowledgeable spectators recognised their destroyers as Tomahawks piloted by the American Volunteer Group which, only hours earlier, had been the object of so much condemnation, and the antiquated Brewster Buffaloes flown by the small and neglected RAF squadrons.

As soon as the news of the attack reached the headquarters of the Rocks, a bugle summoned every man to the parade ground where they received orders to go into the city and give what assistance they could to the civilian services. Twenty minutes later a convoy of Bedford trucks was racing towards the pall of smoke and fire which rose like an Indian signal above Rangoon. By the time they reached the centre the city was in a state of paralysis; everything had ground to a halt. The coolies had stopped working in the docks and joined the mass exodus of terrified people fleeing the devastated city. The streets were strewn with the mangled corpses of those who had not been given time nor opportunity to flee, while those overhead cables which had not been brought down were festooned with strips of human flesh. Above the brittle crackle of burning houses the anguished cries of the wounded and dying rose like a single accusatory voice. Those people trapped in the collapsed shelters, and whose lungs had not been burst by the blast, suffered untold agonies before the air supply was exhausted and they mercifully expired.

Sergeant Harris sat beside Wagstaff in the cabin of a truck as the Cockney carefully threaded a path between blazing vehicles, tangled coils of fallen overhead cables, craters and bubbling tarmac. In the back, Simmonds and Fazackerley could only gape in open-mouthed astonishment over the tailboard at the scenes of death and destruction. Simmonds shook his head in dismay. 'What a turn up for the book. Poor sods didn't know what hit them.'

Fazackerley said, 'You should feel more sorry for the buggers who did have time to find out.'

Harris jumped out of the cab, bellowing, 'Start looking for survivors. Don't worry about the dead. Nothing we can do for them.'

He cocked his head to one side, like an attentive starling listening for the movement of worms below a lawn. 'Listen! I thought I heard something.'

The others copied him, straining their ears for the slightest sound of life.

'Over there,' shouted Harris, pointing to one of the shelters that had caved in. He ran towards it, calling out, 'Follow me. At the double.' His voice was harsh with concern.

He crouched low over the rubble and listened. He heard a faint, anguished cry that was obviously human. 'Get the spades and start digging, lads. Juldi, juldi!'

They dug feverishly, throwing the debris over their shoulders with the frenzied energy of stokers who had been told to raise full steam. As the pile diminished they became more cautious, fearful that their spades might inflict even greater injuries on those trapped below. The faint noise Harris had detected grew louder, and he said, 'Easy now, lads. Bare hands from now on.'

They discarded their spades and began to scoop away handfuls of brick and dust with the painstaking care of prospectors panning for gold. Within minutes a hole emerged, big enough for Harris to poke his head into. The cry which so far had been incoherent became a desperate plea for help. 'For God's sake, somebody help us.' It was a woman's voice, tired and laced with abject fear of being buried alive in a stygian darkness.

Harris squirmed further into the hole like an inquisitive terrier sniffing out a badger's sett. 'Hold on, we'll have you out in a jiffy,' he called. 'Just stay calm, don't move and save your breath. We don't want the whole lot caving in.'

When the hole was large enough he lowered himself down and searched the shelter with a hand torch. His eyes stung from the pollen-fine dust which filled the shelter, and several seconds elapsed before he was able to see clearly. A young European woman whose hand was severed at the wrist was clutching an obviously dead baby with her other hand. A man lay beside her looking calm and relaxed as if enjoying an afternoon siesta, but Harris could tell from the motionless chest that he too was dead. The woman asked, 'Is he all right? He's my husband.'

Harris said non-committally, 'Let's get you out first before we deal with him.'

He gently prised the baby from her arms and passed it up to the waiting hands of Simmonds. Then he put his hands under the woman's armpits, saying, 'Don't move. Leave everything to me.'

He braced his feet against the uneven floor and gently levered her up until Simmonds with his massive strength was able to take her full weight and pull her to safety.

'Any of you know how to apply a tourniquet?' he asked.

Wagstaff grunted assent before turning to Fazackerley and asking, 'Gotta lipstick on you? Better mark 'er head with a big T so they'll know when we get 'er to 'ospital.'

Fazackerley said, 'Always carry one in my handbag, Waggy.'

Harris, thinking it was no time for levity, snapped, 'Knock it off. This is no time for wisecracks. I'll go back and see if I can find her handbag. Bound to be one there.'

He emerged from the shelter clutching a handbag that had once been white but was now rust-coloured. 'Look inside.'

Wagstaff found a lipstick the same colour as the blood which covered the woman's shredded wrist, and he marked her forehead with the letter T so as to alert the hospital to the fact that the tourniquet would need untightening to avoid gangrene setting in and necessitating the amputation of the entire arm.

'Get her to the Rangoon General as fast as you can, Wagstaff, and don't wait to find out how she is. Just get back here as fast as you can — there are others in need of us.'

By the time Wagstaff had returned from the hospital Harris and the other two privates had recovered several people who had been trapped in shelters and below the debris of shops and houses. Regrettably only two or three stood the least chance of surviving, the others were already dead.

48

The Japanese bombers had attacked with premeditated ruthlessness, determined to strike total terror into the heart of the city, and this they had achieved. The incendiaries and anti-personnel bombs had caused widespread panic and started a mass migration of people whose only concern was to get out of Rangoon and put as much distance as possible between them and the enemy who might return at any time. They forgot about homes and possessions, motivated solely by a desire to live.

The raid, as is always the case in war, brought out the best in some and the worst in others. Saboteurs who saw it as an opportunity to get rid of the British oppressor in return for an Asian conqueror who promised freedom from the Colonial yoke, indulged in acts of arson and vandalism simply in order to add to the confusion. There were others, criminally minded, who saw it as an open invitation to loot the windowless shops and stores, and steal valuable items which in the past they had only been able to gaze upon with unvoiced envy. And there were those who forgot their own needs and losses and immersed themselves with the task of helping and saving others.

At her own small hospital, Sister Kitty Bradshaw tried to retain an outward semblance of calm efficiency while wondering how on earth anyone could cope with the avalanche of casualties. Already the wards were filled to overflowing and even the corridors were lined with the wounded and dying. All the available stretchers were occupied so that the less fortunate had to lie on the bare floors. The operating theatre looked more like an abattoir; the surgeons were so busy with the next operation there was no time to clear the floor of amputated limbs or wash away the blood. There was also grave danger of the blood bank running dry.

From the moment the first bombs had fallen the hospital had been inundated with people seeking treatment for the most grievous wounds. Some had been delivered by ambulance or army truck, but there had been insufficient of them to meet the need and so bullock carts, piled high with injured and dying, had trundled into the courtyard like a long funeral procession, followed by a trail of limping, even crawling victims, driven on by the knowledge that the hospital offered them their only hope.

By the end of the evening the mortuary was so crammed with bodies that extra spaces had to be found in some of the outhouses and store rooms. But if corpses were not promptly identified by some relative they were speedily disposed of, because in the heat they rapidly decomposed.

Without pause, Sister Bradshaw scuttled hour after hour from ward to ward, corridor to corridor, giving morphine injections, assisting in the operating theatre, and barking encouragement and issuing rebukes as if it were just another day, all the while managing to look calm and unruffled although her uniform was now more red than white.

Only once, when the theatre was at last being hosed down and the limbs removed, did she visibly relax, but then only long enough to sneak a tot of gin topped up with a liberal measure of orange juice. Without that she doubted whether she could have remained upright. Nevertheless, she was aware of being guilty of a grave offence which, if she had detected it in one of her juniors, would have resulted in instant dismissal or at the very least suspension. The lapse from her own high standards was, she thought, justified in the circumstances, because no one was going to get any sleep that night judging from the numbers of injured who continued to pour in like water from a burst main.

It was well past midnight when one of the equally exhausted doctors ordered her to go to her quarters and snatch some sleep, but she took off only the time it required to wash and change into a crisp, clean uniform. The sudden influx of air raid victims did not mean the other patients could be ignored; raid or no raid, babies would insist on being born, and the seriously ill would demand attention, bedpans would be called for, and no one would be prepared to forego attention because there were others in more urgent need. Anyway, she thought as she studied herself in the mirror to make sure she looked presentable, how could I look my nurses in the face if I went to bed? They need me there, just as a sailor needs a beacon in a long and stormy voyage.

50

At precisely the same time that Sister Bradshaw was contemplating the immensity of the task that confronted the hospital and its meagre resources, Sergeant Harris and his three companions were sitting on the tailboard of their truck enjoying a cup of tea and some bully beef straight out of the tin. Their faces were smoke-blackened and their tunics pitted with holes from specks of burning debris, their bare arms and knees blistered by flying sparks, their fingers and knuckles grazed and bleeding.

As far as was humanly possible they had recovered as many living and dead as they could find, and now had time to ruminate on the scene of utter chaos that confronted them.

The back of the truck was piled high with bodies, reminding Harris of the woodcuts he had seen at school depicting scenes when the Great Plague had devastated London. He had no idea what to do with them, and there did not seem anyone available to provide an answer. One solution would be to dig a mass grave or light a massive bonfire, but if the latter was resorted to there might well be a public outcry, especially from those religious communities who had to be buried facing Mecca. Few of the dead carried any form of identification, and there certainly was not time to lay them out for identification by relatives. The danger of pestilence demanded prompt disposal. A rough and ready estimate was that 3,000 had been killed, although it was readily conceded the figure could be much higher because some bodies might never be recovered from the human warrens in the heavily populated native quarters.

He swallowed his tea and said, 'Right, lads, when you've finished we'll drive down to the harbour and dump this lot into the water.'

That too would probably be unacceptable to some group or other, but he doubted if there were enough people remaining in Rangoon to stage an effective protest, for since the first bombs had fallen thousands had fled along the road to Prome. Hour after hour an unbroken column of people had choked the roads leading out of the ravaged city. Bullock carts piled high with furniture and household utensils trundled along in a cloud of sulphur-coloured dust. Alongside walked women with babies perched precariously on their hips and on their backs. There were Indian women with children clutching at the hems of their saris, and husbands with stark fear registering on their faces and a handful of pitiful personal belongings suspended from bamboo poles slung milkmaid-style across their shoulders. The cars of the better-off raced past them, adding to the already dense fog of dust, while taxis, filled with refugees prepared to pay a small fortune for a ride to safety, roared along at breakneck speed, driven by men who were spurred on by the hope of a return fare if they got back before Rangoon was totally deserted. There were women pushing prams on which babies lay on sacks of rice, young men wheeling bicycles with old people perched on the saddles and crossbars who had not got the strength or will to walk. There were rickshaws and horse-drawn tongas, and ancient buses filled with Indians who for years had dreamed of the day when they would return to the land of their birth and were now forced to contemplate the hazards of achieving it by travelling through vast tracts of uncharted land, rife with malaria and roamed by wild animals, and even wilder tribesmen.

By the time the sun rose again over Rangoon, a major portion of the city's population of 500,000 had departed. An uncertain future lay ahead, but that was preferable to remaining in the capital.

Despite the efforts of the civilian services, aided by the military, the streets were still littered with dead humans and animals. Bullocks and ponies with white wide-staring eyes and bared teeth, their spilled-out entrails covered with bloated flies, were already beginning to fill with gases and putrefy, as were the dead humans. They provided an unexpected banquet of carrion for the crows, kites and the countless wild and homeless dogs that roamed the streets in yelping packs. Fur and feather ripped and tore with talons, beaks and teeth, indifferent to all attempts to drive them off, and not caring if the fare was animal or human.

Sergeant Harris and his men had dumped scores of bodies into the river, but they seemed to make no impact; there were just as many corpses lying around as there were when they started.

'Like trying to bail out a sinking boat with a colander,'

he said dejectedly. 'Let's have a breather and see if we can find somewhere that's still serving beer.'

Wagstaff said, 'If it's okay with you, Sarge, I wouldn't mind going to the warehouse and trying to pick up our booze and extra fags for tomorrow. Everyone else seems to be 'elpin' themselves. No reason why we shouldn't enjoy our Christmas nosh. The Japs won't be back in a 'urry. No need to.'

He was quite wrong in that prediction, but he was not alone in thinking so. When darkness descended on the city, illuminated by the countless still-burning fires, diners strolled through the rubble and glass-strewn streets in full evening dress heading for the Strand Hotel as if nothing untoward had happened.

Wagstaff watched them laughing and joking, wondering whether they should be admired or condemned. Were they being fearless or just blind?

He rummaged through the pockets of his shirt before producing a two ounce tin of Navy Cut tobacco. 'Merry Christmas, Sarge. Courtesy of the 'elp yourself shop I come across.'

Sergeant Harris got his tobacco, but none of them sat down to the long awaited Christmas dinner. The enemy returned next day in even greater strength. At least one hundred bombers with a powerful fighter escort blackened the sky over Rangoon, and the Rocks had to turn out again.

Although casualties were still alarmingly high, the mass evacuation of the previous day had served the useful purpose of keeping them lower than they might have been. But the evacuation had disastrous consequences. Hospitals were denuded of staff as nurses and ancillary workers sought sanctuary with their families up-country, and hundreds of seriously injured people were left unattended. The public services which included the collection of the 'night soil' from the 'long drop' latrines, and the refuse disposal squads, ceased to function, and those Europeans who had chosen to remain found to their chagrin they would have to exist without servants.

Sergeant Harris and his three man team were again called upon to help rescue the trapped, remove casualties

53

to hospital, and assist in the unsavoury task of disposing of the dead.

It had been hoped that the corpses dumped in the river would have been carried out to sea on the tide, or devoured by sharks attracted by the stench, but neither happened. Hundreds of bodies bobbed up and down on the surface of the water, kept afloat by body gases. Many were churned to pieces by the propellors of the big liners, cargo ships and smaller vessels all overloaded with passengers who had booked a passage to India, and by ships still arriving with Lease-Lend equipment and essential supplies for the local population who had departed.

As the city ground to a petrified halt, Harris and his men were shifted from venue to venue as the panic mounted, and the need to restore some semblance of law and order became of prime importance because a large number of police had also joined the exodus.

They were sent to the railway station along with other troops to control the hungry, disorderly and hysterical rabble who packed the platforms, squabbling and fighting among themselves, demanding places on one of the few trains heading north. They disregarded all pleas to remain calm and distrusted assurances that their turn would come if only they would be patient. They refused to accept that some trains could not be moved because there was a shortage of drivers and firemen, and battled their way aboard, often more than one hundred people cramming into coaches designed to take only sixty. Some clambered on to the roof, others clung to the outside, some even sat on the buffers and couplings. Those with enough money tried bribery; others pleaded that they were entitled to be given priority on the grounds of ill health, their status in society, or any other reason which might cause a harassed official to wilt under the pressure.

Assisted by those policemen who had not deserted, the troops literally managed to knock some sense into the more aggressive and demonstrative people with a blow on the head or backside with a stout lathi.

Similar scenes were being enacted at the ferry points where vast crowds had assembled to get aboard Irrawaddy Flotilla steamers which were evacuating people upriver to Mandalay.

The queues were swelled by numerous Europeans who had decided to stay and see it through but had suffered a sudden change of heart with the second air raid. They were not deserting, they told themselves, merely moving out until such time as they could return.

Others had piled everything of value into their cars — silver, cut glass, expensive carpets, pictures, and other prized possessions — and joined the slow moving processions of pedestrians and vehicles on the Prome Road or the other which went to Mandalay via Pegu.

Many were bitterly outspoken over the conduct of the banks which had been hit by staff desertions and holidays, and closed their doors so that customers had been unable to withdraw large sums of money which they would need at the end of their journey. The wiser women sewed valuable jewellery and silver rupees into the hems of their skirts because they would be travelling through jungle-clad hills where dacoits were known to prey on travellers.

There were some, however, who gave no thought to worldly possessions, simply walking out of their homes leaving them like some landlocked *Marie Celeste*. Curtains fluttered at open windows, and doors were unlocked, leaving the entire contents freely available to the mounting hordes of looters.

The looting became so rife and violent that Harris and his party were detached from all other duties and given the onerous task of carrying out a shoot-on-sight order at anyone seen staggering through the streets laden down with pillaged goods. It was an order that Harris carried out with a marked lack of enthusiasm because most people were helping themselves to something or other from deserted shops and houses, sometimes only food to ensure survival. In many cases the looters did the job themselves, shooting rivals with stolen guns or stabbing them to death in order to deprive them of their spoils.

A deep sense of bitterness and resentment at the incompetence of the military leaders and the inertia of the civil administration, many of whom had departed for Maymyo, the summer seat of Government, welled up inside Harris like a bubbling spring seeking to find the surface, and it demanded

55

all his self-control to prevent his anger becoming visible to his men. The Rocks should be marching out to meet the approaching enemy, not wasting their time protecting a city for which the bell had tolled with deafening clarity. A city that had signed its own death certificate because of the ostrich-like attitude of the Europeans who had buried their heads in the sand rather than recognise that without change there could only be decay.

All credit had now ceased and any purchases were on a cash only basis, which even extended to the Governor; something that no one had ever envisaged and a sure sign to the locals who had remained that British rule was at an end.

Harris knew he was not being totally fair; a considerable number of white men and women had stuck to their posts, convinced the tide would turn and the invaders be given a bloody nose. Although their optimism, bolstered by an in-built arrogance, was eroded by the hour, they carried on with efficiency and dedication in the face of insurmountable odds. Even so, many found it necessary to have a scapegoat for their own past neglect and lack of foresight, and they latched on to the unfortunate Governor.

Overnight Sir Reginald became aware that he was now referred to as 'Dormant Myth' and other unkind and totally unjustified vilifications. His denigrators ignored the fact that he had remained and toured the worst hit parts of the city uttering words of encouragement and sympathy, visited the hospitals with his wife, and kept silent about his own innermost fears.

These he confided to the Viceroy of India in a confidential signal in which he praised the valiant efforts of the RAF and AVG, but warned their losses had been so high that replacement pilots and aircraft were desperately needed. He also reported the mass exodus of much of the labour force, and desertions from the medical services of nurses and doctors and orderlies which had left some hospitals in a desperately precarious position. He tactfully refrained from mentioning that among those who had fled was a large proportion of his own servants: that would have sounded too much like stressing the personal inconvenience the air raids had inflicted.

Whatever his critics might say of him, Sir Reginald did not lack courage and he was determined to see Rangoon rise phoenix-like from the ashes.

Alex Carfax had certainly stayed on and from his vantage point above Victoria Lake had seen one of his warehouses go up in flames and his prized export and import business disappear in a ball of orange fire. Undeterred he had sat at the head of the table with his wife, Avril, and a much depleted guest list, and celebrated Christmas as he had done for the past twenty years or more. Mrs Carfax, furious with the servants who had forsaken duty for safety, had dredged her memory in order to cook the dinner and sat with a smile of smug satisfaction at the way she had coped in the face of so much adversity.

When the port had been drunk and the cigars smoked, and the guests had all departed, Alex Carfax packed the Rolls with crated valuables until the springs were in danger of collapsing. Next morning he intended driving his wife to the docks where, by a mixture of bullying and bribery, he had managed to secure a passage for her to Calcutta.

Avil had declined to accompany her, dreading the thought of sharing a cabin with her and still convinced that things were not as bad as they seemed; and even if they were she could easily drive herself to Mandalay and book a flight to India should the need arise.

Alex Carfax, who had waxed angry at the dinner table about rats deserting a sinking ship, was not motivated by anything as abstract as patriotism when he announced his intention to stay on; he was determined to remain until the banks reopened and he was able to transfer the remainder of his capital. He was quite prepared to sell off his other interests to anyone daft enough to want to buy them.

Suddenly Scotland had acquired an allure it had not previously possessed. No matter how things turned out he would still have enough brass to live in the style of a laird, because he had been canny enough to invest in heavy insurance in the event of a rainy day. Maybe there would not be two caddies, but the cigars would not be any smaller and he certainly would not have to import whisky.

Burma, he reflected, had not treated him badly, and if he had to leave before the cow was milked dry that was just too bad. From what he had read the Jerries had not dropped any bombs on Edinburgh, which made it infinitely more attractive than Rangoon.

Then as the days passed and the Japanese concentrated more and more on purely military targets and towns further north, people began to trickle back to Rangoon. The gloom which had sat over the city like a heavy cloud lifted and life inched back to some degree of normality, although everyone conceded it would never be quite the same again. But the ships were being unloaded and the esential services maintained, although a telephone call took hours and the ban on credit had not been lifted. The local radio station delivered regular programmes and news bulletins. However, the latter never seemed to have anything to say: rumour seemed to have usurped hard fact, and intelligent analysis had given way to optimistic speculation.

Many people found the traumatic experiences they had suffered were, like pain, difficult to recall in any great detail. They were like drunks for whom the memory of Wednesday's hangover was not enough to stop them reaching for the bottle on Friday.

The days of January slipped by into irretrievable oblivion, and though the streets of Rangoon were still littered with the relics of the two air raids, life resumed its old established pattern – a hard morning's work followed by tennis, golf, sailing and swimming, and copious drinks once the sun had sunk over the yardarm. On Saturdays the same old nostalgic songs were sung.

It was true that events in Malaya were not going too well and the Australian and British troops were being driven back, but London had assured the watching world that defeat was out of the question and the invader would be hurled back. These bland assurances were willingly accepted in Burma because the alternative was too horrible to contemplate. And so the European community who had stayed on bolstered each other's confidence with their own interpretation of events in Malaya. The visiting team had shown an unexpected batting strength which had resulted in a high score because the home team had momentarily lost line and length. In no time at all the balance would be restored and the invaders skittled out. There was an over-abundance of cricketing metaphors in Rangoon's clubs and bars.

Confidence was further restored by the announcement that more and more reinforcements were arriving in Rangoon harbour, fighting fit and anxious to display their martial qualities. No one mentioned that many of them were raw recruits, mainly Indian and Gurkha, who had yet to sniff the aroma of cordite and who had to unload their own vehicles and equipment because a major part of the labour force was still absent. Neither was it made public that what equipment they did have was inferior and incapable of halting a determined attack.

The Governor also encouraged bulletins that were wholly optimistic, obsessed as ever with the need to maintain morale, and those who remained firm gobbled up the misinformation like fat cats lapping up the spillings from the milking bucket. They were content to be cocooned from reality and had no desire to break out and face the truth.

Unknown to Army Intelligence, the Japanese had been massing troops on the Indo-China and Burma-Siam borders. Without warning two divisions slipped into Siam, where the Thais offered little resistance after being assured that their sovereignty was assured. Then two more divisions crossed into Burma. They were tough, frugal, bestial men who could survive on meagre rations and when they ran out could live off the land. They bore no resemblance to the soldiers who had been caricatured in the information disseminated among the British troops; they were not myopic runts with little stomach for a fight, but seasoned campaigners who had been baptised in the cauldron of battle in the long standing war against China, and at the warfare school in Formosa where there was no shortage of human targets on which to practise with rifle and bayonet. It was an honour to die for the Emperor who was a God, and the thought of surrender was unthinkable. Unlike the British army which had never been allowed to train in the jungle because of the risks of malaria and other tropical diseases, they had been taught

59

to use it to their own advantage. They also brought a new and terrifying form of warfare which frequently unnerved the young untrained soldiers who were sent to combat it. The Japanese troops moved silently and stealthily through the jungle, launching surprise attacks to the accompaniment of whistles, Very pistols and tracer bullets, and adding their own spine-chilling screams to the cacophony of battle.

The British and Empire troops fought with great courage, but they were no real match for the ruthless and dedicated killers, and one disaster quickly followed another. In a short time the army was in retreat on most fronts, although the use of the word 'retreat' was specifically banned by Churchill because it was demoralising.

The man sent out to lead the men in actual battle was Major General Jackie Smyth, VC, MC, recognised as one of the army's most outstanding fighting soldiers. The VC had been won in the First War, the MC in the Afghan War, and to these had been added six mentions in despatches, the last for his outstanding bravery at Dunkirk. His appointment had been greeted with unqualified approval, but in a very short time acclaim was replaced by condemnation. Smyth failed to live up to the legend.

As his troops continued to be driven back he was faced with an agonising decision when they reached the Sittang river, spanned by a vital railway bridge and boarded over to permit motorised transport to use it. If the enemy seized the bridge the road to Rangoon was wide open. Although a large proportion of his troops was still on the wrong side of the river, Smyth gave the order for the bridge to be blown, leaving them stranded. Many managed to swim across, others built rafts or paddled over in any boats they managed to find on the bank. But casualties were tragically high. Large numbers drowned in the swollen river, while many more were killed or captured.

The controversial decision taken by Smyth had little effect on the Japanese advance. They crossed the river upstream, and in an astonishingly short period of time Rangoon was in danger of capture. Soothing bulletins continued to be issued, assuring the jittery remnants of the population that the city was not threatened and there was no question of evacuation, although it did not really matter as Rangoon was finished as a great commercial centre. The city, once pulsating with life, now resembled a patient in the terminal stages of an incurable illness but still clinging pathetically to life. Few shops were open, the banks had moved to Mandalay or Calcutta, and most of the hotels and restaurants had put up their shutters. It was essential, however, to keep the port operating for as long as possible, for the beleagured army depended on it for supplies and reinforcements.

Morale among the remaining population, never extremely high, suffered another severe denting when it was learned that Lady Dorman-Smith and her two daughters had left for the relative safety of Maymyo.

Another mass exodus followed, comparable to those which followed the two air raids, and prompted by further outbreaks of violence which made the streets so dangerous few people dared to venture out. Much of the violence was orchestrated by the Fifth Column which officials had stoutly denied existed. The stores and go-downs the Japanese bombers had not destroyed were burnt down, and anyone who attempted to stop the arsonists was ruthlessly murdered. Apart from the politically motivated saboteurs there were the usual mobs of looters who destroyed anything they considered worthless, and that included huge quantities of drugs and medicine which had arrived in the docks for use by the army.

Sergeant Harris wondered how long it would be before the Rocks ceased to be jacks-of-all-trades and received orders to leave the city and engage the enemy in battle.

61

Chapter Five

Sergeant Harris was escorted into the Commanding Officer's personal eyrie, a spacious room above the officers' mess with a large square window which provided a panoramic view of the parade ground and barracks. He paused before the long, uncluttered desk and saluted smartly, wondering why he had been summoned to the holy of holies and racking his brain to remember where and how he might have blotted his copybook.

Lieutenant-Colonel the Honourable Rupert Selthorpe, DSO, dismissed his adjutant with an airy wave of his hand and gestured to a comfortable armchair. It stood beside a table on which were a bottle of whisky and a siphon of soda nestling in a ice bucket.

'Park your arse, Sergeant, and take the weight off your feet.'

Harris heaved an inward sigh of relief, happy to know that the Old Man did not want his guts for garters. When he was vulgarly familiar it was a good omen.

Rupert Selthorpe resembled a horse that had just overcome a rather severe attack of colic. A sparse moustache failed to disguise a top lip that lacked depth, and his nose was long and thin and seemed about to touch his upper lip which was drawn back exposing a row of tusklike yellow teeth. His thin hair, the colour of sandpaper, was plastered across his skull in a none too successful attempt to conceal his growing baldness. He was as lean as a whippet and, as he liked to claim, 'as fit as a fiddler's bitch'.

Although he would inherit a vast estate and almost

62

immeasurable wealth when his father eventually gave up the ghost, he had no interest in anything but the Regiment. It was the sole purpose of his life. His father had been Colonel, as had *his* father, and *his* father before him. The name of Selthorpe was known in every part of the Empire whose proud boast was that the sun never set on it, and Rupert Selthorpe had served in many parts of it: Aden, Palestine, India, West Africa, Malaya and now Burma. He was a bachelor by choice and not inclination, because the Regiment was his wife and his children and his attitude to his profession was simple and uncomplicated. If Private Jones died in an assault on an unimportant hill on orders given by a senior officer who had never learned the lessons of the Somme, he would continue to storm it until it was taken because he would not want one of his men to die to no purpose. He had won a DSO in the First War, been mentioned in despatches, did not know the meaning of fear, and could drink most men under the table. His troops admired him and trusted him completely.

Despite the effete and somewhat unimpressive appearance, he was a very perceptive man, and while his betters had confidently predicted that Japan would never attack Burma, he had shrewdly deduced that the apathy, complacency and lack of preparation were an open invitation for them to walk in and take it. So, well before the first air raid, he had insisted, much to the annoyance but later gratification of everyone, that the wives should be evacuated to Mandalay. Men, he knew, could not fight to the best of their ability if they were worried about the well-being of their loved ones.

He took the chair opposite Harris and poured out two liberal measures of whisky, adding just a squirt of soda.

He raised his glass. 'Cheers, and good luck, Sergeant. You're going to need it.' His nose twitched like a doormouse's scenting a granary.

Harris lifted his glass and said, 'Your health, sir, and the Regiment's,' while thinking: What's the old rascal cooked up? That nose of his only works overtime when he's about to spring an unpleasant surprise. He can be a mischievous old bugger. The Colonel's next words confirmed his fears.

'You're wondering why you're sitting in a comfortable

63

chair drinking my whisky as if you were a member of my club. Well, I'll tell you. I'm mellowing you for the lousy news I'm just about to deliver. You'll hate my bloody guts.' (The Colonel could match any of his men when it came to strong language.)

Selthorpe's harsh stare pierced Harris like a poniard. 'My news can wait a minute though. First I want to know how you read the present state of things, Sergeant. And I want an honest answer.'

Harris pondered the question, wondering if it would be wise to be frank or more discreet to be tactful. He opted for the latter. 'As we haven't been involved in the actual fighting, sir, I can't express a personal opinion. I can only rely on the official communiques, and they are very encouraging.'

'Take no notice of those rosy bulletins the local radio puts out. We're going to be kicked out of Burma. That's not defeatist, just hard fact, unpalatable though it may be. The campaign has been a disaster from the very beginning.'

Harris tried hard to remain expressionless because non-commissioned officers were not normally taken into a Commanding Officer's confidence. He thought no less of the Colonel because of his bluntness; he was merely expressing thoughts he himself had not had the courage to voice. Even so, he was still bewildered: what had the Colonel's misgivings got to do with him being in his room?

Harris fidgeted uncomfortably through the ensuing long silence but the Colonel showed no sign of wanting to break it. So he decided to end it himself. 'Things should improve now that General Alexander has taken over, sir. A splendid fighting soldier and a fine tactician.'

'He certainly is, Sergeant.'

'He's also very popular with the men, sir, and that's something that is often overlooked by those who've never led others into battle.'

Harris was not being sycophantic, he believed every word he was speaking. Alexander had become a legend in his own lifetime and the men worshipped him. There wasn't a soldier who was ignorant of his achievements. What's more he looked the part. He was remarkably handsome and certainly had panache, wearing his Guard's cap at a

64

rakish angle very much as his naval counterpart Beatty had done. And he possessed the right pedigree, both by birth and example. The third son of an Earl, he had won the MC and DSO in the First War, been wounded three times and mentioned in despatches five times.

'He says he will turn Rangoon into another Tobruk, sir, and if any man can do it he can,' ventured Harris.

Selthorpe knew that Alexander had already abandoned all hope of doing that, for soon after his arrival he had quickly recognised that the retention of the city was out of the question and Burma itself could not be saved. But given a modicum of luck he could save the army.

Selthorpe said, 'I'm afraid you're in for a disappointment, Sergeant. The General will be announcing very soon that Rangoon is to be evacuated, and the scorched earth policy carried out to prevent the Japanese taking over vital installations. The army is going to retreat, sorry withdraw, all the way to India. There it will be rebuilt so that we can return and retake Burma.'

Harris was stunned by the news; he had known things were not going too well, but he had never imagined they had reached such a low ebb. He was still wondering, though, where he fitted in and what the Colonel had in mind.

'The Rocks have been honoured with the task of providing the rear-guard in the withdrawal fron Rangoon and, forgive me if I sound hackneyed, Sergeant, we will be called upon, if necessary, to fight to the last man and the last round.'

'You can count on us doing that, sir.'

'Unfortunately, though you may well think otherwise, you will not be with us.'

'I don't like that very much, sir.'

'Don't look so ruddy down in the mouth, Sergeant! You'll probably wish to God you had been allowed to stay with the rest of us. You aren't going on any picnic, lad. I've chosen you for a special job because I think you're the best man for it.'

The Colonel refilled the glasses. 'I'm giving you the task of taking the Regimental Colours and Silver to safety. They must not be allowed to fall into enemy hands. I pulled every string I could to get them aboard an India bound ship, but the ruddy dock official in charge of evacuation said he had no time to worry about a flag and some silver table pieces. Bloody fool didn't realise what they meant to the Regiment.'

Harris knew that the loss of the Colours and the Silver would be akin to cutting off the Old Man's arms and legs; their value could not be measured in monetary terms. They were the past, present and future of the Regiment. The Colours bore the battle honours which had been won in campaigns all over the world, while the Silver was another proud record of the Regiment's achievements. Many of the items had been plundered from vanquished foes; there was a helmet taken from the body of one of Napoleon's Imperial Guard at Waterloo, a Russian snuff box from the Crimea, a priceless model in silver of the Taj Mahal captured when the Red Fort in Delhi was relieved during the Indian Mutiny, along with numerous other objects, all of which had an accompanying story of gallantry and self-sacrifice.

'Outsiders can't understand how important they are to us,' said the Colonel. 'Like an Olympic medal, you can't put a price tag on them. Ever been in India, Sergeant?'

The question was so unexpected it caught Harris offguard and he heard himself say, 'Yes, sir.'

'Thought so,' said Selthorpe with the slightest hint of a smile. 'Wasn't trying to catch you out. Seen you on a horse, and you don't learn to ride like that in Aldershot. Not that it matters. Know what ma-bap means?' The Colonel did not wait for him to reply. 'Sepoys say "ap mai ma-bap hai", when referring to their regiment. Means "you are my mother and father". That's how I like to think my own men regard the Regiment. Likely as not many of us will be called upon to make the supreme sacrifice, but there'll be no shortage of others to fill their places, and the Colours and Silver will be their inheritance.'

'I'd rather you entrusted them to somebody else, sir, but I'll do my best to see they reach safety.'

'Couldn't ask more of any man. You can take two trucks from the transport section, and pick three men to accompany you. See the quartermaster and he'll make certain you get everything you need for a long journey. Any men you particularly want?'

Harris replied without hesitation. 'Simmonds, Fazackerley and Wagstaff, sir.'

'A good choice. They won't let you down.'

The Colonel took a long sip of his drink, wiped his moustache with the back of his hand, and studied the face of the man opposite. You are a human enigma, young man, he thought.

Several times in the past he had been sorely tempted to make some discreet inquiries into Harris's past, but at the last minute had always desisted. His sense of honour would not allow him to satisfy his curiosity at the expense of a man's privacy. If Harris had some skeleton locked away in a closet he had no right to start opening doors. Of one thing he was certain: Harris was not the person he claimed to be. For a start, he knew too much about the army to have acquired the knowledge purely from years spent soldiering. The slip over India could be a pointer. Furthermore, he had the polished manners that you just did not acquire in the ranks, or even the sergeant's mess. It was not a snobbish observation, for despite his own background the Colonel was the least snobbish of men; his sole criterion was not where a man came from but what he was and, like it or not, Harris was a silk purse pretending to be a sow's ear.

Selthorpe's interest in Harris was genuine and not born out of sheer curiosity, for the welfare of his men occupied more of his thoughts than the affairs of his officers. If the latter lived up to his requirements he left them alone; if they did not, he found a way of getting rid of them. He did not give a tinker's cuss if they womanised and drank a little more than was good for them on mess nights, so long as they surfaced in the morning as bright as buttons. He was not so old he could not remember his own green and salad days. But he was ruthless if they were bullies, incompetent, or ran up mess bills they could not meet. It showed a lack of self-discipline, a fatal flaw if they were to lead men into battle. If they lacked initiative he had no time for them.

His attitude to his men was entirely different. He saw them as the jetsam of an uncaring society. They found the

67

Regiment a spar they could cling to, and without which they would flounder in a sea of indifference. His personal role was that of surrogate father. Unlike the politicians, whom he heartily despised for starting wars soldiers had to fight, he would never ask them to do anything he was not prepared to do himself. Neither could he forgive the Frocks — his favourite term of derision for the people in Westminster — for promising 'homes for heroes' after the First War, then reneging on their pledge. One of his proudest boasts was that you would never see an old Rock selling matches at the kerbside. He personally saw to that.

And it was this affection for his men that made him so interested in Harris, who gave everything to the Regiment and asked nothing in return. He was a splendid soldier, dependable and self-reliant, which was why he had chosen him for the job of taking the Colours and Silver to safety. But it pained Selthorpe to see Harris remaining aloof and detached, and he wondered if there was something in his past that accounted for it.

Selthorpe sighed audibly; Harris's past was his own concern. He stood up and crossed to his desk where he took a map from a drawer and spread it out on the top.

'Not very good, but the best I could manage in the circumstances. You know, we don't possess any decent field maps of Burma; weren't considered necessary because everyone said it was an impossible place to fight a war.' His forefinger traced a route through some of the most daunting terrain in the world. 'My advice is to head for Mandalay where I'm told you stand a good chance of getting aboard an aircraft to India. If the transport lets you down get on a Flotilla steamer and go by water. I don't really mind how you get there, but get there. When you've handed everything over, make your own arrangements for rejoining the Regiment.'

'When do we start, sir?'

'When you leave my office. Brief your three men while I get a working party to load up the trucks. I want you to be ready to leave first thing in the morning. Time's the enemy.'

'Anything else, sir?'

'No. I'll be there to see you off.'

68

Harris saluted and was about to leave when the Colonel said, 'Almost forgot to mention it: you'll have two passengers, a nursing sister who's being sent up country to find a suitable location for a hospital which is about to be evacuated, and a young woman who hasn't been able to find a berth aboard a ship or a seat on a train. Father went down on his knees begging me to help. Seems she planned to drive up-country in her own car, but it was requisitioned because she didn't have an E windscreen sticker, the things they issued to essential personnel when the evacuation plan was drawn up. Why the hell anyone wanted her car is beyond me; the docks are full of Lease-Lend vehicles that are being destroyed to prevent the Japs using them. Didn't have the heart to turn her away.'

Harris pulled a face. 'It never rains but it pours, sir.'

'Look on the bright side, Sergeant. They'll relieve the boredom if nothing else.'

Harris had just reached the door when Selthorpe halted him. 'Tell me, Sergeant, is your name really Harris?'

'No, sir.'

'Thought not, but never mind. If I survive this I'll forget I ever asked. Just damned curious. No right to be. Take the bottle with you, Sergeant. It might help when you chat to your lads.'

As he walked down the stairs, Harris fervently hoped the Colonel and his men would not be called upon to lay down their lives. They deserved the opportunity to return to Burma as the spearhead of a new and victorious army.

Sergeant Harris sent a messenger to the wet canteen to ask the three privates to report to his quarters. It was the only place he could think of where he could talk in private. He saw no point in letting everyone else know what had been planned. There could well be a rush of volunteers for the job, and he certainly had no intention of providing an opportunity for any of the three he had chosen to opt out. Like himself they would prefer to remain and fight; that was one of the reasons he had selected them.

Fazackerley, Wagstaff and Simmonds arrived at his

quarters displaying all the nervous concern he himself had felt when ordered to report to the Colonel.

'Find somewhere to sit and make yourselves comfortable while I pour you a very large scotch. Colonel's compliments,' said Harris. The three privates visibly relaxed and glanced around the spartan and sparsely furnished room for somewhere to sit.

Wagstaff and Simmonds sat on Harris's cot and Fazackerley perched on the top of a small chest of drawers.

The bottle contained only enough for a tot each by the time Harris had finished his briefing.

'That's it, lads. You should be honoured at the privilege.'

'One fing I'd like to say, Sarge,' said Wagstaff. 'I 'ope this don't reach the ears of any of the uvvers because they're goin' to accuse us of puttin' our own skins first. Desertion in the face of the enemy.'

'You didn't volunteer, you were press ganged,' said Harris. 'The Colonel told me to choose my own team. You are it.'

He picked up a note pad on which he had written a long list of the items they should take with them.

'Personal belongings: three shirts, three pairs of shorts. As many socks as you can lay your hands on. Changes of underwear. Shaving kit and personal weapons. I've arranged to draw a Tommy-gun and a Bren from the armoury. I've also managed to get a couple of decent compasses and some medical supplies.' He poured the final tots. 'Knock these back and then you can start packing. One final thing – we'll be having two young ladies in the party, so watch your p's and q's. Especially you, Simmonds. I don't want you to try and impress them with your masculine attribute.'

The three privates laughed, and Harris was relieved that they had not objected to being selected to do the job even though he knew how much they would have preferred being in the rearguard.

He produced a handful of rupee notes saying, 'Buy as many bottles of beer as this will go to. I don't know how long it'll be before you get the chance of another drink-up. And make sure you're on the parade ground at six in the morning, sharp.'

Wagstaff looked at the bundle of notes and said, 'We can't take all this, Sarge. It'll buy enough wallop to float the Queen Mary.'

Harris said, 'I'm not leaving myself short. In any case there won't be much to spend money on where we're going.'

Chapter Six

Sergeant Harris tested the lashings securing the wooden crates containing the Silver and nodded approvingly; it would take an earthquake to shift them. Each of the lorries contained two boxes that had been stowed against the back of the driving cabs, with enough space between so as not to impede the rear view of the drivers. Apart from the need to distribute the weight evenly so that each of the vehicles was capable of the same performance, Colonel Selthorpe had deemed it unwise to put all the precious eggs in one basket. Rumours were rife that marauding bands of dacoits were halting trains and killing the occupants for their miserable possessions, lying in wait like hungry predators along the two main routes of evacuation.

He had said to Harris, 'I don't think anyone would be silly enough to try and hi-jack army vehicles, but better to be safe than sorry. But if you *are* attacked, there's always the chance of one vehicle escaping and returning to beat off any looters.' Harris knew it was an old and simple strategem which had proved extremely effective on the North West Frontier of India against the Pathans who were adept at ambushing army columns in order to seize highly prized weapons. There they had often been wrong footed, parts of the column pretended to flee only to reappear, and so preoccupied were the tribesmen with brandishing the arms they had stolen they were as easy to pick off as targets in a shooting gallery.

The sergeant felt quite unnerved, however, at the daunting task of getting everything to safety. Until he had been handed

72

the typed inventory he had had no idea how many priceless items there were. Wrapped in thick hessian sacking were candlesticks, a statue of a Rock officer in full dress uniform, silver goblets and tankards, an exquisitely modelled tiger presented by a rajah in appreciation of services rendered, cigar and cigarette boxes, decanters in elaborate stands, wine coasters, and presentations from departing officers. Colonel Selthorpe had not exaggerated when he said they represented a complete record of the Regiment's history.

The remainder of the space in the trucks was taken up by jerrycans of petrol and water, all clearly marked, tins of food and condensed milk, spades and pickaxes in case they got bogged down, boxes of ammunition for the Bren and Thompson and their personal weapons, spare wheels, and a steel box containing field dressings and first aid equipment.

Colonel Selthorpe stood on the parade ground beside the trucks, holding the Colours in their protective covering as if anxious to hold on to them until the last possible moment. When he finally handed them over to Harris, he said gravely, 'Don't let them out of your sight, and put a guard on them at night. I wouldn't want them to end up as a trophy in some Japanese mess.' He looked at his watch. 'The first of your passengers should be here any minute now. Then you can be off.'

Harris detected a noticeable gruffness in his voice, and realised the Colonel felt as deeply about his departure as any mourner standing over an open grave. He felt compelled to say something comforting. 'Don't worry, sir. You'll see it all again. On the mess table when it's all over.'

Selthorpe coughed and brushed away a non-existent fly from his eye. He said hoarsely, 'It's not for me, Sergeant. Damnit, they're not my property.'

It was an emotional scene that both men wanted to end, but they had to endure an interminable period of waiting because there was no sign of the woman. Selthorpe tugged at the lashings which Harris had already tested several times, and the sergeant counted the cans of water and petrol yet again, although he knew exactly how many there were.

They waited half an hour, then a further twenty minutes,

with the Colonel glancing at his watch first every five minutes, then every minute, then every few seconds, his annoyance mounting as the second hand ticked its way round the face. Then a Rolls-Royce emerged from a cloud of dust on the perimeter of the parade ground and headed towards the waiting group. A corpulent man in a white duck suit stepped out from behind the steering wheel, and a young white woman and a Burmese girl got out of the back.

The man removed his topee and mopped his brow. 'Sorry for the hiccup, Colonel, but you know what women are: forget their heads if they weren't stuck on. Avril decided at the last moment there were one or two things she couldn't do without.' He seemed remarkably unconcerned even indifferent, to his lack of punctuality.

Selthorpe said, 'You're damned lucky I didn't tell Sergeant Harris to go without her, Carfax.' He looked at the Rolls with ill-disguised distaste and said, almost venomously, 'If I'd known you had that damned great thing at your disposal I wouldn't have agreed to take her. What's to stop *you* driving her to Mandalay? We're not running a bloody bus service.'

Carfax bridled. 'I intend taking myself there, but not just yet.' He became aggressive. 'I've been in this country longer than most people, and all I possess is here. I'm going to sacrifice a lot, but I'm going to make bloody sure I don't lose *everything*.' The blatant untruth did not worry him at all; the fact that he had transferred assets was nothing to do with the army. 'I'm going home to pick up the most important things. The stuff I can't carry has been buried in the garden, and I'm crossing my fingers that the buggers who dug the hole don't dig it up as soon as my back is turned. One day, when it's all over, I'll return.' He stared hard at the Colonel. 'I presume the army does intend returning? Though maybe not as quickly as it's pulling out.' He smiled at the barbed inference and waited for Selthorpe to rise to the bait. He did not like his attitude; if the troops had shown a little more spunk there would have been no need to ask favours. But Selthorpe turned his back on him and spoke to Harris.

Carfax shrugged and muttered, 'Rude sod. Wouldn't have dared talk to me like that in normal times.' Until his taunt about the army's prowess, Alex Carfax had not given any serious thought to the question of returning; now he was anxious not to appear a coward. Not that it mattered all that much; he would see how things developed. If a return, when it was all over, was easy and profitable, he would do so. If not he would happily remain in Scotland. He was, he told himself, a canny cautious man who, metaphorically speaking, wore both belt and braces.

He turned towards the Rolls and spoke rapidly in Burmese to the houseboy who sat in the seat alongside the driver. The boy jumped out and began to unload several suitcases from the spacious boot.

Harris looked on with astonishment. Apart from the cases there were a portable gramophone and record holder, a carton of gin, several siphons of soda, two tennis raquets, three boxes of balls, and a hamper of food.

He looked at the girl and groaned inwardly, wondering what in heaven's name the Colonel had let him in for. She was dressed in a very strange manner for someone about to embark on a long and arduous journey through some extremely inhospitable country. She wore a topee on her head, a mink stole over her shoulders, and a pale blue linen suit. In one hand she held a jewellery case, in the other a vanity box. She looked very much like the bitch who had tried to run him over.

She saw his expression and said brusquely, 'Do you approve, Sergeant?' but before he had a chance to reply she was speaking to the Burmese girl. 'Don't just *stand* there, Nellie. Help the boy put the luggage in one of the trucks.'

Harris said, 'Hold on, Miss Carfax. You can't possibly take all that stuff. Only essentials, I'm afraid.'

'Your idea of what is essential and mine are clearly different,' she said haughtily. 'Nellie, do be careful. Anyone would think you were handling sacks of cement.'

Harris glanced towards the Colonel, seeking support and guidance. 'Let the young lady take everything *she* considers necessary to make life tolerable, Sergeant,' he said resignedly. 'Otherwise we'll be here all day arguing. But you have my permission to jettison anything and everything when and if you think fit. The important thing to bear in mind is not her personal comfort but the treasures which have been entrusted to your care.'

The girl turned, her voice strident with indignation. 'If my car hadn't been requisitioned by some over zealous nincompoop I could have gone under my own steam and with as much baggage as I wanted. Instead my father had to come cap-in-hand begging for a lift.' She stamped her foot in petulant anger. 'If the army had done its job properly, Colonel, there would be no need for this disgraceful scuttle. It almost makes one ashamed to be British.'

Selthorpe's voice was abrasive. 'When I encounter rather spoiled little brats like you, Miss Carfax, I have similar thoughts. No one is ordering you to accompany Sergeant Harris. The choice is yours.'

Carfax blustered, 'Just a minute, Colonel, you have no right to talk to her like that. You're not addressing some coolie, or one of your own men.'

The Colonel's voice was annoyingly casual. 'Why don't you just get into your car and attend to your unfinished business, otherwise you might find you've left it too late. Very soon the signal will be given to start the demolition.'

Harris sensed an explosive situation of quite a different nature was building up and it was time for a tactful intervention. He saluted, 'Permission to proceed, sir?'

'Whenever you're ready, and good luck.'

'Thank you, sir. I hope we won't need too much.'

The Colonel said, 'With all this argy-bargy going on I almost forgot a most important thing.' He extended a hand to his adjutant standing close by, and was handed a stout canvas bag of the type used by banks. 'Two hundred silver rupees, Sergeant. You might find they'll come in useful if you have to buy your way out of trouble. When a country is about to be overrun, notes lose their value. Silver never does.' He turned to Carfax, his tone mellower. 'Better say goodbye to your daughter.'

The others averted their eyes, not wishing to intrude on what they imagined would be an emotional and intimate farewell.

Carfax hugged her briefly and planted a perfunctory kiss on her cheek. 'I'll meet you in Mandalay as soon as I can. Meanwhile I've made arrangements for you to draw money from the Imperial Bank. I've also booked you into the club where you can stay until you find more suitable accommodation. You've enough cash to last until Mandalay. Can't think of anything else.'

Avril said, 'Goodbye, Daddy, and look after yourself.'

'You too, lassie, and remember − if you get the chance of a flight out before I arrive, take it. Make your way to Delhi and book in at the Willingdon. I'll catch you up.'

Harris called the three privates together and told them Wagstaff would be driving the second truck. He would be driving the first himself. Simmonds would ride shotgun beside him armed with the Thompson, and Fazackerley would man the Bren in the second vehicle.

'Mount up as soon as you're ready,' he said. He turned to the girl. 'Miss Carfax, you and your maid can ride in the back of my truck. There's a pile of blankets you can sit on for a little added comfort.'

'I would prefer to ride in the cabin with you, Sergeant. I never travel *with* Nellie, if you know what I mean. It's not the done thing.'

'You should have known we would not be travelling in Pulman comfort, Miss Carfax, so let's not argue. I have another important passenger to pick up, and we're late already.'

'I am not sitting with Nellie, and that is that,' she said. 'Now stop dawdling, Nellie, or you'll be left behind.'

Harris gave an exaggerated sigh of exasperation: the bloody woman was impossible, but he could not turf her out and send her back home. He was tempted to point out that she had not minded sitting with Nellie in the Rolls, but decided it would be a waste of time; she would only remind him that that had been an emergency situation and therefore unavoidable.

'Move over, Simmonds, and make room for the lady. If we run into any trouble and she prevents you from using the Thompson, just open the door and kick her out.'

Harris started the engine, pushed the gear lever into first, and let the clutch out so fiercely the jerk threw Miss Carfax forward and she banged her knees on the dashboard. By the time I've finished, Harris told himself, she'll be bloody glad to ask if she can go in the back.

Through his rear mirror he could see Colonel Selthorpe standing ramrod stiff and saluting. Carfax's Rolls had gone.

As the two vehicles headed for the hospital to pick up the other passenger, Miss Carfax said, 'The way you drive, Sergeant, I'm surprised they let you behind a wheel. You're quite reckless.'

'That, I might say, is a classic example of the pot calling the kettle black. I personally witnessed your driving skill when you almost wrote me off in the Strand.'

She flushed, vaguely recalling the incident. 'You were day dreaming, or drunk, one of the two. I hooted and swerved like mad to avoid killing you,' she said defensively. 'You were entirely at fault. Anyway, this is no time to try and get your own back.'

Without taking his eyes off the road Harris said, 'Simmonds, if she opens her mouth again, I'll stop the truck and you can toss her into the back with her maid. That seems the most severe punishment I can administer.'

The girl lapsed into a petulant silence, musing that her father had been absolutely right in everything he had said about soldiers: they *were* uncouth louts. From the man's accent one could be forgiven for thinking he was a gentleman, but he clearly was not. From the tone of his voice she deemed it wise not to express her thoughts out loud; he was quite capable of carrying out his threat, and what would anyone think if they saw her travelling in the back like a common peasant? She conveniently overlooked the fact that the rear was covered by a canvas hood.

They drove through the now almost deserted streets where fires still smouldered, and armed foot patrols were out in force hunting down the remaining gangs of looters and fire raisers.

Some of the looters had clearly been encouraged by the spectacle of British and Indian officers and men helping themselves to anything of value they could find in the abandoned shops and warehouses, not knowing the patrols had been given strict orders not to open fire on them as they had been issued with 'permits to loot' because most were survivors of the débâcle at Sittang and had been forced to swim or paddle crudely made rafts across the river when the bridge was blown. They had managed to struggle back to Rangoon with nothing but the clothes they wore. In some cases this was no more than a vest and underpants.

The permits had been issued with the strict proviso that they were only entitled to replace lost equipment such as knives, forks, toothbrushes, razors, and any clothing they were fortunate enough to find. But this was so loosely interpreted that officers and men helped themselves to all kinds of luxury items from watches and cigarettes to golf clubs. One enterprising officer had even managed to capture an abandoned cow that was put on the back of a lorry, thus ensuring a regular supply of fresh milk.

The patrols turned a blind eye on their activities, knowing how bitter and resentful many of the survivors were.

General Smyth had been 'sold' to them as a soldier's soldier, the kind of man it was an honour and privilege to fight alongside; but they believed, rightly or wrongly, that he had panicked and abandoned them and many of their comrades to an unknown fate. They were further incensed by the knowledge that during the retreat to the bridge they had been strafed and bombed by the RAF and AVG, and although they had seen the markings on the wings quite clearly they had been assured that they were mistaken. They would have been angrier still if they had known it had been a deliberate decision not to admit the error because that would have been bad for morale.

Drink was still plentiful and many soldiers were staggering drunk; there were few vehicles that did not contain a cache of stolen booze. It seemed pointless to leave anything behind for the Japs to enjoy.

In the harbour, amid the scenes of chaos, newly arrived reinforcements were unloading their own equipment which included tanks and artillery, but they had arrived too late and in too little quantity to have a decisive effect on the war.

Harris observed it all from the cab of his truck as he made his way in the direction of the hospital. He had been forced to make numerous detours because the streets were still cluttered with the burnt out wrecks of trams, cars, buses and other assorted vehicles, while enormous craters made other roads impassable.

He passed army lorries filled with corpses and manned by soldiers wearing gas masks who had the unsavoury task of dumping the rotting bodies into the harbour. He thought that was one task that could have been left to the Japs. At one crossroads he saw a completely naked man directing non-existent traffic, and at another junction was convinced his eyes had deceived him: padding along the pavement with deceptive casualness was a tiger.

'Did you see that, Simmonds?' he asked in disbelief.

'A tiger, I think, Sarge. Too big for a tabby.' He spoke as if such sights were commonplace. 'Didn't like to say so, seeing as you're driving and wouldn't want to be distracted, but I think I saw a giraffe when we passed what remains of Scott's Market.'

'Stop being silly, the pair of you,' snapped Miss Carfax. 'If you think you're going to scare me, you've got another think coming.'

'Miss Carfax, you have a very short memory!' The sergeant's voice was so icily threatening she clamped her jaws tight and stared straight ahead, hoping her silence was an eloquent expression of her total disdain.

The wheels of the trucks threw up handfuls of gravel as they braked to a halt on the drive outside the entrance to the hospital that appeared an oasis of calm after the shambles and confusion they had just driven through.

Standing on the wide flight of steps leading to a revolving door was a woman wearing a khaki drill shirt and a pair of men's slacks. Her head was covered by a big straw coolie hat, and slung over one shoulder was a rusksack. In one hand she carried a red and green gold umbrella, in the other a portable wireless set.

Harris dismounted, walked up the steps and saluted. 'Sergeant Harris. Are you Sister Bradshaw?'

She put down the umbrella and wagged a reproving finger. 'This won't do, Sergeant. Punctuality is one thing I insist upon.' He smiled, knowing from the tone of her voice and the sparkle in her eyes that she was only jesting.

He looked at her feet, enclosed in stout brogue shoes. 'We've got transport, Sister. We won't be hiking to Mandalay.'

'Better safe than sorry. Ever been up-country?'

'Can't say that I have.'

'Stout shoes are every bit as important as a stout heart, especially if the trucks break down. The road to Mandalay, despite Mr Kipling's rhapsodising, is not all it's cracked up to be. The heat's abominable, hence the brolly.'

He looked at the rucksack, and thinking of the mass of luggage the girl had brought, said, 'That all you've got?'

'It's all I need for the time being. The rest of my belongings will catch up with me when the hospital is evacuated. But I do have a largish wooden box I'd like you to find room for. Quinine, morphia, salt tablets, chlorine, bandages, iodine, things like that.'

Harris was aware that malaria was prevalent up-country and how wise it was of her to remember quinine, but the chlorine baffled him. 'Chlorine?'

'For purifying water. I'm not sure what I'll encounter, when and if I find a suitable place for the hospital. Maybe plenty of water, but undrinkable.'

'Let me take your gear,' said Harris, reaching for the rucksack.

'Thank you, young man, but that doesn't leave my sight. Birth certificate, various papers which are proof of my qualifications, a photo of Mum and Dad, and a few odds and ends of sentimental value. Now, hadn't you better introduce me to my travelling companions? I'm very un-British in that respect. I hate to travel in silence and without knowing who everyone is.'

Harris decided that he and Sister Bradshaw were going to get on well together.

He introduced her to the three soldiers who shook hands rather awkwardly, unaccustomed to being treated on equal terms by a memsahib, then to Nellie, and finally, and deliberately, to Avril Carfax.

As the medicine chest was being put into the back of the truck, Sister Bradshaw's eyes caught sight of the tennis raquets and she said mischievously, 'Good idea, Miss Carfax.

81

We might find time for a good three sets on the way. And that mink stole will certainly come in useful.'

Harris had the feeling that while he and the Sister were going to get on, she and Miss Carfax were going to be as compatible as two terriers squabbling over the same bone.

Apart from the sulky, 'Nice to meet you, Sister,' Avril remained stonily and reprovingly silent. The remark about the tennis raquets and the stole had been quite uncalled for, and revealed how little the woman knew of the situation in Mandalay whereas her father had taken the trouble to telephone a friend there to find out the true position.

Sergeant Harris, she thought, can scoff at the amount of luggage I've got and that silly nurse can joke about tennis, but I'm not the fool they take me for. Hand luggage aboard a plane is strictly limited and carefully weighed, but I know that if you wear several layers of clothing and three or four sets of underwear, nobody notices. And I'm sure I'll get away with the mink too. I also happen to know that you can wait forever before getting a flight, and there are some excellent courts at the club where you can pass the time away. It'll be much better than sitting in the 'snake pit' at the club listening to the stupid gossip of the women members.

But she could not be bothered to explain all that to Sister Bradshaw. As far as she was concerned, the nurse was a frustrated old spinster who had come to Burma as one of the 'fishing fleet' but missed out on marriage, which was not too surprising, and resorted to nursing as a substitute. Miss Bradshaw had already been consigned to the 'dustbin' reserved for the socially inferior.

'Where would you like me to go?' asked Sister Bradshaw breezily.

'Please yourself, Sister. You can travel with the driver of the second truck, or if you prefer travel in the back of mine with the Burmese girl.'

Miss Carfax chewed her top lip, reluctant to cause more friction but feeling compelled to speak her mind. 'Sergeant! *If* I'm allowed to say something? She certainly must travel with the driver behind.'

Harris replied, and realised he was being childish, 'He's only a private, Miss Carfax.'

Sister Bradshaw said, 'Don't worry, Miss Carfax, I'll enjoy getting to know your servant. Never had one of my own. Always had to share. Anyway, I'm used to working with coloured and mixed blood.'

Harris grinned, exposing his teeth and making the scar on his face very noticeable. It was going to be a stormy trip, and he had the feeling that Miss Bradshaw was going to prove the most resilient traveller. She had great buoyancy, a sense of humour, and was totally indifferent to the social mores of Burma. And who could tell? Some of her might rub off on to the obnoxious little Miss Carfax.

Avril felt the tears welling to her eyes and wondered why they felt they had to be so beastly. Why couldn't they understand this country? She felt compelled to say something that would take the idiotic smile off the Sergeant's face. 'I was not just thinking of appearances, Miss Bradshaw, but your personal safety. The Sergeant actually saw a tiger in the city.' She made no attempt to conceal how ridiculous she thought the claim was, and was deflated when the nurse said, 'Don't panic, Sergeant, no need to consult an optician. Seems some official panicked and ordered all the animals to be released from the zoo, along with all the lepers, the inmates of a lunatic asylum and the prison. He thought that as there was no longer anyone to look after them, they would starve to death.'

'He deserves to be shot,' snapped Miss Carfax.

'Saved someone else the trouble. Poor devil did it himself when he realised the consequences,' said Miss Bradshaw.

She heaved herself over the tailboard and settled down on the pile of blankets, then hammered on the rear of the cabin. 'Ready to go when you are, Sergeant.'

She smiled at Nellie, then closed her eyes. 'We'll have a chat in a few minutes. Just now I want to be alone with my thoughts for a little while.'

She closed her eyes, wishing she was not engulfed by a feeling of betrayal and guilt. Although she had been ordered to leave the hospital and find an alternative building to which the patients and few remaining staff could be transferred, she could not help thinking it was wrong to abandon the sick and wounded. Suppose the Japs arrived before they could be moved? She heard they had bayonetted and raped the nurses and patients in a hospital in Singapore. Maybe it was just a rumour, but whatever the truth it was an alarming thing to contemplate.

Against her will she found herself drifting into a deep sleep, and by the time the two trucks had turned on to the Prome Road had slipped into temporary but merciful untormented oblivion.

Chapter Seven

Sergeant Harris had been driving for two hours but did not need to glance at the milometer to know they had travelled only eight miles; he had never encountered such congestion. It was far, far worse than the newsreel pictures he had seen of French families fleeing before the German Blitzkrieg. Thousands of people who had fled from Rangoon were choking the road to Prome, one of the main avenues of escape. Cars, ancient buses, ambulances packed with wounded troops, all hooted impatiently at the pedestrians and the families in lumbering bullock carts, horse-drawn gharries, and those on cycles who insisted on using the metalled surface instead of the rutted cart tracks on either side, and stubbornly refused to give way to more mobile forms of transport. The wheels of the countless vehicles churned up great choking clouds of thick red dust which clogged the nostrils, burnt the eyes and reduced visibility to almost zero. Accidents were frequent as impatient drivers left the road to try and leap-frog the slow-moving procession, only to career down the steep bunds on either side which had been erected so that the road was usable during the rainy season. The ground below the raised surface of the road was piled high with dead and injured, whom no one bothered to stop and help, while vehicles which had ground to a halt because of overheating or had run out of fuel, were manhandled off the road, their occupants screaming and white-eyed with fear. Many of the cars had lost wheels, and close examination revealed they had been tampered with by Fifth Columnists.

'Like Epsom Downs on Derby Day,' remarked Simmonds laconically.

'It's going to get a lot worse before it gets any better,' said Sergeant Harris. 'These are the last lot to leave Rangoon. What'll happen when they catch up with those who left earlier? Even more horrible to contemplate is what it'll be like if the army decides to retreat up the Prome Road.'

Miss Carfax remarked impatiently, 'Can't we make a detour and get away from this shambles? There must be side roads.'

'Sorry. Because the rivers provided such a cheap and efficient means of transportation, the roads have been somewhat neglected. As far as I know there are only two roads out of Rangoon capable of taking motorised transport, and this is one of them. There are *some* lateral roads, but they could well peter out into nothing. Not worth the risk.'

'Surely they can see you are army and have priority,' she said angrily. 'They can't be that stupid.'

'When people are concerned with saving their own skin, they don't worry themselves with the claims of others. We'll just have to be patient.'

In the vehicle behind, Wagstaff was cursing as he was forced to use the windscreen wipers and washers to clear the dust obscuring his vision. 'This is a ripe ol' turn up for the book, Zack. I bet 'annibal made better progress when he took his elephants over the bleedin' Alps. Any minute now I'll 'ave to flash the Sergeant an' ask 'im to stop. Engine's so bloody 'ot the radiator's nearly dry. Quite apart from that, my arse feels like I've been sittin' on red 'ot cinders.'

Sister Bradshaw woke from her untroubled sleep and said to Nellie, 'Rude of me to drop off like that, but I had a lot of sleep to catch up on. Feel almost human now.'

Nellie rose from her hunkered position and went and sat beside her. 'It is terrible this is happening to my people. They are running away but have no place to go.' She spat and said, 'The Indians can go to India, but this is our home. We did not ask the British to come here, and we did not ask the Japanese, but no one cares about us.'

Sister Bradshaw patted her hands comfortingly. 'I'm afraid the map is covered with red patches where the

British have turned up uninvited. Now it seems the Japs have been bitten by the same bug.'

'The Japanese say they will treat us well because we are all Asians,' said Nellie hopefully.

'You may find the devil you know is better than the one you don't,' said the nurse. 'Obviously a lot of people think so, otherwise they wouldn't be running away.'

'That was because of the bomb raids.'

'Well, there won't be any more now we're clearing out of Rangoon, so there's no reason why they can't go back, is there? More important at the moment is whether Miss Carfax has mentioned what'll happen to you when we reach Mandalay?'

'The memsahib says she will go over that bridge when she reaches it. I think she wants to fly to India, and then perhaps England.'

'In that case I can't for the life of me think why she wanted to bring you. She can't dump you in Mandalay. Would have been kinder and less selfish to let you find your way to your village and stay there till the war is over.'

Nellie's almond eyes sparkled at the prospect. 'I'd like her to take me to England.'

Miss Bradshaw snorted. 'When hell freezes over she will! I'm afraid your little memsahib is a mite too self-centred to give much thought to the wishes of others, Nellie.'

The maid put her finger to the tip of her button nose. 'She needs me. She would be no good if I am not there. Who would brush her hair, or get ready her bath, or paint her nails? She has never had to do those important things.'

'I suppose she would find that pretty intolerable.' She was going to say more, but decided not to. There was no point in undermining the relationship between mistress and servant, but if the girl was dumped in Mandalay she would do what she could to find her employment.

Harris saw Wagstaff flash his headlights and waited until he found a suitable spot where he could pull off the road. About two miles further on he came across an intersection, and he signalled his intention and stopped on a reasonably flat patch of ground where a few trees and some clumps of bamboo provided partial shade and shelter.

'Trouble?' asked Harris when Wagstaff stopped beside him.

'Nuffin' serious, Sarge. Grindin' along in second gear with all those stops an' starts has made the engine over'eat. Like a pongo in a knockin' shop. Give it a 'our an' it'll 'ave cooled off.'

'Time we had a breather anyway,' said Harris. 'We could all do with a rest. Maybe if the refugees get their heads down for the night we can drive by our headlamps and make up some lost time. If not we can make a really early start.'

The occupants of the trucks clambered out, bending and stretching their tortured limbs, and groaning as they did so, not with pain but from the sheer pleasure of getting away from the constant jolting and jarring.

Fazackerley watched Sister Bradshaw putting her arms high above her head then bringing them down in a revolving movement, and noticing that her breasts were threatening to burst the buttons of her shirt when she reached up. He liked women with big breasts and big buttocks, and she was amply endowed with both. He felt a slight stirring in the area of his crotch, and ruminated on the possible outcome of a mildly amorous approach which could be unobtrusive enough not to be noticed by Sergeant Harris. If *he* saw any shenanigans then the shit really would hit the punkah. The woman, he thought, was certainly no oil painting and might even be flattered.

He feared Harris had read his thoughts, for he bellowed out, 'Fazackerley! Brew up some tea, and don't make too big a fire. Don't want to draw attention.'

'There won't be any flame or smoke, Sarge. Old army dodge I picked up in Palestine when we did desert patrols,' he replied, mildly offended at the slight on his ability.

He rummaged in the back of the truck for an empty petrol can, and when he found one cut off the top and filled it with sand and gravel, then poured a generous measure of petrol into it before lighting it with a match. 'Better than a primus,' he said. He put two billy cans of water on top and added a handful of tea. 'Be able to stand a spoon up in that when it's brewed,' he said with evident satisfaction. 'Rot your boots, Sarge, and put a little bit of lead in anyone's pencil.'

88

When the water had boiled he dripped in spoonfuls of condensed milk. It was hot, strong and sweet, and very palatable. Only Miss Carfax pulled a face, saying, 'Can't we possibly get some fresh milk? This is awful.'

Harris said, 'Even if we could it wouldn't be wise to use it. It'll not be pasteurised as it is from a dairy.'

'How are we off for water, Sergeant?' asked Sister Bradshaw. 'I feel as if I've been rubbed down with sandpaper. That dust is really murderous. I could do with a good wash.'

'Not enough to be wasteful, but plenty for anyone who fancies a sluice down. The ladies can go first, and I'll see there are no peeping Toms,' said Harris jocularly.

'Don't worry about me, Sergeant,' said Miss Bradshaw. 'I've seen so many naked bodies, male and female, that I've lost all sense of modesty. The thought of anyone staring at mine doesn't bother me at all.'

'That may be true, Sister, but I can't say the same for my lads. Private Fazackerley is renowned for his roving eye.' He looked towards the soldier. 'That's so, isn't it?'

Fazackerley felt his cheeks burning. The crafty bugger has been watching me like a hawk, he realised. Now he's reading the riot act.

She said, 'If you can suggest how we can wash down in the middle of nowhere without an audience, I'd be grateful.'

Harris smiled broadly. 'Don't worry. I'd anticipated the problem and took the precaution of packing a zinc bath in my truck. You can wash in the back. The canvas hood will screen you.'

Miss Carfax finished her tea and said, 'If you've no objection, Miss Bradshaw, I'd like to go first.' She attempted a smile. 'This is quite strange for me, quite an ordeal. At home I bathe at least three times a day, but times aren't normal and I'll just have to get used to roughing it. Finish your tea first, Nellie, then bring me a clean towel, soap, and my dressing gown.' She turned to the Sergeant. 'How many cans are we rationed to? Can Nellie take three?'

'Afraid not, only two. Just imagine you're in England where four inches of water is the limit. I've read that even the King has painted a line on his bath so that he won't exceed it.' In a more serious tone he added, 'Until we know what the water supply is like along the road it's better to err on the side of caution. Drinking is more important than washing.'

Nellie rose to her feet, and Harris put a restraining hand on her shoulder. 'No need for you to carry water when there are men around.'

Avril said, 'She really doesn't mind, Sergeant. That's what she's paid for. I hope you aren't going to spoil her. Two cans are not going to break her back.'

Harris said, 'Put the water in the bath, Fazackerley, and don't hang around when you've done it.' He was anxious to make light of a situation Miss Carfax seemed determined to turn into a major issue.

When Avril had disappeared into the back of the truck Sister Bradshaw said, 'You're going to have your hands full with that young lady, Sergeant. She's been thoroughly spoiled and needs to be handled very firmly, otherwise we're going to have trouble.'

'I don't intend carrying any prima donnas, Sister, and I'm hoping she'll quickly realise that. If she doesn't, she'll learn the hard way. If I have to crack the whip, I will.'

As he spoke a series of explosions, like great rolling claps of thunder, reverberated across the sky from the direction of Rangoon, and towering pillars of dense black smoke climbed high into the air, so high they were visible from twenty miles away.

'Good God, what's that? Another air raid,' asked SisterBradshaw.

'No. The denial and demolition order has been given,' said Harris. 'The smoke is burning oil. Means the refinery at Syriam has gone for a Burton. That's comforting. The oil was one of the reasons the Japs invaded. The explosions also mean there won't be much of the docks left for the enemy to make use of.'

As he spoke Nellie let out a terrified scream and jumped out of the truck, followed by Avril who had wrapped a towel around herself.

'Is that an air raid?'

'No. As I've just explained to Sister, it's Rangoon being

blown up by our own side. You can go back and finish your bath.'

When Avril reappeared she was wearing a white towel dressing gown and carrying a hair brush which she handed to Nellie before sitting down by the make-shift stove. Without a word being exchanged, Nellie began brushing her mistress's hair, counting slowly like a child learning its numbers, 'One ... two ... three ...' She handed the brush back when she reached two hundred.

'Be a good girl, Nellie, and give my dirty dress a rinse through before you throw the water away. Not very hygienic, but one mustn't be wasteful, isn't that so, Sergeant?' Her voice was irritatingly sweet.

Sister Bradshaw jumped to her feet and said loudly, 'Miss Carfax! You and I are going to fall out if this nonsense continues. Try washing your own ruddy dress. That's what I'm going to do when I've bathed, *and* brush my own hair.'

Avril looked perplexed. 'What on earth has got into her, Sergeant? It's not my fault she didn't bring a servant.'

Harris tipped away the dregs of his tea with deliberate slowness, and said, 'Miss Carfax, if you don't want that beautiful backside of yours spanked I'd stop making such idiotic remarks. The Sister is quite capable of doing it, you know. What's more, so am I.'

'You wouldn't dare,' she retorted angrily. 'I'll report you to your superior officer. You're not talking to a bazaar bibi.'

His voice was quiet and unruffled. 'If you could find what you call my superior officer, which you won't, he would agree with everything I've said. Now if you don't like what I'm telling you, there's nothing to stop you leaving and taking pot luck with the other refugees.' He gave her no chance to reply but called out to Private Wagstaff, 'Open a couple of tins of bully and boil some eggs. Might as well enjoy them while they're still fresh. Not exactly cordon bleu, I'm afraid, but as Miss Carfax has pointed out, the circumstances are not quite normal.'

Wagstaff began noisily to whistle an old army song he usually sang, but the words were so obscene that out of deference to the ladies he compromised.

91

The soldiers ate with obvious relish, and Sister Bradshaw contented herself with a mild, 'Well, anyone who's eaten hospital food will eat anything.'

Avril declined the food and sent Nellie to get the hamper from the truck. She called out to the others. 'There's no point in eating that stuff when I've got such nice food here. You're welcome to share it.'

Harris said, 'Thanks for the offer, but you hang on to it. Sooner or later you're going to have to eat army rations, so you'd better make hay while the sun shines.'

Explosions continued to kettle-drum in the distance, but everyone had become so accustomed to them that, like people who live beside a railway line, they did not hear the noise.

When they had finished eating Avril said to Nellie, 'Be a useful girl and bring my vanity case. My nails are in a dreadful state.'

Then, oblivious to the outraged stares of Sister Bradshaw, she sat on the hamper while the Burmese girl buffed and painted her finger nails.

When Miss Bradshaw snorted, unable to constrain herself any longer, Avril said quite seriously, 'It's no good grunting like that. Appearances are very important at a time like this. Having my nails done is no more silly than someone dressing for dinner up-country. It's making an important point. Drawing the line between us and the ignorant refugees.'

Wagstaff turned to Simmonds and whispered, 'How far is it to Mandalay, Simmo? It 'adn't better be too long because I'll go stark ravin' bonkers if that little madam don't recognise this ain't the Orient Express and start pullin' 'er weight. Gettin' that kid to do 'er nails! What a bleedin' nerve!'

'She's just a kid herself. You got to realise she's probably never had to clean her own teeth or wipe her own bum,' said the Yorkshireman tolerantly.

'Now that's a job I wouldn't mind taken' on.'

'And another thing,' said Simmonds. 'She's right about keeping up appearances. The Sergeant isn't going to let us drift into shit order. He'll make sure we keep up standards. We may be out of sight of the Colonel but we're still Rocks, and don't you forget it.'

Without any warning Wagstaff suddenly burst into song:

On the road to Mandalay,
Where the flyin' fishes play,
Come you back you British soldier,
Come you back to Mandalay.

'They aren't the right words, Waggy,' said Fazackerley. 'You missed out something about thunder.'

'Zack, me ol' China, I've 'eard enuff thunder to last me a lifetime.' He cocked his head towards Rangoon. 'I can do wivout that lot. The daft sod what wrote that song I was jus' singin' wanted his 'ead examined. I don't wanna come back, I just wanna get to Mandalay, 'and over the silver, and bugger off somewhere safe.'

'The only place you'll bugger off back to is the Battalion, and you know it,' said Simmonds.

'If you was to ask me, I'd say the Battalion is more likely to catch up wiv us. Even the Rocks ain't goin' to be able to 'alt the Japs. They'll chase the army all the way to India.'

Fazackerley said, 'That's bloody defeatist, Waggy. I don't like to hear that kind of thing.'

Wagstaff shook his head. 'That's the kinda remark I expect from a ignorant scouse. I ain't bein' down'earted. Jus' practical. It ain't down to the ordinary pongo; the generals'll decide what 'appens, an' judgin from the way fings 'ave gone so far, they won't stand 'an fight. Stands to reason, don't it? We coulda done that at Dunkirk an' what woulda been the outcome? We'd 'ave 'ad no army left at all. I tell you, we'll bolt out, just like that fox's tail disappears up my jacksie. Then we'll return, which makes sense to me, 'cos that's what General Custer wished 'e'd done. 'E who fights an' runs away, lives to fight anuver day. An' I bet you a pound to a pinch of shit, they is General Alexander's sentiments right now.'

Simmonds said, 'Remind me to look in your bloody knapsack, Waggy, for the Field Marshal's baton.'

Wagstaff said, 'Stop piss takin', Simmo and put your money where your mouth is.' He unbuttoned a pocket and produced the cards. 'I'll take first bank. Pay pontoons and five card tricks.'

As dusk approached Harris walked down to the road to see if the congestion had eased and they could drive through the night while the refugees rested, but the creak of ungreased axles and the clatter of wooden wheels, the bellowing of oxen, and the shuffling of countless feet mingling with the growl of constantly changing gears, told him otherwise.

When he returned he said, 'It's as bad as ever. People are going to carry on until they drop. We might just as well rest and make an early start before sun up. You three ladies can sleep in my truck. The lads will rig up some mosquito netting so that you won't get bitten to death.'

'You mean you want Nellie to share the truck with Miss Bradshaw and me?' asked Avril incredulously.

'Exactly. If you're all together it means I need only post one sentry, which also means each spell can be shorter than if I mount two. And we might as well get one thing clear whilst we are at it, Miss Carfax. There is no sergeants' mess here either. I'll be sleeping with the three privates, not that they'll mind too much. If they can put up with it, then I don't consider it is asking too much of you to pocket your pride and sleep in the same truck as Nellie.'

The harsh timbre of his tone was such that Miss Carfax decided it would be most unwise to argue; anyway, it would only be for a few days. Mandalay was not all that far distant, and there was no reason why anyone should ever find out she had slept with her maid.

Harris said, 'Goodnight,' and made his way to his truck where he sat in the cabin, the Colours resting on his knees, thinking of the Battalion. The explosions meant that the order to commence Red Elephant had been given and the army was withdrawing from Rangoon and heading towards the advancing Japanese. The strategy would be to avoid them if possible, but if that was not so he had no doubt that the Rocks and the rest of the army for that matter, would give a good account of themselves.

Sister Bradshaw climbed into the cabin and sat beside him, saying, 'Penny for them, Sergeant.'

94

Her unexpected appearance startled him. 'I was miles away just then.'

'With your regiment?'

'As a matter of fact, yes. How did you guess?'

'Not difficult. I was thinking of the patients I've left behind. It's no great consolation knowing that I'm only obeying orders. I sensed you must feel the same. I'm beginning to think I should have stayed.'

'Orders are orders, and have to be obeyed; personal feelings don't enter into it.'

'Tell me honestly: do you think Burma can be saved?'

He shrugged. 'I don't think that is a serious consideration. But can the army be saved? It really is a touch and go situation. If the Japs decide on an all out attack it could be a massacre, penned down as our troops will be to a single road. I'm afraid the Japs have taught us a harsh lesson when it comes to this kind of fighting. We're totally dependent on motorised transport, whereas they march. When we come back we'll have to fight them on their own terms, use the jungle and not call a halt because it's the rainy season, and equip the men with close quarter weapons like the Thompson and not deprive them of mortars as we have done.'

Miss Bradshaw tapped the wireless she held in her hand. 'I thought I'd try and pick up Mandalay Radio and get some kind of news. It's awful being so in the dark.'

She twiddled the tuning knob, but the set remained defiantly silent. 'Can't be the batteries, I put new ones in when I left.' She whacked the set with the ball of her hand. 'When all else fails, try brute force.' There was a crackle of static, and as she continued to twiddle the knob she picked up a faint voice that was just concluding an official communique: ' . . . Sir Reginald, who has left Rangoon with his personal entourage, is due to arrive in Maymyo which will then become the new seat of government. All vital installations in Rangoon have been destroyed to prevent anything of value falling into enemy hands, and the Japanese will find the port totally unusable. The army under the command of General Alexander is staging a strategic withdrawal until a suitable line of defence can be established from which the invaders can be driven back . . . '

She switched off. 'Do you think we can drive them back?' she asked earnestly. 'We've been told so many lies it's difficult to accept any of their assurances.'

'I'm no tactician, Sister, and I don't know what's going through General Alexander's mind. But the odds are against him. After the Sittang, a large part of the army isn't really in a fit state to wage a counter-offensive so I'd imagine his plan will be to get as much of it as possible back to India and then rebuild for an invasion of our own. Understandably he can't publicly announce his intentions; it would smack too much of defeatism. The truth is that the ordinary chaps like Private Wagstaff know the realities of the situation. I heard him telling the others. No good tearing him off a strip for speaking his mind when I share his fears.'

'So you think I'm wasting my time looking for an alternative site for the hospital? Burma is lost?'

'I think so, but it'll be a fighting withdrawal and it could be weeks, even months, before Upper Burma falls. The Japs may have established air supremacy because the RAF has been shot out of the skies and the AVG are perilously short of planes, but we do have some tanks now, although this isn't tank country, and should be able to rely on the support of the American General Stillwell who's commanding a sizeable Chinese army. True, Vinegar Joe is said to be a limey-hater and, by all accounts, doesn't rate Alexander, which doesn't help. But his own country is at war, and that fact must outweigh his own prejudices. Chiang Kai-Shek isn't an anglophile either, but I think he'll pocket his differences too and do all he can to help. Even so, I don't think it will alter Alexander's decision to get back to India.'

'You inspire me with confidence. Maybe I should find my own way back to Rangoon where I can still be of use at the hospital.'

'Nothing you can do will alter the fate of the patients,' he said, bluntly. 'You'd be interned for sure, whereas the patients might be treated reasonably well. After all, the Japs have no quarrel with them. But our own wounded still need caring for in Mandalay where I expect they'll be sent as there are a couple of good military hospitals there, in addition to the civilian ones. Every extra pair of hands is going to be a bonus.'

Kitty Bradshaw sighed. 'That's that, then. I stay with you.'

'It's going to be a long, uncomfortable journey.'

'In which case,' she said, 'don't you think it's about time we became less formal? As I'm not on duty you can call me Kitty. Makes me feel a lot less old. And you must have a Christian name?'

'David, and I don't mind you using it when I'm alone with you, but it's Sergeant in front of the lads. I've got to maintain discipline and avoid over-familiarity, and I can't do that if everyone is palsy-walsy. I have to make the decisions, rightly or wrongly, and I don't want them querying anything. Anyhow, that's how they prefer things. Soldiers are simple chaps; they don't want responsibility, and if they have trust and respect in someone they'll do everything they are told to do.'

She gave a mock salute. 'I'll remember that, David.'

'I'm serious, Kitty. I've got to be *seen* to be the boss, especially where Miss Carfax is concerned. She isn't going to put herself out too much, and I can't risk reaching a situation where she, or anyone else, feels entitled to disagree because I'm not going to run things on a consensus basis. There will only be one jockey.'

She held up her hands, palms outwards in mute surrender, and said with a smile, 'You have my total allegiance, but I can't speak for Miss Carfax. I've met her type before. Although you can blame the system more than the individual. She's been brought up to believe that life is some kind of human chest of drawers: the best people are at the top, the inferior ones at the bottom, and soldiers alas are among the discarded, and too darned socks. But adversity often brings out unknown qualities, and this could prove the making of her.'

'I hope so,' he replied flatly. 'I reckon you can have a greater influence on her than I can. She dislikes soldiers and will go out of her way to disagree with me. The trouble is I can't kick her out, as I've threatened, and she knows it.'

Kitty Bradshaw touched the side of her nose. 'Leave it to

97

me. I've had stroppy young girls under me who've developed into absolute treasures. Unlike soldiers, they thrive when a little responsibility is thrust on them. Not all girls enter nursing with a sense of vocation; some see it as a glamorous occupation, all dances and handsome doctors, but they're quickly disillusioned when they empty their first bedpan, and are the better for it.'

Harris said, 'She's unlikely to get such a rude awakening on this trip, Kitty.'

She wagged a reproving finger. 'You never know. You never know.'

He reached for the door handle. 'I've enjoyed our little heart to heart, but I'd better get back and sort out the sentry roster.'

'I'll come with you. I'm going to give everyone a hefty dose of quinine. I want it to become a daily routine. Although it's no guarantee against malaria, it shortens the odds.' She nudged him in the ribs. 'A prophylactic. A condom against mosquitoes, you could say.'

They strolled back to where the others were still sitting round the warm stove, the soldiers cursing Wagstaff for his winning streak, Nellie still attending to Miss Carfax's needs.

Fazackerley and Simmonds were detailed to share the guard duties for the night because, as Harris explained, he and Wagstaff could do with as much sleep as possible as they would be doing the driving.

Private Simmonds sat with his back against one of the wheels of the truck in which the women were sleeping, the Tommy-gun resting across his knees. In the darkness he could hear the grinding of gears and the rumble of wheels as the long procession of refugees continued their ponderous progress up the Prome Road. He lit a Woodbine and drew the smoke deep down into his lungs. This was not how a war should be fought, he mused. War was something that should be sorted out by soldiers; civilians should be bystanders, not victims. Half the poor sods tramping up the road didn't stand a cat in hell's chance of making it. There were mountains to climb, rivers to cross, and great arid expanses to traverse. He reminded himself not to expend too much sympathy on the refugees; their own journey was not going to be a picnic.

His thoughts were interrupted by a strange sound coming from inside the truck and he got up, leaned over the tailboard, parted the canvas, and whispered, 'Everything all right in there?'

He realised the sound was a woman crying. 'Come out and tell me what's wrong. Don't want to wake the others, do we?'

The Burmese girl appeared at the gap, wiping her eyes with the back of one hand while trying to stifle her sobs with the other.

Simmonds put his massive arms round her waist and lifted her out as if she weighed no more than a child. He reached in for a blanket and draped it round her shaking shoulders, then sat her down beside the wheel where he had put his gun. 'Here, Miss, take a drag of this.' He held out his cigarette. 'Sorry I haven't got a cheroot.'

Nellie shook her head, declining his offer. 'I am crying because I do not want to be left.'

'Who says you're going to be?' he said gently.

'My memsahib will leave me in Mandalay.'

'Well, to my way of thinking, that's a lot healthier than being left in Rangoon.'

'I would like to go to England.'

'You and me both, but that's a bit of a tall order, Miss Nellie. But never you mind, I'll have a word with Sergeant Harris.' He winked in the darkness. 'The Sergeant's a bloody miracle maker, and I'm not just saying that to cheer you up.'

Her voice became excited and high-pitched. 'Perhaps he could arrange for me to marry a Tommy?'

'That's an even taller order, even for the Sergeant, but no doubt he'll give it due consideration.' His voice became serious. 'Now listen to me, Nellie. Don't you go talking to Private Fazackerley about wanting to marry a soldier. You can't count on his promises. A bit of an opportunist, you might say. He's one of my best mates, but I wouldn't trust him with the fat lady in the circus. Not that I'm comparing you to the likes of her. Just giving you a warning.'

'Burmese girls who marry soldiers live with them in married quarters and are paid, and when the time comes go to England.'

'Well now, some do and some don't,' he said laboriously, 'and there're a lot who wished they'd looked before they leaped.'

'I would be a good wife.'

Simmonds sat cradling the girl until she fell asleep, then withdrew his arms with extreme gentleness so as not to waken her when the time came for him to rouse Fazackerley. As he handed over the Tommy-gun he said, 'Zack, the Burmese girl is sleeping outside. She's had a fit of snivels, so be nice and kind.' He screwed his hand into a ham-sized fist. 'And don't try your luck. Otherwise ...' The fist was placed under his oppo's nose.

Fazackerley said, 'Knock it off, Simmo. I rather fancy the old nurse. Bit of meat on her.'

'Old! Jesus Christ, she's young enough to be your daughter.'

'I'm not as old as I look,' retorted Fazackerley indignantly. 'When I've got my choppers in, I look ten years younger.'

'In that case you'd better stop wearing them. The Sergeant's got enough on his plate as it is without having to worry about you trying to get your leg over.'

It did not occur to Private Simmonds that he would have been wiser warning Wagstaff not to take advantage of Nellie's eagerness to find a soldier boyfriend. Fazackerley might have a reputation for womanising, but he lacked guile, something the Cockney had in abundance − which could not be said of him when it came to scruples. He had already been attracted to Nellie's fragile beauty, and was wondering how he could enjoy it.

When Sergeant Harris got out of the truck next morning, he glanced instinctively towards Rangoon where a tenebrous rosy hue tinted the sky, and wondered whether it was caused by fires still burning because great mushroom clouds, black as tar, climbed high into the sky, or whether it was the sun heralding another scorching day. On the road the slow millipede of humanity was continuing its imperceptible

100

progress. It reminded him of volcanic lava moving across a landscape.

He called over to Fazackerley, hunched against the wheel of a truck, the Tommy-gun on the ground beside him. 'Get a brew started and rustle up some breakfast. I want to be on the road in an hour's time.' He noticed the blanket-shrouded figure of the Burmese girl and hoped she wasn't going to cause him unwanted trouble. He would ask Fazackerley what she was doing there.

When he had roused Miss Carfax and Sister Bradshaw he returned to Fazackerley who had already got the stove going.

'What's the girl doing outside like that?'

'Private Simmonds said she was crying her eyes out over something and he let her kip down there, Sarge. I expect her ladyship woke up in the middle of the night and wanted her nails doing.'

'That's quite enough of that, Fazackerley. Take her a cup of tea.'

He walked down to the road to see how the traffic was, and by the time he got back Simmonds and Wagstaff were shaving. He was glad of that; it saved him the trouble of telling them. He was determined, no matter how long the journey took, that his men would always look like soldiers. If men looked good they performed well. It was said, he remembered, that when the Guards returned from Dunkirk they were all clean shaven, their boots shining, their rifles resting on the shoulders of uniforms that were smart enough to pass any inspection. Well, what was good enough for the Guards was good enough for the Rocks.

Avril appeared in her towelling dressing gown, and Harris said, 'You'd better get dressed. We'll be off as soon as we've eaten.'

'I'd like Nellie to prepare a bath before I dress. Rather pointless to have to take everything off again.'

'There'll be no morning bath. At the rate we're progressing we'll have to start thinking about conserving our water. One in the evening will be the rule from now on. Just a rinse down in the morning will have to do.'

'But that's ridiculous!'

101

'Miss Carfax,' he explained patiently, 'I estimate we'll be drinking at least five pints each every day to avoid dehydration. On top of that we've got to take overheating of the trucks into account, plus the possibility that with half a million people on the road fresh supplies are going to be extremely hard to come by.'

'Come on, Avril,' said Miss Bradshaw. 'A lick and a promise never hurt anyone.'

Common sense told her to acquiesce; the sergeant's voice was quite threatening, but there was a stubbornness in her make-up which made her ignore the inner voice counselling caution; a stand had to be taken or he would stamp his authority on all her future conduct and ride roughshod over everything she had been taught to value.

Harris willed her to capitulate, knowing he would have to fulfil his threat otherwise his authority would be irreversibly undermined. If they were to survive he had to be obeyed.

'I'll not be bullied by you or anyone else. At the pace we're going a few minutes won't make the slightest difference. There's no need to panic,' said Avril sharply.

'The sergeant isn't talking about time, neither is he panicking,' said Kitty. 'He's talking about rationing. A perfectly sensible precaution. Now stop being silly and get into the truck.'

'If he wants to abandon me ...' she shrugged. 'I'm pefectly capable of fending for myself. I've lived in Burma all my life and know no one is going to molest a mamsahib.'

'Not even those bastards who are lighting beacons to guide the Jap bombers,' snapped Harris.

'You don't scare me. You're just being stupidly petty. Treating me like a child made to stand in the corner.'

'Get in the truck and forget all about it,' said Harris weakly. 'We've a long way to go, so let's try and achieve a little harmony.'

'What you mean is I should accept without question eveything you say.'

'That just about sums it up.'

'And be treated like dirt for the rest of the journey. No, thank you. I'd rather walk.'

'Please yourself, Miss Carfax.'

Kitty Bradshaw tried to curb her growing sense of frustration. 'Avril, for God's sake, it isn't worth upsetting everyone over a bloody bath.'

'I have never started the day without one, and I don't intend to break the habit of a lifetime. Nellie, get the bath.'

Harris said flatly, 'Simmonds, let her have two cans of water and the ruddy bath.'

'That's better. At last you're seeing reason. We can soon make up the lost time.'

'We won't be losing *any* time. We're pressing on, with or without you.'

'You wouldn't dare leave me behind.'

'You've made it abundantly clear that the prospect doesn't worry you in the least.'

'You'd never live it down, Sergeant.'

'I'll learn to live with it then.' He turned to Nellie. 'Get one of your mistress's cases from the truck. One is all she'll be able to carry.'

The bewildered Burmese girl got the suitcase and placed it on the ground beside the bath. She knew how much her mistress liked her bath, but for the life of her she failed to see how it was more important than a lift in the truck.

Harris turned his back and shouted, 'Mount up.'

As the two trucks drove off, Harris glanced in his mirror and saw Miss Carfax standing with her back to the departing vehicles, gesturing to Nellie to prepare her bath.

An hour passed before Simmonds broke the tense silence which pervaded the cabin. 'She may be like a handful of grit under your foreskin, Sarge, but I don't think you should leave her. A white girl in that bloody great crowd of wogs is in real danger.'

'It was her own choice. Apart from that, she isn't the only person I have to consider.'

Kitty Bradshaw's voice came through the aperture. 'I think she'll have learned her lesson by now. *Please* turn back.'

Harris braked sharply, causing Wagstaff who was following closely behind to curse loudly and mutter, 'You might give a fuckin' signal.'

'All right, I'll give in this time, but there'll be no second

103

chances. My job is to deliver the Silver and Colours. Miss Carfax is a secondary consideration and she'd better learn that,' said Harris.

He was secretly relieved at the face-saving intervention. He had not liked the idea of abandoning her and had already decided in his own mind that he would return. Now it looked as if he had been cajoled into changing his mind.

He shouted to Wagstaff to stay where he was, then executed a sharp U-turn and, horn blaring, carved a path through the slowly moving column of refugees, glancing to left and right for a glimpse of Miss Carfax who he assumed would have joined them. His agitation increased when he saw no sign of her or the Burmese girl, and he was immensely relieved when he caught sight of them exactly where they had been left. Avril was sitting on the suitcase and Nellie was using the bath as a chair.

He braked beside them, saying tersely, 'Get in.'

Miss Carfax said, 'That was a foolish thing to do. You must have known you'd have to come back. I'm only surprised you took so long.'

'Don't press your luck. You've Sister Bradshaw and Private Simmonds to thank for my change of heart. Next time, if there is one, I won't be so amenable.'

It was as if Miss Carfax had not heard. 'Put my case back where it was, Nellie, and let the Sergeant have his bath back.'

As she clambered into the truck she heaved an inward sigh of relief; she had not been at all confident that Harris would return, but the moral victory she had scored made her panic fade into insignificance. Sergeant Harris was more vulnerable than she was.

Later, when they halted for the night, she said disarmingly, 'At least you've agreed to us bathing in the evening, Sergeant, so we won't be falling out if I tell Nellie to prepare it.'

As a silent gesture of their disapproval, the others simply washed their hands and face. It was lost on Miss Carfax who appeared in her dressing gown, and as Nellie brushed her hair remarked, 'I really can't make up my mind what to wear. I always think if you look good you feel good. Don't you agree, Sergeant?'

Harris nodded assent. He could hardly disagree in view of his attitude to his own men's appearance, but it still seemed to him that Miss Carfax had her priorities mixed. He also suspected that it was her own way of telling him that no lessons had been taught and the daggers had only temporarily been sheathed.

Chapter Eight

The road ahead wound a serpentine course as far as the eye
could see, although strictly speaking the road itself was not
visible; all that could be seen was the great heaving mass
of people, animals and transport. After three gruelling
hours the two army trucks had barely covered six miles
and Prome was beginning to assume the magnitude of an
unachievable target. The faces of the women and soldiers
were masks of caked dust the colour of red ochre in which
perspiration had carved distinct furrows. Their eyes smarted,
their throats were parched, and every bone ached with the
constant jolting.

Sergeant Harris's wrists and forearms felt as if they were
being pulverised by a hammer as he continuously spun the
wheel to avoid some obstacle, animal, human or geological.
Already the long trek was beginning to take its toll and both
sides of the road were lined with prostrate figures. Some
were people resting in order to regain enough strength to
continue, others would never rise again. Flies buzzed on
and around the corpses, and overhead planed vultures on
rigid wings, patiently waiting for an opportunity to descend
and eat. They possessed an uncanny instinct for detecting
when life had departed, and as soon as they touched the
ground lost all the grace and beauty they displayed in the air,
hobbling with ungainly, obscene steps towards their meal,
their scrawny featherless necks thrust aggressively forward.

Kitty Bradshaw called through the aperture at the rear of
the cabin: 'Sergeant Harris! I don't like the look of this
at all. If cholera and dysentery break out they'll be dying

in their hundreds. The Indians are not the most sanitary people at the best of times − not because they're naturally filthy, but when it comes to bodily functions they aren't too particular about clearing up the mess. Something to do with their caste system, I think. It's a job for untouchables.'

She did not need to elaborate because it was evident to anyone with eyes that the sides of the road were becoming one vast latrine, with people squatting down to obey the call of nature. They seemed to experience no embarrassment at performing such a personal function in front of each other, chatting away cheerfully and treating it as some sort of social occasion. And since it was beneath them to bury their own excreta it was left to attract more flies.

Harris, conditioned by army life not to be over squeamish, had seen similar scenes from the windows of troop trains in India; lines of squatting people, often shaded by umbrellas, calmly reading newspapers as they defecated beside the tracks, and waving cheerfully as the trains passed. Gandhi, he recalled, had ruled against the filthy habit, but even the 'great soul' had been unable to put a halt to it. In the conditions which now prevailed it was inviting disaster.

Avril said, 'My father moaned like billyo when the sweepers who cleared our "night soil" disappeared. It was the worst thing, as far as he was concerned, about the bombing. He just couldn't bring himself to clear up his own mess.'

'I suppose he had to eventually,' said Miss Bradshaw.

'No. He paid our neighbours' sweepers to do it. He bitterly regretted not having spent money on flush sanitation, but then, he never envisaged a shortage of sweepers. Mother and I pleaded with him to move with the times but he just wouldn't listen.' She shuddered at the memory of her visits to the toilet. 'It was awful. So humiliating. The sweepers used to sit behind a hedge with their eyes on the door of the 'long drop'. When it was left open they knew it was the signal to clear up.'

Sister Bradshaw said, 'Well, we're all going to find out what an unpleasant job it was, because we'll have to be our own sweepers.'

Avril said, 'I think you're talking like that just to upset

me. I think you enjoy it. You know something, I think you're jealous of the lifestyle I enjoyed. You honestly think they were unearned privileges, don't you? Well, modern Burma wasn't built by nurses and missionaries and other do-gooders, but by hard-headed businessmen like my father. His type were the visionaries.' She felt quite pleased with herself, even though she was merely repeating words she had heard her father use many many times.

'I'm just trying to point out that we have to forget what things were like and accept what they are,' said Miss Bradshaw. 'I'm not in the least envious. I'm rather sorry for you. It's made you singularly ill-equipped for a journey such as this. You expect to be carried, like some ruddy princess in a howdah.'

'We'll just have to wait and see how wrong you are,' said Avril tartly. 'You really make me sick the way you carry on. Do you think the men who opened up this country, drilled the oil wells, mined the tin and exploited the teak forests, and made Burma a proud part of Empire, did everything for themselves? Of course not. They had porters and sweepers, and cooks and gun bearers, because they had more important things to occupy their minds. They were not trying to be superior, they *were*.

'And you think burdening us with your damned silly tennis raquets and balls, not to mention gramophone and a wardrobe more suited to the Strand Hotel and the club than the back of an army truck, is a sign of that superiority? I think if a little less importance had been attached to what people wore and there had been fewer dances and race meetings, we wouldn't be handing the Burma you are so proud of to the Japs on a plate.'

'You're only trying to goad me into losing my temper, but it won't work. I'm not going to go native because you have a chip on your shoulder,' she retorted.

Kitty Bradshaw groaned. 'You give me a pain in the backside. Trying to instill some sense of responsiblity into you is like banging your head against a brick wall.' Her face disappeared from the aperture and she sat on some blankets, inwardly fuming at the girl's refusal to face up to reality.

Harris maintained a tactful silence, thinking: You silly girl.

She isn't being bitchy, she's trying to make you grow up. The same way I treat a raw recruit who doesn't think polished boots and buttons are as important as a clean rifle barrel. You have to make someone feel ashamed before instilling a feeling of pride.

They travelled in flinty silence for the best part of two hours before it was broken by Miss Carfax. 'I know you think I'm pretty useless, but if you'll let me take a turn at the wheel you'll see I'm a very useful driver.'

Harris smiled, glad the unpleasant tension had been eased; but he could not resist the temptation to say, 'I know that. Remember the Strand?'

Avril smiled and said, 'Miaow,' and Harris was pleased she had taken it as a joke and not lapsed into a moody silence, or even worse thrown another tantrum.

He patted her on the shoulder. 'I'm all right for a little longer. In any case, I'll be calling a halt soon. Time everybody stretched their legs. Later on I'll think about letting you drive, but you'll find it a little different to what you're used to. It's as much as I can do to hold the road.'

'I see no earthly reason why you shouldn't start calling me Avril. It'll be a step in the right direction.'

'I'd like that very much,' he replied, although he had no intention of doing so. She had to become one of the team before that happened.

In the truck behind, Wagstaff, tired of Fazackerley's company which he considered as enjoyable as a conversation with a donkey, began talking to Nellie who, uninvited, had decided to travel in the cabin in order to be close to the Cockney private.

'I coulda been made up to sergeant, or at least lance-jack if I 'ad wanted, but I said to myself, Private Wagstaff, it's men like you wot is the backbone of the army. The feet as we're called. Now some NCOs is good at givin' orders, but not too 'ot when it comes to carryin' them out, an' it stands to reason that if there's any fightin' to do you want blokes who is good at it, an' I consider that when it comes to that I'm much better than the next man.'

He took his eyes off the road and looked towards Nellie for appreciation.

Nellie, who had only understood a fraction of what he had said, seized the opportunity to pursue what had now become a definite purpose in her life. 'That is why I like soldiers. That is why I want to be missus for one.'

'You gotta smart little 'ead on your shoulders, Nellie. Not that marriage to a soldier is all 'oney and clover. Not by a long chalk. You gotta accept the Regiment always comes first, but you get a decent roof over your 'ead, and four square meals a day, an' a marriage allowance, an' there ain't no one around waitin' to kick you up the bum sayin', "Brush me 'air, fill me bath, and scrub me back." An', of course, there's the uvver bit of marriage, which is the best of all. The love bit. When it comes to that you can't teach a soldier nuffink.'

She said solemnly, 'Burmese girls much same. Very good jig-jig.'

Wagstaff began to whistle softly. A wink was as good as a nod to a blind horse, and he certainly wasn't blind or deaf. When it came to the next overnight halt he would volunteer for a sentry do. Tell the Sergeant that he didn't think it was fair to leave it all to Simmo and Zack. Then he would get Nellie on her own, and from there play it by ear.

Fazackerley, sitting on the other side of the girl, said, 'I can read you like a bloody book, Waggy. Got a mind like a sewer. You ought to be out there squatting on the road with those wogs.'

'Up yours,' said Wagstaff cheerfully.

'Let me give you a little warning, Waggy. Don't let Simmo find out you're feeling horny for her. Because when he's finished with you, what's left could be put in a bully beef tin. He's already read me the riot act.'

In the truck ahead, Private Simmonds, craning his head out of the open window to get a better view of the road ahead, suddenly shouted, 'Sarge! Listen!' The urgency in his voice made Harris lean sideways in order to hear better and his ears caught the distinctive high-pitched drone of an aircraft flying low and at speed. Then he heard the unmistakable rat-a-tat-a-tat chatter of machine gun fire, followed by the harsher more pronounced crump of exploding bombs.

'Hang on,' he yelled as he swung the wheel hard right

110

and bounced off the road. They careered down the steep embankment towards the cover of a dense bamboo thicket.

Wagstaff saw the right-hand indicator of the lorry ahead jerk out into the horizontal position, quickly followed by Harris's rigid forearm signalling an emergency turn. He followed, narrowly missing a bullock cart but grazing several people who were walking beside it. He went down the incline so fast his head banged against the roof of the cabin and only Fazackerley's arm stopped Nellie from being hurled through the windscreen.

Before the trucks had come to a halt Simmonds had jumped out and was blazing away with the Tommy-gun at the fast disappearing aircraft, while Fazackerley was trying single-handedly to operate the Bren. When Wagstaff joined him he used his back as a support and began firing in short disciplined bursts. Harris was on one knee working the bolt of his Lee Enfield as fast as his fingers could move.

The air was filled with terrified screams as the bullets from the aircraft thudded into the close-packed refugees, and shrapnel tore into their flesh. The road was quickly strewn with dead and wounded humans and beasts, and a carpet of red was gradually spreading across the surface. Those who were still alive were put out of their misery by the wheels of vehicles which continued to press on. Many refugees tripped and fell as they ran down the embankment and were trampled to death by those behind.

Harris was not strong on aircraft recognition because there had been a shortage of identity charts in Rangoon, but as he watched the plane flying impudently low, bank sharply in readiness for a strafing run in the opposite direction, he thought: Could be a Mitsubishi 'Sally' or a 'Nell' medium bomber. Of one thing he was certain, it was Japanese; the rising sun emblem on the underside of the wings was clearly visible.

As the bomber came back, more anti-personnel bombs tumbled from the belly and the 7.7mm guns began hammering out their staccato tattoo.

Fazackerley muttered, 'Keep still, Waggy, the bloody sight is wobbling about like a pissed sailor on a tightrope.'

Wagstaff took a deep breath and held it, feeling the barrel

111

of the Bren thumping into his back and his skin scorching from the heat as Fazackerley emptied an entire magazine, then clipped a fresh one on without there seeming to be a pause in the firing.

Harris saw a finger of black smoke emerge from one of the engine cowlings and feel its way along the fuselage where it changed colour to a fiery orange.

Fazackerley screamed, 'Got the yellow bastard.'

Wagstaff felt the pressure ease from his shoulders. He looked up to see the bomber, trailing its crimson pennant, turn and heard the engines growl as the pilot struggled to gain height. For a moment it seemed to climb vertically before stalling, then it began a swiftly descending glide before crashing into a distant hillside where it exploded in an angry ball of fire.

Harris ran over to Fazackerley and pounded him on the back. 'Bloody well done, Zack.' He did the same to Wagstaff who, determined to conceal his own pleasure, said morosely, 'Hold on, Sarge, my back's so sore I feel I've been flogged on a gun wheel.'

However, Harris's jubilation was tempered by the knowledge that with complete mastery of the air the Japanese could if they wished send another aircraft to harass and terrify the already demoralised refugees. He acknowledged it was senseless blood letting, but part of a deliberate tactic to create as much confusion and chaos as possible along the route the retreating army would be forced to follow.

Kitty Bradshaw emerged from the bamboo and ran across the patch of ground that separated them from the road and the scene of terrible carnage. Bullocks and mules lay on their sides, their stomachs heaving as they gulped for air in a desperate effort to stave off encroaching death. The machine guns had cut great swathes through the massed crowds, and the anti-personnel bombs had reaped a grim harvest. She knelt beside a boy with a gaping hole in his chest and realised there was nothing she could do. All around she could hear the groans and screams of other mortally wounded people. She ran back to the trucks, shouting, 'I must get the morphine. At least I can ease their last moments.'

Harris shook her. 'Forget it, Kitty. For every one you treat there are ten others worse off. I know it's hard, but now is the time to press on. It sounds callous, but it's the truth.'

Avril said sympathetically, 'Don't blame yourself, Kitty. Just look at the others, they're not stopping to help.'

Nellie was crying hysterically and Avril grabbed her and shook her until she stopped. 'Get back into the truck if you don't want to be left behind. And for God's sake, pull yourself together.'

Harris thought: She's maturing quickly, but what a hard school in which to learn.

When the women were aboard he whispered something to Simmonds and Fazackerley who ran towards the road. Soon afterwards there were bursts of prolonged gunfire.

Avril said gently, 'That was a horrible thing to have to do, but very merciful, Sergeant.'

They set off again with Harris sticking to the cattle track that ran parallel to the road. It was an excruciatingly bruising ride which even the heavy duty tyres were incapable of easing. Huge stones clunked against the underside of the vehicles, and the pot holes were so deep Harris feared the sumps would be damaged beyond repair. But it was marginally safer than the road should the Japanese attack again.

From the window he noticed a beautiful Indian woman in a canary-yellow sari, a small girl perched papoose-fashion on her back, striding barefoot and purposefully along the verge. Her arms and legs were adorned with numerous gold bracelets and anklets, and she wore diamonds in her ears and in her nostrils. Her belly was swollen with child. By her side, trying to match her pace, was her spindly-legged husband wearing a once-white dhoti and clutching a goatskin water container.

The attack had opened up a wide gap in the column and the two trucks were able to make good progress for the next two hours, although Harris was saddened by the knowledge that it had only been made possible by heavy loss of life.

Soon afterwards he rejoined the road proper. A further attack now seemed unlikely and he did not want to inflict any further gruelling punishment on the trucks. But once again they were reduced to little more than a crawl and

113

Harris resigned himself to the fact he was powerless to do anything about it. A day lost here or there was not that important. Mandalay would still be there, and he reminded himself that he should not forget the purpose of the trip was to arrive safely with his precious cargo. Automatically his thoughts turned to Colonel Selthorpe, and he wondered how he and the Battalion were faring in the withdrawal from Rangoon. He was concerned, but confidently imagined they were coping well under conditions which made his own plight of miniscule importance.

It was just as well he had to rely on his imagination, for even in his most pessimistic moods it would never have occurred to him that not only was the Battalion in danger, but the entire army was in imminent peril of being annihilated with the capital almost still within sight.

General Alexander's Rangoon forces were stretched along several miles of the Prome Road – lorries, ambulances, tanks and Bren carriers – never intended to support such a massive volume of motorised transport. And falling back from Pegu to link up with him at Taukkyan were the men who had managed to cross the Sittang before it was blown, and the 16th Brigade.

At Taukkyan, unbeknown to Alexander, the enemy had employed one of their favourite tactics to which the British had yet to find an answer. They had set up massive road blocks of felled trees and iron-staked oil drums, and when the army arrived it was brought to an immediate halt.

Several attempts were made to break through, by infantry, tanks and artillery, but all failed, and in a short time the entire force was bottled up on a forty mile stretch of road and facing total obliteration.

To avoid the humiliation of surrender Alexander was about to issue the career-ending order 'every man for himself' and let his men disperse and make their own way to safety, when a miracle occurred.

Good generals always need a modicum of luck, and that elusive lady was certainly at Alexander's side at Taukkyan. The Japanese general was so eager to press on and take Rangoon he abandoned the road block and by-passed the penned-in army, and so missed a golden opportunity of ending the war in Burma.

Alexander jumped into his staff car and ordered the retreat to continue. It signalled a withdrawal that was to become the longest in British military history; one which made Moore's historic retreat from Corunna seem little more than a leisurely stroll.

'Watch it, Sarge.'

Simmonds' strident warning roused Harris from the momentary torpor induced by the brain numbing growl of the engine labouring in low gear, the constant jolting and the dispiriting, funereal rate of progress. A short distance ahead a bullock had dropped dead between the shafts of a cart and blocked the centre of the road. He swung the wheel intending to swerve outside the obstacle, but the nearside wheels caught the edge of the road and the lorry bounced off and slid sideways down the steep incline, coming to rest at an angle of forty-five degrees. He climbed out of the cabin, calling, 'Everyone all right?'

Simmonds clambered clear and went to the rear of the truck where he was assured that everyone was still in one piece although they were all badly bruised and shaken.

Harris surveyed the truck. 'Shouldn't be too difficult getting it upright and back on to the road.'

The engine had stalled and Harris murmured a silent prayer as he turned the ignition key. He gave a thumbs up sign when it fired first time. 'Panic over. I'll run it down on to the flat, then Wagstaff can tow me back up.'

The other passengers watched anxiously as Harris tried to drive the vehicle down the incline on to the flat stretch that ran parallel to the road, but the wheels spun in the soft dust and the truck became even more embedded. He got out and called up to Wagstaff, peering anxiously down from the road: 'Toss down the tow rope and see if you can haul me clear.'

Wagstaff called back. 'I need a bit of road space for that, Sarge, but these buggers ain't going to give me none. I can't pull you sideways.'

'Tell Fazackerley to turn the Bren on them if they won't move,' bellowed Harris.

115

Fazackerley grinned and fired a short burst over the heads of the milling crowd, and when that failed to clear a way he fired another longer one at their feet which sent them scampering for safety down the bund, leaving Wagstaff with a clear stretch of road for about thirty yards. 'That should do the trick, Sarge.'

When the tow rope was attached Wagstaff drove gingerly forward, gradually taking up the slack, and when the rope was taut began to edge slowly forward, but the truck remained axle deep in the soft dust.

'Right, everyone put some beef into trying to get it more upright,' said Harris.

They all put their backs against the side of the truck and Harris said, 'When I've counted to three, all push as hard as you can. One-two-three ...'

They dug their feet as firmly as they could into the sandy soil and pushed hard with their backs. Simmonds took off his shirt and turned it into a cushion which he placed behind his shoulders. The muscles on his arms and back stood out like steel hawsers as he exerted all his Herculean strength. The engine of Wagstaff's truck groaned in anguish, but the wheels of the stranded truck continued to spin. 'She ain't going to budge, Sarge.'

'We'll give it one more go and if that fails we'll unload everything and try again.'

The second attempt was no more successful and Harris gave the order for all the food, water and petrol to be offloaded.

When the contents of the truck had been piled up on the ground he said, 'Fazackerley, you'd better stand guard over it. Put a bayonet on your rifle and if anyone tries to steal anything don't have any qualms about using it. A glimpse of cold steel may be more effective than the Bren.'

A large crowd had now gathered on the road and around the truck to observe with detached curiosity the efforts of the soldiers and three women to free the bogged down vehicle.

Two or three of them, undeterred by the menacing figure of Fazackerley standing guard with fixed bayonet, seeing an opportunity to appease their rumbling stomachs and quench their unbearable thirst, darted forward and grabbed cans of

116

water and boxes of food. Fazackerley lunged at one and managed to pierce him through the shoulder, but as he pulled hard to withdraw the bayonet others, emboldened by the success of those who had melted into the crowd with their booty, dashed forward and helped themselves to more food and water.

'Shoot the next bastard who tries it on,' bellowed Harris.

The private fired three rounds and heard loud screams although he had no idea if he had hit anyone or if the cries were simply of fear, but his action was effective. The crowd quickly dispersed, scuttling up the road screaming words of abuse as they fled.

'Okay, let's give it another try,' said Harris.

Again they took up position against the side of the truck and tried with all their strength to push it into a more upright position and make Wagstaff's task that much easier, but despite the unloading the vehicle refused to budge. By now refugees who had not experienced the threat of gunfire had drawn level and Wagstaff no longer had room in which to manoeuvre his truck. Furthermore, they were indifferent to any threats and continued to mill foward until he was hemmed in by a solid mass of people.

'We've done our best,' said Harris resignedly. 'We'll just have to abandon it. We'll transfer everything to the other truck. It's going to make life a trifle cramped but that's too bad. Begin with the food and water. We'll leave the Silver till last because that will have to be unpacked.'

They toiled in the blazing sun for half an hour before all the food, water, medical supplies and essential spare parts had been transferred to Wagstaff's vehicle.

'We'll have a brew up before we start on the Silver. No point in overtaxing ourselves.'

As they sat by the edge of the road drinking hot strong tea, Sister Bradshaw remarked casually, 'If my eyes don't deceive me, I think our troubles are over.' She pointed down the road, but all the others could see was the same milling exodus of people, vehicles and animals.

'So, wot's new?' asked Wagstaff.

'An elephant,' exclaimed Miss Bradshaw.

Towering high above the refugee column was a make-shift

117

howdah mounted on top of a huge elephant. 'If you've seen them at work you'll know that a stuck lorry isn't going to present any problems. I've seen them shifting teak trunks that weighed tons. I've been told they can understand a hundred or more commands.'

'It's worth a try,' said Harris with no great conviction. He moved on to the road and waited until the elephant was level. An oozie in a filthy vest and grubby shorts sat with legs astride the dome of its head, guiding the huge beast with his knees and a sharp pointed instrument. Harris signalled for him to stop, and the man muttered something and the elephant came to a docile halt.

A curtain parted in the howdah and a pale, podgy-faced Indian wearing an immaculate white silk turban poked his head out.

'Do you speak English?' asked Harris.

'Passably,' said the Indian in a cultured voice that bore no trace of the typical Indian lilt.

'I need the use of your elephant to get a truck back on the road.'

'That, I regret, is impossible. I have my family with me and I cannot risk weakening the beast. We have a long way to go.'

'I have a lot of silver rupees which should make it worth your while.'

'Sir, I have been offered a thousand rupees by people seeking transport, but I have no need of money. I have paid this man fifty thousand rupees to take me to Assam.'

'Food and water?'

'I have no need of that either. Now I wish to move along.' He called something to the oozie who looked anxiously at Harris, holding up his hand like a policeman halting traffic. To the Indian he said, 'If you don't co-operate I'll order my men to shoot your precious elephant. It's up to you.'

The Indian remained remarkably unruffled. 'Why not shoot me and my family, then take the elephant?'

'I don't shoot innocent people. I'll let you walk to India like the rest of the poor sods.'

'What is it you British say? I have Hobson's choice.' He smiled genially. 'You may borrow my elephant.'

He shouted something to the oozie who gave a series of commands and the elephant sank slowly down until its belly was resting on the ground. Then he placed a short ladder against the beast and the Indian descended, followed by two women and two children. The man was wearing a silk button-up coat, matching pantaloons and highly polished brown brogues. The women wore expensive saris and held their veils firmly over their faces.

'You can rest in the back of my other vehicle until we've finished,' said Harris.

'That is most considerate. My women will accept your kind offer. I'd prefer to watch. It will be good to know my thousands of rupees have contributed to the survival of a small section of the British army.' Instead of being frightened, he seemed slightly amused.

Harris called Nellie over and asked her to explain to the oozie exactly what he wanted done.

The handler grinned, showing betel-stained teeth, and nudged the elephant to the brink of the road. Then, with a series of softly whispered commands, he guided it gently down the slope. He led it to the side of the truck where the beast placed its enormous domed head against the side and slowly began to exert pressure until the truck was almost upright.

Harris bounded down the incline, calling out, 'Get as may biggish stones as you can, lads, and put them under the wheels to give a firm hold.'

When the nearside wheels were on a solid footing he clambered into the cabin and started the engine. The oozie then led the elephant to the rear of the vehicle where it lowered its head against the tailboard and began to push. Harris got the truck into first gear and let the clutch in very slowly. He could feel the force of the elephant's enormous strength thrusting the vehicle forward. The wheels spun madly, then suddenly the truck lurched and he edged it on to firm, flat ground.

The Indian applauded and called down, 'You'd better let him pull you back on to the road. I'd not like to leave you stranded down there.'

The ascent up the steep incline with the elephant pushing

119

from behind proved a remarkably easy task, and when it was completed Harris said, 'I can't thank you enough. I'm most grateful.'

The Indian said, 'Tell me, would you really have shot such a noble beast for the sake of a piece of machinery? In Rangoon they are burning them.'

'It's not the vehicle that matters, it's what's inside.'

'It must be gold.'

'No, it's silver, but a special kind of silver.'

'I have never known silver of such value,' said the bewildered Indian.

'It's the kind money can't buy,' said Harris.

The Indian laughed and slapped his thighs. 'No such silver exists. I know.' He touched the side of his nose. 'You have a secret you will not disclose. That is the truth, yes?'

'Men will die for it,' said Harris.

'Even shoot a harmless elephant?'

'If necessary.'

'But then you would have been, as you say, still in the same sticky position.'

'Not as bad as the one you'd have been in!'

'Perhaps one day, if we should ever meet again, you would show me this silver? I regret there is not time now. May I proceed?'

'With pleasure,' said Harris, grinning broadly.

The ladder was replaced against the side of the elephant and the ladies and children made a sedate ascent. The Indian entered last, parting the curtain before they left to say, 'Are you a student of the immortal bard?'

'I have a fleeting acquaintance.'

'"All is well that ends well" is my favourite play.'

They watched the elephant lumber ponderously up the road, surrounded by Indians calling out for baksheesh.

'Rum kinda sod, Sarge,' said Wagstaff. 'Got the feelin' he kinda enjoyed 'imself. Bet 'e knew you'd never kill 'is jumbo.'

'He'd have been a bloody fool to put it to the test, Waggy. Now let's load up again and check on what we've lost.'

When all the food, water and petrol had been put back

120

aboard the truck, Sister Bradshaw asked, 'Did they get away with much?'

'Enough to make the journey a lot dicier than I anticipated.'

Avril said chirpily, 'At least we won't be squabbling about an evening bath any more.'

That, thought Harris, was the only bright thing in what had otherwise been a thoroughly depressing day.

As they drove off they saw a long queue of refugees waiting by the roadside for a portion of the butchered buffalo that had been the cause of their misfortune. Sister Bradshaw said, 'They remind me of villagers on an Olde English ox roast. Not a care in the world. Amazing how people can shut their minds to the future. How many will make it?'

'Don't worry about them,' said Harris. 'The way things are, that's a question we'll be asking ourselves soon.'

Totally exhausted as they were by their efforts, Harris decided to call an early halt and as late afternoon approached he signalled his intention to pull off the road and settle down for the remainder of the night. Some five hundred yards or more in the distance he could just make out the shape of roofs which suggested a small village. He halted the trucks outside the cactus boma and tall bamboo barricade which fringed the cluster of huts and acted as a protection against wild animals and marauding dacoits. He picked up his rifle and gestured to Simmonds to follow him with the Tommy-gun.

It was a typical Burmese village, consisting of small thatch and timber dwellings standing on stilts with enough space below the large single room for the animals to shelter. There was no sign of life and no lamps shone through the glassless windows, and no dogs barked a warning.

'Looks like it's deserted, Sarge,' whispered Simmonds.

Harris put a finger to his pursed lips and moved cautiously towards a doorway. He peeped round the jamb before edging his way inside. Simmonds stood back with the cocked Tommy-gun at the ready.

He heard Harris call out from the gloom, 'Come on in, no one here.'

The hut was bare except for two crudely made charpoys. Everything indicated a sudden departure.

121

They moved stealthily from hut to hut, where they encountered the same thing.

'Obviously pulled out, taking everything of value with them. Might have heard the sound of fighting in the distance,' said Harris. He shrugged. 'Odd, though, because we haven't heard any gunfire.'

'Maybe they got the wind up when they saw the refugees streaming past?'

'No point in guessing. Might even have been buzzed by a plane. All we know is that they've gone. Could even be hiding out in the forest, waiting to see when they can return.'

He signalled for Fazackerley and Wagstaff to join him. 'Have a good scout round and see what you can find,' he said quietly.

He then walked over to the trucks and whispered to Avril and Kitty, 'Might as well take some blankets into one of the huts. The beds aren't exactly feather-down, but they'll be a sight more comfortable than the floor of the trucks.'

Wagstaff returned soon afterwards to announce with some pride that he had found a small stream. 'Figured no one in their right mind would build a village where there ain't no water. Looks clean enough; maybe not drinkable, but safe to wash in.'

Simmonds said, 'I'll get some petrol and start a brew up,' but Avril halted him, pointing to a primitive clay oven in the middle of the compound. 'Might as well save fuel and use that. The servants had one just like it at home and Nellie will know what to do. Time she earned her keep. Been ornamental too long.'

The villagers had left behind a pile of cut and dried timber, and the Burmese girl quickly got a fire burning under the oven, and five minutes later the tea had brewed.

Harris said impatiently, 'Where the hell is Fazackerley? He's been gone half an hour now. Simmonds, have a look round in case he's found trouble. He'd manage to do that in the crypt of St Paul's.' But as the private got to his feet Fazackerley appeared with a struggling and squealing piglet under one arm and a scrawny chicken dangling head down in the other hand. A look of smug satisfaction illuminated his toothless mouth. 'Spotted the bird up a tree, and when

I went to get it, well, blow me down if I didn't tread on the bloody porker. Had a good chase before I collared it. Only hope someone knows how to remove its innards because I don't, and don't ask me to slit its throat either.'

Simmonds said, 'We ought to hang on to the chicken. Who knows, it might start laying eggs.'

Nellie said, 'I will kill the pig. Give me a sharp knife.'

Wagstaff handed her his bayonet and held the animal while she calmly and skilfully cut its throat. 'Now dig hole. Too big for oven.'

Wagstaff and Fazackerley excavated a hole about a yard square and eighteen inches deep into which Nellie tossed kindling to which, when burning, she added larger pieces of wood. When this had burned to a hot grey ash she laid down several big stones, then placed the pig on top and covered it with layers of wide, thick leaves. 'My father show me,' she said proudly.

An hour later they were licking their fingers having enjoyed a succulent meal of roast pork.

'You're an absolute marvel, Nellie,' enthused Miss Bradshaw. 'If we're ever lucky enough to get another pig, you can do the honours again.'

'This calls for a celebration,' said Avril. 'Anyone join me in a gin and soda? And I don't want any more complaints about my bringing my servant along.'

They drank the gin and soda water from enamel mugs, and Kitty said, 'Save a little for the quinine, it'll go down so much better.'

When they had finished their drink, Sister Bradshaw said, 'Fancy joining me for a dip in the stream while it's still light, Avril? It'll be a good opportunity to wash our smalls and have a natter.'

Harris sensed she was trying desperately hard to be friendly and extend the olive branch after their recent row.

He said, 'I'm afraid you'll have to take an escort, ladies. If any of the villagers are still around they might not take too kindly to us using their huts and eating their livestock. May even be dacoits in the vicinity.'

Neither of the women voiced any objection; Burma was renowned for its banditry which was considered by some to be an almost honourable profession. The *Rangoon Gazette* had often carried stories about entire villages being wiped out and the crops and livestock stolen by the extremely mobile gangs who could vanish as suddenly as they appeared. Now, with a total breakdown in law enforcement, it could be safely assumed they would greatly increase their activities.

Avril said, 'Come on, Nellie, it's time you had a scrub down instead of covering the grime with more of that awful thanaka. And bring any of my clothes that need washing.'

Private Simmonds got up without being told, shouldered his Tommy-gun and followed the three women along the track Wagstaff had pointed out. The big Yorkshireman had appointed himself custodian to the Burmese girl, for in the short time he had known her he had developed an avuncular interest in her welfare and was determined she should come to no harm. He had decided she was in need of his protection because any girl who talked so eagerly of marrying a soldier was either very immature or else unbalanced, and he had neither seen nor heard anything to suggest that Nellie was simple minded. Somehow, somewhere, she had got this bee in her bonnet, and she was asking for trouble being so outspoken about it. Fazackerley, he thought, was the real danger, although Wagstaff would also need watching. He was still a youngster and could not be blamed if he took the opportunity to dip his wick. So it was down to Simmonds to see she came to no harm. It was a responsibility he readily shouldered because Sergeant Harris had other, more important things to worry about, and Miss Carfax, who treated the girl like dirt, wouldn't give a damn if she was knocked up by a soldier.

The stream was crystal clear and fast running, and a pool had formed where the water cascaded over some rocks and been partially stemmed by an obviously man-made dam.

Avril rolled her skirt above her knees, stepped into the water and began to splash her face and douse her hair with handfuls of the refreshing water.

'Don't be such a bloody prude, Avril.'

She turned and saw Miss Bradshaw standing in the water completely naked, rinsing out her shirt and slacks. Without her clothes she seemed to have shed her dumpiness and Avril was surprised and slightly disappointed to see she had quite a presentable figure. Over-large breasts, perhaps, but they did not droop as she had imagined, and some men might even find her attractive. Her thighs were on the heavy side, but her calves were well shaped and the hours she had spent walking the wards probably accounted for the fact that she carried no surplus weight. She reminded Avril of a picture she had seen in a magazine by an artist called Rubens. The women had been described in the caption as voluptuous, and although she wasn't quite sure what that meant she had the feeling it had something to do with immorality.

Her feelings were strangely mixed as she watched the nurse gambolling like a child at the seaside; one part of her wanted to throw modesty to the wind and join her, the other part warned her not to be a fool. If Sister Bradshaw wanted to be vulgarly brazen that was up to her. It was not setting a very good example with the soldier sitting so close, even though his back was turned. She compromised by removing her dress but keeping her underclothes on.

Nellie had moved discreetly upstream for her own ablutions. It was one thing to see her own mistress naked but quite a different matter to see Sister Bradshaw without a stitch on. She was more shocked than her mistress.

When she had finished washing herself she found a suitably flat stone to use as a scrubbing board and began singing in a tuneless high-pitched voice as she soaped the clothing she had collected from the truck. When she was married, she mused, there would be no more laundry, because she had been told soldier's wives always had a dhobi wallah and an ayah for the babies.

Simmonds sat with his back to the stream, listening for the slightest sound that might signal danger. He guessed from the overheard conversation and the splashing and shouting, that Sister Bradshaw was starkers, and he did not approve; respectable women did not do that kind of thing. He had enough on his plate worrying about Nellie without the nurse acting like she was at a nudist camp.

When they returned to the village, Nellie went to the truck and came back holding Avril's hairbrush; she began brushing to the monotonous chant of her own counting.

125

Miss Bradshaw observed the ritual with mounting anger and frustration, and was reminded of Avril's silly story about the 'jungle wallah' who dressed for dinner. 'Appearances,' she snorted to herself. 'How bloody silly can you get?' She accepted that in normal circumstances she would never have dreamed of appearing before her nurses in a uniform that was not spotless and perfectly starched, but they were in the middle of nowhere with people dying like flies. Avril insisting on having her hair brushed, and her cuticles attended to, and her nails polished, was as incomprehensible to her as the way she put on a night dress to sleep in the back of the foul smelling truck. It made much more sense to sleep as she did, in daytime clothes which afforded the maximum protection against the mosquitoes.

She sighed, accepting that she and Avril lived in different worlds, their personal values separated by an unbridgeable gulf. She had hoped the girl would change, but now she realised there was little hope of that. She told herself not to worry about it; when they reached Mandalay they would go their separate ways, she to look for a suitable building or, if that proved pointless, a job in one of the hospitals, while Avril would make full use of her racquets and the wardrobe she had brought with her.

She got up, saying, 'I'm off to bed,' and walked towards the hut.

Avril said, 'Me too, I'm absolutely whacked.'

Private Wagstaff turned to Sergeant Harris. 'I been finkin' I oughta do the first stint of sentry duty, Sarge. Ain't fair to dodge it. I'll still be fit to drive, don't worry.'

Harris nodded. 'I appreciate that.'

Although he could have slept in one of the huts, Harris decided he would prefer the cabin of his truck because he wanted to be able to switch on the headlights if there was any trouble. He thought how fortunate he was in having the three men with him; he could not have made a better choice.

He would not have felt so self-satisfied if he could have known what was passing through the Cockney's mind. Wagstaff was thinking that when the others left he would keep Nellie talking and see how things developed. He was a soldier and she was dead set on marrying one, and you would have to be a prize prick not to exploit such a golden opporunity.

Fazackerley ambled off without a word, and Simmonds said, 'Call me in three hours, Waggy. And I mean that, not two.'

Alone with the Burmese girl Wagstaff said, 'You remin' me a lot of a girl I used to know back 'ome. Very pretty, and a lovely nature. Mighta taken 'er up the aisle if she 'adn't gone off and married a postman. Can't say I blame 'er. A soldier's lot is a dicey do. One minute you're 'ere, the next you're gettin' a 'ero's funeral.'

As he spoke he was already convinced that the mythical girl really existed and was not a figment of his fertile imagination, conveniently forgetting it was an opening gambit he had frequently used with some success in the past.

'Why did she marry the man who comes with the letters? A soldier is better.'

'That was my sentiments, Nellie. Took a bit to get over it, I can tell you. Put me right offa marriage. Made me realise no one wants to get 'itched to a soldier.'

'I would marry soldier,' she said with dogged persistence.

Wagstaff felt encouraged enough to sit beside her and put his arm around her slim waist. 'A pretty little fing like you could 'ave the pick of the field.'

'I do not understand. You explain.'

Wagstaff was not sure either. His brow furrowed. 'Let me put it this way – in 'orse racin' terms it means you could 'ave the odds-on favrit. If it was flowers, you could 'ave the best bloom to put behind your ear. Only I was referrin' to men. Get it?'

Nellie clearly did not. Like a needle stuck in the groove of a record she said, 'I want to be soldier's missus.'

'No reason why you shouldn' if your 'eart's set on it, Nellie. All you gotta do is sit tight an' wait for Mr Right to come along an' pop the question.'

His lips brushed against her cheek and Nellie turned her head so that her own could meet his. She had seen enough American films to know that was how white people liked to kiss. She had done it before and found it very enjoyable.

127

When she felt his hand fumbling with the buttons on her longyi she made no attempt to stop him. He would find her breasts, although they did not appear to be so from the outside, were nicer than Miss Bradshaw's. If the soldier wanted to enter her she would not mind that either. Like kissing, it was very good.

Wagstaff was aware of the growing hardness between his thighs, and he was thinking of taking her to one of the empty huts in order to do something about it when a voice that was unmistakably Miss Carfax's cut through the night air. 'Nellie, it's time you went to bed. Private Wagstaff is supposed to be keeping watch and he won't do that with his hand down your longyi.'

Nellie jumped up and scuttled off like a scalded cat, leaving Wagstaff nursing an erection that made his groin ache.

'Stupid, stuck up cow!' he muttered. 'I was almost home and dry. Now I'm left with the ol' five-fingered widow.'

He lit a cigarette and wondered why the Colonel, usually so level-headed, had agreed to Avril Carfax's joining the party. She had been a pain in the arse from the moment they set off with her hoity-toity airs and graces, and the way things were going they would be stuck with her for a long time. On the other hand if she had not been there, neither would Nellie, so it was all swings and roundabouts. The only consolation was that the journey looked like taking a lot longer than anyone had imagined, and that would give him more oppourtunities of making it with Nellie. Come to think of it, she was a real peach and not a girl you would be ashamed of being seen with at a battalion dance. She was certainly a lot better looking than some of the scrubbers Fazackerley had picked up in Rangoon and rogered after the last waltz.

They set off early next morning as a purple-pink hue was suffusing the sky, and although progress was still laboriously slow Harris felt confident they would reach Prome by nightfall.

It was a largish town and thriving business centre, standing on a bank of the Irrawaddy, and if the Japs hadn't reduced it to rubble would be an ideal spot for an extended halt. Furthermore, with a bit of luck the congestion would be considerably eased because many of the refugees would want to cross the river into the Arakan which provided a more direct route into India, whereas he would follow the course of the river and head north east for Mandalay. From a study of the admittedly not too detailed map, the road was reasonably good all the way.

His thoughts were interrupted by a furious hammering on the door panel and he looked down out of the window and saw an Indian running alongside. He was clinging to the handle with one hand and pounding on the panelling with the other. The man's eyes were white with fear, and he was so breathless he had difficulty in getting his words out. 'Honourable sahib, you must help me. I implore of you to come and see my wife.'

He slowed down to a walking pace, fearful of pulling the man's arm out of its socket. 'Sorry, I can't stop for everyone who needs help. If I did I'd never get anywhere.'

The man placed his hands together in a gesture of supplication. 'Please, honoured sahib. I have seen the memsahibs with you. They will know what to do. My wife is in childbirth, but the baby will not come.'

Harris called to Miss Bradshaw through the aperture. 'Hear that? Do you want me to pull off so that you can have a look?'

'Of course,' she snapped. 'All these people are fleeing in order to stay alive, so it doesn't make a lot of sense if we turn our backs on the woman when we have the chance of saving two lives.'

Harris pulled off the road and the agitated Indian hopped from one foot to the other while Miss Bradshaw filled her rucksack with all she thought she would need.

Harris said, 'I'll come with you. The lads can keep an eye on the trucks.'

'Good. You can carry that stove contraption because we'll need a lot of hot water. Avril and Nellie had better come too. I'll need all the help I can get.'

Harris called to Wagstaff, 'Bring a can of water and some petrol.'

The Indian said, 'Thank you, sahib. Thank you, sahib,'

and darted ahead, constantly glancing over his shoulder to make sure they were following.

Harris recognised the woman immediately from the yellow sari and the bangles and anklets. She was lying beneath the shade of a peepul tree, groaning softly as the pains surged through her body. Her eyes were shut, and perspiration coursed down her face. Her sari was sodden. The baby she had been carrying on her back was on the ground nearby, fast asleep.

Kitty knelt beside her, rested a hand on her distended stomach and began a gentle exploratory examination. 'Poor thing is petrified with fear. Can't relax. Normally childbirth to them is as easy as shelling peas, but when things go wrong they panic. Get some water boiling, Sergeant. Avril and I will need to wash our hands.'

Avril chewed a knuckle. 'I'm not going to be of much help. This kind of thing is entirely new to me.'

'It is to me too,' snapped Miss Bradshaw. 'How many times do you think I've delivered a baby by the roadside? In normal circumstances a woman in her condition would need hospital treatment and the services of a doctor, but as we haven't got either we'll have to do the best we can. If the child dies at least we'll have tried.'

'I really can't,' pleaded Avril.

'Stop thinking about yourself for once, and just do what I tell you.'

She removed what she needed from the rucksack, then handed it to Avril, saying, 'Put that under her head, and reassure her everything is going to be all right. Nellie, boil these for a good ten minutes.'

She gave the Burmese girl three pieces of string about nine inches long, and a pair of scissors.

Miss Bradshaw knelt and felt the woman's stomach, and cursed silently; she hoped it was not a breech and she would have to manoeuvre the child until it was in the head down position.

In a maternity ward that would not have presented any great difficulty to a doctor, but doing it on the side of a dusty road without the proper instruments was a daunting task. The nurse gave no sign of the anxiety she felt. From the

130

outside she looked perfectly calm and composed. If it was a breech there was a danger the baby might be strangled by its own umbilical cord. As she probed further she heaved a sigh of relief; the baby was in a perfectly normal position.

As the contractions increased and the woman entered the second stage of labour, Kitty lifted her sari exposing her lower body, then moved her legs apart and bent her knees to facilitate the birth.

She tore the wrapping from a packet of cotton wool and handed a thick wad to Avril. 'Wipe her if she has a bowel movement, and make sure it doesn't go anywhere near her vagina. There's enough risk of infection as it is without adding to it.'

'Sorry, I just couldn't do it. You'll have to manage without me.'

Kitty rose, raised her fist and swung it in a wide arc, delivering a stinging blow that struck Avril on the mouth and drew blood. 'You'll do as you're told.'

Avril rushed forward, her fists flailing the air. Harris moved swiftly and pinioned her hands. 'If you two want to fight you'll have to leave it till later. Now take the cotton wool and do as the Sister asks.'

Avril took the swab of cotton wool saying, 'You'll regret that, Miss Bradshaw.'

'Just get on with it, the pair of you,' said Harris wearily. 'When this is over I want you both to shake hands. We've still got a fair way to go and two squabbling women is more than I can bear.'

'I really can't. Can't Nellie . . .' but she was cut short.

'No she can't. She's got her hands full boiling things. I need *you*. Now don't be such a ninny. This is the most natural thing in the world, so stop acting as if you're being asked to help with the impossible.'

Avril knelt beside the woman and began dabbing her brow with some of the cotton wool, while her other hand was poised in readiness for the task she prayed she would not be called upon to carry out. She tried hard not to show the revulsion she felt.

Kitty glanced at her watch, timing the contractions and thinking: It can't be long now.

131

The father was making incoherent whimpering sounds like a puppy that has been beaten. 'For God's sake, get him out of the way, Sergeant. I'll tell him when he's a proud father.' She gave vent to her frustration which was fuelled by the fear that she would not be able to cope with the unexpected emergency, and muttered angrily, 'If he could have kept his mind off his bloody lingam for five minutes his poor wife wouldn't be in danger of losing her life from septicaemia or haemorrhaging.'

He replied gently, 'Don't take it out on him, Kitty. Poor devil didn't know Rangoon was going to be bombed.'

'I'm sorry, I shouldn't have said that; moralising is no part of a nurse's job, but Hindus *do* have this obsession with sex and fertility and they'd be better off if they didn't.'

Harris could not refute that because he had witnessed it in India and had been appalled that in a country so poverty stricken and over-populated the lingam and the yoni, the male and female sex organs, were the objects of religious worship. He knew too from the well-thumbed copies of the *Kama Sutra* that had been passed round the barracks that love-making was considered a fine art that required the skills of a contortionist. But who could blame the Indians? It was one thing that cost nothing and took their minds off their awful plight.

To cool her anger he said jokingly, 'Maybe one day someone will launch a religious crusade and make a goddess of contraception.'

'A damned good idea, but in the meantime I'd better see about delivering this baby.'

Harris told the man to pick up the sleeping child then took him by the arm and led him to the shelter of some nearby trees.

There was a steady trickle of amniotic fluid which told Kitty the woman's 'waters' had broken. She spoke aloud, to no one in particular, 'She's a bit undernourished which, thank God, means the baby won't be too big. Even better, she's had other children.' Her voice sharpened, 'Avril, try and get her to grasp her knees, bend her head forward and hold her breath, then press down hard.'

132

Avril put her mouth close to the woman's ear and whispered the instructions, then said despairingly, 'She doesn't understand.'

'Then damn well help her do it.'

Nellie, in contrast, remained perfectly calm, doing everything she was commanded without any fuss and with a face as expressionless as a Buddha, yet wondering why they should be bothered with one more Indian baby when there were too many in Burma as it was. Kitty wrongly assumed that her indifference was due to the fact that she had witnessed too many similar scenes in her own village for this one to have any dramatic significance.

An hour after they had first arrived on the scene, the baby's head was just visible at the lower end of the birth canal. Kitty's hands supported the head as it emerged, and she called to Avril, 'Tell her to stop pushing, the worst is over. Make her open her mouth and start gulping in air.'

Kitty removed the membrane from the baby's face and checked to make sure there was no risk of strangulation. She continued to support the head until the shoulders emerged, and when the baby had been safely delivered cleaned out its mouth then laid it gently on its side so that any mucous would drain away. When the placenta appeared she waited until the cord had stopped pulsating before she tied the pieces of sterilised string around it six inches and eight inches from the abdomen, the pieces nearest the baby very tightly, to prevent excessive bleeding. Then she asked Nellie to hand her the scissors. When the cord had been cut she tied a third piece of string four inches from the abdomen.

She wrapped the child in a clean towel, gave it a gentle slap and pressed on its chest to encourage breathing. The child began to cry and Kitty, unable to conceal her delight and relief, said, 'That's it. Delivered safe and sound. Mother and baby fine.'

She straightened up and said to Avril, 'You can chuck the afterbirth into the bushes for the crows.'

Avril cringed at the prospect of handling the gruesome-looking mess. 'I'm going into the bushes, but not for what you want. I'm going to be sick.'

Kitty sighed. 'Oh, go on then. At least you waited until it

was all over. I'll do it.' She was pleased the girl had stood up to it so well.

With Nelllie's reluctant assistance she washed the mother as best she could, then walked over to where the sergeant stood with the quaking father. 'Pull yourself together, man,' she snapped. 'You've got a lovely daughter. Now go and say something to your wife.'

The man stumbled towards his exhausted wife and Miss Bradshaw was amazed that although he seemed concerned for her, he was not at all interested in the baby. She did not know that far from being delighted he was disappointed: he had wanted a son, whereas he had got another daughter which did not call for any celebration.

She said to Harris, 'She's too weak to move under her own steam. Can we fetch one of the trucks and let her rest until we reach Prome?'

'I'll get it. How is she?'

'As well as can be expected in the circumstances. I'll tell her husband that she needs to rest for a couple of days before moving on. They have remarkably good recuperative powers, but she needs nourishment and from what I've seen food is on the scarce side among the refugees. If she can't feed the baby, our efforts will have been a waste of time.'

'I'll see they have enough food and water to see them through for some time. How about Miss Carfax?'

'She's in the bushes throwing up. She didn't exactly relish it, but she did far better than I imagined she would. She's a decent kid at heart, David. It's just up to us to make her realise that.'

When Harris returned with the truck they lifted the woman into the back and made her as comfortable as possible on a heap of blankets. Kitty placed the child beside her and soon it was nestling at her breast. 'She'll have forgotten all about it by the morning. Women never remember what they've been through, which is a damned good thing otherwise they'd never have another baby.'

Avril emerged from the bushes, looking whey-faced and tense, the front of her dress coated with dried vomit. 'How are they?' she asked.

134

'Go and have a look, and give yourself a pat on the back. Without you they'd never have made it,' said Kitty.

Avril permitted a slight smile to pucker her mouth. 'I'm already regretting I didn't bother to attend any of those first aid classes. Wouldn't have made such a fool of myself if I had. But I don't ever want to go through that again.'

'If it's any consolation, neither do I,' said Sister Bradshaw.

Harris said, 'You both deserve a medal. When we get to Prome we'll open a bottle and wet the baby's head. And now you can both shake hands.'

Kitty Bradshaw extended a hand and stood looking at Harris when Avril failed to respond. Several seconds elapsed before she said, 'Oh, all right,' and took the proferred hand. 'I still think an apology is in order.'

Kitty smiled wryly. 'Anything to make you happy and preserve the peace,' she said disarmingly, indicating the flag of truce had been hoisted and hoping it would not be hauled down.

Chapter Nine

As soon as Sergeant Harris passed the twin gryphons marking the entrance to Prome, he knew that he would have to abandon his plan for a prolonged stay before continuing the journey to Mandalay; it was obvious the news of the reverses in the south and the abandonment of Rangoon had reached the town and triggered off a panic departure. Prome, which had once been grandiosely described as a sod detached from mainland England – a claim that owed much more to sentiment than any physical likeness – was a ghost town. The inland port which sprawled along two miles of the east bank of the Irrawaddy had ceased to exist as a thriving commercial centre supporting a comfortably off European community.

Harris drove carefully through the filthy, refuse-strewn streets which carried the sickly odour of decaying vegetation and excreta for, as in Rangoon, the natives employed by the municipal services had been among the first to leave. He wrinkled his nose in disgust, not only at the offensive stench but the speed with which everyone seemed to have deserted their post. It was not a place in which to linger.

The road took them along the embankment overlooking the river that was so wide it seemed more like the sea, past the ram which jutted out into the water, then into the area which had been the centre of the civil administration. Standing like a well-preserved relic commemorating the grandeur of a bygone era was the lofty courthouse where a short time ago the great business of Empire had been transacted, and life or death decisions made.

The bazaar, so recently canopied by the countless multi-coloured umbrellas of the fruit and vegetable vendors, was empty; and the large girdered structure of the main market, normally teeming with cobblers, sellers of silk, makers of embroidered trappings for horses, and the inevitable cheroot stalls, now resembled an empty stage set.

The quayside area presented a vastly different picture. There the normal working population had been replaced by thousands of refugees waiting patiently for a passage aboard one of the few ferries willing to take them across the river so that they could continue their trek along the Arakan and finally to India. Many had been there several days, waiting with stoic resignation, accepting the fact that several more days could elapse before they obtained a space on the overcrowded decks, because many of the steamer skippers were reluctant to travel so far south for fear of air attacks, and those who did were often more concerned with shifting the mountains of rice that had accumulated in the warehouses and which was so desperately needed for the army and townships further north.

Harris's eyes searched in vain for a road sign that would point to the European civil lines, but when he passed a building that was unmistakably the club he knew he was heading in the right direction. No Union Jack flew from the white-painted pole outside and the adjacent tennis court was already beginning to spout weeds. The neat rows of European houses were shuttered and bolted, and the gardens had an unkempt look about them.

He studied the bungalows, looking for a suitable place to stop, and when he saw a solid-looking building standing at the end of a drive he signalled his intention to turn into it. The big double gates at the entrance were open and the house stood far enough back from the road for a sentry to have ample warning of any approaching strangers. There was no point, he told himself, in running risks, especially with so many desperately hungry people around; an empty belly could make the mildest person bold and aggressive.

He got out of the truck and told Simmonds to keep him covered with the Tommy-gun whilst he walked up to the porch. When he climbed the flight of wooden steps he saw a handwritten notice pinned to the front door which said: 'Don't bother to loot. You've been beaten to it.' The unexpected touch of humour amidst so much panic gave him a feeting of encouragement; it was comforting to know that there were still Britons around who could display the qualities which had helped their country survive so many stormy passages.

The door was unlocked. He went inside and found himself in a large, comfortably furnished room. He made a quick tour of the other rooms and decided that if the house had been looted the culprits had only removed what they considered would be of immediate use. The kitchen larder contained no food, but a paraffin refrigerator was still working. There were pictures on the walls of the lounge and books stood in neat regimental lines on a row of shelves, while the chintz-covered chairs and settee with their puffed up cushions gave the impression that the occupants had just gone out for a short stroll. In one bedroom there was a double bed that looked as if it had just been made, and in a smaller adjoining room children's bunks and a floor littered with toys as if a game had been suddenly interrupted.

He went out onto the veranda and signalled that it was safe for the others to come in.

Fazackerley and Simmonds carried the still exhausted Indian woman into the house, followed by Kitty Bradshaw who held the sleeping baby. After a cursory examination she told them to put the woman on the double bed. She turned to Avril and said, 'And I don't want you moaning about sharing the same roof with her.'

She knew it was a cruel taunt, but she was determined to accelerate the process of maturing Miss Carfax.

Avril said, 'That was quite uncalled for. Where else could you put the poor thing?'

Harris's voice had the frightening bark he normally reserved for a recalcitrant soldier. 'Pack it in, you two. I've enough to worry about without having two bloody silly women at each other's throats. You should know better, Miss Bradshaw, and as for you, Miss Carfax, it's time you learned to muck in with the rest of us.' He spun on his heel before she had the chance to reply and called to Wagstaff, 'Get what

138

food we need from the truck and give it to the ladies. The kitchen seems in working order.'

When the private returned with some tins of corned beef, canned vegetables and biscuits, Harris said, 'Take the wrapper off one of the tins of bully and give it to the Indian. Tell him it's mutton, otherwise he won't eat it.'

Sister Bradshaw said, 'Haven't you forgotten something, Sergeant?'

'I don't think so.'

'The gin. Remember, we agreed to wet the baby's head? It'll also help to cool your temper.'

Despite himself Harris smiled. 'I prefer your leg pulling to your rather tiresome efforts to upset Miss Carfax. At least I've got a thick hide, whereas she hasn't.' And to Wagstaff he said, 'Get a bottle and bring some beer in for yourself and the lads. The fridge is still working which means you're in for a rare treat – chilled beer.'

Kitty Bradshaw's reminder had eased the tension and a more relaxed atmosphere prevailed.

When the private returned with the gin and beer, he said that while they were cooling he and the other two soldiers were going to scout around and see if they could find a suitable spot for them to settle down for the night. Harris did not suggest that the bungalow was large enough to accommodate them all because he suspected the men wanted a little privacy of their own; a place where they could relax without him watching their every move. They probably wanted to cuss and swear, drink more beer than he would have approved of, and get out the cards and play another interminable game of pontoon. He did not really care what they did as long as they arranged a sentry roster for the hours of darkness.

Harris and the two women drank their gin, sitting in the comfort of the lounge, with undisguised pleasure, noisily rattling the ice cubes in their glasses, and when the food was ready they ate the rather unappetising fare in real style around the large teak dining table.

A good two hours of daylight still remained by the time they had finished eating, and Harris announced that he was going down to the riverside to get a better idea of the situation that confronted them.

As he walked through the streets he realised that the privations of the long trek from Rangoon were beginning to take their toll. The occasional dead body lay on the pavement, and when he reached the quay area the situation was even worse; corpses were more frequent and vultures were gorging on the blackened flesh. In the nearby trees more vultures, looking like ancient sextons, sat waiting their turn.

The majority of the refugees were Indians, and lay sleeping by the side of their un-yoked oxen or in the shade of cumbersome carts. On the quays the better off were brandishing great wads of rupee notes and expressing their willingness to pay *any* price for transportation across the river. The owners of even the smallest craft were making fortunes they had never imagined possible. He noticed that those who offered silver rupees or gold fared better than those with paper money who, if they were lucky, had to pay three or four times as much. He silently blessed Colonel Selthorpe for his foresight.

Secured alongside one of the quays was a big Irrawaddy paddle steamer with a large red cross crudely painted on the top of the main deck awning. The conversion into a hospital had been hurried and more concerned with providing the maximum space above and below deck than with the comfort of the wounded and sick. The boat had been commandeered by the army to ferry casualties from the Sittang and other earlier battles to Mandalay, and the scene reminded him of accounts he had read of hospital conditions in the Crimea. Every inch of space was occupied by stretcher cases, and the stench of gangrenous limbs, mingling with disinfectant, urine and excreta, was nauseating. There were men whose arms and legs had been amputated in field hospitals under the most primitive conditions, whilst others nursed head and stomach wounds caused by shell and mortar fragments or were doubled up in agony with dysentery. Morphia was so scarce that only the very worst cases could hope for any relief from their pain. They had endured the persistent jolting of a long ambulance journey along crudely made roads that would have tested the fittest men, and ahead lay an even more uncertain and hazardous voyage before they could receive the expert attention they needed.

Lined up on the quay were even more stretcher cases waiting to be carried aboard, and sitting on any available object that offered momentary respite to their tortured limbs were the walking wounded who would be the last to board.

Harris estimated that there must be four or five hundred British and Indian soldiers, and he had counted only four medical orderlies.

He walked down to the gangway, wondering how many would be thrown over the side before the steamer reached its destination. A voice bellowed in his ear, 'You'll have to wait like the rest, Sergeant. No bloody queue jumping.'

He turned and saw he had been spoken to by a captain in the Medical Corps. His tunic was caked with dried blood and his face was grey with exhaustion.

Harris saluted. 'I had no intention of boarding, sir. I've a party of my own, some are women. I've got to get to Mandalay, but we have transport. I was just hoping to pick up some news.'

The captain said, 'If I were you I wouldn't hang around this place a second longer than is absolutely necessary. Cholera and typhoid have broken out among the refugees, and the way they're living it'll spread like an oil fire on water. I've tried telling the daft buggers that it's their own filthy habits which have caused the outbreak, but it's like talking to a brick wall. Wisely, the powers that be decided it was safer and healthier to transport our own wounded by river instead of sticking to the road. I'm beginning to have doubts about it though.'

'I wish there was something I could do to help, sir.'

The officer, who looked no older than twenty-four or five, said wearily, 'There's nothing, unless of course you happen to have a vast amount of blood plasma and a lorry load of medical supplies.'

'I have a nursing sister with me who has a little,' he said hopefully.

'Save it for yourselves. You may need it. Anyway, I need so much any contribution you could make wouldn't make any difference. The poor devils will just have to grit their teeth and suffer — not in silence, that's asking too much — until we get them tucked up in a decent bed. It's too much to ask the Almighty to come up with the fishes and loaves solution, but I'm praying that the Japs will take notice of that red cross.'

'I wish you the best of luck, sir,' said Harris before turning his back on the nightmarish scene and retracing his path back to the bungalow. He was filled with a deep sense of depression; the deep-rooted complacency in the higher echelons of the army and civil administration was unforgivable. Countless soldiers and civilians were going to die, or already had, because no preparations had been made for the large-scale evacuation of the wounded and the refugees, and the situation was going to get worse when the retreating army caught up with them.

When he reached the bungalow he found Nellie asleep under a blanket on the veranda. He peeped into the darkened room Kitty and Avril were sharing, and could just make out their dim shapes on the children's bunks. He closed the door quietly behind him and went into the lounge where he poured himself a tumbler of gin. He emptied half the glass and felt the raw spirit scorch his gullet. He flopped down into the armchair, pulled off his boots and hoped the alcohol would help him snatch some sleep, although he doubted it. His head was still echoing with the cries of the men he had seen aboard the steamer.

Avril was awakened from the troubled sleep by the sound of her own sobbing. She sat bolt upright, her body bathed in a cold sweat and shivering uncontrollably. She slipped off the lower bunk, anxious not to wake Miss Bradshaw, and crept silently into the lounge where she was surprised to see Sergeant Harris sitting in one of the armchairs with a bottle of gin at his feet.

'I'm sorry, I didn't realise you were here. Couldn't sleep.'

The sergeant said unsympathetically, 'Conscience troubling you?' Then seeing her distress he relented and got up and poured her a drink to which he added cold water. 'Here, have this, it'll steady you up. Sorry to be so snappy. Couldn't sleep myself. I've just got back from a sight I never want to see again. What was troubling you? The Indian woman and the baby?'

'I don't know. Do you think the brain can do that deliberately? Blot out unpleasant things?'

'No idea. What makes you ask?'

'A feeling of guilt. Perhaps that's what kept me tossing and turning.'

'What have you got to feel guilty about?'

'I wanted to run away,' she confessed.

'You didn't, so forget it,' he said brusquely.

'But I wanted to. I'm ashamed of myself.'

'Don't be. Let me tell you something, Miss Carfax. There are two kinds of bravery. There's the blind courage where a man performs an heroic deed because he doesn't know what fear is, and there's the kind where a man stays put even though he's in a cold funk and everything tells him to make a run for it. The latter kind of bravery is the most admirable.'

'That's kind of you, but Sister Bradshaw despises me and that's difficult to live with.'

'She doesn't despise *you* but what you represent: privilege, patronage, and a fearful sense of your own importance and superiority. That's understandable. She's dedicated her life to serving, and she thinks you've devoted yours to being served.'

'What she can't understand,' said Avril fervently, 'is that is what I was brought up to think life was all about. She can't expect me to change as if someone had waved a magic wand. My father said that only the best was good enough for me, and the very best in his eyes is all the things she detests.'

Harris said wearily, 'Personally, I'm not particularly interested in dissertations on the sins of the father. My job is to get the Colours and Silver to safety. I intend doing that. I also intend to make certain that you are there when I hand them over. I didn't ask for it, but you are my responsibility too. You wouldn't be if the burra sahibs and the tuans hadn't acted as if they were God's appointed, because the Japs wouldn't have found Burma such easy meat.'

'You sound just like Sister Bradshaw.'

'That could be a compliment,' he said with a wry smile.

'It wasn't intended to be,' she said angrily. 'Can't you

143

understand that we had to live as we did to command the necessary respect?'

'Earning it might have been more fruitful.'

'You sound just like one of those hot-headed Burmese agitators.'

'I'm trying to make you see things through a soldier's eyes. We're asked to fight for a country we never asked to visit, and to preserve a way of life we aren't allowed to share. And what have we found? A country so ill-prepared it seems to have a death wish. With a bit of luck the army will make it to India where they'll encounter the same privileges and prejudices, and when the Japs start hammering on the door the army will be asked to save that too.'

'Surely,' she said with astonishment, 'that is what soldiers are for?'

'True, but it helps if you're able to believe in the cause.'

'The Indians would hate not being part of the Raj. It's the jewel in the crown. Surely that's worth fighting for?'

Harris sighed, tired of the argument, but feeling the need to explain how he felt. He was sick and tired of seeing soldiers taken for granted and treated like ignoramuses who had no right to question what they were being asked to die for. The 'theirs not to reason why' mentality was still alive and flourishing. 'Try to remember, Miss Carfax, that the sepoy makes up the bulk of the army, so of course he'll fight for his country, but when it's over he'll expect to be rewarded with independence.'

'You couldn't possibly agree to that,' she said, quite horrified at the suggestion.

'Wholeheartedly. Quite apart from the fact that it's inevitable, they've earned it by fighting in other countries they don't care a damn about.'

'You're a strange man, Sergeant. Not at all what my father led me to expect. He said all soldiers were wet behind the ears and, like donkeys, had to be led. You really think about things, not like your three privates who never question or complain about anything you tell them to do.'

'They trust and respect me.'

'That's because you have three stripes on your arm,' she

144

said with a note of triumph. 'It confirms what I said about status.'

'It does nothing of the kind. You get promotion through ability and no one appreciates that more than they do. They may be poorly paid, forgotten most of the time, but they're the salt of the earth and they know they mean a lot to people like me and the Colonel. And that's all they care about. They don't give a damn for the rest of the world's indifference. Ever read Kipling?'

'Not really. He wasn't considered suitable for young convent girls.'

'You should try. He understood the British soldier and the public attitude towards him:

> For it's Tommy this an' Tommy that, an'
> Chuck him out the brute!
> But it's "Saviour of 'is country", when
> the guns begin to shoot ...

'I can almost hear Private Wagstaff's voice,' she said mockingly.

'The sentiments are true, though. We're seen as a necessary evil, to be kept out of sight until needed.'

'You sound bitter.'

'I am, because I happen to be a soldier − never wanted to be anything else, and very proud of the fact − but it doesn't deny me the right to think.'

'For someone who thinks so much, you're singularly lacking in ambition.'

'What prompted that?'

'Well, you seem to be content to be an ordinary ranker. Haven't you ever tried to become an officer? I'm sure you'd make a very good one. You certainly look as if you could be.'

He replied with a detectable note of contempt: 'There're a lot of men in Burma who *look* like officers, but they couldn't lead a thirsty horse to water and I'm not referring to the fighting officer, just some brass hats.'

'But seriously, wouldn't you like to be ...'

He cut her short. 'It's a subject I don't want to discuss,

for the simple reason that it has nothing whatsoever to do with you. To be frank, I object to your curiosity and stupid snobbishness. Would I be a better person with pips on my shoulders instead of stripes on my arm? Of course I damn well wouldn't! I'd only be more socially acceptable.'

She sensed she had touched a raw spot and hastily changed the subject. 'When we set off in the morning, will you let me have a spell driving?'

'Let's see what the road's like first,' he said non-committally.

Avril began to feel the gin taking effect and said, 'Goodnight, Sergeant. I've enjoyed the chat. I'll try hard to see things differently from now on.'

He couldn't make out if she was being sarcastic or whether she was going to make a genuine effort to fit in.

When Avril got into her bunk she was still unable to sleep; her mind was filled with thoughts of her father and she wondered if he had managed to get out of Rangoon safely. She felt a flush of guilt suffuse her cheeks, realising that although she had talked about him quite a lot she had not given any thought to his welfare since they parted and her concern had only been aroused by the conversation with Sergeant Harris. He was a man who seemed only to care about others, whereas her father was totally self-centred. She accepted too that she had never questioned his views, firstly because there had never been any need to because they coincided with those of everyone else she knew; and secondly because he was so dogmatically forceful. She also realised that she respected him rather than loved him which confused her even more, because the sergeant found him obnoxious.

She turned her eyes towards the bunk above and listened to the regular breathing of Sister Bradshaw, thinking: And you despise *me*, but I never knew people like you and the sergeant existed, people who are completely unselfish. I might have been different if I had, so don't blame me. Daddy always said, 'You can only crow if you're on top of the dung heap.' That was his way of telling me that material success was the only thing that mattered and anyone who thought differently was a failure and soured by envy. You can tell me he is wrong,

146

but I know one thing: he'll survive, which is more than can be said for a lot of people. You make me feel guilty, whereas he would dismiss your criticisms with utter contempt. He doesn't need to be liked by people like you and the sergeant. Aloud she said despairingly, 'You both don't seem to realise, I'm still very young. I need time.'

Alex Carfax had left Rangoon just ahead of the retreating army. He had packed everything of value which he had been unable to crate and put aboard the ship with his wife, or dare not risk burying, and stowed it in the boot and on the back seat of the Rolls. He had also loaded enough food, water and fuel to see him safely to Mandalay where he would join up with his daughter. His sole travelling companion was the head boy who would fill the role of head cook and bottle washer. Resting between the front seats was a twelve-bore shotgun and a hunting rifle and two boxes of cartridges, just in case he came across any hostile Burmese. He did not anticipate encountering any Japanese for, from what he had heard, they were too busy racing for Rangoon to bother with the odd stray traveller.

Round his neck was a silver chain to which was attached the key to the steel deed box which contained a large sum of money, a copy of his Will that he had retrieved from his Solicitor's office, all his share certificates and other documents which were tangible proof of his worldly possessions.

He had followed the Prome Road until he reached the large fork, then instead of taking the left-hand road he had turned right and headed for Pegu, confident he could follow the railway to Toungoo and Meiktila, a shorter and more direct route to Mandalay.

He had made excellent progress, often maintaining speeds of up to twenty miles an hour, for even the refugees had an inbred respect for a Rolls-Royce which was to them the symbol of wealth and authority and frequently pulled off the road to make way for him. He had encountered no enemy troops, and apart from one occasion when he had had to seek shelter in the trees when an anemy aircraft had strafed a refugee train on the nearby line, it had been

147

uneventful. At night he had pulled off the road and found a suitable place to sleep, somewhere safe and concealed. He had locked the doors, loaded the shotgun and given the boy strict instructions to stay awake and rouse him if anyone approached. He had assured the boy that he would not in the least mind if he dozed off during the day because they had to rely on each other for mutual protection.

Three days after leaving the capital he had passed through Toungoo, hardly able to believe his good fortune; no one would have thought there was a war on. Apart from the refugees there was no sign of the widespread devastation he had expected. He spotted a dak bungalow, one of the many that catered for peacetime travellers, and wondered whether it was possible to obtain overnight accommodation. There seemed no point in tiring himself to the point of exhaustion.

He switched off the engine and walked up to the bungalow, and was a trifle unnerved to see a tattooed Burmese man sitting on the veranda sharpening a frightening looking dah on a flat stone. The man, who had the look of an opium addict, was poorly dressed in a faded blouse and long baggy trousers that looked as if they had been discarded by some European as being of no further use.

Carfax spoke rapidly in Burmese, asking the man if there was food and a room available, but the man shrugged indifferently and said the house had been abandoned by its owners. Carfax was tempted to tell him to stand up when spoken to and not be so bloody uppity, but he did not like the look of the knife which the man kept testing with the ball of his thumb, and as he had left the guns in the car he decided to thank him instead. There had been rumours in Rangoon of an active Fifth Column, an increase in dacoitry, and a growing band of deserters from the Burmese and Indian Armies who had thrown their lot in with the Japanese. Alone and unarmed as he was, it was not time to take foolish chances.

When he turned to walk back to the car he was surprised to see it surrounded by a number of equally disreputable-looking Burmese who were fondling the lamps and other fixtures, as if they were valuable objects.

148

He shouted, 'Take your filthy bloody hands off other people's property,' but they merely returned insolent and toothy grins. He turned towards the man on the balcony intending to ask him to intervene, but he had got up and was following Carfax towards the car too.

He wished he had a stout lathi in his hand to put the buggers in their place. Christ Almighty, he thought, what's the country coming to?

He quickened his pace, intending to reach into the car for the shotgun; there was nothing better than a dose of buckshot for reminding bloody-minded natives of their station in life. His head boy, he noticed, was doing absolutely bugger all to stop the wretches from running their grubby paws over the car, just sitting there with an inane smile on his face. Spineless sod.

He bellowed, 'Get away from that car. I'll not warn you again. When I reach the next town I'll report you to the police and you'll all end up in leg irons.' He realised his voice was shrill with fear and he rebuked himself: Pull yourself together, Carfax. The least sign of weakness could be disastrous. Show the buggers who's on top. Kick a few arses.

The men around the car were laughing loudly and mockingly, and Carfax knew what they thought of his threat to inform the police. They were telling him that law and order no longer existed.

Although he felt his bowels churn he straightened his back and lengthened his stride. After all his years in Burma he had learned how important it was to retain the upper hand. Show the least sign of uncertainty, he told himself, and the buggers will try and walk all over you. Stand up to them though, and they'll be off like a cat with a can on its tail.

'Right,' he roared, 'don't say I didn't warn you.'

He felt a stunning blow at the base of his skull which sent his topee sailing through the air, and saw flashes of incandescent light before he stumbled and fell to the ground. When he opened his eyes he saw the man who had been sitting on the veranda standing over him, a cheroot clamped between his betel-stained teeth. The man fingered the blade of his dah

149

before leaning down and putting it against his neck and begin sawing.

Carfax screamed and remained alive just long enough to know that he was about to be decapitated.

The dacoit chief looked down, unmoved by the stump of neck still bubbling blood, and saw the silver chain and key.

The chillingly cold bestiality of the murder which had attracted the admiring eyes of the other bandits, gave the house boy time to vault out of the car and run for his life on wobbling legs, but as two men set off in pursuit their leader waved dismissively telling them to forget him, he was not worth chasing. Apart from being a fellow Burmese he had nothing worth stealing.

The dacoit leader, indifferent to the spouting gouts of blood, reached down and ripped the chain away, then he removed Carfax's wrist watch. He tugged at the signet ring on the dead man's hand, but when he found he could not get it over the thickened joint calmly severed the finger with his dah. He straightened up and walked towards the car, twirling the chain from a forefinger.

He leaned into the car and retrieved the two guns, breaking the breech of the shotgun and peering down the barrels, then working the bolt of the hunting rifle as if to satisfy himself that both were worth purloining. Then he gave a casual gesture, indicating that his men should start a systematic search of the car. He sat on the running board like a king waiting for his loyal and servile subjects to bring him gifts. They broke open the suitcases, and he told them they could help themselves to any item of clothing they wished. When the wooden crate containing the valuable articles was prised open he pointed a finger at himself to let them know they belonged to him.

When the deed box was laid at his feet he opened it with the key, crusted now with congealed blood, and rummaged through the contents. The money and jewellery he stowed in his blouse; the deeds and documents he tossed contemptuously aside. They meant nothing to him, just meaningless and valueless scraps of paper. He knocked the winged lady, the Spirit of Ecstasy, off the bonnet with a spanner and tucked that into his blouse too. It would serve as

150

his emblem of authority, along with the dead man's topee.

When the bandits had completed their plunder they smashed all the windows of the car, ripped off the headlamps, cut the upholstery, and felt inside for any concealed valuables before setting fire to it.

The car was engulfed in flames that quickly blistered the well-polished paint, then exploded with a great whoomf when the flames reached the cans of petrol.

The leader barked a staccato order and his men began to walk away without a backward glance. As the head dacoit passed the body of Alex Carfax he calmly kicked aside the head which was in his path. It rolled away, and the wide open eyes seemed to be gazing in admonition at a man who had treated a lifetime's accumulation of wealth and property with such flagrant disrespect. A black crow descended from a tree and hopped warily towards the head then, seeing there was no danger, perched on the hair and began pecking at the sightless eyes.

One of the bandits paused only long enough to strip the body of its clothes, but he was not allowed to keep them. The leader poked his own chest with a finger indicating that he wished to wear them.

The dacoits went inside the deserted bungalow, once the privileged preserve of Europeans, where they shared the contents of the suitcases while their leader counted the money. After retaining the major portion for himself, he distributed the remainder in equal amounts.

Sergeant Harris, dozing in an armchair, the empty glass at his feet, heard Avril's shrill cry of terror. He jumped up and hastened to her room where he found her sleeping like some sculptured figure on a tomb. He shook her and was surprised when she said, 'I was sleeping the sleep of the dead. Why did you wake me?'

'You woke *me*, with your screaming,' he said.

Her cry also woke Sister Bradshaw who scrambled down, saying, 'You poor child, you're shivering. You've had another nightmare.' She cradled Avril in her arms, crooning softly, 'There, there, it's all right now, you're among friends.'

151

Avril shuddered and said, 'It's so odd, Kitty. I can't remember anything of the dream.' She felt an odd sense of elation on hearing that Kitty considered herself a friend. A few hours ago she would not have believed that possible.

Private Simmonds also heard the piercing scream and, half asleep, grabbed his Tommy-gun and almost threw himself out of the door of the servants' hut where he and Fazackerley were sleeping. He almost tripped over Wagstaff lying on the veranda outside, a smile of deep contentment on his face, and his arms embracing Nellie. He had the look of a man who had slipped into that abyss of total bliss the French call 'le petit mort'.

The giant Yorkshireman grabbed him by his shirt front and yanked him to his feet with terrifying ease, while Nellie cowered against the wall in terror.

'Was that her screaming?' demanded Simmonds.

'Come off it, Simmo, she might 'ave been squealing with delight but certainly not screamin'. Don't you start accusin' me of rape.'

'Waggy, I have made myself her guardian, so naturally I don't take kindly to finding you've got your leg over while I've been asleep.' He shook his head in dismay. 'And all the time I've been thinking it was Zack who needed watching! Now listen to me carefully. When we get to Mandalay I'm going to haul you up before a padre and you're going to do the decent thing by her. Till then I'm watching you like a bloody hawk, and if you take it out for anything but a slash I'm going to break every bone in your body.' He pushed the private to the ground with a gesture that indicated his distaste and disapproval, and was surprised when he looked towards the girl and saw a smile of smug satisfaction on her doll-like face.

Wagstaff, who thought the pleasures he had so recently enjoyed were worth a mild roughing up, said plaintively, 'Simmo, ain't you bein' a bit 'ard? Seein' as 'ow I've got to get 'itched to 'er, it ain't really fair to expect me to go wivvout what a future 'usband can consider as 'is rights.'

Private Simmonds' brow creased at the complexity of the reasoning. 'Waggy, I'll have to think about that, and real seriously.'

152

Sergeant Harris appeared on the veranda. 'It's nothing to worry about; Miss Carfax had a bad turn. Panic's over. She's all right now. You can turn in again. Who's on guard?'

Wagstaff said, 'Me, Sarge.'

'I'm surprised you didn't hear anything.'

'I did, Sarge, but I though it was ol' Simmo 'ere, trying 'is luck on the Sister.'

Harris looked hard at Simmonds. 'If I believed for a moment that you even entertained such thoughts I'd tie you to the wheel of one of the trucks, and I won't say by what.'

Simmonds said, 'There isn't a word of truth in what he's just said, Sergeant. Cross my heart.'

'There had better not be,' Harris said as he turned and went inside. He had no doubt in his own mind what had happened, but he felt certain Private Simmonds would settle it without his intervention. In any case, the girl did not seem to mind, and neither did he as long as Wagstaff carried out his duties.

Simmonds said, 'You're a real bastard, Waggy, you just tried to drop me in the shit, but it don't make the slightest difference to what I've just said to you. It just makes me dig my heels in a bit deeper.'

The Burmese girl said, 'You see he becomes my hubby?'

Simmonds said, 'You're bloody right I will, if only to get my own back.'

Private Wagstaff sat on the veranda steps, his rifle resting on his bare knees. All in all, he mused, things were not going too badly. He had managed when everyone else was sleeping to slip Nellie the odd length by promising to marry her, a pledge he had no intention of honouring. Admittedly they were making slow progress, but if they could find a few more comfortable billets like the bungalow they now occupied it wouldn't matter how long it took to reach Mandalay. And when they did get there and the Silver was handed over, they would all have to rejoin the Battalion and get into the thick of things. While the prospect of battle did not worry him unduly it was something he was quite happy to put off until the last possible moment. Burma was a shit hole of a place and not worth fighting for, and so for the life of him he could not see the logic of fighting your way out with the sole purpose of coming back again.

His thoughts were interrupted by the sound of a car horn, and he looked up and saw a dark blue saloon car drive through the gates. He instinctively stood up and moved the safety catch on his rifle to the firing position. A door swung open and a middle-aged European wearing a white topee, white shirt and slacks stepped out, followed by the Burmese driver in a police constable's uniform.

The European stabbed a swagger stick at Wagstaff. 'Just what do you think you're doing?'

'Keepin' guard.'

'Sir,' he bellowed.

Wagstaff looked bewildered. 'Sir?'

'Yes, *Sir*! That's how you should address me. And stand to attention when you do.'

'Beggin' your pardon, I ain't in the 'abit of sirin' nobody whose rank I don' recognise.'

'Well, you'd better recognise mine. I'm a senior civilian officer and I've been sent here from Maymyo on the express orders of His Excellency to put a bit of snap and ginger into the place and stop the rot that's set in. Mass desertions and evacuations galore. It's a positive disgrace.'

'Wiv all respec' Sir, we're wot you might call in transit. We're 'eadin' for Mandalay.'

'You'll stay here and wait for the army, when you'll be expected to act and fight like real soldiers.'

'It ain't exactly up to me to make decisions, Sir. That I leave to Sergeant 'arris.'

'And since when did sergeants start making decisions?'

'Well, in the absence of anyone 'igher, 'e 'as to.'

'You had better take me to him.'

Wagstaff led the official into the room where Harris was still slumped in an armchair. The sergeant rose to his feet. 'Can I help you?'

'I've been sent here to knock this place into shape, and from the little I've seen it's not a minute too soon. First, tell me what you're doing in Prome, and secondly why you've had the damned impertinence to move into someone else's home.'

His eyes roamed round the room and fastened on the empty bottle. 'I see it didn't take you long to find the drinks and turn this into a public house.'

'The drink is my own property, Sir,' replied an unruffled Harris. 'Now, if you'll give me the chance, I'll answer your questions. I'm on my way to Mandalay on the orders of my Colonel to deliver the Regimental Silver and Colours into safe keeping, then rejoin him. I also have two English ladies travelling under my protection.'

'I won't mince my words, Sergeant, it sounds a distinctly fishy story to me. The army is screaming out for transport, yet you have two valuable vehicles allotted to you to transport some silver.' His disbelief was obvious. 'As for the two ladies, why didn't they evacuate with the other European women? They aren't fancy women, are they?'

'No, Sir. One is a nursing sister, the other is the daughter of a prominent Rangoon businessman. They can explain better than me how they came to be in my party.'

'They had better be damned convincing. More than you are.'

'I'll take you to them, Sir,' replied an unruffled Harris.

He led the two visitors to the women's room, knocked on the door and called out, 'There's a gentleman from Maymyo who wants to talk to you.'

'Show him in. We're up and about and decently clad,' called Miss Bradshaw breezily.

The official gestured to the constable who turned the handle.

Avril was sitting in front of the dressing table mirror putting on her lipstick and make-up, while Sister Bradshaw was browsing through a book she had picked at random from one of the shelves.

'The Sergeant tells me you are his passengers. I want to know how that came about.'

When they had explained he said, 'I find myself unable to swallow that story. I think the best course of action is for you two ladies to return to Maymyo with me. I am placing the Sergeant and his men under house arrest until I can round up

155

enough troops to transfer them to the town jail. I am relying on their word of honour that they will not abscond. Their transport will be handed over to someone who can put it to better use.'

Sister Bradshaw said, 'I think you're being incredibly stubborn, and what's more I don't like your high and mighty attitude. The Sergeant and his men are only carrying out orders, and I know that personally. *I* will decide for myself how and when I travel. I'm a civilian nursing sister and I do not have to take orders from you.'

'I have the authority of His Excellency the Governor to act in the manner I think proper,' said the official haughtily.

'I have only your word for that, and as you refuse to accept Sergeant Harris's explanation that he is acting under orders, I fail to see why I should believe you.'

'We'll see about that later. Meanwhile I have to know what *you* intend, Miss Carfax.'

'I have no objection to travelling with you, but I do have a lot of luggage plus my personal maid.'

'There is a limit to what any evacuee is allowed to carry and I can't bend the rules for anyone. You must limit yourself to basic essentials. There's a war on, in case it's escaped your notice. Your maid can stay here. Mandalay and Maymyo have enough native refugees as it is without adding to their number.'

'I think I prefer to remain with Sergeant Harris.'

'You'll do as you're told,' he snapped. 'Now, Sergeant, I want to see over the remainder of the house, and I warn you, you will be held personally responsible for any damage.'

Harris showed him over the bungalow and paused at the door where the Indian woman was. 'There's a woman who's just had a baby resting in there. I don't think she should be disturbed.'

'Just want to satisfy myself.' He gestured towards the constable who again turned the knob while he prodded the door open with his stick. He saw the woman sleeping with the child nestling against her, and signalled to the constable to close the door.

'What do you think you're doing putting a native woman in the bed of a European family? Have you no bloody sense

156

of decency? You can't use other people's homes like an open house. Imagine what'll happen if any of the other Indians lining the quay get to hear of it. They'll take over every damned property in Prome. What's more, it's a bloody outrage to have her under the same roof as two white ladies.'

'When you've finished I'd like to say this: Sister Bradshaw decided she should be put there, so *she* isn't being outraged. As for myself, I have no intention of handing over my vehicles to anyone, and if there is an attempt to seize them forcibly, then whoever takes on the job can expect a bloody fight. And I don't use the word as an expletive.'

'You are guilty of rank insubordination, and I'll see you are court martialled for it. I am now going down to the jetty where I'm sure I'll find enough fit and armed men to carry out my orders.'

'I've met a few fools in my time, but you take the biscuit! Why don't you forget about us and get on with the job of restoring some semblance of law and order to this place? Do you think three soldiers and two trucks are going to make the slightest difference to the outcome of this war? You'd be better occupied getting some of the officials who have buggered off to safety to come back here and do the jobs they're paid for.'

'I am not going to bandy words with you, Sergeant. You have received my orders, I want them obeyed.'

'I'll do that, Sir.'

'Good. I'm glad you've seen reason.'

Harris walked to the veranda and watched the car drive off before turning and saying, 'Daft bastard. Now if you two ladies still want to travel with us you'd better get a move on. We're leaving immediately. I want to put as many miles between me and that silly arse as I can in the shortest possible time.'

157

Chapter Ten

Ten minutes later they left the bungalow and stopped at the quayside just long enough to unload the Indian family, the father, despite Kitty Bradshaw's protests, having insisted they wanted to wait until they got a passage on one of the ferries. Kitty had remonstrated with him but he was adamant, and she finally bowed to his wishes, acccepting the woman had made a good recovery and the baby was in no danger. The chances were they would fare no better if they remained with the party until it reached Mandalay because the city would by now be overflowing with European refugees from Rangoon, not to mention its local dignitaries who would be given priority over all others when it came to flights to India.

Harris gave them some water, tins of food, and twenty of his valuable silver rupees and wished them luck.

The conditions in the rear of the two trucks had been considerably improved thanks to the foresight and acquisitive instincts of Private Fazackerley who had put two armchairs in one and a settee in the other, plus some clean sheets and two mosquito nets. It was not exactly Pullman class, but the furniture did a lot to cushion the constant jolting.

Harris was disappointed to find the congestion on the road, instead of easing, had in fact increased. Ambulances filled with wounded men trundled along in convoy, impeded as ever by the river of fleeing people, and he assumed that someone had told them — soldiers and civilians — there was little hope of getting aboard a steamer or ferry at Prome.

Harris pressed hard on his horn, forcing vehicles and

people to make way until he drew abreast of the leading ambulance. He called across the gap between the two vehicles, 'What's the latest gen?'

The corporal who was driving said, 'I'm as much in the dark as anyone, Sarge.' He grimaced. 'Ever seen such a cock up? Talk about order, counter order, disorder. No one in charge seems to know his arse from his elbow.' His head jerked towards the rear of the ambulance. 'A lot of these lads aren't going to make it, and we'll have to bury them by the roadside. I've got a pocketful of identity discs as it is without wanting to add to them. Don't have time to mark the graves properly, and I only hope they can be found when we come back.'

Harris said, 'I thought the wounded were going by steamer?'

'So did I. Take them to Prome, says the brass hat, where a steamer will take them up river. But what happens? When I get there another red-tabber says we should never have been sent there in the first place as there's no room on a boat and he wants to know the name of the silly sod who gave me the order; and of course I don't know because the last thing you do if you've got any sense is ask a senior officer what his name is. So he tells me not to worry he'll look into it, although I know he'll have forgotten all about it in five minutes.'

Harris waved good luck and drove on, reflecting that if someone did not put an end to the bumbling and indecision, disease and the harshness of the terrain would decimate the retreating army and save the Japs a lot of trouble.

He pressed on as best as he could through the heat of the morning until he was forced to call a halt because of a massive pile-up of vehicles. He dismounted from the cabin, and with Simmonds at his side walked up the road to investigate. Abandoned in the middle of the road were three brand new Lease-Lend lorries which should have been driven up the Burma Road for the Chinese but had seized up because the inexperienced drivers did not know oil had to be replenished or water put into over-heated radiators. On either side of the road were the blackened remains of more American lorries which had been pushed down the banks and set on fire, because the drivers could not change a punctured tyre.

As a massive tail-back built up, creating even more of a shambles, Harris called to Wagstaff and Fazackerley to help him and Simmonds manhandle the three vehicles off the road to join the mechanised graveyard below. They heaved and strained until their backs and legs were one agonising pain, cursing the refugees who just stood looking at them, but they kept at it until the road was clear.

An hour later they caught up with another convoy of Lease-Lend lorries being driven by reckless men who had no interest in such trifles as the rules of the road; they drove on the left; in the middle and on the right, happy in the knowledge that nothing would be coming from the opposite direction.

It was Fazackerley who hit upon a means of forcing them to give way; he told Wagstaff to stop the truck as he had a bright idea. From the side of the road he gathered several lumps of dry clay the size of a cricket ball, and when he got back into the truck said, 'Pull up as close as you can to the tail-end bastard who's hogging the middle, and let's see if it works.'

Wagstaff drove until the bonnet was almost touching the tailboard of a Dodge truck, then with an underhand throw Fazackerley tossed a lump of clay high into the air. It was miserably off target, as was the second, but the third landed with a loud bang on the bonnet of the lorry where it exploded like a grenade. The panic-stricken driver, fearing he was under aerial attack, swerved violently, forcing the nearside vehicle to career off the road. Two more well-aimed bombs widened the gap and they were able to drive through.

After that it became a regular routine whenever progress was impeded, and to Harris's surprise Miss Carfax proved the most adept. She threw the lumps of clay with unerring accuracy and power, and when Harris complimented her she replied, 'Put it down to the misspent hours I put in on the tennis court.' Inwardly she was delighted to have done *something* that met with his approval and shown him she was not utterly useless.

In the rear of the truck, comfortably ensconced in an armchair, Kitty Bradshaw was trying to pick up Mandalay on the radio, and when she finally managed to was appalled to

160

hear an official announcement to the effect that the refugee programme was proceeding according to plan and that food piles were being established on the major evacuation routes and air drops being organised from India. She fervently wished she could parachute some of the lying officials into the mass of fleeing humanity so that they could repeat their bland assurances.

She tossed aside the radio in disgust; it was far better to have no news at all than listen to such misleading drivel. She could understand a doctor telling a dying patient he was well on the road to recovery because that was human, but what was emanating from Mandalay was shameful.

The gruelling monotony of their routine made them lose all count of time as days and nights became repetitions of the previous ones. They drove for as long as possible, sometimes covering as little as fifteen miles, for the clay bombs, so effective against motorised transport, had no impact whatsoever on bullock carts or the footsore people who plodded on like sleepwalkers.

As soon as darkness approached they found a suitable spot to pull off and eat and sleep.

The victims of cholera and typhoid were now such a common sight they no longer bothered to avert their eyes, and ominous signs began to appear by the side of some of the smaller springs and pools: Danger! DO NOT DRINK. POLLUTED. CHLORINATE.

They had obviously been put there by Europeans or the army, but no matter how well-intentioned, Harris regarded them as a rather sick joke because few of the refugees could read and those who could would take no notice because they had no chlorine.

It seemed so perverse for people to continue drinking the foul water when all around was visible evidence of the horrifying death that awaited them. Sometimes it took an agonisingly long time before they were put out of their misery, during which they endured severe vomiting and diarrhoea with excruciating cramps in the legs, feet and abdomen. The surface of the body became cold and purple and the eyes deeply sunken, the skin dry and wrinkled, the voice reduced to a hoarse whisper. The final stages were marked by violent contractions which forced the limbs into the most grotesque positions, and blood became thick and tarry. The fortunate were those whose collapse was sudden and without warning. They died within the hour. Typhoid, cholera's companion in death, was just as rife. Yet the craving for water was so great it made the refugees blind to the terrible consequences.

Sister Bradshaw suffered more than the others because she knew that with a little common sense it could all be avoided. So when Harris had asked despairingly, 'Can't *anything* be done?' she had exploded with uncharacteristic anger. 'Of course. All you need to do is get them into hospital and give them intravenous injections of sodium bicarbonate and sodium chloride in sterile water. Failing that, issue them with permanganate pills to be taken every fifteen minutes. Then they'll be as right as rain. That's all we do in hospital.'

Seeing how deeply disturbed she was, Harris mumbled, 'I'm sorry Kitty, that was a damn silly question to ask.'

'It's not your fault. How were you to know? I lost my temper because these asinine fools in Mandalay are deliberately misleading people.' She smiled and said with mock gaiety, 'I read somewhere that in Simla during the 'flu epidemic at the end of the First War, the dead were piled several foot high by the sides of the road, but people passing on their way to a ball at the Viceregal Lodge did not notice. That's what we'll have to learn to do.'

Harris knew that it was her way of saying that no lessons had been learned since then.'

It was largely due to the skills of Private Wagstaff that the two trucks gave such little trouble. Every evening when they halted he would spend at least an hour with his head under the raised bonnets, listening to the ticking-over engines with the intensity of a doctor listening to the heartbeats of an ailing patient. He cleaned the plugs, adjusted the points, repaired punctures, fixed up leaking hoses, and topped up the batteries.

One morning, when Harris's vehicle would not start, Wagstaff said, 'Not only is the battery kaput, all that

162

stoppin' and startin', but the starter motor's packed up.'

'Anything you can do about it?' asked Harris anxiously.

'Dunno, Sarge, but I can always 'ave a try. If Simmo comes and keeps an eye on me with his Tommy-gun, I'll drive back down the road where there's a lotta piled-up stuff. Any ol' battery'll do, an' there are enuff write-offs to nick a starter motor from.'

He was absent for three hours and Harris was worried that something might have happened to the two men. It required all his self-control not to show his relief when he saw the truck bouncing along the road enveloped in a cloud of dust.

'The battery was no sweat, Sarge. Just a question of fixin' it secure. Starter motor was a bit of a bastard though. The ones in the Yank trucks was no good, so I 'ad to scrounge around till I foun' one inna wrecked ambulance. Gimme a couple of hours at top whack and we'll be off an' away again. Just a nuts an' spanner job.'

He drew the sergeant aside and lowered his voice. 'You should let Miss Carfax 'ave a turn at the wheel, Sarge. That way we can spend a lot longer on the road, an' that'll be easier on the trucks. Apart from that, the sooner we get to Mandalay the better because the refugees is startin' to fight among themselves. The stronger ones is nickin' the grub off the weaker ones, an' if that ain't enuff, one Indian said they'd 'ad trouble with some bandits what want money and valuables.'

Harris said, 'I'll think about it. I'm not keen though, a truck isn't a car, and if we lost one through her inexperience or through the state of the road which turns the truck into a bucking bronco, we would be up the creek without a paddle.'

As it turned out Harris did not have to make the decision; circumstances made it for him.

The day after Wagstaff had carried out his emergency repairs, Sergeant Harris woke feeling decidedly unwell. He had been sleeping stretched out on the bench seat of the truck with the Colours resting beside him. He did not need a doctor to tell him what was wrong: he had malaria. He had had attacks before and, if previous experience was any

163

guide, he would be out of action for several days. It might take much longer this time because then he had been carted off to the sick bay where he received expert attention.

He felt chillingly cold and began to shiver, while his teeth rattled like a pair of Spanish castanets. His fingers felt dead, and when he looked at them they were bone-white in contrast to the nails which were a startling blue. He also felt an urgent need to urinate, and he just managed to stumble out of the cab to pass a copious flow of watery urine. He staggered back inside and pressed hard on the horn. When Wagstaff's face appeared at the window enquiring, 'Everyfing all right, Sarge?' he could only mutter, 'Get Sister Bradshaw, please, Wagstaff.'

When she appeared he said apologetically, 'I'm afraid I've got a bout of malaria.'

'I can see that for myself,' she said. 'Can't be helped. You've taken your quinine like a good little boy, so I won't scold you.'

'This creates a problem with the driving. I really don't think I'll be up to it. I can't ask Miss Carfax. Not fair on her.' His teeth were chattering so loudly he had difficulty in making himself understood.

'We've all been complaining about her being a passenger, so we've no right to deny her the opportunity of proving herself otherwise. After all, she's offered often enough. I think she might surprise you.' She turned to Wagstaff. 'Help me to get him into the back. He can rest on the settee. He's going to get a damned sight worse before he gets any better, so let's make him as comfortable as possible.'

Harris was wrapped in several blankets, but they did nothing to stop the shivering.

'I'm going to take your temperature, Sergeant, and you're not going to like it because I'm going to put the thermometer up your bottom.'

When she had read it she gave it a flick, and whistled. 'Hot enough to boil an egg,' she said cheerfully.

Harris had little recollection of the second stage when his skin was burning and his complexion was the colour of an over-ripe plum. There were times when he was semi-delirious, but he was always conscious of wanting to urinate and when he did it was only a trickle and highly coloured. When they stopped at night he was aware of Kitty giving him large doses of quinine and Miss Carfax sponging him down with tepid water. He tried to object, disliking the idea of her seeing him naked, but she ignored his protests and after a time he ceased to care. He was sweating so profusely the blankets had to be frequently replaced, they were so drenched, and his urine left a thick red sediment on them.

The cycle kept repeating itself, although between attacks he felt quite lucid but extremely weak.

One morning, he had no idea how long he had been on the settee, Kitty Bradshaw said, 'You'll be up and about soon. You've broken the back of it. Lucky you haven't died of quinine poisoning, but I was so worried it might develop into blackwater fever then you'd have turned your toes up.'

'I'm very grateful, Kitty.' He managed a feeble smile. 'I'll even forgive you sticking that thing up my rectum.'

'Don't thank me, save that for Miss Carfax. When she hasn't been driving she's been looking after you. She's washed you down, and done a lot of other unpleasant tasks I never thought she was capable of doing. She's absolutely exhausted, so find something nice to say when she comes back.'

When Avril came to sponge him down, he was shocked at her appearance; her face was drawn and her eyes were sunken in dark hollow pits, and her hair looked damp and unkempt. Clearly she had dispensed with Nellie's nightly attention.

She sat beside the settee and took his hand in hers. 'How's the invalid?'

'Alive and well, thanks to you and Kitty.'

'She was the doctor, I was only the nurse.'

'She said you've hardly had any sleep, Miss Carfax. You'd better try and catch up on it.'

'I promise to do that as soon as you're fit enough to drive.' She lowered her voice. 'Now that I know you so intimately, isn't it time you called me Avril?'

'I'm glad I wasn't compos mentis because I'd have been reticent about letting you get to know me so well,' he quipped.

'Externally you're an open book, but I still know nothing about you as a person. One day I'm going to have the nerve to ask you about that scar. You certainly didn't get it shaving.'

She lowered her head so that her lips, dry and parched, briefly touched his, and she experienced a momentary pang of regret that this resolute and remote man would very shortly not require her ministrations. A feeling of protective caring surged through her body, so intense it made her feel guilty. She was frightened yet exhilarated; she had fallen in love with him. If she told him he would laugh, and tell her not to be silly. He might even treat it as a joke and say all nurses fall in love with their patients. The realisation was an exquisite agony; she had found something she had never imagined possible, and she wondered how long it would be before her love was reciprocated.

She said as flippantly as possible, 'My father would hit the ceiling if he could see what I've just done. You know how he feels about soldiers.'

Harris, bewildered at the sudden display of emotion and not at all sure what his own feelings were, said, 'Avril, don't mistake sympathy for something bigger. You'll think differently when you meet someone of your own age.' He knew it was an inane remark, but he had been so surprised he blurted out the first thing that came to mind.

A tidal wave of emotion swamped her. How could she possibly convince him that what she was experiencing was not some girlish infatuation but the flowering of something she found quite awesome? It reminded her in some confusing way of a day in her childhood when she had stood breast-high in pounding surf that threatened to drown her, yet aware all the time that the fear she experienced was nullified by an even greater feeling of exhilaration.

She was not too worried that he had advised caution because she was certain that, given time, he would share her feelings.

166

Chapter Eleven

Harris was delighted to find that Avril's driving skills were no idle boast. Admittedly she was rather aggressive, but she was not reckless, knowing when to give way and when to chance her luck. Nevertheless he was depressed at their slow progress, feeling like someone walking up the down escalator. But Kitty Bradshaw had insisted during the worst period of his sickness they should not spend too much time on the road because the constant bumping would only delay his recovery. Neither did she think Avril was physically strong enough to withstand prolonged spells.

Harris spent much of his time stretched out on the settee, slowly regaining his strength, and although the inactivity irked him he knew it was essential for him to be fully fit, mentally and physically, for the crucial decisions he would be called upon to make. Sometimes he sat in the leading cab driven by Wagstaff, studied his map, and ordered him to leave the metalled road and branch off on to one of the unmade subsidiary tracks in an attempt to leap-frog the traffic, but the extra concentration it demanded and the additional strain it inflicted on the vehicles was not justified by the pitifully few extra miles gained. In any case they were soon bogged down again when they rejoined the main road. In the end he accepted that they would just have to be patient, like ships in a convoy whose progress is dictated by the speed of the slowest vessel.

Whenever they halted for food or the night, Avril would fuss over him as if he was still critically ill, and although he was rather brusque with her, saying he did not need molly coddling, he was secretly pleased with her concern and began to look foward to seeing her. The visits did a lot for his morale.

One particular incident did raise all their spirits, causing them to wave and cheer. One afternoon they passed a battered bus, the windows of which were splintered and dust-caked, but they were able to catch a momentary glimpse of a woman in a yellow sari nursing a baby. Any doubts they may have had that she was the same woman whose baby Sister Bradshaw had delivered were dispelled when a bangled forearm appeared at a window, waving in recognition. They were delighted that she had been given a lift and was not stranded in Prome.

Two days after the encounter Harris was well enough to resume driving and no one was happier than Wagstaff who was utterly exhausted because in addition to driving he also had to do his nightly spell of sentry duty.

Nellie was also delighted for it meant that a refreshed Wagstaff might show a renewed interest in her.

Days and nights passed with unvarying monotony. They passed through towns and villages which were only names on the sergeant's crude map: Kama, Pato, Dayindabo, Pauknou, Kyaukgyi, Thayetmyo ... tongue-twisting names that never sounded anything like the way they were spelt on the map. Harris carefully ticked each one off, like a prisoner writing on a cell wall the number of days he has served. And if the days had a stultifying sameness, so too did the places they passed through or skirted; each presented the same dismal scene of desertion, death, despair for some and desperate hope for others. The odour of defeat was everywhere, like the stench of decaying flesh.

However, away from the towns the scenery was ever-changing; one day they drove along a road fringed with thick tropical vegetation, the next through dust that was almost pure sand. Dense forests gave way to areas that had been cleared by fire to expose the rich loamy soil to the plough, and always in the distance were mountains, sometimes purple hued and topped with white clouds that resembled grazing sheep, or carpeted with custard-apple orchards and wild plums. The road twisted and turned in a series of never ending hairpin bends, but seldom out of sight was the great Irrawaddy, sometimes so wide the far bank was barely visible. And following its course was another great river of humanity.

At night, which descended with the abruptness of a lowered blind, the air was filled with the screech of homing parrots, the shrill whistling of Gibbon monkeys, the incessant chirruping of crickets, and the occasional growl of an audible but unseen tiger that had strayed from its secret haunts to take advantage of the easy prey that lay sleeping by the roadside. Huge flying foxes darted back and forth overhead, like ghostly spectres from another planet. In time they ceased to hear the noises, but were unable to ignore the attention of the countless insects which battened on to the smallest portion of exposed flesh, so that they woke each morning looking as if they were the victims of an outbreak of chicken pox.

When they reached Ye-gyan-zin, Harris estimated they had arrived at what was commonly called the 'dry belt' which was wide and sparsely populated. From being lush green and densely covered, it became brown and arid with occasional patches of parched jungle. The chaungs which cut through the low undulating hills were bone dry, and the heat and dust were oppressive. It was also punishing territory for the trucks, for the road wound like a serpent intent on devouring its own tail. The engines and gear boxes groaned in protest as they laboured to reach the summit of a high gradient and protested even louder on the descent. Sometimes it seemed as if the wheels were suspended in space, and after a while they learned not to look over the precipitous drops; not only did they create a disturbing feeling of vertigo, they also enabled the travellers to see immediately below the stretch of road they had traversed half an hour earlier and emphasise how far they had travelled to get nowhere.

The craving for water became intolerable, and it was intensified by the knowledge that their meagre daily ration would very soon have to be cut again. They were sweating so much that Kitty Bradshaw issued salt tablets. When they left the trucks to stretch their legs, swarms of butterflies

169

descended on any exposed flesh to drink the perspiration; they were so multi-hued it looked as though everyone was wearing sleeves of gaily patterned material.

As always in the distance the outline of the Arakan Yoma, the mountain barrier between Burma and India, was clearly visible, dauntingly high and virtually uncharted.

As the need to conserve water became more urgent they had to forego the much looked forward to evening brew up, a deprivation which even Avril accepted with good-humoured grace. Neither had she objected when Harris had barred the luxury of the occasional tot of gin; the pleasure it gave was not commensurate with the dehydration it caused. She also accepted the fact that Wagstaff and Nellie seemed to prefer each other's company, sitting apart and conversing in lowered voices. Avril's gradual mellowing had not gone unnoticed, but no one spoke about it, not even when she began brushing her own hair and doing a stint as cook.

In turn she did not mention that she now realised that life for her had changed and she was just one more member of a group who depended on each other for survival.

Without being advised, she had also forsaken dresses for a more practical pair of slacks and a khaki drill shirt which she had stolen without the least qualm from a deserted shop.

The portable gramophone and the case of records, once the subject of ribald derision, were now prized possessions, and every night they were put to use; and although played over and over again, familiarity only served to enhance the attraction of the records. And Avril, who had been resentful of remarks about her way of life, had changed so much she was able to say, 'You won't believe it, but my father actually had someone to wind the gramophone at home, although he never allowed him to put a record on. Can you imagine anything sillier?' She had not thought so at Balmoral.

Early one morning when it was scarcely light, Simmonds who was keeping guard was startled to hear the sound of gunfire, not a steady fusillade but a series of short, sharp bursts.

He shook Harris and said, 'Fighting somewhere, Sarge, but it don't sound like a pitched battle. Can't believe the Nips have got this far.'

170

Harris roused the other men and told them to bring their weapons and full ammunition pouches. To Wagstaff he said, 'You stay and look after the women. If anyone approaches with a gun in their hands just shoot, don't ask any questions.'

The other two clambered into Harris's truck where Fazackerley rolled down the canvas cover in order to give a free field of fire to the Bren. He had not finished before Harris was racing down the road towards the sound of the intermittent gunfire. The road ahead was clear, the refugees having scuttled for cover in the thorn scrub by the roadside.

Half a mile along the road they saw the cause of the shooting; a group of oddly dressed Burmese — several wore European slacks and shirts — were firing into a cowering crowd of refugees. One man was leaning over a prostrate figure with a stone in his hand which he was using to knock out the dead person's gold teeth.

'Bloody dacoits,' shouted Harris. 'Give them a burst from the Bren.'

Fazackerley rested the barrel on the top of the cabin, moved the catch to automatic fire and sprayed the bandits, praying that he did not hit any innocent people in the process. Three men fell to the ground, two dead and one screaming with agony from shattered legs.

When they were two hundred yards away, Harris braked to a halt and shouted for Simmonds to follow him. He advanced towards the bandits at the double, pausing every few steps to fire his Lee Enfield. Simmonds running alongside fired the Tommy-gun from his hip, emptying an entire magazine. Several more dacoits fell. The remainder, half a dozen at the most, dropped their weapons and raised their hands above their heads.

Harris roared, 'Keep shooting, Simmonds. We can't be burdened with prisoners.'

Simmonds attached a fresh magazine and shot them as if they were no more than targets on the range. Harris saw a man wearing a white topee and a white duck suit running towards some scrub. He took careful aim and shot him through the head. He then calmly put the muzzle of his rifle against the temples of the wounded bandits and put them out of their misery. Only then did he begin to make a count of the dead and wounded among the refugees, all of whom were Indians. At least forty men and women had been brutally murdered for their pitifully few possessions and what little food they had. There was blood everywhere, and several of the women had been savagely mutilated with dahs in order to remove their jewellery.

Among the dead was the Indian woman they had seen in the coach. Her yellow sari had been ripped off and a knife, buried to the hilt, protruded from between her breasts. Her feet and hands had been amputated so that her anklets and bracelets could be removed and her ears and nose cut off for the diamonds in them. The baby lay nearby, its brains spilling out on to the dust. Close by was her husband and the other child.

Harris could not believe that the mass slaughter was due entirely to theft; more than likely the Burmese had also seized it as an opportunity to vent their hatred on the despised Indians.

He said, 'Collect all their weapons and ammo.' The two soldiers collected as many weapons as they could find, and the returned to the truck with armloads of muzzle-loading muskets, several crudely made shotguns, and a hunting rifle and a twelve-bore which were relatively new and expensive and clearly of European make.

'I feel ashamed at having to leave them to the vultures and jackals; after all they've been through they deserve a decent grave. Trouble is, they will cause even more pestilence.'

Simmonds said, 'Don't blame yourself, Sarge. We'd need a ruddy bulldozer to dig a hole big enough.' He added in an anxious tone, 'You won't mention the Indian lady to Miss Carfax and Sister Bradshaw? That would be a bit hard for them to take.'

'Of course not. Serve no useful purpose.'

Already the road was crowded as the refugees resumed their journey into uncertainty. They had become so accustomed to the sight of death it had lost its ability to shock; if anything it gave them an added incentive to hasten on.

When they returned to the other truck Harris explained as

172

briefly as possible what had happened, and how unfortunate it was that the dead would have to be left to rot.

'Why don't we try burning them?' said Kitty Bradshaw.

He looked at her quizzically, although his voice was surprisingly gentle. 'Ever tried burning a human corpse, Sister?'

'No, but I went to the burning ghats in Rangoon once. All you need is plenty of wood and oil. The Indians use ghee. We could use petrol.'

'We may need all the fuel we have, and we certainly haven't got the time to collect the amount of wood we'd need.'

'Get the refugees to collect it. There's plenty about. They won't mind, surely? Maybe they would appreciate the opportunity of showing some respect.'

Fazackerley broke in, 'We could siphon some petrol out of the abandoned vehicles, Sarge. That charabanc the Indian woman was in must have a big tank.'

Simmonds growled, 'Zack, your bloody tongue'll be the death of you! Now what did you have to go and say that for?'

Thankfully neither of the two women seemed to have noticed the significance of Fazackerley's remark.

Harris said, 'All right, we'll see what can be done. Nothing lost in trying. We've managed to capture some guns and dahs from the dacoits and I'll offer them to the refugees on the condition they collect the wood and help with the bodies. I know Indians are very touchy about handling corpses, but if it means saving their own lives they may not be so squeamish.' He turned to the three privates. 'Right, lads, let's get on with it. The sooner we start the quicker we'll finish.' Then turning to the women the added, 'It would be best if you remained in the back of one of the trucks. It's not going to be a pleasant sight.'

Sister Bradshaw said determinedly, 'It was my idea and I've no intention of asking you and your men to do something I won't do myself.'

'Nobody has to prove anything. That is an order, and you'll obey it. I'll send one of the lads back to tell you when you can come down.'

The two women clambered into a truck, where Avril began

173

casually to inspect the captured weapons. Kitty Bradshaw saw her turn a deathly white, stiffen, then thrust a knuckle into her mouth to stifle a scream.

'What on earth's the matter, Avril? You look like you've seen a ghost.'

'I have,' she murmured. 'Two of those guns are my father's.'

Kitty put her arms around the girl who was desperately trying to suppress the sobs which convulsed her body. 'You poor child. Are you sure?'

'I've been shooting with them too often to be mistaken.' She sniffed loudly and wiped her hands across her eyes. 'Don't tell the sergeant; at least, not yet. He's got enough on his plate.'

Kitty thought ruefully: I wanted you to grow up and you have, but this is something you could have been spared. Aloud she said, 'Now have a good cry. There's no one here to see you.'

But there were no tears, and she was surprised to hear Avril say, 'At least they'll come in useful. I've fired both many times. Might get something for the pot.'

Many of the refugees refused point blank even to contemplate assisting with the mass cremation, protesting that they were devout muslims who feared offending Islamic law by inadvertently consigning any member of the Faith to eternal perdition, but there were enough who were subverted by the tempting offer of arms to carry out the task; even so they stripped the bodies of any remnants of clothing of possible future use.

The sole reason Sergeant Harris had insisted on the two women remaining behind until sent for was because he wanted time to get the body of the Indian woman out of sight before they saw it.

A pyre several feet high and several yards long was quickly erected from the plentiful supply of tinder-dry wood lying on the ground, and Harris told the soldiers to douse it with cans of siphoned petrol When he was satisfied the wood was thoroughly soaked, he told the refugees they could start putting the bodies on, a task they did with a total lack of reverence or respect, and in a short time a pile of corpses

174

that looked like broken dolls had covered the timber. Near the bottom of the heap was the Indian woman and her family, tossed there by Wagstaff and Simmonds.

When Harris paused from his grisly supervision and looked around, he was furious to see that the two women had disobeyed him and were swinging a body by the arms and legs before releasing it in a high arc to land with a sickening thud on the growing heap.

He was livid with anger, not because he had been disobeyed, he just could not understand why they felt the need to participate in the gruesome task. He strode over to them, his voice strident with suppressed fury. 'This is bloody ridiculous. Stop it immediately. This isn't some ruddy test of character. You've proved nothing but how bloody silly you both are.'

Avril replied, 'I was only ...' but he cut her short. 'I'm not interested in your reasons. Both of you, get back to the truck.'

Avril said, 'Sergeant Harris, may I *please* say something?'

'No you can't.'

She saw from his expression that it was useless to try and explain that she had acted as she had because she felt so guilty about depriving the refugees of the two best weapons. They had been bribed into carrying out the horrible task by the promise of arms and, as she intended to keep her father's, the least she could do was help with the disposal of the corpses.

As they turned and headed back towards the truck, Kitty Bradshaw said comfortingly, 'You did the right thing. It's a pity he's in no mood to listen.'

Avril said miserably, 'He thinks I was trying to impress him.'

'I certainly was, and I don't feel apologetic either. If I hadn't suggested it they would have been left there to rot.'

The smell of the bodies attracted vultures, jackals and packs of ravenous pi-dogs who, sensing they were about to be deprived of food, summoned up an unexpected courage and darted forward to seize scraps of flesh, entrails, detached limbs, and small children. They were indifferent to the hurled

175

stones, screams of outrage, the blows from sticks and the kicks from the soldiers' boots, and the bullets from their weapons. When one was hit the carcass simply provided more food. Some of the more dauntless beasts even burrowed into the mountain of corpses.

Harris told his men to save their ammunition; the carrion eaters were only doing the job nature had created them for, the prevention of pestilence. 'It doesn't really matter,' he said 'if a plague is prevented by their gastric juices or fire; the outcome is the same.'

When the last cadaver had been tossed onto the pyre, he shouted for everyone to stand clear and when the crowd had moved away wrapped wads of petrol-soaked cloth round the ends of three long bamboo canes, lit them and threw them javelin-style into the pyre. It ignited with an enormous whoof that scorched the hair and eyebrows of those incautious enough not to have moved well away. There was a fierce crackle of burning timber as the flames spread, and the stench of rotting flesh was replaced by the smell of scorched and burning meat that clung to the back of the throat and made the stomach heave.

Sergeant Harris watched as dense clouds of smoke, mingling with sheets of crimson flame, obscured the reduction of flesh to ashes, his face expressionless, his eyes as dead as marble. He was not indifferent to human suffering but, like all soldiers, accepted that violent death was a fact of life and far better than a long lingering one.

When he was satisfied there was no danger of the fire going out he gave an abrupt gesture with his arm signalling that the time had come for them to leave. The vultures, jackals and pi-dogs driven back by the intensity of the fire, sat or stood in silent groups, reluctant to accept defeat.

The refugees who had assisted with the mass cremation returned to the roadside where they squatted down, waiting with the patience of the carrion eaters for the promised handover of arms.

Back at the trucks Kitty Bradshaw, still smarting from Sergeant Harris's outburst, countermanded his order to drive off. 'We do not move an inch until everyone has washed. It'll have been a waste of time burning those corpses if we don't take that elementary precaution.' And she added coldly, 'And don't argue with me, Sergeant. *Some* things I'm better qualified to rule on. And don't tell me we can't spare the water. We'll use what's left of the gin if necessary.' Avril thought she detected an imperceptible flutter of Sister Bradshaw's left eyelid as she turned away.

Four hours later when the two trucks breasted the top of a high ridge, the smoke from the funeral pyre was still visible.

Five days after the encounter with the dacoits they drove into Alanymyo which, like so many of the towns and villages they had passed through, was almost uninhabited, the population having fled to escape from the Japanese air force now engaged in the systematic destruction of as many towns as possible. The town, even when occupied, had little to commend it, so that when they settled down for the night in a sheltered grove near the river bank there were looks of bewildered surprise when Avril declared that their arrival called for a celebration drink of extra water.

Wagstaff commented sourly, 'Wiv all respec', Miss, I fink it's more a question of drownin' our sorrows. Like findin' yourself on the end of Southend Pier when it's rainin' cats and dogs and you ain't got a brolly to your name.'

'It may not be much to look at, but it certainly does call for a bigger swig. My education may have been patchy, but I recall this place was named after Major Alan Grant who, donkeys years ago, drew an arbitrary line from east to west and declared that everything north of it was Upper Burma, the rest Lower.'

Apart from a line of white pillars, most of which were buried under weeds or in the jungle, nothing else remained as visible testimony of the demarcation, but the news instantly cheered everyone for they realised they had reached a mile-stone in their journey.

Chapter Twelve

During the hours of daylight the canvas cover of the rear truck was rolled up to give Fazackerley a clear field of fire for the Bren, as aerial activity had markedly increased. Fighters and bombers often flew low over the stretched out column of refugees, but did not open fire or drop bombs, their pilots possibly thinking the target hardly merited the expenditure of bullets or bombs. In any case, there was no point in creating terror when it already existed in abundance. Apart from such tactical considerations, there was ample evidence that disease, malnutrition and sheer exhaustion were proving as effective as any man-made weapon.

Fazackerley questioned the wisdom of removing the canvas cover because it made the back of the vehicle intolerably hot and, as he pointed out, on the occasions he had opened fire it had invited retaliation. Harris, however, remained adamant; the cover would remain rolled up because there was no way of knowing when, and if, the aircraft would change tactics, but he compromised to the extent that he gave Fazackerley permission to open fire only if they were attacked.

There were times when Sister Bradshaw was tempted to try and pick up Mandalay on her portable, feeling like the people she had read about in faraway England who secretly tuned in to Lord Haw-Haw, knowing in advance they would hear only bad news. But she resisted the urge because, as Sergeant Harris pointed out, if they maintained their present rate of progress they would be in Mandalay in a week or thereabouts and then they could see at first hand what was the true situation.

'The good news you'll hear on the wireless will only make you lose your temper,' he chided.

Late one night when the others were sleeping and Harris had volunteered to keep guard, Avril found herself sitting beside him around the still-hot stove. His face was covered with several days' stubble for he had decided that the protection a beard afforded against the insects far outweighed any minor decline in discipline, and he had told the three privates that dry shaving was no longer a compulsory morning routine. As a precaution, however, he had warned them that this concession did not mean they could relax in any other direction and he was encouraged to hear Simmonds say, 'A beard never affected morale in the navy, Sarge.'

They had been sitting enjoying the silence when Avril said in a strangely detached manner, 'I think those dacoits murdered my father.'

The remark, coming as it did out of the blue, caused Harris to remark, 'What an odd thing to say, Avril. Whatever prompted it?'

'The shotgun and the rifle you brought back were his. I can't see how they could have got them any other way.'

She sounded so matter-of-fact he did not know what to say, and he wondered if the calm acceptance was a warning that she might be on the verge of a nervous breakdown; he had seen it happen before to men who had gone through a period of great stress.

'You could be mistaken. Just try and put it from your mind until we get to Mandalay. There we might be able to get some news. Even better, you might see him.'

She shrugged. 'I know you're trying to be considerate, but you saw what those dacoits did; they wouldn't rob anyone, *then* let them go free. At least I know it would have been quick.'

'Why didn't you tell me sooner?'

'You haven't exactly been in the best of health, and I saw no point in burdening you with my troubles. What could you have done?' She felt like saying she had tried to tell him about the guns at the mass cremation until his foul temper had prevented her, but she refrained. She did not want to

179

score cheap points. He meant too much to her for her to want to hurt him.

He admired her fortitude and thought how much she had matured since they left Rangoon; then she would have argued nonsensically and said the dacoits had no right whatsoever to act as they did and something should be done about it before they lost all respect for law and order.

'I'm not too worried for myself,' she continued in the same rather detached way. 'It's time I learned to stand on my own two feet, but I'm awfully worried about Mummy. Goodness knows what'll happen to her when she hears.' She sighed, as if in sympathy with her mother's shortcomings. 'She's never had to lift a finger before except to click them, and at her age it's going to be hard to start. I'm saddened naturally, but it's odd how detached I feel. Almost like being in the cinema and weeping when someone dies, then forgetting all about it as soon as you get outside into the sunlight. I might feel differently if he'd died in bed and I'd been there to witness it.'

Harris was confused. Avril was talking about her mother as if she had enjoyed privileges that had been denied to her and been brought up in an environment she herself had been unable to share, but he was more concerned over her attitude towards the death of her father; she was talking about him in a too vague and remote manner.

'I thought he was someone you looked up to,' he said.

'Only because there was no one else around to mould my character. But for him I might have developed into quite a different, and much nicer person.'

'Jesus, Avril, people aren't putty in the hands of some potter. You can't blame him for everything.'

'I suffered more over the death of that poor Indian woman,' she said, as if she had not heard what he had said.

Harris was unable to disguise his surprise. 'I didn't know you knew. You're piling one surprise on top of another. I'm not sure I understand what you're trying to say. Are you apologising for your upbringing? There's no need to. A person can break out of the mould without apportioning blame.'

180

Again it seemed as if she was deliberately trying to misunderstand him, for she said, 'That yellow sari was unmistakable. It was visible a mile away.'

'I thought I'd saved you from seeing her.'

'I know, that's why I didn't say anything. I didn't want you to be disappointed. But Kitty and I saw you put her on the wood with her family.'

'You shouldn't have disobeyed my order, then you would have been saved that.'

'Would it have brought her back if we hadn't?'

'Of course not, but I wanted to spare you the agony of knowing what you and Kitty had done was all wasted.'

She shrugged. 'I've been spared from seeing too many of the unpleasant aspects of life. I thought that was what you and Kitty have been trying to spell out.' She shrugged and sighed. 'I suppose you think I'm heartless, over my father I mean?'

Harris shook his head. 'Of course not. It's what's called growing up. But you don't have to do it with one enormous leap. It should be a gradual process.'

'You think I'm cold and unfeeling?'

'Nothing of the kind. I've seen many men die, some quickly, some slowly; at first it shocks but then, to your own surprise and not without some inner qualms, you find yourself immune. It's not callousness but self-protection. It's happened to you. But Sister Bradshaw could explain it better than I can. In her profession you have to be case-hardened in order to carry on. That's what you're learning to do.'

Harris knew he was expressing himself badly. He was trying to talk to her as one soldier to another. As he had talked to rookie soldiers on the North West Frontier who had thrown up and cried on witnessing the death of a comrade, unable to comprehend how older and more experienced men had just carried on firing as if the dead man had never existed.

She spoke as if addressing someone who was not present. 'I envy her in some respects. She's so self-reliant and able to take all this in her stride, whereas I feel like a cossetted pet that's been turned out of a comfortable home to fend for itself. I'm so inadequate.'

181

Harris suspected she was seeking sympathy, then realised she was not and felt deeply moved. 'You don't have to torture yourself with recriminations, Avril. You've every right to be proud. You've been tossed in at the deep end to sink or swim and you've surfaced. When we started off I honestly thought you'd be a hindrance, a human ball and chain, and frankly you didn't go out of your way to convince me otherwise. I knew the journey was going to be hard, but certainly not as tough as it's turned out to be, and I was worried you'd crack up. Thank God you've proved me wrong, Avril. That's not just empty flattery, intended to bolster your determination, but words sincerely meant. And when the going gets even worse, just remind yourself that this could be a blessing in disguise. But for the war you might have carried on in the same vain and empty-headed fashion.'

She said, 'Good heavens, you do a lot for a girl's confidence! Isn't that what they call damning with faint praise?' Inwardly she was pleased with his reappraisal of her character and glowing at his use of her first name. She suddenly felt the need to say something that would arouse even greater admiration and a further admission that she was pulling her weight.

'I've done a fair amount of shooting in Burma, and if you're agreeable I'd like to go out in the morning and try and bag something to eat. We haven't had fresh meat since we ate the chicken that wouldn't lay. Personally I'm sick and tired of tinned food and I'm sure everyone else is. Perhaps you could spare Private Wagstaff to come with me?'

It was a sensible request that she knew he would agree to because other dacoit bands could be in the vicinity, but she had specifically mentioned Wagstaff because she wanted to pump him about his relationship with Nellie for whom she now felt some responsibility. In Rangoon the girl's amatory pursuits had been of little interest to her other than as a topic of idle conversation when she liked to tease her maid; now, aware as she was of Nellie's near obsession with becoming a soldier's girl, she wanted to make absolutely certain that Wagstaff was not exploiting it to his own advantage. Nellie had had no choice about accompanying her on the journey, so it was Avril's responsibility to see she came to no harm at

182

the end of it. She had already decided that when they reached Mandalay she would see to it that the girl had ample funds to go wherever she wished and do whatever she wanted. It was the very least she could do considering how badly she had treated her in the past.

Harris said, 'I think it's an excellent idea, but don't stray too far off the beaten track. Private Wagstaff is a great man to have in a tight corner, but he's not a one man army so give us time to reach you if he sounds the alarm.' He tapped his pipe against the heel of his boot and began to refill it with attentive care.

She reached out for the pipe and pouch. 'Here, let me do that for you.'

He expressed mock horror. 'Not on your life, Avril. You may have washed me down and done a lot of other things I get embarrassed thinking about, but filling my pipe . . .' He shook his head. 'It's like volunteering to reload a soldier's rifle.'

Somehow she felt closer to him than if he had agreed; his words were so intimate.

They started out when the rim of a salmon-pink sun was rising above the distant mist-covered mountains. Avril carried the broken shotgun under her right arm, just as her father had taught her. Wagstaff had the Tommy-gun slung over his shoulder, and a heavy razor sharp dah dangled from his belt.

Ten minutes later they entered scrub jungle, lushly green, dense and dotted with spiky thorns that Wagstaff was forced to hack through.

'If there's anyfin' aroun' 'ere worth shootin', Miss, it'll soon scarper wiv the din I'm makin'.'

'Don't worry, Wagstaff. Whenever I've been on an organised shoot we've had beaters to put the birds up. You'll do the same job.'

The scrub jungle soon gave way to more thickly wooded forest, where the trees were so tall they almost shut out the sun. Great vines, as thick as a man's thigh, twined round the trunks like the giant tentacles of some primeval monster squeezing the life out of its prey, while others were festooned

183

with waxy orchids. There were also clumps of impenetrable bamboo, the diameter of drain pipes and as tall as a flagstaff, and a coarse type of weed the seeds of which worked their way through their clothing and pierced the skin. A deer barked and others responded, but Avril had no idea where they were. A flurry of green pigeons hurtled out of a tree like a volley of well hurled stones, and were out of range before she had time to lock the barrels and raise the gun to her shoulder. She cursed aloud, appreciating for the first time that beaters were not simply ignorant people who made a noise but skilled trackers who knew the habits and habitats of birds and game. She realised too that her father's protests that they were a load of rogues being paid good money for doing nothing was a travesty of the truth.

Their clothes were soon sticking to their bodies, and they frequently stumbled over unseen roots in the semi-gloom which was only occasionally lightened by the yellow shafts of sunlight which managed to penetrate the leafy canopy above. Needle sharp thorns tore at exposed flesh, and unseen insects plagued them, and all around they could hear the calls of birds that refused to show themselves.

'Wot exactly we after?' queried Wagstaff.

'There's just about everything here, or should be: snipe, guinea fowl, pigeons, parrots, jungle fowl ... ' She broke off and said lamely, 'But they don't seem to want to know us.'

'If you don' min' me suggestin' it, Miss, I fink we'll do a little better back where we come in. The jungle ain't so dense an' at least you can see what you're doin'. As it is it's like tryin' to shoot a black cat in a coal cellar.'

She nodded agreement. 'I think you're right. We'll sit under a bush and wait for the mountain to come to Mahomet.' The frustration was evident in her voice, but it was not the missed opportunity to gain food that worried her so much but the idea of returning empty handed and admitting failure to the sergeant.

As they made their way back to the scrub, swarms of butterflies alighted on them and their topee-covered heads pounded in the oppressive heat, and when they paused to drink from their water bottles they immediately sweated it out.

When they emerged from the forest they concealed themselves behind a clump of feather-leafed bushes and waited
for their eyes to become accustomed to the sudden brightness
after the gloom of the forest which rose in front of them like
a green cliff.

Sweat trickled into their eyes making them sting, and they
were tormented by red ants with vicious pincers and unseen
insects that stung like needles. Wagstaff slapped at his bare
knees and the back of his neck, which seemed to be areas of
particular attraction. 'Min' if I light up, Miss? The smoke
might keep the beggars off.'

He wished the girl would call off the shoot because
personally he did not think a few birds were worth being
eaten alive for. In any case, he was very partial to bully
beef, and despite the frequency with which it was dished up
had yet to tire of it. He toyed with the idea of suggesting
they call it a day, but rejected it; she would never be able to
look the sergeant in the face, and it was obvious to anyone
who did not need a white stick that she was stuck on him.
Not that he blamed her, because Sergeant Harris would be
a feather in any woman's hat. Trouble was he was such a
dark horse. For all anyone knew he could have a wife and a
brood of kids he had run from tucked away some place. On
the other hand, Miss Carfax was no Nellie but someone out
of the top drawer, and he could not imagine her not asking
Harris if he was hitched before pulling her skirt up. She was a
proper little madam who would want a ring on her finger and
be able to wear white with a clear conscience when she walked
up the aisle. He hoped it would never come to that, though,
because Sergeant Harris deserved something better.

Avril was beginning to wish she had never mentioned her
shooting ability; if she returned empty handed Sergeant
Harris would think her a braggart. But it was true, she
had shot a great many birds and other game; her mistake
had been thinking she could do it without the help of skilled
beaters.

She felt Wagstaff's hand nudge her elbow. ''Ow about
that for a sittin' bird, Miss.' A forefinger was pointing to the
lower branches of a big tree about thirty yards away where a
largish bird, oblivious of their presence, was cooing gently.

It looked plump and very pot-worthy, and she thought it was an Imperial pigeon but was not sure. When she had gone shooting she had always relied on her father's expert knowledge. She announced with a conviction she did not feel, 'Imperial pigeon. Very common.'

She raised the gun to her shoulder; the butt felt warm against her cheek and when she took aim she was shaking so much the twin barrels were quivering. She heard Wagstaff say, 'Take a deep breff, then 'old it an' squeeze, don't pull.'

She did so, then remembered she had forgotten to release the safety catch. Her fingers seemed to be made of plasticine as she fumbled for the catch, and as she squinted along the barrels she prayed to God not to let her miss. She pulled both triggers simultaneously, and the recoil almost bowled her over. The smell of cordite filled her nostrils, but she saw the bird topple from the branch and hit the ground with a soft thud. She thought her father would have been horrified at her shooting a stationary bird.

When Wagstaff retrieved the bird she held it against her cheek; it was limp and still warm, and she thought she had never felt anything so soft. She experienced a feeling of great tenderness for the bird whose life she had ended so abruptly. But it had not died in vain. Harris would be most impressed. In her exhilaration she forgot that the prime object of the expedition had been to provide food.

The shots sent up a flock of green pigeons which flew round and round in circles twittering in fear, the sun glinting on their emerald plumage. She reloaded and fired two more cartridges, and several birds planed to the ground, followed by clusters of slowly drifting feathers.

'They good to eat?' asked Wagstaff.

'The Burmese think so. I've never tried them myself, but I'm sure Nellie will know what to do with them.' She found it difficult to suppress the elation she felt, even though they were rather small.

As they started on the journey back, Wagstaff thought how fit she must be; her stride was so springy and purposeful, and she seemed to have already forgotten how uncomfortable they had been.

186

When she dropped the birds at Sergeant Harris's feet with a feigned nonchalance, his face lit up with pleasure and she could not recall ever having felt happier or more light hearted.

'Good shooting,' he said approvingly. 'Top marks.'

She looked down at the heap of red-stained feathers and thought the birds had shrunk in death, but she would not have exchanged them for a prize tiger.

Nellie plucked the birds without leaving the slightest bruise on their flesh, and cooked them on wooden spits over an open fire, and they ate them with their fingers. They were dry, boney and utterly tasteless.

Avril felt she had never eaten anything so exquisite. She was glowing all over, especially on the back where Sergeant Harris had thumped her saying, 'Absolutely marvellous. You've got yourself a regular job.' She had not felt like this even when she was presented with the tennis trophies. It was only then that she realised that in her excitement she had quite forgotten to raise the subject of Nellie with Private Wagstaff.

Soon after they had finished the meal they set off again and drove until darkness came. Next day they made another pre-dawn start, and by late afternoon they had reached Yenangyaung where the derricks of the oil wells rose like a forest of metal in a lunar landscape. The ground resembled volcanic lava and the heat was unbearable, but the place was inhabited and oil was still being pumped from deep below the surface.

They drove through the residential area of neat houses, many of which had their own pools and tennis courts, up a drive marked by whitewashed stones, and stopped outside the club where the Union Jack still fluttered proudly.

Harris clambered out of the truck, saying to Simmonds, 'I'll probably be told it's out of bounds to us, but there's no reason why the ladies can't go in and have a decent bath, even a swim.'

Simmonds said, 'Oil men aren't the same as Rangoon's burra sahibs. It's a hard life and they don't have much time for snobs. I've met a few in Rangoon, and you can take it from me, Sarge, they know how to let their hair down and

187

don't give a monkey's who they do it with. Not interested in seeing your mother's marriage lines before they drink with you.'

Harris entwined two fingers and held them aloft. 'Let's hope you're right,' he said as he climbed up the flight of wooden steps on to a veranda where two men were dozing on reclining wicker chairs. He saluted and asked, 'Is the secretary around?'

One of the men jerked his head towards the club. 'In the billiard room.' Harris went into a large and lofty room, the walls of which were lined with hunting trophies, showcases of stuffed birds, and some framed prints of English country scenes. Dominating everything else was a big gilt-framed picture of King George VI and Queen Elizabeth in their coronation robes. Their eyes seemed to follow him as he walked towards some off-duty oil men who were sitting in rattan chairs browsing through issues of very old magazines that had been shipped from England, the last they would receive for a very long time.

None of them seemed surprised or in the least bit interested in his unexpected appearance. He heard the click of ivory balls striking against each other, and followed the sound into the billiard room where two men in shirt sleeves were engrossed in a game. He saluted again and asked, 'Which of you gentlemen is the secretary?'

One of the players brushed some cheroot ash from the green baize, peered along his cue, and made a cannon. Only then did he look up and say, 'I am. Part-time and unpaid. Gerry Smith with no y or an e at the end. What can I do for you?'

Harris explained that they were making for Mandalay and there were two ladies in the party who would greatly appreciate the luxury of a bath or swim as they had been travelling rough for some time.

'Bring your men in too, Sergeant. This isn't the time to stand on protocol. All in the same bloody boat now, and if you ask me, it's sprung a leak and is sinking fast.'

After Harris had introduced his party to Mr Smith, who in turn insisted they meet the off-duty oil men, the secretary said, 'The club's facilities are at your disposal. Sun's not over the yardarm, but the bar's open for anyone who wants to wet their whistle. There's a whole lot of booze to be shifted before the Japs turn up, and rules have become a little flexible.'

The three privates grinned appreciatively, and Smith went on, 'Order what you like and tell the steward I'll sign the chitty for everything.' He smiled, exposing yellow, nicotine-stained teeth. 'Not that it matters a tinker's cuss, no one's going to be blackballed for unpaid bar bills. I've been instructed to destroy all records when the time comes for us to pull out.'

Harris said, 'I think the ladies would like to freshen up first. This is like an oasis in the desert for them.'

'They'll find plenty of towels in the changing room at the back of the tennis courts, showers too, but if they prefer a swim there's the pool. Afraid all the women and children and most of the men have been moved to Mandalay and Maymyo. Only key staff remaining. The rest of us are feeling lonely being bachelors again, and the drinking has been on the ferocious side. Tonight we'll have a little party and celebrate like civilised people. We're a bit like Mother Hubbard's cupboard but we'll do our best. We'll have a blow out and see the last of the food out. We want to be left with just enough to see us to Mandalay.'

The two women thanked him, and as they were leaving he called after them, 'If you've got any clothes that need washing, just give them to the dhobi. He's still being paid so he might as well earn his corn.' He turned to Harris. 'Let's get into the bar. Cleanliness may be next to Godliness, but a cold beer is more important.'

The three privates stood drinking at the bar while Harris and the secretary took their drinks out on to the veranda where Harris asked him if he could be brought up to date with the present situation as they had been without reliable news for some time.

Smith said, 'I'm not sure you won't regret having asked me, because the news couldn't be worse. We're still in contact with the club in Mandalay, so we haven't had to rely on the official version of events. It seems the Japs are sweeping through Burma like a dose of Epsom salts, and our lads can't do a thing about it. The top brass may talk about strategic withdrawals to positions of strength, but it's a rout. Now the army's main concern is to get across the Chindwin before the monsoon breaks. If they don't they'll never make it.'

Harris said, 'You paint a gloomy picture. Why are *you* staying on if things are so bad?'

'Because General Slim asked us to. The army and what's left of the air force, and I include the Yanks, are dependent on us for petrol. He asked us to keep the wells and refinery going until the last possible moment, then we'll have to destroy the lot. They mustn't be in working order when the Nips arrive. General Slim has said he'll let us know when the time comes to blow the lot to buggery. Some experts have already laid the charges.' He grimaced. 'Been here twenty years and I hate to see a lifetime's work go up in smoke, but there's no alternative.'

'So you've met General Slim personally?'

'Briefly, but I was most impressed. He certainly commands the respect of the troops who think he's the new broom we need so badly.'

Kitty and Avril swam naked alongside each other in the club pool. The water was surprisingly cool, and they matched each other stroke for stroke as they spouted water like gambolling dolphins. When they had finished they sat at the side, tilting their heads from side to side and banging their ears with the palms of their hands.

Kitty Bradshaw looked at the young girl beside her and said solemnly, 'You've really taken a tumble for the Sergeant, haven't you?'

Avril said quietly, 'Is it so obvious?'

The nurse smiled, 'Don't worry about it. It would be most unnatural if a young girl in love didn't show it.'

'Sergeant Harris doesn't seem to have noticed.'

'Well, he does have a lot on his mind, and you can hardly expect him to rush into a hectic courtship. He's got a job he must see through to the end, plus three women to look after, which doesn't give him time for anything else.'

'I didn't ask to fall in love with him. It just happened. It wasn't as if I went out of my way, or anything like that,' she said petulantly.

'That's how it should happen. You don't want to be thought a scheming woman, do you?' The smile took away any suggestion of malice.

Kitty realised just how young Avril was; although the privations of the journey had matured her, she was still someone who was accustomed to getting her own way and incapable of concealing her disappointment at the sergeant's lack of response.

'I know nothing at all about him, and for all I know he could be married. Do you think it would be out of place to ask him?'

Kitty laughed. 'I once read a recipe for a very splendid dish which began: first catch your hare.'

'Just what is that supposed to mean?' asked Avril, baffled.

'Until you know how *he* feels it doesn't matter if he's got more wives than Bluebeard. If I were you though, I'd try and find out why a man like him is only a sergeant. He's not the normal run of the mill NCO, not by a long chalk. It might make all the difference to your relationship.'

'I tried to ask him, but he told me to mind my own business. He called me a snob.'

'I didn't suggest you try and find out because you should be ashamed of his rank, but simply in case there was some other reason for him being what he is.'

'You're talking in riddles.'

'Not really. If someone came to me as an ordinary nurse and I spotted unusual talent and potential, I'd ask myself the same kind of question.' She patted Avril on the shoulder. 'Let's forget it and get dried and dressed. You've got goose pimples.'

Avril said, 'You're not exactly helpful, or encouraging.'

'Sorry, Avril, I'll try to be. When we get back, why don't you change into one of those nice dresses you brought along? Wisely you've gone without wearing them, but as we're having a party tonight it'll be quite in order. And who knows? Maybe Sergeant Harris will notice.'

As they vigorously towelled themselves, Avril asked, 'Have you ever been in love, Kitty?'

'Goodnes me, yes. More times than I can remember, and each time it was the last time.'

'Yet you never married.'

'Only because I was never asked. Hence my homily to you about catching your hare.'

'I'm sorry, Kitty, that was unkind of me.'

'Not at all. I've still managed to be very happy.'

'He's a lot older than me,' she said hesitantly.

'Forget the difference. Men are like wine, they improve with age.'

The two women waited by the poolside, enveloped in large white towels, until the club servant arrived with their freshly laundered and ironed clothing, then they made their way back to the trucks where Avril sorted through her clothes looking for something suitable to wear at the party. She decided upon a pearl grey grosgrain evening dress with a wide fluted skirt, hardly any back, and a revealing décollété.

Kitty Bradshaw declined the offer of a loaned dress. 'I'll stick to my shirt and slacks. I'm twice your age and size, and there's no way I'm going to get a quart into a pint bottle. Anyhow, I've no one to impress.'

Later she looked at Avril admiringly and said, 'You look very beautiful. You'll make his eyes pop out of their sockets.'

But as soon as she walked through the door, Avril realised she had made a mistake, at least as far as the sergeant was concerned.

Several tables had been joined together to make one big one, and resting on the crisp white cloth was the club's best silver and crystal. Already seated round it were the members wearing dark trousers, white shirts, black ties and cummerbunds. They stood up as she entered, and applauded. Harris rose too, but his hands remained on the back of his chair.

To hide her embarrassment she gave a cross-legged curtsy and placed a forefinger under the point of her chin in the manner of a dimpled starlet. The dress was for Harris, not them, and from the expression on his face he clearly did not approve.

The sergeant had shaved and his uniform was clean and well pressed, and he looked like a man with no time for flippancy when a foreign invader was tearing apart a country that had been too hedonistic for its own good.

Kitty said, 'Don't look so sour, Sergeant. It doesn't do any harm to shut out reality for a little while.'

'They did that on the *Titanic*, if I remember,' he replied frigidly.

'You really are a miserable bugger,' she said, more out of sympathy for the girl than in protest at his remark.

The kitchen staff had provided no more than an adequate meal from the club's depleted larder (for which Smith apologised), but the wine flowed liberally. Nevertheless the air of festivity was marred by the underlying feeling of tension, possibly even guilt, and the laughter had a forced joviality, rather like the strained guffaws that greet stale and poorly told after-dinner jokes.

As the evening drew on and more drink was consumed the atmosphere improved and the enjoyment became more genuine. When the table was cleared one member played the piano and everyone gathered round it for an impromptu sing-song.

They reminded Harris of Christian martyrs singing on their way to the Colosseum.

The secretary asked the pianist to play a waltz, then bowed to Avril with old world courtesy and requested the pleasure of a dance. Another asked Kitty. But they had only executed a few steps before someone interrupted with, 'Excuse me,' and partners were exchanged. They did not complete one dance in the arms of the same partner.

An hour later Avril had danced with a dozen partners and excused herself in order to look for Harris, whom she found sitting alone at a table with a glass of whisky in front of him.

'Do I have to ask you for a dance, Sergeant?'

'I'm afraid I'm a clumsy partner.'

'If my feet have to be trodden on I'd rather it was by you. I could enjoy that.' She took his hand and tugged him upright, saying, 'Don't be such a spoilsport. Soon it will be midnight and the golden coach will turn into an army truck, and those

193

unfortunate oil men will start thinking about destroying their livelihood and future. So don't begrudge them and me a little fun. They aren't fiddling while Rome burns, just drowning their sorrow.'

He allowed himself to be led to the dancing area, saying, 'Perhaps you're right. There was a ball before Waterloo, and we still won.' He smiled, his teeth glowing whitely. 'That dress certainly took their minds off things.'

He danced well, if mechanically, and was light on his feet, but she was more conscious of his hand resting on the bare flesh of her back. 'I put this on for you, but when I saw your face I wished I hadn't. You looked so disapproving.'

'You reminded me too much of the girl who joined us in Rangoon.'

'It was Kitty's idea. I complained to her that you never took any notice of me.'

'I never take my eyes off you. Remember I'm responsible for your safety,' he said flippantly.

'That's not what I meant, and you know it.' She fanned herself with a hand. 'It's awfully stuffy in here, can't we go outside?'

It was cool on the veranda and the chorus of crickets and the twinkling of the fireflies gave it an air of tranquility, but the fierce red glow of the uncommercial gases burning from the top of the exhaust chimneys was a reminder of reality.

Harris stared into the darkness. 'I know what you are trying to say, Avril, but I'd forget it if I were you. When we reach Mandalay we'll part. When the war's over, and one day it will be, I'll go back to peacetime soldiering. I can't imagine you fitting into that small and compact world.'

'I thought you said I'd changed.'

'So you have, but that has been brought about by circumstances. When things revert to normal there'll be no earthly reason why you shouldn't enjoy the kind of life you did.'

'I don't want to go back to being a memsahib. In any case, now my father is dead there's nothing to make me want to return.'

'I imagine your father is, or was, a very wealthy man. His money will be yours one day.'

'I expect it will all go to Mummy. Anyway, money is the

194

last thing I'm concerned about at the moment. I'm in love with you, and I want you to feel the same.'

'This is all rather pointless, let's drop it.'

'Don't you feel anything at all for me?'

'I would be lying if I said no, but right now I've more important things to occupy my mind.'

'People do get married in wartime.'

'If they've got any sense they don't. There's a lot of nonsense talked about it being better to have shared a little happiness together than never to have known any, but wars don't just kill, they maim and mutilate. Ever thought what it would be like to nurse a wheelchair case when you're still young enough to enjoy life?'

'Women have always been prepared to take that risk.'

'This is all rather academic. We'd better get back inside, you're getting cold.'

'Before we do will you answer me one thing, and honestly?'

'I'll try.'

'Is there something in your past that makes you act as you do?'

'Yes.'

'What was it?'

'That wasn't the question. You said you'd ask one, and you have, and I've answered it.'

'It's important to me.'

'Me too. Although I've started afresh it will always follow me like a shadow.'

'Was there a woman?'

'Up until the time it happened there was. Then she said she had made a mistake and would I release her. I did so happily, because I realised I also had made a mistake.'

'You can't tell me the whole story?'

'Won't is a better word. There's no earthly reason why I should.'

'I love you.'

'That is no fault or concern of mine.'

'I intend to see that it is.'

Harris laughed. 'You're a most determined girl.'

'I've been very spoiled, remember. I know I've changed, but not all that much, I still like to get my own way.'

'When we get to Mandalay, will you let me take you out to dinner? And will you wear that dress?'

'The answer to both questions is yes. Does that mean you're weakening already?'

'No. I just want to show you that in the right circumstances I can relax and enjoy myself. Right now I can't.'

It was long after midnight before the party showed any signs of breaking up. Kitty was the first to leave, then one by one the slightly tipsy oil men excused themselves and drifted off to their quarters. Avril was reluctant to leave Harris's company, but her eyelids were drooping and she yawned continually. 'Sorry, I can't keep my eyes open. I'll see you in the morning.'

The three privates who had been propping up the bar hesitantly suggested that it was perhaps time they left, but the secretary said, 'Stay as long as you like, and drink as much as you can. It's only going to be poured away.'

It was an invitation they could not resist and they stayed, making a concerted assault on the stock of cold beer. Harris was unperturbed; he knew they would surface in the morning perfectly fit for duty. A healthy thirst went hand in hand with soldiering.

Harris remained in the lounge with Smith who said, 'No point in me turning in, I'm on duty soon. If you feel like staying for a chat I'll order one for the road. We really haven't had a chance to natter.'

Harris signified his willingness to remain because he thought it would be churlish to leave the secretary alone after such generous hospitality.

He felt slightly embarrassed when Smith asked him why two women were considered important enough to merit a personal escort, and he had to explain that they had been foisted upon him; his main task was to convey the Regimental Silver and Colours to safety. It seemed so unimportant when the man opposite was about to destroy an entire oil field. To his surprise, Smith did not think it at all strange to attach so much importance to them.

'One of our chaps left behind a lot of valuable personal

196

belongings because he insisted on taking all the old score books and photographs which chronicle the history of our cricket club. Was adamant the Japs wouldn't get them. I didn't have the heart to tell him the Nips didn't play it or live according to the rules or spirit of the game, so would hardly spare them a glance. But a man has to believe in something, even if it's only a lot of statistics. When I pull out I'll take the flag that's flying on the pole outside, and the picture of Their Majesties. No bloody Jap's going to use it for bayonet practice. You may think that's half-baked because the photograph is only one of hundreds of similar ones, but it's more than that to me and I'm not going to bother trying to explain.'

'You don't have to,' said Harris.

They chatted on for another hour, and Harris said, 'If you'll excuse me, I'll nip off to my truck.'

'Don't have to rough it tonight, Sergeant. There's plenty of comfortable beds available.'

'Thanks, but I won't be sleeping. My chaps are in no fit state to keep an eye on the Silver. And thanks very much for an enjoyable party.'

'Think nothing of it. I'll see you before you go. I'll let you have anything we can spare. Petrol is no problem, but water and food are. We've contaminated the fresh water tanks, and we've just enough grub for our own needs.' He sounded genuinely apologetic. 'We had no idea you'd drop in.'

'We'll cope,' said Harris, suppressing his disappointment, although he appreciated the need to deprive the Japanese of everything that would help them to advance without having to wait for supplies to catch up. But the collapse of his hopes for the replenishment of his own depleted water and food was a bitter spill to swallow; now he was beginning to doubt their chances of making it. The men might be able to cope with the privations, but it was too much to expect of the women who had not been trained to endure intolerable hardships.

Wagstaff waited until Simmonds and Fazackerley announced that they had drunk enough beer to float the *Queen Mary*, and when they staggered off to find an empty bungalow where they could sleep off their over-indulgence, he slipped into the room the mess steward had allocated to

Nellie. He had drunk as much as he needed, but he had not attempted to match his comrades drink for drink; much as he loved his beer, the need to share a bed with Nellie was greater.

He found her asleep in a big bed, shrouded in mosquito netting, and gently shook her before slipping in beside her.

He woke in the morning with her honey-coloured, cream-smooth body nestling against his, and could smell the sandalwood in her hair. He had possessed many women in his time, but none had given him greater pleasure or satisfaction than the beautiful Burmese girl. Although she might rabbit on about wanting to be a Tommy's girl, and how much she loved him and wanted to make him happy, she clearly enjoyed the old pork dagger. So he did not feel too badly about stringing her along. Simmo had warned him that he would have to do the right thing by her, but there was no need to worry too much on that score. Mandalay was still a fair distance away, and the important thing was to continue to make hay while the sun shone. When the Silver and Colours had been handed over he would think seriously about his position. It presented no real problem; the ranks of the regular army were filled with men for whom jilted women were unsuccessfully seeking.

Kitty Bradshaw had fallen asleep as soon as her head touched the pillow. It was a long time since she had enjoyed the luxury of clean sheets next to her skin and a feather-soft mattress beneath her, and she was determined to make the most of it.

When Avril joined her in the abandoned bungalow, she sat on the edge of the bed and thought about her discussion with Sergeant Harris. No matter how indifferent he tried to appear, she was determined to marry him. She knew her mother would not be overjoyed at the prospect and would no doubt use one of her contradictory phrases and describe such a union as a 'not awfully good idea'. She would also hold the blunderbuss of poverty over her daughter's head, and threaten to cut her off without a rupee until she came to her senses, but the threat did not worry her. She needed Harris more than she needed her mother's approval. In any case, if she became a soldier's wife the lack of money would not mean a thing because she would be surrounded by women who had to struggle to make ends meet. Apart from that, she had enjoyed enough comfort to last her a lifetime, and one could quickly tire of a diet of eclairs.

Sitting in the cabin of the truck, Harris mentally drew up a list of all the essential tasks that would have to be tackled in the morning and the supplies he would ask Smith for – until he realised the oil men were in as parlous a state as his own party. It was touch and go if they would make it to Mandalay. But he could ask the secretary if he could spare any ammunition for the shotgun. They had a better chance of survival with the occasional supply of fresh meat, and he was unable to forget the evident pleasure Avril showed when she shot the birds. She was a different person when she felt she was pulling her weight and not being a burden on the others.

Private Simmonds passed a troubled and disturbed night, no doubt brought about by the considerable amount of cold beer he had drunk, and when he woke in the morning he willed himself to recall in detail what had disturbed his sleep. But his head pounded and he was so confused he was unsure whether he was recalling something that had actually happened, or whether it had been a dream. He had been standing ram-rod stiff in his best uniform in front of the altar in the garrison church and saying in a loud defiant voice, 'I do,' when the padre had asked in a rich plummy voice, 'Who giveth this woman to be married to this man?' He knew the woman had been Nellie but he could not recall the groom, although he remembered Wagstaff standing in the packed congregation blowing a raspberry. Surely he should have been standing beside her? As his head cleared, he realised it had been a dream. Even so he felt a warm satisfaction at having been Nellie's choice as a stand-in father. He remembered too that his mother had once told him, after he had experienced a very unpleasant dream, that they should be reversed to appreciate their real meaning. That at least was some comfort. It meant Waggy would be the groom.

Private Fazackerley had not managed to reach the bed the

199

night before. His legs had given way and he slumped to the floor unconscious. He had not even woken when he walked in a somnambulent state out on to the veranda to empty his over-filled bladder. When Simmonds shook him he sat on the floor with his head between his hands, groaning softly and wondering why the big Yorkshireman was so anxious to know where Wagstaff had spent the night.

'Christ knows, Simmo. I flaked out. Maybe he did too. We certainly shifted some sherbert between us.'

Simmonds grunted, 'That's all right then. Just so long as he didn't get up to any mischief.'

Fazackerley said, 'In his state? He couldn't have raised it. Brewer's droop.'

He wrapped a towel round his waist and walked out into the blazing sunshine which felt like hammer blows on his head. But a plunge into the cold water of the pool revived him and he was able to recall in delectable detail the big hole he had made in the club's stock of bottled beer. It had been some piss up, he thought, and he felt quite capable of taking on the Jap army single-handed.

Harris was aware of a loud knocking on the door, and when he opened it was confronted by a clearly agitated Smith. 'I've just had an urgent call from Mandalay. We're to pull out immediately — the Japs are on their way. The army is going to hold them back for as long as possible, but everyone knows they'll eventually overrun the place. Then the order for total denial will be issued.'

'When will you be leaving?'

'In half an hour's time, and I suggest you don't hang around to witness it.'

As if to underline the need for speed, a loud rolling rumble was heard in the distance, like the thunder that precedes a violent storm.

'Artillery,' said Harris. 'Can't be more than twenty miles off.'

He abandoned all thought of checking the lorries or replenishing their supplies; he needed to take full advantage of any rearguard action and put as much distance between his party and the advancing army.

200

Smith handed him three bottles of whisky. 'Take these, they'll help shorten your journey.'

'Thanks. I won't crack them, though, till we reach Mandalay. Then we'll really celebrate.'

'Nothing like looking on the bright side,' said Smith.

·

Chapter 13

They covered a reasonable distance throughout the morning, and when they stopped to eat the great mass of Mount Popa, the sacred extinct volcano, was clearly visible rising like a giant cone on the blue hazy plain between the road and the Irrawaddy. It was a place venerated by the Burmese who believed it to be the home of powerful nats or spirits.

Avril sitting beside Harris related the story Nellie had told her.

The sacred volcano was the home of a blacksmith who was the strongest man who ever lived, and his sister, the most beautiful maiden. By means of devious tricks the king lured the girl to his palace in Mandalay and made her one of his brides. Malicious rumours were spread by his other wives that the blacksmith was planning a revolution and he too was lured to the palace where he was burned at the stake. In her grief the girl threw herself into the fire. A giant fig tree grew on the spot housing the spirits of the devoted couple, and they asked a holy man to return them to the volcano where they could live in peace.

'To this day people still lay out food for them,' said Avril. 'It's a lovely story, but I shouldn't think there's a word of truth in it.'

'True or not, I'm glad to see it,' said Harris. 'It means we aren't far from Pakokku. That's our next port of call.'

'Isn't that taking us out of our way?' she asked anxiously.

'Marginally, but it's the centre of the ferry and boat building industry and I've been thinking it's worth going

202

there and trying to get the trucks aboard a big steamer which can take us all the way to Mandalay. It'll save no end of time. We'll also get away from the mainstream of refugees. Apart from that it'll be a change to travel in relative comfort.'

They arrived at Pakokku early next day and Harris's expectations suffered a nasty jolt for the township, really more of a port which had once been so prosperous, was a scene of frenzied turmoil. It was there that the Irrawaddy and the Chindwin, Burma's two mightiest rivers, merged, and it had also become the meeting place of two great rivers of humanity. While huge paddle steamers were being loaded with more wounded to be ferried to Mandalay, a flood of people was arriving from the city as they had been told there was little chance of them being evacuated by air because of a shortage of planes.

As most of Pakkoku's European population had departed, Harris had no difficulty in finding another empty house where his party could rest whilst he reconnoitred the town. When he reached the tamarind-lined waterfront where the boat building industry was centred, he witnessed a scene of appalling incompetence. While one group of officials was commandeering vessels, another was ordering their destruction, and the contradictory policies were leading to violent rows which often became extremely physical.

Down by the waterfront he encountered a harrassed army lieutenant who was trying to rectify the situation. 'I'll sort it out,' he told Harris, 'but it'll take time, and by then a lot of valuable boats will have been lost. Can't blame the people who are sinking them, they're only carrying out the orders of some prick in Mandalay who hasn't bothered to come down to see for himself. The Japs are breathing down our necks and every boat will be worth its weight in gold.'

Harris explained his predicament and received the advice that he would be better off forgetting about Mandalay. 'It's a hotbed of gossip and panic. Everybody is clamouring to be evacuated, and everyone has a sound reason why they should be given priority. No one is going to put your Silver aboard an aircraft because civilians are running the show and they don't share your sentiments about its value; humans come before snuff boxes. One alternative is to go up the Chindwin, but I doubt if you'll find a master who'll take your vehicles and Silver. They're mostly stern paddlers with very shallow draughts, and the weight wouldn't be welcome.'

Harris knew the officer was talking sense and it would be futile to argue in Mandalay that men were prepared to die, in fact were dying, for what the Silver represented, but he had travelled too far to abandon his precious cargo.

'Any suggestions, sir?'

'My advice, for what it's worth, is to scrounge a lift as far as the Ava bridge where you can cross the Irrawaddy, then drive on to Monywa. From there, if your luck holds out, you can make it to Shwegyin, cross the Chindwin and make it to Tamu which is on the Indian border. It's a bastard of a journey, but a lot of people are tackling it.'

Harris thanked him and returned to the bungalow where he told the others of his intentions. To Avril and Kitty he said, 'I suggest you, with Nellie, continue on to Mandalay where you'll have to take pot luck with all the others who want to fly out.'

Kitty Bradshaw said, 'Before we agree to that, can Avril and I talk it over?'

He nodded assent. 'Of course, but don't take too long. Time isn't on our side, and I want to arrange a passage as quickly as possible.'

The two women retired to an adjoining room. Ten minutes later they returned and Kitty Bradshaw said, 'We've decided we'd be better off sticking with you, Sergeant. We have enough petrol, water and supplies, and we'd rather do that than hang around Mandalay. I'm not running away, but it seems to me there's no point in looking for a hospital site there and I'd be more use doing something constructive in India. There's no need to explain why Avril wants to stay with you.'

Harris returned to the waterfront where he sought out the young officer and asked him if he could arrange for passage up river.

'I can't promise anything, but I'll have a word with the master of one of the bigger steamers that has been converted into a hospital ship. Meet me here in an hour's time and I'll let you know the score.'

When they met again the lieutenant announced that the skipper was prepared to give them passage but there was no room for the trucks; every inch above and below decks was needed for the wounded, in addition to which two barges containing more casualties would be lashed alongside.

'He says, if you have any money, not notes but silver rupees, you might get some local people to build you a couple of rafts which can carry the trucks. If you can, then he's perfectly happy to tow you astern. If you haven't got money, they might take jewellery or anything else of real value.' He shrugged. 'You'll just have to put out a few feelers. Not so long ago they'd have done anything for a few rupees, now they strike a hard bargain. Question of supply and demand, and they've cottoned on quickly.'

Harris made his way back to the bungalow where he called another meeting and explained the position. He knew his men would do as they were told, but he wanted to give the women the opportunity to change their minds. They did not.

'Right then, I'll go back with Nellie and see if we can find someone who's prepared to build the rafts. The Colonel gave me some silver rupees before we left with strict orders to keep them for an emergency; well, I suppose this ranks as one.'

Avril said, 'If it isn't enough you can have my jewellery. I'll be glad to know it can be of use. I was beginning to regret bringing it. I've also got some silver rupees sewn into the hem of a dress. You can have those too.'

Harris and the Burmese girl wandered up and down the riverside searching for someone who would build two rafts, but no one seemed interested until they found a wizened old man whose peacetime occupation had been constructing big bamboo rafts for peasants to ferry their cattle, wagons or bales of cotton across the wide river.

Nellie said, 'He ask me how much you pay.'

'Tell him we have plenty of money, which he can have as soon as he finishes. He has my promise.'

Nellie conversed with the man, and Harris waited impatiently for her to deliver his answer. 'He say he want to know how much you pay him. He also want money first.'

'Tell him half now, rest later.'

Another prolonged conversation followed before Nellie

announced, 'He agree. He want two hundred and fifty rupee now, the same when finished.'

'Tell him that is too much.'

Nellie addressed the old man again, her rising voice suggesting she was encountering difficulties. She said, 'Old man say you find someone else, but you won't.'

Harris capitulated, mutely accepting that war brought out the best in some and the worst in others. The patriot had to share the same bed as the profiteer.

He took out the canvas bag from inside his shirt and slowly and methodically counted out one hundred and fifty rupees. 'Tell him he can have this now, the rest later. And tell him I will sit here with a soldier with a gun in case he thinks of running off with the money.'

The down payment had taken all the money the Colonel had given him, and when he added the amount Avril had contributed he was still short of the amount demanded, but he would sort that out with the raft builder later. If he would not accept jewellery then he would forcibly seize the rafts at gun point. Frankly he did not anticipate any trouble, for the amount he had handed over was more than the old man would see if he lived to be a hundred.

He told Nellie to go back and tell Private Simmonds to come down with the Tommy-gun.

When the old man saw the sub-machine gun he clapped his hands and screamed out an unintelligible torrent of words, and a group of young men and women appeared as if from nowhere and gathered around him. He poured out another flood of instructions and the men and women dispersed, returning with great lengths of bamboo six inches across, and great coils of home-made rope. They worked silently and swiftly, sawing and cutting the bamboo into lengths of the same size which were then lashed together until a platform large enough to support a truck had been completed. Then cross beams of stout timber were laid sideways across the bamboo and secured into place. With a great deal of grunting and heaving the raft was up-ended so that the wood supports were undermost, then it was slipped into the water. For added buoyancy four large empty oil drums were lashed to the sides. When twilight approached oil lamps were lit so that they could continue working in the dark, and by eleven o'clock two rafts as alike as identical twins had been finished.

Harris thought it was a remarkable achievement, although they looked rickety and he hoped they would not sink under the weight of the vehicles.

He stood on the rafts and tested the lashings, then jumped up and down, but he found they had been solidly built. Satisfied that no more could be done he told Nellie to go back and fetch the others.

The rafts were poled a short distance down-river through the cocoa coloured water to a hard slipway which had been trampled and pounded until it was rock hard, and down which the trucks could be driven.

Despite the lateness of the hour, Harris insisted the trucks should be loaded without delay because he wanted to secure the rafts to the steamer at first light. Fortunately the head-lights provided them with sufficient light to see what they were doing.

When the lorries were safely lashed into position, the old man demanded the rest of the money and Harris told Nellie to tell him there was no more and ask if he would accept jewellery.

Nellie spoke to the old man. 'He say he want look first.'

Harris turned to Avril. 'Show him a few things, and let him take his pick.'

Avril opened her jewellery box and produced a finely engraved watch that she used to wear pinned to an evening dress. When the cover was opened to expose the face, a tune was played as if a music box was concealed inside. The old man grinned from ear to ear, exposing stumps of blackened teeth, and he nodded greedily. She also showed him two pairs of screw-on ear rings and demonstrated how they should be worn. Again the old man was obviously delighted, for he snatched them away, secured one pair to his ears and tucked the other inside his filthy blouse. He also pointed to a bracelet, and when that was handed over Harris intervened: 'Nellie, tell him that is all. No more.'

He expected an altercation, but to his surprise the man made no protests and Harris wished he had haggled at the beginning of the transaction.

They slept in the trucks until it was light enough to move and the Burmese could see well enough to pole the unwieldy rafts along the congested river to where the steamer was moored alongside.

Although the river was shallow inshore the current was fast, and it needed all the skills and strength of the natives to manoeuvre the rafts under the stern of the paddle steamer where they tossed lines to the waiting seamen who hauled them inboard and secured them to deck bollards.

The young lieutenant stood leaning against a guard rail, and as soon as he saw the rafts he called out to Harris, 'Clamber up and I'll introduce you to the Master, Mr McIntyre.'

The sergeant climbed, monkey fashion, up one of the hawsers and joined the army officer who led him towards the bridge. 'He sounds an irascible old sod, but don't let that fool you; he's a wonderful chap. Doesn't want anyone to know it. More worried about his ship than he is about his own skin. Been his home and life for thirty odd years,' said the officer.

McIntyre was a stocky, compact man with a white pointed beard. His face had the yellowed look of a man who had spent too long in the tropics, and the corners of his eyes were wrinkled from staring too long into brilliant sunshine. A white-topped cap was perched at a jaunty angle on his greying hair, and his uniform looked rumpled and grimy as if he had been wearing it for several days. He spoke with a broad Scottish accent which would have met with Alex Carfax's full approval. 'As you can see, it isn't going to be a joy ride.' He gestured towards the deck below.

In peacetime the three hundred feet long vessel had been the pride of the Irrawaddy Flotilla when it had resembled the paddle steamer from 'Showboat'. Then the brasswork had glistened and the ropework had been blancoed to a bone-white. The First Class passengers had relaxed in the comfortably furnished and exquisitely appointed lounge, and slept in airy cabins at night, with servants at their beck and call. The native passengers had travelled in much less comfort on the upper deck, much of which had been taken over by stalls and a bazaar. Now the ship had the look of a dandy who had suffered an unexpected decline in fortune.

The decks were covered with stretcher cases, most of whom endured the most appalling wounds in stoic silence. They were too grateful to have secured a berth to complain. The air was heavy with the stench of rotten flesh, filthy dressings and excreta, for many of the casualties had severe dysentery.

'Just one army doctor and two wee nurses to cope with that lot,' said the Master grimly. 'And they're still bringing more cases aboard.'

At the gangway every man capable of walking aboard carried two large billets of timber which were added to the rapidly mounting pile which would fuel the boilers.

'That's their fare,' said McIntyre. 'Normally there's a labour force to do it, but most of them have buggered off.'

'One of my party is a qualified nursing sister, sir, and if she can be of any assistance I'm sure she'll be only too willing to volunteer,' offered Harris.

'I'm only the driver, Sergeant, so have a word with the army doctor. I'm sure he'll be most grateful. I'll take you down to him.'

McIntyre led him to a screened off section of the lounge where the doctor had set up an operating table on one of the ornately carved dining tables. He was stripped to the waist, wearing only a pair of surgical gloves and a gauze mask over his mouth. A European nurse in a blood-stained uniform handed him instruments as he called for them in a crisp emotionless voice. A private soldier lay on the table being fed blood plasma by another nurse. His stomach was opened with a large incision several inches long, and the doctor laid his intestines on his chest, and then began searching gingerly through them for pieces of shrapnel. He ignored the presence of Harris and the Master until he straightened up and pushed the intestines back in such a haphazard manner that Harris felt the sour taste of bile rise in his throat. The nurse put her hand to her mouth, and the surgeon snapped, 'Don't be so squeamish. They'll sort themselves out.'

He sewed up the incision with cat gut and shouted, 'Right, take him away.'

209

Two soldiers appeared, placed the patient on a stretcher and carried him out onto the upper deck.

The doctor removed his gloves, and rinsed his hands in a bucket filled with disinfectant. The gorge rose again in Harris's throat when he saw a large zinc bath filled with amputated limbs.

The surgeon spoke to the two nurses. 'Nip out and have a smoke before the next patient comes in.' He turned to McIntyre and said irritably, 'What is it? Can't you see I'm busy.'

Exhaustion had carved deep furrows in his face, and his eyes had the dead look of a man desperately in need of sleep. He reached down and picked up a bottle of whisky standing by one of the table legs, and took a deep swig.

The Master said apologetically, 'Sorry to bother you, sir, but the sergeant here says one of his party is a nursing sister and wonders if you can use her.'

'I can use anybody who won't throw up at the sight of blood. Some of the chaps out there haven't had their dressings changed for days and gangrene has set in. Thankfully the maggots are helping to keep it from spreading. Not a pleasant thought, and one that would bring frowns of disapproval at St Thomas's, but it's nature's way of compensating for shortages.' He lit a cigarette with visibly shaking hands saying, 'Not the Scotch, just tiredness.'

When Harris told Sister Bradshaw that the doctor would appreciate any help she could give, he was surprised to hear Avril say, 'Surely there's something I can do? I don't want to be a wallflower.'

He thought it was an odd choice of words, but he knew what she meant. 'Let's go and ask him,' he said.

The doctor asked Kitty, 'Done any theatre work?'

'A fair amount.' She glanced around the make-shift theatre. 'Not in such grim conditions though. I've certainly never seen limbs left lying around like this.'

The surgeon smiled wanly. 'It's not my normal practice either, but there're cases out there queuing up to come in, and I don't want them to see arms and legs being tossed overboard so I do that when it's dark. When they get in here I don't give them a chance to look around. They're put out with chloroform before you can say knife.' He grimaced. 'That was not an intentional pun.'

Kitty said, 'Where do you want me to start?'

'Here, right away. It'll give one of the nurses a chance to grab a little sleep. Haven't had any for forty-eight hours, and that's too long.'

To Avril he said, 'As for you, young lady, there's a whole lot of unsavoury chores to be done. For a start you can help in the galley where a couple of soldiers are boiling up dirty field dressings and bandages. That kind of thing needs a woman's supervision. Then you can give a drink of water to any of the lads on deck who need it. Don't overdo it, some of them have internal injuries; apart from that, we need to conserve water.'

By late afternoon Kitty Bradshaw had assisted with more operations than she had in her entire nursing career, and when the surgeon decided it was time for her to be relieved she went out on deck to rest against a rack containing life rafts. She closed her eyes, and immediately fell into a deep tormented sleep.

Avril, with the assistance of Nellie, went along the decks with a bucket of tepid water and a dipper. She also supervised the boiling of the filthy dressings and the hosing down of the latrines which had become blocked and foul from over use. Then she found time to tell Sergeant Harris that the decks were in a filthy state, and bucket squads should be organised to swill them down. She could not be expected to do everything.

He smiled, saluted and said, 'Very good, sir.'

She flushed and said, 'I'm sorry, Sergeant. I suppose you think I'm talking to you like one of the servants? I didn't mean to.'

He ruffled her damp hair. 'You're worse than a sergeant-major, but I'll forgive you because you're so pretty.'

She felt herself blush and wanted so much to embrace him, but she feared his rejection because he had still not given the slightest indication that he shared her feelings.

Harris shinned down a rope to his truck and collected three bottles of whisky he had been given in Yenanyaung: one for the surgeon, one for the master, and one for the lieutenant who had been so helpful. He also counted the jerry cans of water and decided two could be spared without any great loss. They would not go far, but it would be a welcome change from the brackish water on the steamer.

The lieutenant declined his bottle, saying, 'Give it to the quack. He's so short of anaesthetic he'll be grateful for it. He's giving the less serious cases a shot instead. Apart from that he's dead on his feet and the odd slug, although it might be frowned upon by the BMA, will help him keep going.'

McIntyre accepted his gift with undisguised pleasure. 'I don't normally drink during a voyage, and because I've so many troops on board I had most of the stock dumped over the side. Just a precaution, mind you, and no reflection on the soldiers, but I didn't want temptation put in their way. Didn't realise at the time how much the doctor would have appreciated it. Keeps him awake, and puts his patients to sleep.'

Harris asked, 'When are you aiming to sail, sir?'

The master shrugged. 'Not my decision. I've been told I can't sail till the two barges, each containing five hundred men, have been lashed to the port and starboard paddle sponsons. But there's no sign of them as yet.'

The tugs towing the barges did not appear until nightfall, and it took two hours working under the steamer's arc lights before they were nudged into position and secured. By then McIntyre decided he would wait until dawn before casting off.

'Come to the wheelhouse, Sergeant, and share a dram before I get my head down for a couple of hours. Be nice to have a chat. My missus used to sail with me, but I packed her ashore when the Japs got too close for comfort. If you feel like it, you can join me on the bridge when we sail. Wouldn't have allowed it in peacetime, but standards have had to be lowered.'

It was still dark when the deck serang, the Chittagong man who was in charge of the small crew, found Harris sleeping against the bulkhead and shook him awake. He said in fractured English, 'Master say ship go. He on bridge now, waiting.'

The lieutenant emerged from the gloom, shook his hand

212

and said, 'Bon voyage, Sergeant. Sorry I'm not coming with you.'

Harris found McIntyre sitting on a tall rattan stool behind the steering wheel which was manned by one of the secunnies (helmsmen) wearing nothing but a faded pair of discarded army shorts.

Standing at the engine telegraph eagerly awaiting orders was the puriwallah, the only member of the crew who shared the slightest intimacy with the master. Below the wheelhouse, on the flats, two men stood by the massive circular paddles.

McIntyre picked up a megaphone from the deck, put his head out of the port bridge window and bellowed in Hindustani, 'Stand by below'. He lit a cheroot, puffed at it until his cheeks bulged, then surveyed the glowing end to make sure it was burning evenly before giving the order for the mooring lines to be released from the onshore bollards.

The windlass creaked and groaned as the heavy manillas were hauled inboard, and smoke plumed from the twin funnels as he gave the puriwallah the order to set the telegraphs to 'Slow Ahead'.

Deep in the bowels of the ship the Chief Engineer, another Scot, tended the pulsing engines and verbally abused the stokers to make them do even more as they tossed the timber into the insatiable furnaces which fired the boilers.

McIntyre gave his orders to the helmsman, again in Hindustani, and supplemented them with gestures of his hand signifying a turn to port or starboard. The steamer juddered from bow to stern as it butted into midstream to meet head on the swift down-river flow. Speed was increased to half-ahead, and the hawsers securing the barges alongside groaned and screeched as they taughtened. The paddles churned up a yellowy wake and Wagstaff, Fazackerley and Simmonds, sitting in the cabins of the two trucks, were blinded by a curtain of muddy spray as the tow ropes tightened and the foremost part of the rafts rose high in the water, so that it seemed as if they were skimming across the surface.

'Christ Almighty,' moaned Wagstaff. 'If 'e keeps this up the ruddy ropes'll break and we'll be back in Rangoon before you can say fart.'

From time to time McIntyre, who seemed to know the river like a keen gardener knows his allotment, picked up a telescope and studied the river ahead, looking for the bamboo buoys that marked the channel, sandy shallows and submerged rocks. An empty tin rested on the deck by his feet and he tossed his half-smoked cheroot into it before lighting a fresh one.

Harris noticed that he had found time to change into a clean uniform.

Avril and Nellie went round the upper and lower decks and the barges lashed to the sponsons with large panniers of thick sweet tea, which they poured into the dixies of any soldier who expressed interest. The tea round completed they returned to the galley and helped to prepare a meagre meal of soggy rice and bully beef. Then Avril supervised the washing and drying of more filthy dressings, whistling cheerfully and seemingly immune to the ever present spectacle of suffering and pain, but in awe of the way in which the men bore their wounds with such uncomplaining good humour. She collected some dressings which were drying in the air and went out and replaced soiled ones.

She was particularly impressed by one man who still carried five bullets in his body; when she changed his bandages, she asked if there was anything else she could do for him and he replied, 'Yes, Miss, bugger off and stop pestering me. I'll have to be dead before I'll allow any woman to give me a bed pan. So there.'

During one break when she managed to smoke a cigarette, she wondered what her father would have said if he could have seen her washing down naked men, emptying buckets of excreta over the side, and whispering words of comfort to men who had only a short time to live. He would turn in his grave, she thought, then immediately regretted being so callous and spiteful. If he had found himself in a similar position she hoped he would have knuckled down and pulled his weight. Unlike her, he had never been given the opportunity of being put to the test. Now it was too late. She felt vaguely grateful that she had been given the chance to prove her own worth, but could not shed the guilty feeling that it was more for Harris's benefit than her own.

She sought his approval rather than self-satisfaction.

Despite the vastness of the river, which at times seemed more like the sea, passage upstream was frustratingly slow because of the enormous increase in traffic which made navigation a nightmare. The barges lashed alongside and the two unwieldy rafts astern, made their craft difficult to handle. In the panic conditions that existed on the river the normal rules of the road went by the board, and McIntyre frequently had to take evasive action to avoid collision with sampans, paddy gigs, dug-out canoes, and huge uprooted trees capable of holing a ship or smashing the paddles to matchwood. Some of the massive trunks were water-logged and submerged, and therefore impossible to spot, and they hit the hull with a terrifying thump that made the passengers fear they had run aground.

McIntyre took it all in his stride, the calm voice with which he gave orders to the helmsman giving no indication of the inner tension he was experiencing. Only once did Harris hear him curse, and that was when a knau, with richly carved stern and shapely prow and carrying no sails on her forest of masts, seemed hell-bent on ramming the steamer, for when McIntyre called for, 'hard a starboard', the solid wooden vessel seemed intent on following, and only by superb seamanship and an intimate knowledge of the river did he avoid a head on collision. It was only when the knau had passed, with less then twenty yards separating the two vessels, that he realised it was crewless and must have broken adrift from its moorings. 'Like Rangoon on a ruddy race day,' he said.

Corpses, animal and human, floated downstream. There were grossly bloated bullocks and horses that drifted past, their legs rigidly upright, and black crows pecking at them until the sharp beaks pierced the skin and they mercifully sank out of sight. The humans floated face upwards and face downwards; some had been thrown overboard from hospital ships, others were refugees who had been murdered or had died from disease or sheer exhaustion.

The master sat upright and expressionless on his high stool, his eyes fixed purposefully ahead, sometimes cocking his head to one side to better hear the cries of the leadsman standing on the bow calling out the depth.

Harris spent many hours standing by his side, seldom speaking unless spoken to because he did not wish to disturb his concentration. He did not mind the silences; they provided him with the opportunity to study the ever-changing scenery. Sometimes the banks rose on either side in sheer red cliffs, the abode of millions of sand martins, to be replaced a few miles later by dense jungle which encroached to the water's edge. There were also wide, flat, muddy areas over which elephants moved on rubbery legs to reach the water for a drink and a bath. Then for miles there would be nothing but paddy fields where the peasants, bent low, worked like automata in the thigh-high muddy water. But no matter how wild, rugged or remote the shoreline appeared, there were always the inevitable cluster of small sugar-white pagodas.

Sometimes a strong breeze blew up from nowhere, whipping the surface of the river into angry white-topped waves, while a surge of water from a funnelled tributary brought a sudden and unexpected rise in the level and the steamer, even with engines at 'full ahead' seemed to be stationary.

McIntyre broke a long silence. 'I'll have to go alongside soon to stock up with wood, Sergeant. Can you muster enough men for a timber party? The Engineer tells me the pressure gauges are perilously low.' The Scot sighed in an exaggerated manner to emphasise his falling faith in mankind. 'The Company has a contract with the suppliers of fuel who are supposed to stockpile it at the various landing stages, but most of their coolies have skedaddled so we'll have to do our own refuelling.'

None of the walking wounded were fit or strong enough to carry more than two or three billets at a time, and four hours passed before enough fuel lay on the deck to satisfy the demands of the Engineer, and when the steamer cast off there was little daylight remaining.

There was no twilight, except for a fleeting period when the setting sun turned the surface of the river into burnished copper, then a liquid darkness descended as if a lamp had been snuffed out. High overhead the sky was filled with a myriad of stars that twinkled like diamonds on a jeweller's velvet, but shed no light on the earth below.

McIntyre called out in Hindustani, 'Put on the big lamp,' and a cone of brilliant white light pierced the darkness ahead illuminating the shoreline and glinting off the gold domes of the bigger pagodas, and picking out the ghostly shapes of passing ships that carried no navigation lights. From out of the inky darkness the leadsman's monotonous chant floated into the wheelhouse warning that the depth was dangerously low, or the bed of the river was unexpectedly sandy.

McIntyre said, 'I'd like a golden sovereign for every trip I've made up and down the river. I'd be a very rich man indeed. But familiarity must never be permitted to breed contempt. You must never take the Irrawaddy for granted or believe you can treat it with impunity. I may know where every submerged rock lies, but I'm in the dark when it comes to shoals and sandbanks; you'll find fresh ones have been deposited somewhere since your last voyage.'

Harris was finding the wheelhouse unbearably hot and airless, and he excused himself, saying he needed to check up on the rafts astern. He walked aft, carefully threading through the recumbent bodies that lined the deck. Some moaned softly, sleep releasing them from the need to suffer in silence, others snored in morphia-induced slumber. Occasionally he heard a loud splash and knew that more bodies, and more limbs, were being dumped overboard.

He leaned over the stern rail and called out, 'Sergeant Harris here. Everything all right?'

Simmonds and Wagstaff replied, almost in unison, that everything was.

'Managing with food?'

Wagstaff's voice floated out of the darkness. 'No problem there, Sarge, unless you object to eatin' grub off of your lap. Won't stay on the plate. Not, you might say, my idea of a pleasure cruise. More like those bleedin' big dippers I rode on in Southend Kursaal when I was a nipper. You go right to the top of this bloody great slope, then you come down like a stone, an' you only stop when you 'it the water at the bottom.'

Harris laughed. 'Never mind, at least you aren't having to pay for it.'

Wagstaff said, 'Would you do me a favour, Sarge, and

tell Nellie I ain't forgot 'er and I'll come and see 'er when we 'ave a decent stop-over. Oh, an' don't mention it to Miss Carfax. I get the feelin' she don't approve of soldiers, not unless they's sergeants, that is.'

Simmonds' voice came from the other raft. 'I keep warning him, Sarge, that I'll get my bayonet out and ruin him socially is he leads that poor kid up the garden path.'

'She seems to enjoy the attention,' replied Harris.

'That's only because she's got some stupid idea that marrying a pongo is like being given a ticket on the gravy train,' said Simmonds.

'You seem to have taken her under your wing, Simmonds.'

'If I don't no one else will. You've got to remember I've known Waggy from the time he didn't know the difference between a pull through and a blow through. Even now he knows more about one than the other, and that's why I'm keeping an eye on Nellie. He's not going to dump her like an old boot when we get to wherever we're going.'

Harris retraced his steps for'ard, thinking it would be a shame if they fell out over the girl. But he consoled himself by deciding that was most unlikely; Wagstaff could talk himself out of anything.

He saw the glimmer of light between a chink in the curtain covering a galley porthole, and told himself that he ought to find out how Sister Bradshaw was getting on, knowing that what he really wanted was a chat with Avril because he was not likely to see Kitty in the galley, but he excused this as being no different to Simmonds' avuncular interest in Nellie. The only people in the galley were the lance-corporal and a private who were poking with sticks at a tangled mess of dressings boiling in two big cauldrons.

'Seen anything of the nursing sister or the young lady from my party?' he asked.

Without stopping the stirring the lance-corporal said, 'I think they've sloped off to get some shut-eye. The MO came in here and told the young one she was overdoing it. Said he'd got the Master's permission for the two of them to use his cabin, seeing as how he couldn't leave the bridge.'

Harris said, 'That's decent of him. Know where it is?'

'Under the bridge. Can't mistake it. Got his monica on

218

the door. And don't do anything I wouldn't do, Sarge.'

'Opportunity would be a fine thing,' Harris replied, knowing that there was no ill intent in the remark; it was simply one that was expected of a soldier.

He found the cabin without any difficulty and rapped gently on the door, telling himself he would leave them in peace if there was no reply. They needed all the rest they could get.

When he heard Kitty call out, 'Who is it?' he replied, 'Sergeant Harris. Just enquiring if there's anything you need.'

'Come on in, the door's not locked.'

'Are you decent?'

'If you're referring to my morals, the answer is no. If to my attire, the answer is yes,' she called out breezily.

She was sitting at a table that was secured to the deck, with her feet resting on the seat of another chair and clutching a tumbler of whisky in one hand. Her appearance bore no resemblance to the chirpy voice that had called out to him. Her clothing was caked with congealed blood, her usually well groomed hair was untidy, and falling in wisps from the pins she had not bothered to adjust, and her eyes had a dead, ashen look. He glanced hurriedly around the cabin and saw Avril lying in a foetal position on one of the two bunks. On the locker by the side was a family portrait of the Master and his wife, a handsome high-cheeked woman, and two girls in blazers and straw hats; he assumed it was the bunk she had used when she sailed with her husband.

He said, 'You should be trying to catch up on your sleep instead of knocking back neat Scotch.'

'Oh, come off it, David. I can do without a lecture. I'm not having a secret nip; the surgeon recommended it. Even poured it for me. I said I was too tired to sleep and he said it would help.'

She thrust the glass towards him. 'Here, take a swig. I can't manage it all. Anyway, it might help you to sleep, you look all in.'

He took the glass although he did not want it, thinking that for once the doctor's orders could be more harmful than beneficial; she would probably wake up feeling like death.

The spirit seered the back of his throat and he felt it

burning its way to his stomach, and was seized with a fit of uncontrollable coughing. His eyes watered and his ears rang. When he had recovered, he looked up and saw Kitty's shoulders were shaking and she was sobbing silently. He put his arms around her saying, 'This won't do. This isn't the Kitty I know. You're the one who's expected to set an example to the rest of us.'

She wiped her eyes with the back of a hand and said weakly, 'Sorry, but I've just made a very disquieting discovery. I thought I was hardened to the sight of human suffering; I'm not.'

'What's so terrible about that, Kitty? You don't want to lose all sense of feeling, do you?'

She sounded almost angry. 'I'm not talking about *feeling*, I'm talking about the ability to be detached when on duty. I've lost that, and a nurse who becomes emotionally involved can't do her job properly or efficiently. I watch the surgeon operate, and I wonder whether the patient will survive or end up feeding the fish. I've never entertained such thoughts before. Maybe it's just the volume of work. In a hospital the conditions are hygienic and a theatre is thoroughly scrubbed out before another patient is admitted, here it's like a slaughter house.'

'I don't suppose the doctor likes it any more than you do, but he has no alternative. He can't refuse to operate because the odds are against him. Neither can he clean up after each op because of the risk of infection. The delay may mean certain death for someone.'

'Trust you to be so practical. When I've had some sleep I'll feel better, but it was nice to have a shoulder to cry on.'

He looked towards Avril. Tiny beads of perspiration covered her upper lip, and there was a sheen to her forehead and her hair was plastered to her head as if she had just showered. The rise and fall of her chest was almost imperceptible.

'I'm worried about her,' he said. 'If the strain is getting at you, how will she stand up to it?'

'You need have no fears on her account. She has great strength of character.' She saw Harris's eyebrows arch. 'Don't look so bloody sceptical. I'm surprised too. She hates what she's doing, but she carries on. She reminds me

220

of a man we had at the hospital who was responsible for fund raising. Sometimes he was forced to eat three lunches a day and two dinners, in the course of duty. He confided to me that he hated the sight of food, but had to entertain prospective donors then he made himself throw up before tackling the next meal. Avril's like that: she throws up over the side and comes back for more.'

'She's following the example you've set.'

'Me? It's nothing to do with me. She's scared stiff of disappointing *you*.'

'Hold on, Kitty, you make me sound like some monster.'

'Hell's bells, you're blind! It's not fear, you idiot, it's love. If I tell her you popped in, she'll be furious I didn't wake her.'

'Then don't tell her,' he said harshly.

'I'll tell her, and face the music. The fact that you took the trouble to see how we were is the best tonic she could have.'

Harris said, 'I don't want you to encourage Avril into thinking there could ever be anything between us. In fact, I'd rather you actively discouraged it. She's very young, and when this is over I'll rejoin the Battalion no matter where it is, and she'll forget I ever existed. It's a girlish infatuation. Apart from that, there's a major obstacle that prevents us from becoming more than friends.'

'Something in your past? I suspected as much.'

'Let's not pursue it, Kitty. If I told you, and I've no intention of doing so, you'd realise I'm not talking nonsense. The man she thinks she loves would no longer exist, and where would that leave her?'

'I'm too tired to try and unravel riddles. If you don't care for her in the same way, have the decency to tell her. Don't leave her dangling on the end of a hook. She'll take no for an answer, but if you don't give it she'll continue to live in hope and that would be cruel, and you aren't a cruel man.'

'I've tried to tell her, but all she said was that she was a person who's used to getting her own way. I can't walk around with a ruddy placard round my neck saying, "Leave well alone" and tinkling a bell.'

He left the cabin, slamming the door behind him much

221

harder than he intended. He did not want to think about the girl, or the future, because there was not any, the past had made certain of that.

When he emerged on to the upper deck he walked to the guard rail and stared down at the snowy foam being churned up by the paddles. His mind was a haze of contradictory thoughts and feelings. He was angry that Kitty had told him what he already knew but did not want confirmed. Yet in some strange way the knowledge that Avril loved him made him happy. He had been alone too long, and although he did not intend doing anything about it, it was comforting to know someone cared. It was like receiving a letter after years of learning to do without.

He decided that he did not want to dwell on it, and so he made his way to the make-shift theatre to see how the doctor was coping; he would be grateful if someone dropped in for a chat.

He found the two on-duty nurses sitting down smoking cigarettes. One put a finger to her pursed lips and gestured towards the operating table where the surgeon was stretched out like one of his anaesthetised patients.

'He just collapsed onto the floor from sheer exhaustion; like a pricked balloon. We had the devil's own job getting him up there, but we couldn't leave him on the floor with all that mess. Like a drunk in the gutter,' said one of them. 'It's as well he did pass out because if he'd carried on he'd have lost more patients that he could have saved.'

Harris looked at the rust-coloured stains on the deck. 'You two pop off and get some sleep. I'll stay with him. I'll call you when he wakes.'

When the nurses had gone to their cabin, Harris swabbed down the deck before sitting down on one of the vacated chairs, and willed himself to stay awake; but his head began to droop and he dozed off. When he awoke shafts of dust-flecked sunlight were filtering through the curtains and he heard the monotonous clunk-clunk-clunk of the paddles as they propelled the steamer upstream. The surgeon was still sleeping soundly and Harris rose carefully, anxious not to make the slightest sound, but as he tip-toed towards the curtain that partitioned the theatre from the rest of the lounge, he heard the doctor call out, 'Sergeant! Did you put me on the table?'

'No, sir, the nurses did.'

'They had no right to let me sleep, but I'm damned glad they did.' He rubbed his red-rimmed eyes. 'You might tell them I'm ready to start again whenever they are, and by the way, I'd like to say how grateful I am for the loan of your two girls. Worth their weight in gold.'

His words reminded Harris of his own men, and that it was time he let them know they had not been forgotten.

Wagstaff and Simmonds were sleeping, and Fazackerley was sitting cross-legged on the port side raft, oiling and cleaning the dismantled Bren. Washing fluttered from a length of rope.

'How are you enjoying your solitary confinement?' Harris called down.

'Better than being up there with those poor sods, Sarge. A good soldier should never be afraid to die, but he shouldn't have to go like an animal without dignity or self-respect; wallowing in his own shit and vomit.' The soldier's voice was strident with indignation.

'They'll be in Mandalay soon, then they can be moved to a proper hospital where they'll get all the proper drugs and treatment. Then they'll be glad they hung on.'

Fazackerley peered down the barrel of the Bren. 'Remember how we all bitched about not seeing any action? I'm not too sure I'm unhappy about it now, Sarge. I feel ashamed that the army can treat its own men the way it's treating those poor devils. It's against everything we've lived by. We were always led to believe the welfare of the men came first, but that isn't happening. I hate to say it, but it makes the question of the regimental Silver and Colours seem unimportant. I'm seriously beginning to think it's a load of bullshit, and that makes me sad.' The private was as near to tears as he ever would be; he was like a devout Christian who had been confronted with irrefutable proof that God does not exist.

'You're wrong there, Zack,' said Harris gently. 'It makes them all the more important, because they represent all the *best* things *we* believe in. Some of the top brass have had

223

a temporary loss of memory, that's all. But if they don't recover it quickly they'll be queuing for their bowler hats.'

Fazackerley sounded sceptical. 'You don't think they'll close ranks and cover for each other under the old boy's network? I've heard rumours that some of them are already blaming the ordinary soldiers for the lack of success. That's buck passing.'

'I never thought I'd hear an old sweat like you talk like this. It doesn't help, and I'll forget I heard it.'

'Sorry, Sarge, but I've never had cause to spout off like this before. It's shame, not anger, that makes me. The army's my life, and I reckon if the Old Man could have heard me he'd have agreed with every word.'

'That's what we've got to keep in mind, Zack. The army is the Rocks, the Simmos, Zacks and Waggies. What Masefield called "the scum of the earth", and he meant that as a tribute.'

Fazackerley grinned, exposing his toothless gums, his momentary lack of faith dispersed like a puff of smoke in a strong wind. 'You left yourself off that list, Sarge.'

Harris smiled. 'Arse licking will get you nowhere, and just remember that. We've both spoken our minds and the subject is now closed.'

Harris was near to tears himself. He loved the three uncouth, ill-educated men who trusted him so implicitly and saw him as some kind of demi-god who reached decisions with total confidence, whereas he knew how difficult it was. He would rather die than risk their lives, but he would unhesitatingly do so because they would despise him if he faltered in his duty. That, after all, was what the Colours and Silver was all about. They were the tangible form of what no words could adequately express.

224

Chapter 14

'Are you a man of religious persuasion, Sergeant?' The master chewed the question out around the cheroot clamped between his teeth.

Harris, who was peering through one of the bridge portholes observing the ever-changing river scene, was startled by the question and wondered what had prompted McIntyre to ask it.

'I don't go down on my knees at night asking for this and that, although I attend church parade; but I'm not sure I would if it wasn't compulsory,' he replied rather flippantly. 'To be honest I don't give it a lot of thought, and when I do I become confused. I agree with the Sermon on the Mount but can't reconcile that with people having private pews in churches. I thought we were all equal in the eyes of God.'

McIntyre tossed his mangled cheroot into the tin at his feet. 'I wasn't trying to promote a theological discussion. I asked the question because I wondered if you know what today is.'

'Haven't the foggiest. One day is pretty much the same as any other, and has been since we left Rangoon. There's not much point in knowing whether it's Monday or Thursday, distance is more important.'

'Today is Good Friday, which seems a contrary way to describe the day on which Christ was crucified. I'd have thought *bad* was more appropriate.'

Harris smiled. 'You are in an introspective mood this morning, sir.'

'It's a habit one gets into with this kind of life. Normally it's a very solitary existence. Can't talk to the helmsman except to tell him which way to turn the wheel. So one has plenty of time to ruminate on imponderables. Trouble is one never comes up with any answers.'

Harris said, 'He died that we might be forgiven. He died to make us good. I remember that much from my religious upbringing.'

McIntyre shook his head. 'The latter part certainly hasn't been achieved, has it? Half the world is dead set on destroying the other half, and all parties are claiming their cause is right and just and God is on their side, whether it's Christ, Buddha or Mohammed.'

'As a soldier I tend to believe that God − whatever name you give him − is on the side of the big battalions.'

The Scot offered Harris a cheroot, who said, 'I'll take it, but only if you don't mind me putting it in my pipe. I'm out of tobacco.'

'It's a shame to spoil a good smoke, but do as you please. Talking of spoiling a good thing, I wish you could have seen Burma in peacetime.'

'I was in Rangoon before the war started.'

'Rangoon isn't, or rather wasn't, Burma,' snorted McIntyre. 'It was the City of London with topees instead of bowlers. The real Burma was this river and the country it cuts through. Beautiful beyond imagination, and populated by happy-go-lucky people who didn't need the opium we foisted on them as part of their wages. Now look at it! One unwanted conqueror replaced by another one, and the defeated one already making plans for a reconquest. Why? The Japs say they've invaded to free the country from the colonial yoke, never mentioning petrol, and the British are equally hypocritical about their motives.'

Harris found the conversation tedious; it was an argument he had heard too many times. *Real* was an individual conception, and as far as he was concerned it meant characterless barracks, periods of stultifying boredom, and the companionship of men who, like firemen, lived in isolation, waiting to be called out only when they were needed.

'Empire builders must have an excuse in order to live with themselves. And what noble reason brought you here, sir?'

226

The gently chiding tone in his voice removed any suggestion of malice or sarcasm.

'Pure chance. I joined a ship that did a regular run from Tilbury to Rangoon as Second Officer, replacement for a man who hit the bottle too hard and too frequently. I remember we had a hold full of cars, and other western symbols of superiority. We had some trouble with the engines and our turn around in Rangoon was delayed much longer than we anticipated. Life consisted of nothing but shore leave for several weeks, during which time I met an Anglo-Burmese girl and fell in love. But when I asked the Master's permission to marry her – you had to have his blessing in those days – he made no attempt to disguise his horror. His home was in Rangoon, and his Birmingham-born wife was very Cheltenham and very much the memsahib; great pillar of society, with housemaid's knees brought on not by scrubbing floors but an excess of piety. It was out of the question, he said, and if I had any ideas of a future with the Line I should give up any thought of marriage. All doors in polite society would be closed to me. So I jumped ship and married her. I buried my past – I won't bore you with the details – but after a spell of coasting I ended up in Mandalay where I joined the company as a trainee, and by the time I was thirty I was a fully qualified master.'

'We seem to have strayed a long way from our original topic of Good Friday,' said Harris with a grin.

'Not at all. Know what day it was when I jumped ship? Good Friday. The blackest day in the history of mankind, but the day I was handed the key to paradise. Now it's all going up in smoke.'

Harris said, 'Milton wrote a sequel. Don't forget that.'

McIntyre chuckled noisily. 'You've a literary turn of phrase, Sergeant. I'm surprised. Like sailors, soldiers aren't expected to be educated. According to the thakins of Rangoon we're drifters with no real roots. The sailor's only home is his ship, the soldier's his regiment.'

'I know exactly how you feel.'

'Frankly it never bothered me. The river became my life. I spent more time afloat than I did ashore, and my wife was with me. And no matter what anyone thought or said,

227

I was always the Master and she was the mistress, of our self-contained little kingdom.' He stamped his foot on the deck. 'This bridge was *my* throne. Only *I* could say who stepped foot on it, and I exercised that authority very firmly indeed. Sometimes I've invited a village headman up here and turned away a burra sahib. You might think that childish, because only a man who has been forced to bury his past can understand.'

Harris felt an irresistible urge to unburden himself. 'In a sense, you could say I also jumped ship. I buried my past too, but not for quite the same reasons because I lost the girl I was going to marry and was publicly disgraced, although there were winks and nods and assurances that it was only a temporary fall from grace. It was merely politically expedient at the time, and after a suitable interval I would be fully restored with dignity and honour intact. I couldn't stomach that ...'

McIntyre interrupted. 'There's bile in your words, lad. You're dying to tell me about it, and you'll have my undivided attention.'

Harris said, 'Occasionally I've wondered if I made the right decision. I could have weathered the storm, and after a period of hibernation emerged and picked up where I had left off and continued a promising career that everyone confidently predicted would end up with red tabs on my collar. But they were only temporary doubts. The price was too high. It was rather like you giving up the woman you loved in order to become acceptable. My honour was at stake.'

'I'm afraid that honour never entered my mind. I simply opted for happiness, and I've never regretted it because the river has taught me one thing: I am immaterial. Long after I've gone, and irrespective of whether the Japs or the British occupy Burma, the Irrawaddy will continue to flow.'

'Let me tell you what happened.'

But Harris had no time, for McIntyre craned his head sideways like a wary bird sensing the presence of a predator. 'Listen,' he said urgently. 'Aircraft.'

The two men hurried out of the wheelhouse on to the bridge wing and stared at the sky above. Some thirty or forty bombers, the sunlight glinting on their silver fuselages,

228

were flying in perfect formation, and to emphasise their superiority had dispensed with any fighter cover.

'I take back everything I said about religion,' said Harris huskily, 'because I'm praying like hell that they don't spot us.'

McIntyre stabbed a forefinger at the aircraft. 'They'll not be bothering us. They're right on course for Mandalay, and you'd better offer up another prayer that someone sounds the alarm. Mandalay is a very complacent place.' He shook his head. 'Can't figure out whether the Japs have a respect for the Christian calendar or contempt. Rangoon got it at Christmas, Mandalay today.'

The army doctor emerged from his operating theatre and stared at the disappearing armada before hastening on to the bridge. 'If they're heading where I think they are, sir, I suggest you moor alongside the next most convenient place and stay there till we know what kind of havoc the raid has caused. There's no point in taking these very sick men to a town where all the medical facilities have been destroyed. I know that's looking on the gloomy side, but it's better to be safe than sorry.'

Harris said, 'I can drive one of my trucks up and have a look. The only problem is how long will it take me to get there and back? If conditions are anything like those we've encountered it could be a long journey.'

The doctor said, 'Can you ride a motor cycle, Sergeant? Because if you can there's one somewhere aboard. Brought here by a D.R. with a badly shattered leg. Christ knows how he managed to ride it, but he won't need it again because I've had to amputate his leg.'

'I could give it a try,' said Harris. 'I had an old Panther when I was at Sandhurst, and maybe it's a bit like swimming — once you've learnt you never forget.' It occurred to him too late that he should not have mentioned Sandhurst.

The master said, 'There's a refuelling station just below the Ava bridge. I'll tie up there and wait as long as the doctor thinks it advisable. Speaking personally, I'd rather press on to Mandalay because my wife and family are there. But it's Good Friday, and a man should be thinking of others, not himself.' Harris knew the great effort it had required to sound so casual.

The motor cycle was found aft, lashed to the guard rail and covered with a tarpaulin sheet, and Harris wheeled it to the side of the stretcher on which the injured despatch rider was lying. He told him he was going to try and make it to Mandalay and would be very grateful if he could have a brief refresher course on how to ride it.

As he listened to the D.R., he realised that the machine differed very little from his old Panther, and he was surprised to find how easily he could recall what he had to do once he was astride it.

The wounded soldier said, 'I know I'm not going to need it again, Sarge, but I'd like some kind of receipt saying you've taken it. I'm not looking on the black side, but if you don't make it I don't want to be handed a bill. You know what the army is.'

Harris used a sheet of McIntyre's notepaper to write out a receipt which included the machine's official serial number, appreciating the soldier's concern; the army was very strict over lost equipment.

McIntyre moored the steamer alongside a none too substantial wooden jetty, and a gangway was run ashore for Harris to wheel the motor cycle across.

The master said, 'It's not the best of roads, but you shouldn't have too much trouble on a motor bike. I can't imagine many people are heading for Mandalay right now.'

The doctor stepped ashore to speak to Harris without being overheard; his voice grave with concern. 'Find someone in authority who knows what the heck is going on. Don't be fobbed off by some silly arse who thinks the truth is bad for morale. Tell him I have hundreds of extremely sick men on board and I want to know exactly what the hospital position is. I don't want to turn up and find there's nowhere to put them. If we can't go to Mandalay then get firm instructions as to the next best thing to do. Don't stand for any bullshit. Just tell whoever you talk to that you're acting on my orders, and I'll take it to the very highest level if one man dies because of someone's incompetence or indifference. Don't worry about being threatened with insubordination, you're only the errand boy, and you can take it from me that even generals don't argue with doctors.'

He held out his hand. 'Good luck, and don't think you're taking part in the TT. The most important thing is to get there in one piece and return with the information I must have.'

'How long will you wait, sir?'

'Three or four days at the maximum. It's not a long trip in terms of miles, and if you aren't back by then, well, frankly you never will be.'

'What'll you do if that happens?'

'I'll cross that bridge when I come to it. Maybe get the master to head downstream again in the hope of linking up with the retreating army, and pray to Christ they'll have enough transport for the wounded. Frankly I just can't bear to think about it.'

'Well don't, sir, because I'll be back. You have my word for that.' Harris hoped his assurances sounded convincing, because he was riddled with doubts.

The master appeared at Harris's side and handed him a sheet of paper. 'My home address. If you have the time, I'd appreciate it if you called round. Tell my wife that if she and the girls are offered a flight out they must take it. They're not to worry about me. Until you get back I don't know what my own moves will be, but tell her I'll end up in Mandalay some time or other, because the ship belongs to the Company and they'll want it handed over. Tell her not to bother about the house either, I'll attend to everything.'

Harris balanced the motor cycle on its rest, then walked to the stern to tell his men what he was doing. 'Keep an eye on Sister Bradshaw and Miss Carfax. I don't know how long I'll be, but I shan't dawdle.' He paused. 'Obviously you can't wait here indefinitely, and if I'm not back in three days then you'll have to carry on without me. Remember our job is to get the Silver to safety.'

Simmonds said. 'You want to take the Tommy-gun, Sarge?'

'No. I'm going to find it hard enough riding the damn thing without being weighed down with unnecessary equipment. Once I'm off I don't intend stopping for anything.'

Wagstaff said, 'Why not let me go, Sarge. I can ride a

motor bike.' He grinned widely. 'Like you, I'd also like the opportunity to pick up some smokes.'

Harris winked. 'Trust you to know I'm doing this with an ulterior motive.' He was grateful to Wagstaff for relieving the tension and making the trip sound like a jaunt to the corner shop to get something he had run out of.

'See you when you get back, Sarge. An' that ain't whislin' in the dark. If anyone can do it you can.'

As he walked back to the machine he heard his name being called, and looked up and saw Avril and Kitty standing amidships. Avril said, 'Do be careful, *please*.' Her fingers touched her lips and she blew on them.

Kitty Bradshaw called out, 'Mandalay General is the best place to find out what the score is regarding hospital facilities.'

He tied a handkerchief over his mouth to protect himself against the dust, checked to make sure the spare petrol can was full, then kick-started the machine into life and almost came off as he took one hand off the handlebars and tried to wave over his shoulder. He wobbled erratically for three or four hundred yards, like a child taking its first solo ride on a cycle; but the long forgotten skills returned, although he took it cautiously until he felt that he and not the machine was the master. With his newfound confidence he settled down in the saddle and began to enjoy the ride. The slipstream ruffled his hair, and he felt a wild sense of exhilaration as the spokes hummed and the wind whipped his face, drawing tears from his eyes. He regretted not asking the D.R. if he had a pair of goggles.

The road was bumpy and deeply rutted, but no great problem for the powerful well-sprung Norton, and as the road was pretty well clear of traffic he was able to maintain a steady forty miles an hour. It was only when he was approaching the outskirts of the town that the congestion started and the road was clogged with refugees from Mandalay, but these he was able to skirt round. He had heard vague rumblings in the distance, but the encircling hills made it impossible for him to decide for certain whether they were explosions, although he assumed they were.

When he reached the town he did not need to be told

that Mandalay had been caught completely unawares. It was Rangoon all over again, only worse. The streets presented the same dreadful scenes of brutal slaughter, and fires were still burning fiercely. Groups of soldiers were carrying out the same gruesome tasks he had carried out in Rangoon, and fire fighting teams watched impatiently as buildings burned to the ground; a shortage of hose pipes and water had turned them into reluctant spectators.

He stopped by a sergeant in charge of a rescue squad and murmured, 'Not a pretty sight.'

'I'm surprised it isn't worse. They came over in perfect formation and dropped their bombs simultaneously. HEs, anti-personnel, fragmentation, incendiaries ... you name it, they dropped it. And the streets were filled with people, all looking up and thinking how impressive it was.'

'Wasn't the alarm sounded?'

'Well, sort of. They have some screwy system here whereby they have different degrees of alertness – yellow means standby, and red bombers approaching. But the red never got sounded. The people who should have given it all buggered off. Or so I've been told.'

'Where's the best place to get some information, and where's the General Hospital?'

'Information or gossip? There's plenty of one around here, but precious little of the other. You could try the club first, that's where everyone who matters seems to congregate. Never been inside it myself, but that's where the brass wet their whistles. Official HQ is at Maymyo, but that's forty miles away, so if I were you I'd go to the club. If you don't get any joy there at least someone will tell you where the hospital is. Sorry I can't be more helpful, but the only orders I ever get are from my platoon commander. And good luck mate, you'll need it.'

The club proved a waste of time, because it no longer existed. It had received a direct hit and, because the timbers were oiled to combat the voracious ants, had quickly burned to a cinder. There was a large crowd looking at the smouldering ruins and bemoaning the loss of one of Mandalay's favourite watering holes and the destruction of the finest cellar in Burma, but there wasn't an officer

233

in sight. He asked several people to direct him to the garrison headquarters, but the answers were so vague and contradictory that he decided not to bother, reminding himself that the prime purpose of his trip was to find out what the medical facilities were. So he asked the way to the General Hospital, the location of which was not such a closed secret as army HQ.

The hospital had also been hit and though burning was still functioning, although the staff were finding it extremely difficult to cope with the ever increasing influx of casualties. He wandered along corridors lined with stretcher cases, and looked into the wards which branched off and saw that even the spaces between the beds were filled with more victims. Everyone he spoke to was too busy to interrupt their life-saving work to answer his questions; they were too involved with their own critically ill to bother about the fate of some anonymous soldiers many, many miles away. They regarded him as an intruder, someone who was blind to what was happening under his nose and more concerned with far off events.

Eventually Harris was able to find a senior medical officer who was prepared to listen to the reason for his arrival in the city.

'There's not a lot left of Mandalay.' He spoke tersely, enumerating in a crisp dispassionate voice that Harris imagined was the one he used when asking for instruments in the theatre, the extent of the damage. 'The native quarter – mainly wood shanties – had been blown off the map. No one knows how many have died, several thousand at least. The exact number is in doubt because so many are still under the rubble. The marshalling yards are also hit. A consignment of RAF bombs was in some wagons there, and it didn't help when they went off along with some ammunition trucks. Blast was so enormous it blew people into the moat of the fort. There's no electricity, and we've been operating in semi-darkness. There's a problem with the drinking water because it's been polluted. But, believe it or not, we're better off than some of the other hospitals.'

It seemed to Harris that the doctor had suddenly tired of listing the catastrophes, for he said irritably, 'Christ, man, you must have seen it for yourself if you rode here. But to answer the question which brought you here: some trains are still running, and the sick and injured who are movable are being taken to Maymyo and Myitkinya. So if I were you I'd go back and tell the doctor that his best chance is to come here and take pot luck. There's no future in staying aboard a steamer tied up alongside some God forsaken jetty. There's no hope there, but there's a slight one here. Tell him to give up any thoughts of turning back because he'll end up with a ship load of corpses. The Japs are not far off now, so time is very important. Get back and pass that on. I've answered you to the best of my ability. Now if you'll excuse me I've work to do.'

Harris thanked him, sensing he was being dismissed, and was grateful for the abruptness of it because when he got outside he was just in time to floor an army deserter who was about to steal his motor cycle. As the man lay on the ground nursing a fractured jaw he looked up and said aggressively, 'Fuck me, how was I to know it was yours? It's every man for himself now. You can't blame me for that. The fucking place is full of soldiers wandering around looking for someone to tell them what to do. Well, I know what I'm going to do, nick the first thing I find on wheels and piss off, and if you had any sense you'd do the same.'

Harris kicked him twice, solidly in the ribs, feeling the bones crack through his heavy boots. 'Any running you do is going to be bloody agonising,' he said in disgust.

He had one more call to make before he headed back to Ava. He consulted the scrap of paper McIntyre had given him. Below the scribbled address was a crudely drawn map explaining how he could get to his house.

The map was of little use because so many streets were impassable. Some had huge craters, others were blocked by wrecked vehicles and huge mounds of rubble. Even when he found a street he could pass through it was too risky to ride because of carpets of shattered glass, and he was forced to wheel the machine. Eventually, after a most circuitous journey, he found the house, not badly damaged but shuttered and bolted, and no one answered his persistent hammering on the door. Just as he was about to turn away, an old man shuffled up to him. He spoke in broken English. 'Family gone, Myitkyina. Me look after house till come back.' He searched inside his blouse and produced an envelope. 'For when Master come home.'

Harris took it, saying, 'I'll see he gets it.'

As he rode and wheeled the motor cycle through the devastated streets, weaving a perilous course between the countless obstacles which blocked his way, delayed action bombs were still exploding. He thought of making a last minute search for a senior officer, but quickly abandoned the idea; it would be a waste of time. The situation was too chaotic. A major city had been destroyed, the Japs were racing pell mell for it although it was hardly a prize worth seizing. Even if he found a full general he would get no better advice than he had been given at the hospital. No one was going to worry too much about a steamer full of wounded soldiers. Everyone was in the same boat.

He turned a corner and was halted by a barbed wire barrier which concertinaed the road. The one gap in it was blocked by a red and white striped pole resting on wooden trestles and the checkpoint was manned by four armed Red Caps sitting in a jeep. A sergeant got out and said belligerently, 'Just where do you think you're heading?' He was well over six feet tall with shoulders to match. The peak of his cap followed the lines of his nose and was almost touching it.

'Ava, where I've come from. There's a hospital ship moored there filled with wounded. I drove here to spy out the land.'

'Unarmed? A likely fucking story. I'm pissed off rotten rounding up deserters who have cock and bull stories as to why they should bugger off and leave everyone else in the shit. You're worse than the pi-dogs roaming the streets. You're under arrest. I'm taking you to the nick.'

He gestured to his men who clambered out of the jeep and pointed their rifles at Harris.

'Put him in the back, and if he makes a fuss, handcuff the bastard. Jack, you follow on his motor bike.'

Harris sucked in a lungful of air; being arrested for no reason seemed to be an occupational hazard. He tried to explain in more detail how he came to be in Mandalay but the big policeman was not interested. 'Produce some written authority, otherwise save your breath till you see the Provost Marshall. And you'd better be convincing because he's sick and tired of dealing with spineless fuckers like you.'

The jeep stopped outside a gaunt red-brick building which had been taken over from the civil police, and Harris was quick marched at gun point into the guard room where the sergeant took a seat behind the desk, entered the prisoner's name, rank and number into a book as large as a family bible, then charged him with desertion in the face of the enemy.

'Isn't this all very improper?' queried Harris. 'Shouldn't there be an officer present? Someone who will at least listen.'

Without looking up the sergeant said, 'In normal times, but times aren't normal, are they?'

'You're being stupidly unreasonable,' protested Harris.

'All right. Produce some written authority as to why you're here.'

'It was my own decision, but I do have a note from the D.R. I borrowed the Norton from.'

'Save it for wiping your arse. That doesn't prove a thing. unless you can produce the bloke who wrote it. Okay, lads, take him away.'

Harris broke free from the restraining arms that were about to lead him off. 'Just what were you in civvy street?' he asked incredulously.

Again the sergeant did not look up. 'What I am now. A copper. A Detective Sergeant in the Met. And the same rules apply: you're guilty till proved innocent.' He tapped the side of his nose. 'I can sniff villains out, and you stink to high heaven. Now piss off out of my sight. If there's one thing I can't stomach it's cowardice. They'll throw the book at you, Harris. If you don't face a firing squad I just hope and pray you do your time in an Indian clink, because then you'll wish to Christ they *had* shot you.'

The sergeant made a gesture and Harris was marched off and bundled into a cell with a grilled window well above head height. There was a wooden bunk against the wall, a solitary chair, and a bucket in one corner. One of the policemen said,

'Don't be too harsh on him. He's got an impossible job. The place is full of deserters.'

Harris heard the cell door being locked and he stretched out on the bunk trying to curb his anger and frustration, telling himself that all would be well once he had seen the Provost. But hours passed without anyone coming to see him. He pounded on the door and bellowed at the top of his voice, but no one took any notice. Eventually he returned to the bunk and drifted into an exhausted sleep.

He was awakened by the first rays of sunlight shining through the window and striking his eyelids. He sat on the edge of the bunk and massaged his cramped limbs. The bed was as hard as a slab of concrete. He heard a key rattling in the lock and the door opened and a private came in carrying a tin tray with a mug of tea and a thick slice of buttered bread on an enamel plate.

'When do I get to see the Provost?' asked Harris.

'Christ knows, mate. I'm in the same sodding boat as you are. Waiting to be court martialled for desertion. A ripe bloody joke that is. I'd just been discharged from hospital and was wandering around looking for my outfit when the Red Caps picked me up. That was five days ago. Since then I've been doing fatigues. Not complaining though. Better than being shipped to the front.'

Harris said, 'I *must* get out of here. There are several hundred men and some white women depending on me to get back. If I don't, God knows what will happen to them.' And he explained in detail why he had come to Mandalay.

The soldier shrugged. 'Nothing I can do. You'll just have to sit tight and sweat it out. You'll have to be patient though, that bastard of a sergeant is in no hurry to sort things out.'

Harris remembered the deadline he had set for his return. If he did not meet it, the hospital ship might return down river, and that would be fatal, while his own party would continue on to India. Without his presence it was doubtful if they would make it. Who would assume command? Would the others, especially Miss Carfax, take his orders? Wagstaff was the obvious choice and he wished he had made his own views clear before he left, but Wagstaff was junior to the

238

other two privates, and loyal though they were they were both proud men.

'I don't suppose you could be a bit absent-minded and leave that door unlocked?'

'More than my life is worth to shit on my own doorstep. That sergeant would string me up by the balls.'

Harris got up. 'No use brooding. Might as well make the best of it.'

'That's the ticket. Just keep your fingers crossed and hope you're weighed off before the Japs arrive and use you for bayonet practice.'

Harris said, 'Put the tray on the bunk. It doesn't look very appetising, but I'm famished.'

As the soldier put the tray on the bed, Harris picked up the chair and brought it down on the back of his head. 'Sorry to have to resort to violence,' he muttered. He hauled the unconscious man to his feet and hefted him on to the bunk, then rolled him over until his head was facing the wall. He tossed the contents of the mug under the bunk and threw the bread after it. Then he picked up the tray, retrieved the key, locked the cell door behind him and put the tray, empty mug and plate on the floor outside.

He found himself in a long corridor lined with cells from which loud shouts came pouring. It was comforting to know they would go unheeded. He passed an open door, peeped inside and saw four Red Caps sitting at a table immersed in a game of cards. He slipped past, opened a door at the end of the corridor and found himself in a courtyard where a row of jeeps and lorries were parked in neat rows. The Norton was upright on its stand near to where a sentry sat in a purloined deck chair reading a book. His rifle was at his feet. He looked up and asked in a disinterested voice, 'Where you spring from Sarge?'

'Just came up with a message from the Provost to tell the sergeant here that all men under detention are to be turned out for rescue work. The sergeant said I could take the Norton as the bloke who arrived on it won't be needing it again.'

'Help yourself. But if you ask me I think it's a waste of time expecting those bastards to help anyone. At the first opportunity they'll bugger off again, and who can blame them?'

Harris's heart was thumping like a riveting hammer and he could feel the sweat breaking out all over him. But he knew he had to remain calm; if he showed the slightest agitation the sentry would become suspicious and sound the alarm. Although he was innocent, Harris knew damned well that he would have sealed his fate if he was caught trying to escape.

His mouth felt dry and parched, and he said as casually as he could, 'Give me a hand with the gates.'

'I'll wheel your ruddy bike too,' said the soldier sarcastically. 'Let yourself out, it ain't locked.'

Harris said, 'Don't ask me to do you a favour when you need one.'

He kicked the rest upright and wheeled the machine towards the gate, expecting any moment to hear a voice bellow, 'Halt, or I'll shoot you,' but when he turned his head he saw the sentry had returned to his book. He pushed the wheel against one half of the gate and felt it swing open. He went through and closed it behind him. Then he mounted, kick started the machine and drove off.

He turned down the nearest side street driving very slowly, resisting the almost overwhelming temptation to open the throttle, knowing a speeding motor cyclist would immediately arouse suspicion. He kept off the main roads thinking they were more likely to be patrolled, and took a circuitous route through a series of narrow alleys. He passed gutted and still burning buildings and the occasional rescue party which did not give him a second glance. It took him some time to reach the outskirts, not being at all sure where he was, but when he reached the road he recognised as the one he had travelled up he felt he could give the machine its head. He knew it was extremely unlikely that anyone would bother to give chase.

The mobility of the motor cycle enabled him to drive round the mass of natives fleeing from the ruined city with no definite destination in mind, spurred on by the knowledge that no matter where they ended up it could be no worse than what they were leaving behind. Unlike

240

the Europeans, there was no question of being evacuated by air.

By the time he arrived back at Ava the motor cycle had lost all its appeal. The inside of his thighs where his shorts had ridden up were red and blistered, and his face felt as if it had been pitted by a thousand needles. He let the machine lie where he let it fall on the river bank and went aboard to seek out the doctor. He had no further use for the Norton, and he did not give a damn if the receipt he had signed ended up in the hands of some officious officer who would pass it on to the appropriate authority urging disciplinary action. So much equipment had been abandoned in panic that the deliberate loss of a motor cycle seemed irrelevant: it was almost a gesture of defiance. Of one thing he was certain, he would never abandon the priceless cargo in the two trucks. They were a symbol of hope in a sea of despair.

Harris recounted the chaos he had witnessed in Mandalay and the advice he had received at the hospital, wisely refraining from mentioning his brush with the Red Caps. The medical officer listened intently, then said, 'Thanks for everything, Sergeant. If I ever find someone who'll listen, I'll recommend you for an award. I'll also say how invaluable your two young ladies have been. Seems it's Hobson's choice for me. It's risky going to Mandalay, but even riskier staying here. I know the Japs have a reputation for being inhuman bastards, but if the worst comes to the worst I can't believe they won't let us look after our wounded. The Geneva Convention still exists. I'll ask the master to get cracking as soon as possible. I know he's just as anxious as I am to move off.'

The words reminded Harris of the letter in his breast pocket, and he set off to find McIntyre who was on the bridge peering in the direction of Mandalay.

'How is it there, Sergeant?'

'Pretty grim, sir, but I think this will cheer you up.' He handed over the letter, saying, 'It was given to me by an old man who said your wife and family had gone to Myitkyina.'

'That will have been Samuel. Been my head boy all the years I've been in Mandalay. Couldn't have left the place in better hands.'

241

He tore open the envelope and read the contents, his brow furrowed in concentration. He passed the letter to Harris. 'That's a load off my mind. Seems they've been guaranteed a flight out.'

'What'll you do, sir?'

McIntyre shrugged. 'Report to the Company office, and do as I'm told. They may want to sink the ship to stop it falling into Jap hands, but if I have my say I'll offer to take it down river again and see if I can help the army in any way. Sooner or later they'll have to cross the Chindwin in order to get to India, and they'll need every vessel they can lay their hands on. My draught is a bit much for the Chindwin, shallow draughted stern wheelers are more suited to the conditions, but hell, in these times it's shit or bust. You don't turn your nose up at the offer of a mule because you'd prefer a thoroughbred.'

Harris said, 'It's been an honour and a privilege to have met you, sir, and I hope the future is full of your own brand of Good Fridays. I'm sorry I've got to shove off, but I have my orders, although a lot of people may think they're unimportant in times like this.'

'Don't think like that, lad. I know a lot of skippers who'll want to remain on their bridge if they have orders to scuttle their commands. That'll seem crazy to some, but that's only because they don't understand. Get your Silver and Colours to India, and make sure they're with you when you return. And if you were to ask those poor devils below I think you'd find the majority share my sentiments. They've taken a terrible hiding and they want their dignity and pride restored. They may come from different regiments, but they're all linked by the same traditions.'

Harris went aft and told his men to round up enough fit soldiers and members of the crew to beach the rafts and unload the trucks, then he went forward to find Sister Bradshaw and Miss Carfax.

He found them in their loaned cabin lying down on the bunks. They started to say how relieved they were to see him safely back, but he cut them short. 'Get your things together. We haven't much time. The Master wants to cast off as soon as possible.'

242

Kitty Bradshaw said softly but firmly, 'I've changed my mind. I'm going on to Mandalay. I can still be of use to the doctor during the trip, and I can find a job in a hospital when we get there.'

He said heatedly, 'Don't be so foolish, Kitty. I know how you feel, but there's nothing left of Mandalay, everyone is being evacuated. There's no shortage of nurses there, it's more question of getting them and their patients to safety, so come to India with me. You'll be much more use there. When the army turns up they'll need looking after. They will have marched the entire length of Burma.'

She shook her head. 'Sorry, Sergeant, but I must do what I think is best.'

He shrugged resignedly. 'I can't order you to do anything against your will, but I do wish you'd listen . . .'

She silenced him with a curt wave of her hand. 'That's that then. So don't try and talk me out of it. I'll go and tell the MO I'm staying.'

She returned a few minutes later looking extremely crestfallen. 'Seems I'm coming with you after all. Doctor's orders. He said he had no option but to press on to Mandalay, even though he didn't know what was waiting, but he sees no point in my going. Said I might even end up in a POW camp where I'd be no ruddy use to anyone.'

Avril got up from the bunk. 'I'd better see if Nellie wants to go to Mandalay. If she's got any sense she won't, but I must give her the choice. I'll give her the names of some people at the club who'll see she gets everything she needs.'

'There isn't any club,' said Harris harshly, 'and it's extremely unlikely your friends will still be there. Far better to let her come with us.'

'I must let her decide. She can have what jewellery I have left, and I'll give her signed authority to draw whatever money she needs.'

'The banks have closed,' he said angrily. 'They've transferred everything to Calcutta. India's the only place where you can get any money.'

'Burma is her homeland, India is a foreign country. The Japs won't harm her if she chooses to stay. There's no reason.'

'She worked for you, and they may take that into account. The Fifth Column are going to be falling over each other to ingratiate themselves with the Japs and they'll name everyone who was even remotely pro-British. Apart from that, what on earth will she do in a city that is in ruins?'

She shrugged. 'Perhaps make her way to her own people, I don't know, but I'll put all the points you've made to her. But she must be allowed to decide.'

Harris smiled. 'All right, Avril, do it your way. When we started out I thought Nellie was just someone who brushed your hair and did your nails. I'm glad I was wrong.'

'No, you were right. I was wrong, and I'm not ashamed to admit it. I want to look after her as her friend not her mistress, which is why I won't order her to do anything.'

She found the maid helping to manhandle the two trucks ashore, and when Avril suggested she might prefer to remain in Burma Nellie firmly rejected the offer; she was adamant, she wanted to go to India as she had no wish to leave her mistress. What she did not say was that she had no intention of letting Private Wagstaff out of her sight. He had been too persistent in stressing the advantages of her remaining in Burma, so insistent she suspected he was trying to get rid of her.

When the trucks were ready to leave, McIntyre and the doctor went ashore to see them off.

Harris said, 'I feel a bit of a swine deserting you like this, sir, but as I explained to the Master I have a job to do.'

The doctor gave a wan but understanding smile. 'I know, he told me, and like him I understand. So don't feel guilty about it. We both have precious cargoes. Let's just keep our fingers crossed and hope we can see them to safety.'

They shook hands, and Harris gave the order to, 'Mount up,' and when everyone was aboard he gave the signal to move off. He gave a long blast of farewell on his horn, which was answered by a louder, bolder hoot of the ship's siren, and when he looked back he saw the Master and the MO standing on the bridge waving.

Harris set course for Monywa, from where he hoped to follow the course of the Chindwin as far as Kalewa where he planned to cross the river into the unknown Kabaw

Valley that was also known as Death Valley because of the particularly virulent form of malaria which flourished there. The thought did not daunt him; with good reliable transport it should not provide any great problems.

The road was not good but it was motorable, and although there were still countless refugees stretching as far as the eye could see, they were not the hindrance they had been earlier on for by now most of their mechanised transport had broken down and been abandoned, most of the bullocks had died from exhaustion, and everyone was on foot. The dead were still very much in evidence, but the fleeing multitude seemed to be spurred on by some new sense of urgency. Unknown to Harris it was the thought of water, but unlike animals sensing water ahead they were running away from it, for the monsoon would soon break and when it came there would be little hope of ever reaching India. Dried up chaungs would become torrents, and fordable rivers impassable for all but the very strongest.

The heat in the trucks was unbearable, but spirits in the party were surprisingly high for they all felt that in terms of distance travelled they had completed the major part of their journey. As Wagstaff cheerfully remarked, they were 'Well past Tattenham Corner and 'eadin' for the 'ome straight.'

Chapter 15

Monywa was now well behind them, and although the road had petered out into little more than a dust track that ran through dense jungle, they continued to make what in the circumstances was reasonable progress. Occasionally they passed a village, but often hours went by without them seeing any humans other than refugees who plodded on with dogged persistence.

As the miles rolled away under the wheels of the two trucks, Harris could not recall ever seeing country which provided so many startling contrasts in such a short period: some areas were almost Tyrolean, others reminded him of the Scottish Highlands, then the scenery would change like a slide in a magic lantern and lush green hills would be replaced by ridge after ridge of brown, arid crags, when the track was covered with razor sharp rocks brought down by the monsoon rains which threatened to tear the tyres to shreds. And always the view ahead drew them like a beckoning finger, for in the distance was safety.

To the west the Chin Hills rose above a fertile plain through which the Myittha flowed toward the Chindwin at Kalewa and nearby Shwegyin, which was only a short distance from the Kabaw Valley which led to Palel, the first town in India. To the north towards Homalin were the imposing heights of the Naga Hills dominated by the peak of Suramati, the highest in Burma, shrouded in mist, largely unexplored and reputed to be the wettest place in the world and the habitat of head hunters. In less harrowing circumstances they would have found it breathtakingly beautiful; as they would not be

246

going that way it held no fears for them, but it did serve the purpose of reminding them that the route they had chosen could have been far worse.

One morning before the sun burnt like a blow lamp and while the breeze which blew through the open windows that fluttered the canvas hoods was still fairly cool, Harris became aware of the continuous hooting of Wagstaff's horn, and through his rear window he could see the constant morse-like flashing of headlights. He braked to a halt and poked his head out of the window and saw Wagstaff hurrying towards him.

'Trouble?'

'You can say that again, Sarge. Couldn' be worse. Fink a big end's gone. Bangin' away like a 'airy arsed pongo in a Port Said knockin' shop. It might be okay for a few more miles, but I'm certain of one fing, it's a job wot's too big for me.'

'We'll just have to keep going until it packs up. Then figure out the next move.'

'I'll 'ave to nurse it like a sick baby, so don't go racin' a'ead, Sarge.'

The truck lasted another dozen or more miles before it died on Wagstaff with a frightening series of clatters and bangs. Steam hissed from the radiator which was so hot Wagstaff ordered everyone to dismount in case it blew up.

'She's a write off, Sarge, an' no mistake.' He sounded as disconsolate as someone saying farewell to a much loved friend.

Harris was less emotionally affected. 'Wagstaff, get the wheels off and stow them in my truck. I'll also have the battery and anything else which might come in useful as a replacement. Anything that is not absolutely essential will have to be dumped out of my truck, and I'm afraid that includes the chairs and settee. From now on it's strictly steerage.' He called out sharply to Avril, aware that what he was about to tell her to do added harshness to his voice, 'Miss Carfax, you'd better sort through your things and decide what you can do without. You'll have to be ruthless.'

Avril puckered her lips, but to his surprise expressed no disagreement; in fact she seemed to go out of her way to

247

treat the whole thing with a degree of flippancy. With a cry of, 'Who's for tennis?' she thumped the tennis balls high into the air, then hurled the racquets after them. Then she got back into the truck and tossed out the gramophone and records which were quickly followed by her suitcases and vanity box which hit the ground and burst open, spilling their contents. The dresses, mink, expensive lingerie, shoes, bottles of perfume and beauty aids, lay strewn around like a requiem for a never-to-return way of life. She retrieved the dress she had worn at the party at Yenyanyaung, because she suddenly remembered that Harris had asked her to wear it when he took her out to dinner.

Then to his amazement she suddenly burst out laughing and he feared she was hysterical over the loss of her precious wardrobe. He was relieved when she said, 'I can't help thinking someone is going to get the shock of their life if they pass this way and see the local women all dressed up as if they were going to the races.'

Harris felt ashamed and compelled to excuse himself. 'Sorry, Avril, but food and water and petrol are going to be much more important. I'll also have to transfer the Silver, and I'll be carrying twice the number of passengers as before. It's going to be touch and go.'

'I honestly don't mind at all,' she said, and he knew she meant it. 'I'm yours to honour and obey. With all my worldly goods I thee endow to do with as you wish.' She bowed as if in obeisance, and he could not restrain the smile that creased his face.

'You've taken it in good spirit.'

'That's only because I love you, and I'm scared of putting you off.'

'Off what?' he asked, bewildered.

'Loving me,' she replied disarmingly. 'You know you do, but you can't bring yourself to admit it.'

He said, 'I wish you'd drop the subject, it's very tedious.' He knew his voice lacked the conviction he intended and was aware, much against his will, that he enjoyed hearing what she said. He heard himself adding rather feebly, 'In different circumstances, and I'm not just talking about the present, things might have been different.' What he wanted to say but could not,was that, yes, he had, to use a trite phrase, fallen in love with her, but the past presented an insurmountable barrier to any hopes of future happiness.

Before he had time to walk away, as he intended, she embraced him and kissed him firmly on the mouth. 'David, you can't run away for ever from whatever it is you're running away from. I don't care what it is, but I know I'm not going to let you run away from me. I've never been in love before, and now I am I'm not going to relinquish it, not without a fight anyway.'

He repelled her with a force he did not intend, knowing the violence was a cloak for the unexpected feeling of tenderness which surged through him like a warm glow. But it was no time, he told himself, to become involved in a personal relationship that would require total honesty on his part about the past, and that he was not prepared to do, for it was buried as deep as any legendary pirate's treasure; except that in his case if it was ever unearthed it would not bring wealth and happiness but only the knowledge of disgrace.

Avril held back the tears she felt prickling her eyes and walked away, saying as light heartedly as she could, 'I'm sure there's some other stuff I can toss out. I'm an expert when it comes to unburdening.'

Kitty Bradshaw, who had observed it all with wry amusement, said, 'Pity I have no jumble to clear out. I think she enjoyed it.'

Harris said sharply, 'You don't think I did, do you?'

'God, you can be a prickly so and so. You mean far more to her than those belongings. Most men would be flattered if a young girl told them she loved them, but all you can do is go off in a huff. You don't deserve her, but I'll tell you one thing − as sure as God made little green apples, you've got her whether you like it or not, and your attempts to humiliate her will only make her more determined.'

Harris ignored her, turned away, cupped his hands, and shouted to his men to transfer the Silver from the broken down truck to his own. 'If it's too heavy to lift, then unpack it and ruddy well recrate it. And get a move on.' His tone was uncharacteristically bullying.

Fazackerley muttered, 'Jesus, the sooner we get to India

249

and he sees the back of that girl, the better it's going to be for the rest of us.'

Wagstaff said, 'Zack, you ain't no student of 'uman nature, an' that's a fact. 'E's been bit by the love bug, but there's no way 'es gonna admit it. 'E's gonna just go on scratchin' hisself till he goes roun' the twist.'

'Why? She isn't a bad looker.'

'If I was able to answer that I wouldn' be a 'umble soddin' private sweatin' my bollocks off an' bein' ordered to shift a ton of silver from one truck to annuver.'

Simmonds said, 'When you two've finished poking your noses into what don't concern you, maybe we can get around to the Silver because if we can't shift it without unpacking we'll be here all ruddy day.'

Wagstaff said, 'All right, Simmo, but let's not rely on your brute force and ignorance. A little savvy is required 'ere.'

He took the dah from the truck and walked over to a bamboo thicket and cut down four stout poles. When he returned he said, 'When those wogs built the pyramids they didn't cart the stones on their backs, they used rollers.' He winked. 'An' that's what we're going to do. We can rest 'em against the tailboard an' slide the crate down, then we do the opposite to get it in the Sarge's truck.'

Simmonds lashed a tow rope to the crate and stood in the truck like the anchor man in a tug of war team, while the other two placed the poles in position. They were suddenly aware that Sergeant Harris had joined them.

'What in God's name are you three idiots up to?' His voice was mellow and lacked any real criticism.

Wagstaff grinned. 'Jus' cuttin' the 'ard bit out of the labour, Sarge.'

'Why not let me reverse my truck onto this one, then we can use the poles as rollers?'

Fazackerley said, 'I was going to suggest that myself, but you know Waggie — he thinks he's the only one with brains.'

Wagstaff grinned. 'No wonder I can never crack nuts proper.'

It took them half an hour to transfer the crate and secure it, and on completion of the exhausting task Harris said,

'Well done, lads, I reckon we're entitled to an extra ration of water.'

The water was warm and brackish, but to the privates it was nectar. The sergeant had got over his bad-tempered mood, and their relationship was back to normal.

Harris decided there was little point in pressing on as too little daylight now remained and they might as well settle for the night.

After they had eaten, he suggested that it would be a good idea if everyone got as much sleep as possible as he wanted to make an earlier than normal start; with only one vehicle which was considerably overloaded, progress would be even slower than before and they would be forced to make extra halts to avoid overtaxing the engine and springs. He also volunteered to keep the first guard, and as he sat with the Tommy-gun resting across his knees he recalled the scene with Avril during which he had lost his temper and decided, if only in fairness to her, that at the first suitable opportunity he would explain why it was pointless for her to think their relationship could ever extend beyond friendship. When they parted he wanted her to know that, if only things had been different, his attitude would not have been the same.

They woke next morning to find that every inch of exposed flesh was covered with little blood blisters which, with the prickly heat from which they already suffered, made them want to scratch themselves until they bled, but that was something they dare not do for risk of turning the bites into festering sores. They had not felt or seen the insects that had bitten them and it was no consolation when Nellie said they were polaung, a species of tiny black fly, because there was nothing they could do about them.

The men had discovered that by removing their shirts and exposing their bodies to the sun they obtained some relief for their prickly heat, and it proved equally effective against the irritations of the polaung bites. But that same luxury was denied to the women who were forced to endure the torment of flesh that felt as if it had been rubbed down with sandpaper.

Two days after transferring the crate of Silver, they encountered their first rain, and although it was of short duration it fell in penny-sized drops which quickly turned the track into a muddy quagmire in which the wheels spun uselessly, forcing them to get out and cut small branches to put under the wheels to get extra purchase so that the vehicle could be manhandled onto firmer ground. The rain literally stung when it fell on them, and served as a reminder of how impossible conditions would become when the monsoon started in earnest.

In the excessive humidity which came with the rain, they also encountered their first leeches. They were not aware of their existence until they found them clinging to their skin by the dozens.

They discovered them when they woke up one morning: black loathsome creatures which crawled into every orifice and even found their way through the lace holes of their boots. Some which had not had time to feed were no bigger than matchsticks, others had gorged themselves on blood until they were longer and fatter than a man's thumb.

Avril screamed in horror when she saw them and tried to tear one off with her fingers, but Kitty forcibly restrained her. 'Just hang on, I'll show you what to do.'

The scream brought the four soldiers running to the truck, and Harris said, 'Don't panic, Avril, we've all managed to pick some up.'

Kitty said, 'You'd better listen very carefully to what I have to say, otherwise you'll end up with sores that won't heal. You mustn't try to pull them off because they'll inject some kind of liquid that prevents the blood clotting, and there's the added risk you'll leave a bit of them behind. A cigarette end, or a pinch of salt on their tail, is best. They'll just drop off then.'

Harris said ruefully, 'It'll have to be salt; we've no cigarettes left.'

Wagstaff coughed apologetically, 'That ain't exactly true, Sarge, what I said about 'avin' no fags left, I mean. I've 'ung on to a private little 'oard because I didn' want them two scroungers to be on the ear'ole. I been ration'n myself to the odd drag 'ere an' there when no one was lookin'. I didn' see why I should share them, because they've puffed away their own like there was a NAAFI just up the road.'

Kitty said, 'As you've cleansed your conscience, Private Wagstaff, Miss Carfax and I will rely on salt and you can share your cigarettes with your comrades.' She turned to Harris. 'From the little I know about leeches, once they've found human blood they'll pass the message on and there'll be others queuing up to take their place, so from now on every morning we'll strip off and thoroughly search each other. Apart from the risk of infection, if they aren't removed properly there's a danger that the loss of blood will lead to something really nasty. I'll hand out some iodine which may not help, but it can't do any harm.'

From then on the body searches became a regular routine, and to their surprise they lost their earlier dread and became quite accustomed, almost resigned, to seeing their legs, arms and bodies covered with the slimy black creatures.

'What puzzles me, Sister,' said Wagstaff as he worked on Simmonds with the glowing end of a cigarette, 'is what the little buggers do when there ain't no one around like us to provide a tasty meal.'

'That's a question I can't answer. God really does move in a mysterious way, his wonders to perform. Not so long ago the medical profession believed that a little blood letting was a cure all, and they used leeches for the purpose. Maybe that's why they were created and not to make our lives a misery.'

Simmonds said, 'My old Dad was a keen gardener, and I remember when I was a kid him saying, "God in his infinite wisdom created the black fly." I reckon he'd say the same for leeches.'

Kitty said, 'He was a man who had clearly learned to come to terms with nature.'

Simmonds grunted as Wagstaff missed his aim and contacted bare flesh with the end of his glowing cigarette. 'I don't think you're right, Sister. My Dad hated black flies and used to jump up and down with joy as he sprayed them, so I don't think he was paying the Almighty a compliment. More likely it was his way of saying He had had an off day.'

Two or three days later, no one could be sure how long it was and no one could be bothered to work it out exactly, they halted for the night in a small clearing well away from

253

the main stream of refugees who continued to foul the ground and pollute the water, and Private Simmonds called Sergeant Harris inside. He was enveloped in a blanket, looking far from well, and he said, 'Sorry to be a nuisance, Sarge, but I feel real ropey. I wondered if Sister Bradshaw could give me some kind of pick-me-up.'

Harris had never known the big Yorkshireman express concern about his health before. As he liked to say, he was 'built like a brick shithouse' and the unexpected admission worried the sergeant.

'I'm sure she can, Simmo, but what exactly is wrong?'

'If you don't mind, Sarge, I'd prefer her to have a look first because I'm real out of sorts, and if I take this blanket off the others are bound to see and I don't want that. No point in worrying them with my problems. They've got enough of their own.'

Harris clapped him encouragingly on the shoulder. 'It'll be a secret just the three of us will share. Nip inside the truck and I'll send Sister Bradshaw. I'll see the others are kept occupied.'

Behind the protective cover of the canvas hood, Simmons said, 'I'm afraid I'll have to strip off to show you properly, Sister. It isn't a pretty sight.'

'Let me worry about that.'

When Simmonds dropped the blanket, undid his shorts and removed his shirt, Kitty Bradshaw, accustomed as she was to many forms of sickness, was unable to suppress a whistle of concern, but she quickly composed herself and adopted her best and most comforting bedside voice. 'As you say, not a pretty sight, but I've seen it before and we'll soon have you on the mend.'

The huge private's joints and limbs were abnormally swollen, and even his face was excessively puffy. When she pressed firmly on the flesh of one thigh her fingers left a depression which took some time to fill out again.

'How do you feel in yourself?' she asked matter-of-factly, anxious not to pass on her own alarm.

'Well, I've got awful guts ache, and a kind of burning pain all over, and walking is sheer agony.'

'Any palpitations?'

254

'No worse than indigestion.'

'What you need is plenty of rest, so for a start you'll be excused all duties. I'll give you something to help you sleep, then I'll sort through my little chest and see what medicine I can find.'

'How bad is it, Sister?' he asked anxiously. 'I'd rather know the truth.'

'It's not good, but it's not as bad as you fear.' And she added with a conviction she did not feel the medical profession's time-honoured soporific, 'You'll be up and about in no time.' She was not being deliberately complacent, she just wanted to relieve him of the terrible fear that must have been gnawing away at his insides and give herself time to consider the situation a little more calmly and with greater detachment.

When he was asleep she slipped out of the truck to find Harris. 'We'd better sit in the cabin and have a quiet heart to heart,' she told him.

They sat side by side on the bench seat in total silence, each waiting for the other to speak. Harris was the first. 'All right, Kitty, let me have it, both barrels.'

'I've seen many similar cases during my years here, and I'm pretty sure it's beri-beri which is endemic in most tropical countries. It's a Sinhalese word which literally means weakness. A lot of research has been carried out, particularly in the Philippines, and here, but there's still a lot more to do. From what I recall from a lecture I attended in Rangoon a long time ago, it's generally accepted that it's caused by malnutrition and a vitamin deficiency. Some experts say the main cause is the eating of polished rice in preference to the more nutritious unpolished variety. Others pooh-pooh the idea, saying it has a bacteriological origin. But it still has something to do with rice, and as you know we've been eating a lot of it.'

'We've been eating other stuff too.'

'I know, but that doesn't help me much. You've got to realise that when I attended that lecture it was all rather academic at the time. When you're a nurse, as I was then, in an efficient and well-equipped hospital, you don't worry too much about the medical aspects of a particular illness.

You just administer the treatment the doctor prescribes.'

'And in the case of beri-beri, that is?'

'A well-balanced diet with additional vitamins, but that is a tall order, placed as we are.'

'I'll admit our meals have lacked variety, but we've all eaten the same and I've been scrupulously fair to see we all get equal amounts. So why poor Simmonds?'

'I don't know,' she replied, raising her voice. 'Why did you get malaria when no one else did? Why do some people get cancer and others don't? You could ask the same damn question about every disease. What I do know is that Private Simmonds is a very sick man. Because he's the biggest and strongest, perhaps he needs to eat more, so I suggest you revise your policy of fair shares for all. There's one other thing: we can't hope to keep this from the others; all we can do is play down the seriousness.'

For several days following, Private Simmonds was carefully nursed by Sister Bradshaw and Avril who took it in turns to see he was never left unattended, and his diet was as varied and plentiful as the now rapidly diminishing stocks of food permitted. When they had left Yenyanyaung there had been no fear of acute shortage, but the contents of several tins when opened had been off. Possibly they had been punctured and contaminated in some way. Whatever the reason, they had to be discarded. Only one thing was certain, the condition of Private Simmonds showed no signs of improving.

In a desperate attempt to obtain fresh meat, Harris frequently sent out Wagstaff and Fazackerley in search of game, but they invariably returned empty handed. They either lacked the rudimentary skills of hunting or their quarry was too wary or had been decimated by the natives who had fled their villages. When a further week elapsed, Kitty Bradshaw was forced to confide in Harris, 'We've done all that's humanly possible. All we can hope to do is keep him alive until we get to a hospital.'

Simmonds lay in the back of the bouncing, jolting truck, bearing his suffering with incredible courage and fortitude, suppressing an almost irresistible urge to scream aloud because he was so pain-racked, and even managing to crack the odd joke about his bloated and deformed limbs.

Harris ordered the canvas hood to be erected to provide some relief from the relentless sun, but it turned the interior into a cloche and he wondered if it was an improvement. Simmonds did not seem to care.

Fazackerley and Wagstaff tried to entice him into playing pontoon, but that was too much even for the gentle Yorkshireman who constantly apologised for being such a nuisance and meekly did everything he was told because he did not wish to cause any offence. He found little relief in the occasional sponging down that Avril and Kitty subjected him to whenever they came across water, but submitted to it because he knew they thought it was doing him good. He just wished he could drink it. He even smoked the odd lighted cigarette that Wagstaff placed between his parched lips, although it tasted vile and did nothing to ease the dagger sharp pain in his chest. He appreciated everyone's ministrations, but told himself he wouldn't mind being put out of his misery, he was such a burden.

One evening, as Wagstaff and Fazackerley were stretched out under the tailboard of the truck having eaten their meal, the Cockney said, 'We've often joked about old Simmo bein' like a cart 'orse – well, I wish 'e bloody well was. No one'd let a animal suffer like that; they'd put a round in its 'ead.' He started weeping silently, his shoulders rising and falling as he tried to stifle the sobs that racked him.

'Waggy, you've got to take a hold of yourself. Bawling your eyes out like a kid isn't going to help him. We've just got to cross our fingers and hope for a miracle.'

Chapter 16

Day after never-varying day they drove at a tortoise pace along the truck-wide dust track that ended where they would have to cross the Chindwin at Shwegyin, their speed dictated by several factors: they needed to save Simmonds from any further and unnecessary jolting, the need to nurse the grossly overloaded truck, the short but heavy downpours that were recurring with more frequency and violence, and the mounting plight of the refugees whose tenacity and determination were being increasingly eroded by thirst, starvation and decimating epidemics. Often leaderless and deprived of any information many lacked the inner drive so essential if they were to continue, and simply lay down to die, all hope abandoned. The more determined pressed on, their eyes sunken and bright with fever. Some mothers clutched long-dead babies to their breasts, their feet driven on by the need to save the lives of their children whose death they refused to accept.

Apart from these considerations, the nature of the terrain demanded extreme caution. The track was a series of bends that wound through the jungle-coated hills like a writhing snake, and went up and down like a fairground switchback, so that one moment it seemed as if they were trying to climb a wall, the next in danger of toppling over a near precipice, and disaster was only avoided by the harsh application of the brakes which filled the cabin with the throat-searing smell of burning rubber.

Flat, open spaces were a rarity, as welcome as a desert oasis, and it was while traversing one of them that Wagstaff's

258

strident voice called for silence. He craned his head out of the open window thinking he had detected the sound of an aircraft, and when he knew that his ears had not deceived him he shouted a warning to Harris, who responded automatically and veered off the track and accelerated towards the safety of the encroaching scrub with the reflex action of a destroyer captain responding to the look-out's warning of an approaching torpedo.

As soon as the truck stopped Harris vaulted out with his rifle, and Wagstaff followed with the Tommy-gun, while Fazackerley tumbled out of the back clutching the Bren and tripod.

They flopped down on to the ground, their legs spread wide apart, feeling their hearts thumping against the earth beneath them.

The aircraft was not yet visible, although the throaty grumble of its engines was becoming increasingly louder. Harris whispered, although there was no need to keep his voice down, 'Remember! No firing unless he does. No point in drawing attention.'

A cumbersome twin-engine aircraft whose wings wobbled so violently they seemed in imminent danger of dropping off, flew perilously low over the surrounding treetops. RAF markings were clearly visible on the fuselage and underside of the wings, and as it banked sharply, sheets of paper cascaded earthwards like confetti from the balcony at a New Year's Eve ball.

Wagstaff bellowed jubilantly, 'It's one of ours. Fought the Brylcreem Boys had forgotten we existed.'

Harris said, 'I'm not sure, but it looks like a Douglas transport. Yank-built.'

Wagstaff replied with a grin, 'I don' giv' a monkey's who built it, I'm only interested in who's flyin' it.'

The aircraft climbed steeply, banked again, levelled out, then made another low approach run, and large canister-shaped objects tumbled out of an open door and plummetted down, their rate of descent abruptly slowed as parachutes billowed out behind them. The plane was so low they could clearly see the two men standing at the open door waving. When the canisters hit the ground sending up great gouts of

259

dust, they split open like over-ripe fruit falling from a tree, spilling their contents over a wide area.

Fazackerley abandoned his Bren and sprinted towards them, calling over his shoulder, 'This could be the miracle old Simmo needs. Might be grub, even medicine.'

'Give him a hand, Wagstaff, I'll cover with the Bren.' said Harris.

As the two privates ran towards what they hoped was manna from heaven, the entire dropping zone became a running, hobbling, crawling sprawl of humanity as hundreds of refugees hastened as fast as their condition allowed, to grab something before it had all gone.

The aircraft seemed to rock from side to side, its wings tilting in what Harris could only assume was some kind of good luck gesture, before it disappeared from view. He waved back, then turned his eyes towards the two soldiers who were trying to drag by the parachute harness a canister that had not burst open, but were being impeded by kicks and blows from a group of desperate refugees intent on relieving them of their booty. He fired a short burst from the Bren high in the air, and he saw them pause then fall back and leave the two soldiers to carry out their task unmolested.

He was astonished to hear the rattle of gunfire long after he had removed his finger from the trigger, and was even more amazed to see several of the refugees slump to the ground.

'Bastard dacoits,' he muttered to himself. He caught a brief glimpse of Avril at the tailboard of the truck, and called out urgently, 'Get back inside. Don't want them to see white women.' Memories of their last encounter with dacoits came vividly to mind.

He turned his gaze towards the trees from where the shooting seemed to be coming, and saw small greyish puffs of smoke betraying the position of the attackers. Then a dozen or more men burst from cover firing indiscriminately and seemingly with no specific target in mind, as they ran towards the spilled out contents of the canisters. He was surprised to see they were wearing British army uniforms.

He swung the Bren in a sweeping arc, fired several shortbursts of automatic fire, quickly reloaded and resumed firing. He saw three men fall before he became the target

260

of retaliatory fire; bullets whined over his head and kicked up small puffs of dust around him. The men were partially obscured by the dust their boots kicked up, and he wished to God that Wagstaff and Fazackerley would get a move on because he needed their support. He saw one man kneel and take careful aim, and he shot him before he could pull the trigger. He heard a loud report close to his ear, and he turned his head sideways and saw Avril lying flat on her stomach with the hunting rifle.

'I thought I told you to stay in the truck, but I'm damned glad you didn't. Take your time and pick your target. No good trying to scare them off.'

She fired twice and held up two fingers, inviting him to acknowledge her marksmanship.

More uniformed men emerged from the jungle, shouting unintelligible war cries and firing in wild abandoned volleys. They struck Harris as being remarkably undisciplined for trained soldiers; their firing was so inaccurate they seemed more concerned with grabbing what they could than with hitting anyone.

He and Avril continued to fire calmly and methodically as if they were in the practice butts, pausing only to reload. Wagstaff and Fazackerley thudded to the ground beside them, exhausted by their exertions but elated to have retrieved their canister intact.

Wagstaff unslung the Tommy-gun and raised it to his shoulder, but there was no target at which to fire. The attackers had reached the strewn out supplies and were clubbing with their rifle butts anyone who stood in their way, and if he pulled the trigger he was just as likely to hit a refugee.

'Who the 'ell are they, Sarge? They got our uniform, but I can't believe our blokes would act like that.'

'What's the next move?' asked Fazackerley, more practically.

'Mount up and drive towards them, making as much din as we can, but aim high. They may be kidded into thinking we're the spearhead of a bigger force and shove off.' He grinned, lessening the tension. 'It works in the cinema.'

Harris drove slowly towards the milling crowd, his hand

261

hard down on the horn, the wheels throwing up an obscuring cloud of dust. Fazackerley, spreadeagled on the canvas hood, fired long bursts from the Bren, while Wagstaff fired the Thompson out of the open window. A few looters paused in their work to kneel and fire at the approaching truck, and bullets hit the mudguards and roof of the cabin with a shrill pinging sound before ricocheting off with a low whine; but most of them, apparently satisfied that they had seized all they could carry, were now staggering towards the safe haven of the trees. Those who had fired at the advancing truck quickly followed them, but Harris was now close enough to see they were Indian sepoys.

He shouted to make himself heard above the noise of the engine. 'Try winging one, Zack. I want to find out who they are.'

Fazackerley switched to single shot and fired three rounds in rapid succession, and one heavily burdened Indian staggered, fell, rose, fell again, abandoned his hoard and began to crawl like a dog with a broken spine, towards the trees. He thought it was pretty good shooting from such an unsteady perch: a Bren was not exactly a sniper's rifle.

Harris stopped the truck, jumped out, told Wagstaff to take the wheel and ran, bent low, to where the wounded man lay on the ground clutching a leg that was pumping blood. He aimed his rifle at his head. 'Speak English.'

'Yes, sahib.' The Indian's eyes were white with fear, and he shook like a retriever emerging from water.

'Good. Tell me who you and the other soldiers are.' He waved the muzzle menacingly. 'And don't try to lie.'

He listened as the man told him, between loud groans of pain and pleas of mercy, that they were deserters from a non-combatant unit stationed in Mandalay who had only run away because there was no officer to tell them what to do.

'We only want to go home, sahib, but to do that we must eat. We have as much right to the food as the refugees. You know that must be true, sahib.'

'Well, you and several of your chums aren't going to make it, not unless you sprout wings,' he said callously.

The Indian put his hands together in a gesture of supplication. 'Take me to your truck, sahib,' he pleaded. 'Left

262

here I die. Look at my leg, sahib. Please, you will see I cannot now walk.'

'You can cut out the sahib bullshit. I'm a sergeant. If you want to get to India you'll have to get your pals to come back and carry you,' he said coldly, and turned away and walked back towards the truck, deaf to the desperate pleas behind him. When he reached the truck he told Wagstaff to drive to the edge of the hysterical crowd who were clutching what they had managed to grab from the air-drop. Lying on the ground were several dead refugees, some badly wounded ones, and three injured and cowering sepoys.

'Collect their weapons,' he told the privates, 'and give them to the refugees. They may not know how to use them, but the sight of them may put off any other would-be attackers.'

An Indian woman whose black hair was striped with white like a badger's mask, stepped forward and said in very correct English, 'You must help us, Sergeant. They cannot be left for the jackals to devour.'

'I wish I could do something, but my truck is overloaded and I have a sick man of my own, but if you carry your wounded — not the soldiers — over to the truck I have a nursing sister who will do all she can for them. It won't be much.'

The woman spoke rapidly in what he thought was Hindi, and several men picked up the wounded and carried them to the truck where, Kitty, assisted by Avril, began treating them as best she could, but with so few drugs, bandages and field dressings, it amounted to little more than first aid.

Kitty thought: I'm giving them a short reprieve from certain death which amounts to no more than a humanitarian gesture which does more to salve my own conscience than help them.

She turned to Harris, 'Is the Silver so important? Without it we'd have room for quite a few.'

'If we made room for everyone who needs a lift we'd end up walking ourselves,' he said curtly.

'Pity the aircraft didn't see fit to drop some medical supplies as well,' she sighed.

Her words reminded Wagstaff of the leaflet he had stuffed

unread into his shirt. He rummaged around and when he found it, smoothed it out. He read it and then passed it to Harris. 'This should cheer 'em up, Sarge.'

Harris scanned the crudely printed leaflet that had clearly been printed in great haste, before reading it aloud: 'Do not despair. More help is on the way. More airdrops will be made of food, medical supplies and water purification tablets. A road is being constructed into Assam, and arrangements are being made in India to establish stockpiles of food and field hospitals along your route. So be stout hearted and press on. You have not been forgotten. Until fresh supplies are dropped it is important, repeat important, to boil all drinking water.'

He handed the leaflet to the Indian woman. 'You had better translate it for those who can't read English. It'll give them some encouragement.'

She smiled. 'They saw them on the ground, but they were too busy scrambling for food to bother with them.' She extended her hand. 'Thank you for the generous assistance you and the two ladies have given, and for saving us from those wicked men. I wish you a safe voyage.'

'The same to you. When you halt at the next open space, put down some markers to let the airmen know you are there. Take some of the parachutes and use them.'

She gave him a strange smile that was more an expression of bewilderment. 'It is a very strange and confusing world we live in, Sergeant.' Her voice had an attractive sing-song lilt. 'I did not wish to leave Burma, I was happy. I was headmistress in a small town with a sizeable Indian community, mostly shopkeepers and their families. When the war started, the Burmese, whom we had always looked upon as friends, ran riot through the streets, burning our homes, pillaging our dukas and shouting, "Death to the Indians". Like the others I was forced to flee. Then we are attacked by soldiers from our own country.'

'They are deserters and a disgrace to the thousands of Indian troops who are fighting their way home in order to return again.'

'That is most comforting,' she said disarmingly. 'And will the Burmese forgive them for coming back?'

264

She walked away and joined the refugees who already seemed to have forgotten their recent ordeal: they were squatting on the ground enjoying the unexpected meal that had descended on them before resuming the long slow trek home.

Wagstaff asked, 'Wot about the deserters? Can't leave them.'

'What do you suggest? Giving them a piggy back?'

'Course not, Sarge, but we could shoot the poor sods or give 'em back a couple of their own weapons so they can do it themselves.'

'They've no one but themselves to blame, but I'll mention your scruples to the Indian lady who seems to have assumed command, and leave the decision to her. I'm not taking any of the weapons back.'

He returned, having spoken to her. 'She thinks they should be left behind in the hope that their friends will come back and assist them. A forlorn hope, but better than none.' He seemed to Wagstaff to be remarkably indifferent to their fate, and when Harris said, 'Waggy, desertion in the face of the enemy is a capital offence, so if they die here instead of in front of a firing squad they'll only have got their just deserts,' the private thought he must have been reading his mind.

Before setting off again, Harris told the Cockney to examine the truck to make sure that it had not been damaged by the rifle fire, while Kitty Bradshaw was sent off to examine the contents of the cannister.

Wagstaff began his inspection with a careful look at the exterior of the truck, and after prowling round it three or four times he felt pretty certain it had escaped virtually unscathed. There were several bullet holes in the mudguards, a couple in the roof of the cabin, and some deeply gouged furrows in the woodwork, none of which would affect the performance. It was only when he lifted the bonnet and peered inside that he emitted a long drawn out whistle which, to Harris, indicated trouble. Water was trickling slowly but steadily from a leak halfway up the radiator and soaking into the dust below.

'Think you can patch it up?' asked Harris, trying his utmost to stifle the despair he felt.

Wagstaff studied it intently, like a pathologist examining

265

a growth under a microscope and faced with the awesome decision of deciding whether or not it was malignant or benign, aware that his verdict could spell life or death.

The hole was about the diameter of a pencil, but as most of the water had drained away he was unable to say for certain how serious it was until he had filled the radiator. He topped it up with water from a jerry-can, started the engine and watched the water spurt out. It was comparable in size to a small leak in a garden hose. 'I can try pluggin' it wiv a bit of wood, but it'll be touch an' go, an' even if it do work we'll 'ave to keep toppin' it up.' He shook his head. 'Amazin' how much water can drain out of a little 'ole. Bit of chewin' gum, or putty'd be better, but as we ain't got neither it'll 'ave to be wood.'

'Just think what that little Dutch boy did with his finger in the dyke,' said Harris, exuding a cheerfulness he did not feel.

The Cockney scratched his head and wished the sergeant would not talk in riddles. He knew nothing about a Dutch boy or a dyke. He was not even sure what a dyke was.

With a dah he prised a piece of wood from one of the furrows ploughed by a bullet and fashioned it into a tapered plug. When he was satisfied he got a hammer from the tool box and gently banged it into the hole. Too much force would only enlarge it, too little would serve no useful purpose at all. 'There's a good fing about a engin', Sarge, it can't get cholera, so we don't 'ave to worry about wastin' drinkin' water, we can pour any ol' stuff in. Even pee.'

'We haven't reached that stage yet, so fill it up and run the engine. If it's reasonably watertight I want to push on. We've lost too much time already.' He tried to sound calm and unruffled and conceal the fear that gnawed away inside him like a maggot in the core of an apple. If the truck broke down he would be confronted with the near impossible task of getting the Silver to safety. The thought daunted him, and he dismissed it from his mind, telling himself he had the utmost confidence in Wagstaff's mechanical skills, but fearful of hearing any more bad news, he clambered into the truck to see what Kitty Bradshaw had found.

'More ruddy bags of rice than we'll need, so we can

pass some on to the refugees – let them get beri-beri.' She sounded quite cheerful and not at all malicious. She enumerated the items on her fingers: 'Some packets of nuts and raisins, bars of chocolate, a tin of biscuits with a nice oatmeal flavour, tea, powdered milk, sugar, dried egg, a bag of salt – watch out, leeches – and a carton of 'V' cigarettes – manufactured in India – tins of sardines, toilet paper. There's some other stuff I haven't had time to look at yet, but the important thing is that a lot of it is going to be very useful in getting Private Simmonds well again.' She sounded like a small child who has been allowed to unpack a Christmas hamper.

Avril who was fanning the big Yorkshireman with a palm leaf looked up and said, 'Nothing like good news to brighten up a rainy day. Did you hear that, Simmo?'

If he had he made no reply, and Harris knelt beside him, gently shook him and said, as if speaking to a child feigning sleep, 'I know you heard, so tell me how you're feeling today?'

'A lot better, thanks, Sarge. Almost feel like getting up and taking a short stroll,' he lied. He felt as bad as ever but saw no point in telling Harris that; everyone was falling over backwards to help him, and he didn't want to sound ungrateful. He had heard the sound of gunfire and heard the bullets strike the truck, but he couldn't be bothered to ask what it had all been about. His one regret was that one of the bullets had not got his name on it; it would have been a welcome release. Hell couldn't be hotter than he felt, and with a bit of luck he would go to the other place.

Harris winked and patted his shoulder. 'Good for you, Simmo, Wagstaff has fixed the truck and we'll be off before you can say knife. Then it won't be long before we reach civilisation and we can get you into hospital. The RAF lads have been over and dropped supplies and leaflets telling us not to worry.'

'I'll be on my feet soon, Sarge, don't *you* worry. Don't like being a passenger.' He felt desperately weary, and if it had not been for the others he would have been quite happy to hear the truck would not start. The bouncing, bumping and jarring was purgatory, and he would happily end his days where he was.

Wagstaff had started the engine and let it tick over, and there was only the slightest seepage from the leak. 'Tight as a duck's arse, an' that's watertight,' he said to Harris, but he urged him to take things easily. 'Treat it like a good jockey on a 'umpty 'orse, not too much whip an' spur, an' don't give it 'er 'ead, if you get my meanin',' he pleaded.

Harris looked around for Fazackerley in order to tell him it was time to mount up as they were about to leave, and saw him standing in the distance surreptitiously washing his right leg with a water-soaked cloth. When Harris called him over he noticed he was walking with a pronounced limp.

'You all right, Zack?'

'Slight scratch, Sarge. Had bigger ones from a kitten. One of them spent bullets must have nicked me; didn't feel a thing at the time. Only noticed it when I felt blood in my boot. Nothing to worry about though.'

'Let's have a look. Can't take any chances in this place. Cuts become infected very quickly if they aren't looked after.'

Fazackerley showed his leg, and Harris was relieved to see that it was not a bad wound; it was about two inches long and not very deep, but it was clogged with dirt.

'Get Sister Bradshaw to clean it up, put some iodine on it and a dressing.'

'Crikey, Sarge, it's nothing,' he protested, but he did as he was told.

When they drove off, Harris kept an anxious eye on the instrument panel for any sign of overheating, and they had barely travelled ten miles when he saw the needle on the water pressure gauge was hovering over the red sector and heard an ominous bubbling sound from beneath the bonnet and saw a plume of white steam hissing from the radiator cap. He cursed audibly and braked to a halt, and asked Wagstaff to check the wooden plug. Wagstaff got out, lifted the bonnet and saw that, although the piece of wood was still in position, steam was pouring out. When he put his hand against the grille he had to withdraw it quickly.

'Can't do a effin' fing till she's cooled down. The plug obviously ain't doin' the trick.' he said plaintively.

Harris paced up and down impatiently for half an hour before Wagstaff decided it was safe enough. He wrapped a piece of cloth around his hand and gingerly unscrewed the cap, jumping back as a spout of scalding water pumped out. He waited another ten minutes before he shone a torch down the filler-hole and emitted the tuneless whistle that Harris now knew was the harbinger of bad tidings. 'Dry as me tonsils the mornin' after the night before,' muttered a dejected Wagstaff. 'Bloody puzzling 'ow it's drained so quick.' He examined the plug, gave it a gentle tap with a hammer, then buried his head inside the bonnet and started to look for some other explanation. He straightened up, wiped his oil-grimed hands on the cloth, and said, 'You in a fit state for more rotten news, Sarge?' His voice mirrored his own dismay.

'Put me out of my misery. They say it's always darkest before the dawn.'

Wagstaff grinned. 'It's blacker than Newgate's knocker right now. This ain't rain, Sarge, it's a bleedin' deluge. The fan belt's on its last legs, an' I bet a poun' to a pinch of you-know-wot we ain't got a spare. I checked everyfing before we left to see we 'ad what we needed, but I don't remember seein' one, an' it never struck me we might need it.'

He clambered into the truck and rummaged through the spare parts box. He returned shaking his head in consternation like someone who had put something in a safe place but can't recall just where it was. 'I was right, an' I can only say 'ow sorry I am. One of the first fings I shoulda asked for.'

'Not your fault. It should have been seen by the transport section. But there's no point in apportioning blame. Is it repairable?'

''Ave a bash at tryin' to strengthen it wiv some wire an' a pair of pliers, but it'll be a dodgy do, an' even then it might turn out there's somefing else up the spout. I ain't a expert, Sarge, as you know, a bit a bodgin' 'ere an' a bit there, but nuffin' skilful.'

'You've performed ruddy miracles. Just one more is all I ask.'

They became aware that Fazackerley had joined them. 'How about the abandoned truck, Sarge. I could go back and get the fan from that.'

Harris sat on the running board deep in thought, trying to estimate how many miles they had travelled since they had transferred the crates of Silver, but it was impossible to work out with any accuracy. It could be forty, fifty, sixty miles, perhaps even more. Whatever the distance it would have to be doubled because Fazackerley would have to get back. It was too much to ask; no man could walk that distance carrying necessary rations and water. Apart from that, how long would it take? At the most conservative estimate five or six days, by which time Simmonds could have had it.

He got up saying, 'Forget it. Just do what you can, Wagstaff.'

Fazackerley said earnestly, 'I'm more than willing to give it a try. You know what I'm like on route marches: still on my feet and ready for more, when everyone else is knackered.'

Harris slapped him on the back. 'I know that, but I've worked it out and it's just not on. How long would you expect us to wait? I don't even know how far you've got to go. Say we agreed on five days and you hadn't turned up? I'd think it was further and decide to hang on ... there's no end to it. It's like the old conundrum: how long is a piece of string?'

Wagstaff busied himself twisting a length of tough thin wire tightly round the frayed section of the fan belt with the pliers, while Harris sent Fazackerley off with two empty jerrycans to search for water, but he returned empty handed. He had been unable to find a spring, and the chaungs were bone dry, even though there had been some rain. The parched earth absorbed it like blotting paper.

Harris shrugged in resignation. Until the track got close enough to the river's edge, or it was near enough to walk to, they would just have to use drinking water, precious though it was. They could survive on very little, the engine could not. He had discovered during the trip that everyone felt better and was less thirsty later on in the day if they were allowed to drink most of their ration in the morning. The Chindwin, he knew, was never far away, but the surrounding hills prevented it from being seen, so until they got a glimpse of it they would have to err on the side of caution and forget their thirst. Although the situation was extremely critical, they still had a long way to go. He estimated they were anything from sixty to seventy miles from Shwegyin, and with the truck in its precarious state it could take as long as a week. He could not apply his mind to the problem of how they were going to cross the river − getting there was all that mattered at the moment. Like a man climbing a ladder who suffers from vertigo, one rung at a time was target enough.

Although the fan belt held out, the radiator continued to leak and the engine overheat, sometimes to such an extent it stopped of its own accord, and the halts became more frequent than Harris had dreamed of in his most pessimistic moments.

Wagstaff sitting beside him swivelled his eyes in vain for a suitable vehicle from which he could remove the fan belt, but all the abandoned transport was well astern of them.

They witnessed three air drops in as many days, but ignored them; they had all the food they needed, at least for the time being, and the one thing they did need, water, was not delivered by air. Harris had suggested trying to collect some medical supplies, but Kitty was against it; Simmonds under his varied if monotonous diet, was beginning to show slight signs of improvement, and although still very ill she considered it more important to get him to hospital rather than try out medicines she was not knowledgeable enough to administer with any degree of confidence.

Nellie, although willing to carry out any duties assigned to her, was a problem, becoming more sullen and withdrawn as the days passed. Everyone wrongly suspected she was homesick and regretting her decision to remain with them, when all that was tormenting her was Wagstaff's lack of interest.

She was at her wit's end to know what to do about it. And it was no good going to her mistress for advice because her memsahib had distanced herself so much she felt she was no

271

longer employed by her; her duties were non-existent. She was not required to wash her hair, do her nails or wash her clothes, because her memsahib now wore the same slacks and shirt every day, which she did not bother to wash. In the circumstances she felt she could not complain about not being paid because the memsahib worked harder than she did herself, especially when it came to nursing the big soldier. Not that she ignored Nellie, she did not, she spoke kindly to her and treated her in a way she had never done in Rangoon, but she was no longer a memsahib in whom to confide. She was always too busy to listen, not at all as she was at Balmoral when she had so much time to spare and encouraged her maid to talk about her lovers.

Wagstaff was different; he ignored her completely.

Whenever they stopped he seemed to have his head buried under the bonnet of the lorry, or be lying flat on his back on the ground looking up at the engine, his forehead creased in deep furrows of intense concentration, his eyes blind to everything except a drip of oil or a trickle of water. It was as if the truck meant more to him than she did. And at night he seemed to prefer Private Simmonds' company to hers, talking quietly and gently, not at all worried that he seldom got any response, and when he was not with his friend he was either keeping guard or sleeping. She was not even able to talk to him when they were travelling, because he rode in the front with Sergeant Harris and her mistress, while she was consigned to the back with the sick man and Miss Bradshaw, who was even less inclined to listen to her when she raised the subject of Wagstaff's indifference. She kept telling her not to be a silly girl, and that it was no time to natter on about promises of marriage.

'Just keep your legs crossed until we reach India,' she said crossly. 'Private Wagstaff has to keep this damned thing going at all costs, otherwise we'll never make it. On top of that he's worried about his friend, so how can you expect him to find the time to keep you happy? Five other people are also relying on him, so stop being so bloody selfish and tiresome.'

When she had protested, pointing out that the sick soldier also wanted Private Wagstaff to marry her – she would have

272

like Simmonds to have confirmed that, but he was past caring about anything — Kitty's voice had mellowed a little. 'I'm not saying you shouldn't marry him, Nellie; all I'm asking is that you stop mooning around like a sick cow in calf and wait until we reach safety. Then, for all I care, get yourself pregnant. But for God's sake don't ever mention it again. Just send me an invitation.'

Nellie had been so surprised and shocked by the angry outburst she had not spoken to the sister since. How could anyone be so heartless? she asked herself. Her own heart was bursting at the waning prospect of becoming a soldier's missus, for if she was denied that the whole awful journey would have been for nothing.

At night she had to stuff her longyi into her mouth so that no one could hear her crying herself to sleep.

Chapter 17

They reached Shwegyin late one afternoon in the middle of a pre-monsoon rainstorm. The tiny port lay in a horsehoe-shaped basin surrounded on three sides by sheer escarpments and jungle-covered hills topped by shifting clouds of grey mist. Huddled round the basin were thousands of drenched and starving refugees waiting for a stern-wheeler to take them up river to Kalewa, for it was only from there that they could begin the long and perilous trek through Kabaw, 'the valley of death'. The wealthier Indians were brandishing fat wads of rupee notes and shouting aloud, like bidders at a badly run auction, their willingness to pay any price in order to jump the queue; but paddle steamers were few and far between and the masters of those willing to make the short but hazardous trip were not in the least interested in bribes. They were solely concerned with treating their passengers on a first-come-first-served basis, having witnessed too much greed and blatant self-preservation at the expense of others to be influenced by money that could turn out to be worthless. Far better, they reasoned, to witness the collapse of Burma with a clear conscience.

Harris parked the truck well away from the refugees – he did not want their despair transmitted to his own party – and told Wagstaff to get a wood fire going. He was reluctant to use the improvised stove which had stood them in such stead because of the need to conserve fuel, but the timber the private gathered was too sodden and when lit produced smoke but no heat.

'Hang the expense, use some petrol. We all need a hot

274

drink,' he said. 'I'll see about collecting some rain water for the engine.' He dug a hole and lined it with a tarpaulin sheet then stood in the teeming rain, hands on hips, surveying the scene in front of him. But for the rain it could have been the North West Frontier of India, limitless and forbidding. He heaved a deep sigh of contentment and relief; against all the odds they had made it. The journey that lay ahead might be arduous but it was not at all daunting. Unlike the wretched refugees they would not have to hike through the Kabaw Valley, they would do it on the relative comfort of four wheels.

When darkness came the temperature plummeted and it became cruelly cold. The three women huddled together in the back of the truck for added warmth. The rain hammered on the canvas hood and on the roof of the cabin like the drumming of impatient fingers, and they had to raise their voices to be heard above the din. Simmonds alone was indifferent to the rain and cold.

Harris, sitting in the cabin with Wagstaff, said, 'At least we have the consolation of knowing that this is only a heavy shower. Imagine what it'll be like when the monsoon starts in earnest and it rains non-stop for weeks on end.'

'Makes you wonder about the refugees, Sarge. Those wot don't get over before that will 'ave 'ad it.' Fazackerley lay on a blanket underneath the truck because he did not want anyone to smell his leg. He had religiously cleansed it and put on a fresh dressing, and although it had shown little sign of improvement it had not got any worse. Then two days ago he noticed his leg had a black puffy look about it and was giving off an unpleasant sickly odour. He had thought of going to Sister Bradshaw, but could not bear the thought of being scolded for not looking after himself. Apart from that, he was aware of her mounting concern for Simmonds and did not want to add to her worries. He had hoped that if he rested his leg as much as possible it would clear up, but it got worse. The one good thing was that it was not painful and he was confident he would see the journey through without having to bother anyone.

In the back of the truck, Avril lay listening to the brain-numbing tattoo of the rain beating the canvas like the muffled drums at a military funeral, and wondered how the others could sleep through it. She decided she could stand it no longer and picked up a blanket, muttering to herself: This is driving me potty.

She clambered out into the blinding driving rain to find a dry spot somewhere. There was no such thing, but she found a space beneath a big tree with rhubarb-shaped leaves that was damp but infinitely better than the claustrophobic clamminess of the truck. There she lay down, drew the blanket up around her chin and dozed off. From the cabin of the truck Harris saw her dark silhouette move off into the darkness and assumed she was obeying the call of nature, but when she did not reappear he decided to look for her. It was a dangerous place for a young woman to wander around alone.

He stood looking down at her, thinking how childlike she looked. Her wet hair was sleeked across her forehead, and she looked less gaunt than when she was awake, for like the rest of the party she had lost a lot of weight; there were dark prune-coloured patches beneath her closed eyes and her cheekbones were now as prominent as Nellie's.

He knelt beside her recumbent form, content just to look at the pale face that had an almost luminous glow. The rain rattled on the leaves above and fell in heavy drops on to her exposed face, but she did not seem to feel them. He leant over and brushed his lips against hers. They felt dry and parched, almost corpse-like, and he was surprised when they responded warmly and he realised she was not asleep.

Her arms moved from inside the blanket to embrace him, and he felt her kiss burning through him like flickering tongues of fire. His own arms cradled her, and he responded with an intensity he had never imagined himself capable of.

'It took a long time for you to get around to it,' she said.

'I thought you were dead to the world.'

'Never to you,' she said with a tinkling laugh that set his heart racing like a trip hammer. She sat up, letting the blanket fall away. The rain trickled down her face in rivulets. 'Don't say you wouldn't have kissed me if you'd known I wasn't sleeping? That's cowardly. Apart from that, stolen kisses are never as sweet.'

'Not cowardly, just sensible.'

'That doesn't make sense. At least to me it doesn't. Either you wanted to or you didn't.'

'I wanted to and did,' he said awkwardly. 'I can't continue pretending any longer. I am in love with you; you've been wanting me to admit it and I have, but it can't lead to anything.'

'Why on earth not?' she said angrily. 'We've found something that most people spend a lifetime looking for, and all you can say is it's a waste of time.'

'I've been wanting to tell you why for some time now but there never seemed to be an appropriate moment. Always something that needed to be attended to, or someone was close at hand to overhear every word I uttered. I wanted only you to know.'

She cradled her knees with her hands. 'Well, we're alone and I'm all ears, David.'

He exhaled noisily and started talking, hesitantly at first, then as he narrated his story his confidence grew and he felt he was shedding the guilt of years much as a snake sheds its skin before starting life afresh.

'I've suspected for some time that you knew Harris was not my real identity.'

She nodded, anxious not to interrupt what she had waited so long to hear.

'From the time I was a small boy it never entered my head that I would ever be anything but a soldier. My father was the son of a soldier, as was his father before him; the tradition stretches back hundreds of years. My mother comes from a military family, and her pedigree is just as pure. I was born in Quetta and christened in the garrison church there, and my earliest recollections are of splendid parades on the maidan where the Indian troops filed past the dais, drums banging, bugles blaring, bagpipes swirling, and every turbanned sepoy marching with the precision of a metronome, heads high, uniforms immaculate, pride in the pounding of their highly polished boots. On the dais the officers' ladies, white-gloved and wearing wide-brimmed straw hats basked in the reflected glory.

'At night in my nursery, after the ayah had bathed me,

277

my mother would come up and tell me stories of valiant deeds on the polo ground and battlefield, the wonders of shikar, and occasionally when he could tear himself away from regimental duties, my father would come in, sometimes smelling of horses and sweat, sometimes in full mess kit, all crimson and gold, and tell me what a wonderful, fulfilling life lay ahead for me. I never doubted it. I was destined to follow the drum as some men, on hearing church bells, know they're being called to holy orders.

'When I was seven or eight, I can't remember exactly, I was sent to a preparatory school in England because a young boy had to learn to stand on his own two feet and not remain tied to his mother's apron strings.' He laughed drily. 'Cold baths, icy dormitories and appalling food seemed to be regarded as essential ingredients to manliness and preparation for a future in which you would be called upon to command men. It was also necessary in order to remind me that although India was my birthplace England was "home".

'From there I went to the same public school my father had attended, and when I was eighteen I entered the Royal Military Academy at Sandhurst. There I worked like a beaver to pass out with very high marks because only the best were chosen for the Indian Army. I passed out twenty-fourth, which meant I was assured of a place. Apart from that, I had "friends at court", so there was no question of my not joining my father's regiment. But first I did a year's attachment to a British regiment. Is this boring you?'

'Of course not, I want to hear it from the beginning. After all, your past seems to have a deciding influence on my future.'

'Peacetime soldiering was all I had hoped it would be. We worked hard and played hard, and although my father was by then a major-general and detached from the regiment, he made it clear that I was to be treated no differently to any other subaltern, which meant I was treated far worse. But I loved it. I played polo, tennis, billiards, went hunting, rode in point to points, and in between I learned the art of soldiering. It was drummed into me that the regiment and the welfare of the men under me came before anything else. I got my initiation into real fighting

278

when I was sent to the North West Frontier – every young officer's dream in those days – to quell an uprising by the Pathans.

'My future seemed assured. Although there was no formal engagement, there was what they call an "understanding" between me and the Colonel's youngest daughter. She was an extremely pretty girl, and although I wasn't sure I loved her I was quite happy with the arrangement. Girls were not that plentiful, and she seemed as good a choice as any. The important thing was she would fit in. She would accept long separations and concede that the Regiment always came first.

'Soon after the spell on the Frontier, two platoons were sent to a small town outside Bombay in readiness for what is called "duties in aid of the civil power". It was a time when Gandhi was actively promoting his campaign of satyagraha or "soul force", which was a form of passive resistance with Independence as the outcome. The trouble was that many of his followers were not averse to resorting to violence to obtain their objective, and riots were erupting all over the place, agitators daubing the walls of public buildings with "British Out" slogans.

'The town I was sent to had its fair share of marches and demonstrations, but they were mainly peaceful for which we were extremely grateful. Memories of General Dyer and the Amritsar Massacre were still very fresh in the minds of the military authority, and there was a natural reluctance to use the troops unless things got out of hand. Although it was true, no one liked to admit that the army was a repressive presence.

'Well, things did get out of hand. Some agitators moved in from Bombay with the sole intention of provoking trouble. They were members of the Congress Party who made a series of rabble rousing speeches exhorting the until then peaceful demonstrators to resort to violence. It doesn't take much to rouse an Indian crowd and send it on the rampage, and in no time they were marching through the streets chanting slogans and calling for immediate Independence. A European bank was looted and set on fire, and the windows of the courthouse shattered. Then the mob moved on to the railway station where they derailed several coaches and an engine and indulged in a fair amount of looting, which is an irrestistible temptation to an Indian mob who tend to forget the original purpose of a demonstration.

'The police moved in and several rioters were arrested and taken to the police station and put in the cells.

'When the mob heard of this they stormed the kotwali demanding their immediate release. Several policemen were injured and a senior officer was knocked unconscious by a stone. The prisoners were rescued and the mob went on the rampage again. Reluctantly the Deputy Commissioner called in the army to restore law and order.

'The mob was now out of control, streets were barricaded and several cars belonging to Europeans were doused in petrol and set on fire, and a group of Britishers leaving a cinema were attacked and savagely beaten with lathis.

'I was in charge of a platoon that was sent to the part of town where the trouble was greatest. I led my men down a wide street, cleared a barricade of ox wagons and charpoys, and walked towards the crowd that stood defiantly in our path. Stones rained down from the rooftops and several of my men were hit. A man rushed out from a doorway and slashed at me with a sword, leaving me with the scar you've no doubt noticed. His action was greeted with great roars of approval, and the sight of me, a white officer, bleeding like a stuck pig, encouraged them to greater violence. Tiles were ripped off roofs and boiling water poured on to my chaps. I gave the order to fix bayonets and some rifle shots were fired from the window of a nearby house. One soldier who was hit in the shoulder fired back in self-defence as he was perfectly entitled to do. I looked for the ring-leader as we were taught to do, and saw a young man in a Congress cap standing in a bullock cart urging the crowd on. I told one soldier to pick him off and make certain he did not miss. He did not.

'The rioting continued on a small scale, but by next morning the town had returned to some semblance of normality. Although the Indian press contained a very one-sided account of the rioting and accused the army of deliberate murder in order to suppress the genuine aspirations of a downtrodden people, the feeling among the European community was that we had acted with commendable restraint. The Colonel praised me for my coolness in a situation which could have developed into something much bigger, with the resultant loss of many lives.

'No one took much notice of the editorials in the local Indian newspapers, but when the more influential Delhi and Bombay newspapers stepped in, accusing the British of ruthless slaughter and demanding a full public Inquiry, questions were raised in the House of Commons by a vociferous group of MPs who favoured Indian Independence, and seized upon every opportunity to further their cause. It was also disclosed that the man I had ordered to be shot was the son of a lesser Rajah who was renowned for his pro-British opinions, and he had stated that although he did not share his son's political views he accepted they were genuinely held, and it was tragic that the British had deemed it necessary to silence him because he was an ardent supporter of Gandhi and an advocate of non-violence.

'An Inquiry was instigated and, I won't bore you with the details because it lasted several days, a whole string of witnesses were called who swore that the dead man had been pleading with them to stop the bloodshed. If it was not perjury it was a travesty of the truth.

'The decision the Inquiry reached was that, possibly owing to my inexperience and immaturity, I had overreacted and exceeded the minimum force required to restore law and order. I was court martialled, severely reprimanded, and punished with the loss of one year's seniority. Honour seemed to be satisfied all round. The Rajah was mollified and the Congress Party seemed content with the outcome. The army had been revealed for what it was: the tool of the British administration. The Conservative newspapers in England welcomed the decision which they said put an end to the claim that India was ruled by force. The more left-wing newspapers which had no time at all for the Empire, welcomed the punishment although they thought it erred on the side of leniency, but an example had been made and that was what really mattered. A soldier could not stalk the streets of Indian cities shooting innocent people like landed gentry on the Yorkshire moors bagging grouse, even when he was a general's son.

'My father visited me and explained that it had all been a matter of political expedience; talks were due to be held in Delhi aimed at paving the way towards Independence and the Indian delegation had threatened to boycott it if I was not punished. He said that whilst I might feel a bit like the sacrificial lamb, I should accept that it had been done with a noble purpose in mind. It would all blow over and no one would think any the less of me. I remembered saying that did it not matter if I thought a lot less of them? He told me, on the wrongful assumption that I would appreciate I was some kind of Sidney Carton, that Dyer had also been wrongfully punished although everyone, including himself, regarded him as the Saviour of India, the man who averted a second mutiny. "Remember," he told me, "he was eventually vindicated as you will be in time. That must be your buckler until them. Individually we are as unimportant as a grain of sand on a beach when balanced against the importance of a stable and peaceful India. At the talks which are due soon, promises will be made but not kept, but the treatment meted out to you will be seen as evidence of our fairness."

'The next day my fiancée came round and suggested it would be wiser if we delayed any formal announcement of our engagement, otherwise it would look as if she disapproved of the decision. With her father holding the position he did, that would be quite untenable. What was untenable to me was the shabbiness of the whole thing.

'I packed what I needed, said goodbye to my parents and walked out of their lives. I did not even resign my commission, I just disappeared. Understandably my departure was accepted in political circles as a sign of my guilt. It was anything but that. It had been a betrayal of all I had been taught to honour.'

Avril said, 'It was a horrible injustice, and I know you must feel very bitter, but how does that affect us?'

'How can I possibly marry you? I am not David Harris. I'm not even sure it would be legal. Can a man marry under a false name? Don't you have to produce some proof of identity?'

282

'I don't know and what's more I don't care. We've survived so much together I'm sure we can cope with such a minor obstacle.'

He smiled in the darkness. 'We'll talk about it in India. Maybe I'll see a lawyer.'

'There's just one thing you've omitted from your story, David. Who are you really?'

'Sergeant David Harris. That's the only person I want to be.'

'That'll suit me fine.'

The rain stopped early next morning and clothes which had clung to them like wet seaweed quickly dried. Harris and Avril walked up to the jungle's edge listening to the sound of elephants crashing through the undergrowth, the shriek of monkeys, and catching the occasional sight of wild boars nosing for food in the clearings. Once they thought they heard the clanging of a bell. They seldom spoke, content with each other's company.

'We'd better get back. I ought to see about getting us aboard a steamer.' said Harris.

Before setting off for the riverside he suggested to Wagstaff and Fazackerley that it might not be a bad idea if they went into the jungle to try and bag a couple of wild pigs, but to watch out for the elephants, one of which seemed to have a bell attached to it.

Nellie said, 'Must keep away. Elephants from timber mills now escaped. One with bell killer elephant. Very bad.' She used one arm like a trunk, waving it wildly from side to side and stamping the ground with her feet to indicate what it would do if anyone was foolhardy enough to get within reach. Fazackerley was grateful; he was in no state to go hunting.

Harris said, 'While I'm gone, check on that tarpaulin to see if it's collected enough rain to top up the radiators.' But when Fazackerley looked it was as dry as a bone; there was a leak in the seam. 'It never rains but it fucking pours,' he muttered disconsolately, blissfully unaware of the inanity of his observation.

When Harris reached the rickety wooden jetty he saw

283

a Chindwin stern-wheeler moored alongside taking aboard refugees who had been made to form an orderly queue. He went in search of the Master and found him on the bridge supervising the loading. He introduced himself, and, glibly lying, said he had a cargo of important government documents which had been entrusted to his care with orders to see it safely to India.

The Master, another Scot, asked suspiciously, 'What are they? Paper before humans is not my idea of a fair deal.'

'I've no idea, they're crated up. All I know is they must not be allowed to fall into enemy hands. They're in a truck with an escort of three soldiers, and I have two white women passengers.'

'The ruddy army has let everything else fall into the hands of the Japs, so I fail to see why they should sweat blood over some paper. Maybe it's the top brass's written explanation as to why there's been such a cock up.'

Harris laughed. 'Probably dangerously near the truth.'

The Master held out a hand. 'Hamish Crawford. Be here waiting in two days' time and I'll see what I can do. Kalewa may not be far, but it's a treacherous voyage. All rapids and whirlpools, but you'll find out for yourself. Fancy a dram before you step ashore?'

Harris said he would be delighted, and as he drank a half tumbler of neat Dewar's, said it was the second time he had reason to be grateful to a Scottish master.

'And who was before me?'

'Chap called McIntyre. Wonderful man. When I get to India I'm going to submit a report. If anyone deserves a medal he does.'

'Pity he won't be around to collect it,' said Crawford.

'He's dead?'

'Very much so. Tried to take his steamer down to Pakokku to pick up some of the army but the Japs spotted him and blew him and his ship out of the water. Good man. He'll be missed.'

'I'm sorry to hear that.'

'Aye, and a lot of others too. Now if you don't mind I've a job to do. Remember, be on the jetty and ready

284

to go. I'll not wait for any stragglers.' He snorted. 'If it's only bumf you'll be carrying, why on earth not burn the bloody stuff?'

'I can't answer that, sir.'

'And if you could, you ruddy well wouldn't'. He slapped Harris on the back to show there was no ill feeling. 'Now if it was gold I wouldna have any qualms. I'd jump ship and come with you. Help you spend some of it in the cess pits of India.'

The two days passed with agonising slowness, and Harris had the truck in position on the jetty some twelve hours before he expected the steamer to hove into sight. The refugees, embittered that a party of white people were being given preference, gathered round in a menacing crowd, but the sight of the Bren-gun and the brandished Thompson prevented them from venting their feelings in anything other than words and jets of betel-stained spit.

Hamish Crawford tied his steamer alongside the jetty with much hooting on the siren and cries from the bridge for everyone to stand back and stay calm otherwise he wouldn't take one heathen soul aboard. The crowd on the jetty relapsed into sullen silence, too tired to quarrel among themselves and too fearful of the Master to risk being sent to the back of the queue.

When the steamer was secured, Crawford left the bridge to seek out Harris. 'I'll get some of my crew to help get the truck aboard. It's up to you to see it's securely lashed to the bollards and deck bolts. The Chindwin is a rough and cruel river and if we hit a bore, as more than likely we shall, your truck and its precious cargo will go overboard. And that'll be the end because parts of the river are fifty, sixty fathoms deep.'

By dawn the Master was ready to slip and proceed upstream, and he invited Harris on to the bridge.

'Sergeant, I would deeply appreciate it if you could mount your two fit men on the bridge wings with the Bren-gun and that gangster-looking weapon. As I warned you, this is going to be a very perilous journey and the Indians are likely to panic. I want your laddies there to be ready and willing to quell any disturbance. When the going gets a wee bit rough they may take it into their minds to try and make me turn back.'

Crawford had not overestimated the hazards, and the journey to Kalewa which took almost twenty-four hours was not one that Harris would volunteer for again. Washed down teak trees thudded against the side of the hull with pulverising impact, and in stretches of the river the current was so swift the steamer, which had a draught of two feet, was tossed around like a cork in a mill stream. Unseen eddies sucked at the hull threatening to turn the craft in a complete circle, and at times the ship seemed to be heading in the opposite direction to that the Master intended. From time to time a high wave swept across the river like a barrier, buffetting the vessel until it reeled like a punch-drunk boxer.

Crawford remained amazingly calm and in complete control. 'Don't say I didna warn you, Sergeant. She's a very cruel mistress.' He winked. 'But then, what man with red blood in his veins wants a mistress who's compliant and docile? Like fucking a mattress.'

In his mind's eye Harris visualised the immense problem that would confront the army when they reached Shwegyin. How on earth would they get ambulances, transport, artillery and tanks across the river?

The refugees offered none of the violence that was feared; they simply lay on the decks wallowing in their own vomit and not caring if they did not reach Kalewa. They had feared death for so long; now they were prepared willingly to embrace it.

Crawford said, 'We'll be there in two hours, maybe less. Better get the fire hoses turned on to wash down the decks and let the refugees know we're nearly there.'

'That seems a rather drastic alarm clock, sir.'

'Never. The sun'll dry them in minutes, and as soon as they set foot ashore they'll have forgotten they wanted to die.'

The skipper tugged at a length of rope which ended in a monkey's fist, and the siren bellowed mournfully, warning those ashore of the approach of the steamer. As they turned a bend the river appeared to become wilder and more turbulent and Crawford said, 'Let's hope Pewe is in a gentle frame of mind today. She can be a real bitch.'

286

'Pewe?' asked Harris, thinking the master was referring to some harridan ashore who exercised considerable authority in the town.

'Most treacherous whirlpool in Burma. If she's playing up we could have a long wait. Known steamers held up for several days.'

Pewe it seemed was in a benevolent mood for Crawford made no attempt to move inshore and tie up but ordered the man on the engine room telegraph to ask for more revolutions. The stern paddle groaned and juddered under the strain and as they rounded the bend they were enclosed by a continuous wall of sheer cliffs, at the base of which stood small islands which had been carved into grotesque shapes by the ferocity of the current where the two rivers met.

As they approached the dilapidated sprawl of hovels which constituted the town there was little sign of human presence; the only people in sight were near-naked natives salvaging great logs which had been washed ashore. 'Turn them into rafts and canoes that are incapable of capsizing.' said Crawford.

With much clanging on the engine room telegraph and the roaring of helm orders, the steamer was manoeuvred alongside the jetty which stood at the end of the promontory where the small town was situated. Crawford barked out a series of orders to his own deck hands and to a group of natives who were squatting on the jetty chewing betel nut. They disappeared into a ramshackle warehouse that seemed in imminent danger of collapse and emerged struggling under the weight of several wide planks which they placed in position amidships. In a short time they had erected a gangway wide enough for the truck to be pushed ashore.

'This is a one horse town, Sergeant, but there's a bazaar and if you'll take my advice you'll stop and buy a couple of dahs.' He gestured with a forefinger to a ridge of saw-toothed hills. 'Kalemyo is on the other side of those. It marks the start of the Kabaw Valley. Get through that and you're home and dry, but for God's sake take your quinine. The place is littered with the bones of silly arses who ignored that advice.'

287

The narrow high street was lined on both sides by palm-thatched shops draped with betel vines and scarlet-tasselled hibiscus. There were tailors sitting cross-legged beside ancient Singer sewing machines, cobblers repairing shoes with strips of old tyres, stalls selling curios and fruit, and one outside which hung zinc buckets and baths, crudely fashioned hoes, and sturdy looking dahs. Harris bartered some rice and biscuits for two of the knives.

The track over the ridge leading to Kalemyo was strewn with boulders and the truck bounced so violently Harris had trouble holding on to the steering wheel. The engine groaned in agony and the radiator hissed in steamy protest. Through the aperture at the rear of the cabin, Kitty Bradshaw pleaded with him to go easy as Simmonds was being tossed around like a pea on a drum.

'Tell him to hang on. Once we get to the other side it'll be plain sailing.'

When they had cleared the top of the ridge, Harris decided to freewheel the remainder of the distance into the small town of Kalemyo in order to rest the engine, and when they reached the huddle of native huts he announced it was time for a brew-up. While the petrol stove was being prepared he went into the back of the truck to ask Kitty Bradshaw how Simmonds had coped with the journey.

She spoke in a very low voice. 'The rest of the trip had better be plain sailing because if not he isn't going to make it. Anyone else would have thrown the towel in long ago. Just look at the poor devil.'

Harris looked down at the blanket-shrouded figure. Simmonds' face was almost obscured by a heavy growth of beard which had been allowed to grow because shaving had been sheer agony. His eyes which had almost disappeared into their sockets were bright with fever, and but for the slow rise and fall of the blanket he could have been mistaken for a corpse. 'It's only about a hundred miles from here to Tamu. We'll have a good long rest, build up our strength, then make an early start in the morning,' said Harris.

After they had eaten, Wagstaff volunteered for the first guard and settled down by the fire smoking a 'V' cigarette, wondering what lay ahead when they reached India. Would

288

they ever link up with the Battalion, or would they be shunted off to another outfit to make up the numbers? It would be a pity if after all they had gone through they were split up. He was roused from his reverie by Fazackerley's voice. 'You got a minute to spare, Waggy?'

'Why ain't you got your 'ead down, Zack? You gotta take over from me in four hours.'

'Couldn't sleep. My leg's playing me up something rotten.'

'Better let me 'ave a decko.'

Fazackerley unwound the bandage that covered his leg from thigh to ankle and Wagstaff looked at it in the flickering flame of the fire. 'Jesus, I don't like the look of that, Zack. It smells somefink awful. I reckon you gotta touch of gangrene.' He stood up, and Fazackerley asked, 'What you going to do?'

'Wake Sister Bradshaw. You can't go aroun' wiv a leg like that.'

He shook the Sister awake and she stumbled half asleep to the fire where Fazackerley sat, the unrolled bandage in his hand, his face a picture of guilt.

She looked at it. 'My God, why didn't you tell me before?'

'It happened rather suddenly, Sister, and I thought it would go away just as quick. What'll I do?'

'For the life of me, Zack, I don't honestly know. If you were in a hospital they'd take it off below the knee and save the rest, but that's clearly not on. I suggest you let the air to it, and if it gets maggotty don't worry, they'll help clean it up. If the Sergeant is correct, it's only a hundred miles to Tamu where there's bound to be a doctor.'

When Harris was told about it next morning, Fazackerley was relieved to find he was not at all angry but full of commiserations and confidence that they would reach Tamu before irreparable harm was done.

The valley was lush and green, and in the first hour they maintained a steady ten miles an hour although they had to stop frequently to hack a path through the clumps of prickly bamboo which often blocked the track and Harris was grateful that he had heeded the advice given by Crawford and purchased the dahs. Whenever they did dismount they had to be extremely wary for the place seemed alive with snakes. Some were small ones which reared up, flattened their heads and hissed before darting off into the undergrowth; others were fat and sluggish and several feet in length, easily avoided.

Then without warning the truck lurched violently and the rear sagged, tossing the occupants from one side of the vehicle to the other.

Wagstaff said, 'If you ask me, Sarge, that's a rear spring gone for a Burton.'

He jumped out and crawled under the truck and merged a few minutes later to say, 'Even worse. Back axle's gone. Now there's nuffink can be done about that.'

If Harris was dismayed he did not show it. 'I suppose it was too much to hope that it would last us right through. We'll unload, take what we need and walk the rest of the way.'

'What about the Silver, Sarge?'

'We'll bury it and come back for it later.'

He became all brusque efficiency. 'Kitty, you sort out what medicine we'll need. Keep it down to basic essentials. I'll work out what water we'll need. Avril, you do the same with the food. Cut down on the tinned stuff, too heavy. Rice, biscuits, tea and dried milk. Fazackerley, Wagstaff, cut a section out of the hood and chop down some stout bamboo poles; we'll make a stretcher for Simmonds. Nellie, you do whatever Sister Bradshaw tells you. I'll start digging a hole.'

He took a pickaxe and spade from the truck and moved several yards off the track into a clearing where he began to excavate a deep trench. The ground was rock hard and the sweat was soon trickling down his bare torso. He was grateful when the two privates had finished the stretcher and were able to give him a hand.

When the trench was about four feet deep, Harris signalled that they need dig no deeper. 'We'll unpack the Silver and bury it. I'll have to take some sights so we'll know exactly where it is.'

When the Silver had been packed into the hole, Harris told Fazackerley to fetch the Bren. 'Cover it with oil from the sump and wrap it in canvas. It's too heavy to carry,

290

but it might as well be collected when we come back for the Silver.'

The heat was intense and they were totally exhausted by their labours. Harris decided they all needed some strong tea and a good rest before they filled in the hole and started walking.

'We'll establish a routine that won't vary. Walk for an hour, rest for an hour. Stop dead on the stroke of five, sleep, and be off at dawn. Wagstaff and I will take the stretcher. I want everyone to check on their boots and find room for an extra pair of socks, our feet are going to be the most important part of us from now on.'

They rested for four hours before Harris announced it was time to go. 'Kitty, help us to get Simmonds on to the stretcher. He'll need gentle handling.'

Harris, Wagstaff and Kitty Bradshaw clambered into the truck where Kitty knelt beside Simmonds, saying, 'This is going to be uncomfortable for a few minutes. We're going to put you on a stretcher.'

Simmonds said, 'Don't bother. I'm not going anywhere.'

'Stop talking rubbish,' said Kitty harshly. 'You're coming to Tamu.'

'Sorry, Sister, you won't get there if you have to carry me. If you don't you will. I'm not going and that's that.'

Harris said, 'When you're ready we'll pick him up.'

Simmonds said, 'Sergeant, will you call Nellie in, please?'

Harris leaned out of the back and called for the Burmese girl. When she was standing beside him, Simmonds raised himself on one elbow and said, 'I want you to bear witness to this. Waggy, I want you to give your solemn word of honour that you'll do the right thing by the girl and marry her. If you don't I'll haunt you till the day you join me in whatever place I end up.'

Wagstaff said, 'Course I promise, Simmo, but don' go on like that. This ain't like you at all. Just fink wot you're gonna give up! The wet canteen, pontoon with me an' Zack. An' you can be best man, 'ow about that?'

'I've decided the moment's come for me to become time-expired, Sarge.' He managed a weak smile. 'I don't want to go on, honest.'

291

A silence descended on the clammy airless interior.

'Simmo, listen to me,' said Harris croakily, but there was no response. Kitty knelt beside him, felt his pulse, then stood up, saying, 'We won't need the stretcher. He's dead.'

Harris said hoarsely, 'It's almost as if he wished it on himself.'

'He did,' she said curtly.

The tears were streaming down Wagstaff's cheeks. 'Can we bury him with the Silver, Sarge. He would like that.'

'Of course.'

They wrapped Simmonds in a canvas shroud cut from the hood of the truck and lowered him reverently on to the Silver. They stood in a solemn group as Harris recited the Lord's Prayer and then what he could remember of the 23rd Psalm, for that seemed a most appropriate requiem in view of the nickname the Kabaw Valley had acquired.

When they had filled in the trench Wagstaff fashioned a small cross from floor boards prised from the truck and scratched Simmonds' name, rank and number on it with the point of a dah. They placed the dead man's topee on top, and Fazackerley said, 'The Silver couldn't have a better watchdog, Sarge.'

The three soldiers stood rigidly to attention and saluted, then turned smartly on their heels.

Harris said, 'We'll still need the stretcher. We can carry the food on it. Now before we set off, everyone make sure they only have what is absolutely necessary.'

Avril felt a flush of guilt, but nothing would have made her disclose the fact that in the bundle she carried was the dress she was determined to wear in India when Harris took her out.

The Sergeant pocketed the chain and brown identity disc he had removed from Simmonds' neck. 'Let's go then.'

Chapter 18

Without transport they were forced to join the straggle of refugees who moved down the Kabaw Valley like a column of ants whose nest has been disturbed, although at night they made camp well away from them. The leaflets dropped from the air had done nothing to make them mend their ways when it came to the question of hygiene. Not that it would have made much difference if they had tried because most were suffering from chronic dysentery and had no control over their bowels. Even when they walked they continued to pass a thin foul-smelling stream of liquid. Many were so debilitated they dropped in their tracks, and the valley now resembled a corpse strewn battlefield.

Harris maintained a rigid discipline he would not depart from; they walked for an hour, rested for an hour. They drank first thing in the morning and were not allowed to touch another drop until they halted for the night. Sometimes they expressed a desire to break the routine; they felt fit enough to press on a little longer, but he would not budge.

If Fazackerley's leg was giving him pain he gave no hint of it. He had contrived to make a crutch for himself and never complained about the pace, keeping abreast of everyone with his putrefying leg swinging uselessly off the ground. He even managed to make them laugh by putting on a Devon accent and bellowing in a Long John Silver voice, 'Them that dies'll be the lucky ones.'

Every evening they examined their feet, and when it rained put out their socks for a soaking, but they could do nothing with their boots which were now in shreds. The soles had become detached from the uppers and had to be held in place by lengths of vine they stripped from trees. They were also plagued by the voracious mosquitoes and the bloodsucking leeches, and their skin was covered with angry red blotches and open sores.

As dawn broke over the valley, bathing the lush green vegetation with a warm bronzy hue, Fazackerley knew he was in no fit state to carry on. He had spent the night half delirious, tossing and turning and burning with a fever that scorched his skin, and when he tried to pull himself upright with the aid of his crutch the pain was so excruciating he toppled over. It took three tremendous bursts of physical and mental exertion to haul himself into a vertical position, and when he tried a few tentative steps he felt as if he was paralysed. His good leg would not respond to the messages his fuddled brain transmitted. He stood immobile as a statue and called out in a low, hoarse whisper that was laden with fear, 'Waggy, give me a hand, for God's sake.'

Wagstaff's head emerged from under his blanket. ''Ave a 'eart, Zack. I could done wiv annuvver fifteen minutes shuteye.'

'I'm done for. The old leg's as big as a bloody bolster. Can't move.'

Wagstaff got to his feet, sensing the urgency. 'I'll get Sergeant Harris. Don't move.'

'Trust you to be the ruddy comic.'

Wagstaff roused Harris saying, 'Zack's in a real state, Sarge. Standin' there like a stork.'

Harris flung aside his blanket, leaped up and followed the private to where Fazackerley stood like a Masai warrior leaning on his spear.

'Sorry about this, Sarge. First Simmo, now me.'

'Stop being so damned dramatic. It's not like you to throw the towel in. You've probably got no more than a touch of cramp, sleeping on the ground,' and to Wagstaff, 'Fetch Sister Bradshaw.'

The tears streamed down Fazackerley's cheeks, more in frustration than self-pity. 'I can't walk, for Christ's sake. Don't think I haven't tried.'

Kitty Bradshaw knelt and examined his putrefying leg,

294

black, swollen and maggot-infested. 'It certainly hasn't improved, but it hasn't got any worse.' She knew she was lying, and so did Fazackerley.

'Look, why don't you just leave me here with some water and some grub? The army can't be far behind us now. I can thumb a lift. I'll be all right, honest.'

'We have a stretcher, and you're going on it. No arguments. Look after him, Kitty, till we've sorted things out,' said Harris brusquely.

He gestured Wagstaff to follow him. 'We'll have to dump some of the rations. Limit ourselves to the absolute minimum for survival.'

They knelt beside the stretcher containing the food. 'Chuck out what's left of the tinned stuff,' said Harris decisively. 'Keep the rice, biscuits, tea, salt and water. If you want to hang on to any of the cigarettes you'll have to carry them yourself.'

When they had finished they looked down at the mound of discarded food. It amounted to more than they had retained.

'Some of the refugees are gonna 'ave a beanfeast, Sarge.'

'Nothing to stop you having one yourself, Waggy. Tuck in until you have to let your belt out, but I'd advise against it. Your belly is going to be flapping against your backbone, so you might as well start getting used to it.'

Wagstaff stuffed two packets of cigarettes into the pockets of his shirt. 'For the leeches.'

'Salt is just as good.'

'I know, Sarge, but there ain't nuffink like combinin' business wiv pleasure. Anyway, I've found I don' get so 'ungry if I've 'ad a fag.'

They carried Fazackerley to the stretcher and lowered him on to it, and as soon as they had brewed up and eaten they moved off, Harris at the front, Wagstaff at the rear.

They walked slowly and methodically, worried that Fazackerley would topple off. The uneven ground made them stagger and Harris found he had to keep his eyes on the ground to avoid the bigger stones and let Wagstaff act as his guide.

295

'Like tryin' to get a piana up a narrer flight of stairs,' said the Cockney.

The rough pole-ends soon raised blisters on their hands and they quickly discovered that four or five hundred yards was as far as they could travel before they needed to stop and get their breath back. And when they did halt they flopped exhausted to the ground, gulping down air like men who have been released from entombment.

Without being asked, Kitty and Avril took up position in the middle of the stretcher and did their best to lessen the burden. Nellie did what she could to help Wagstaff, not minding at all that he did not speak; just being close to him was enough.

When they halted for the night they were so tired it required a great effort of will to light even a fire and prepare a meal of rice and biscuits. They just wanted to sleep and forget the pains that shot through every limb like red hot pokers.

Fazackerley lay on his back staring at the stars, recalling how Wagstaff had said Simmo should be put out of his misery. He had disagreed with him then, but now he did not. He lay there waiting for the dawn, and when the hills to the east began to assume a visible outline he reached across to where Wagstaff lay sleeping and shook him.

'Waggy, give me a hand. Help me up and pass the crutch. I've got a bad dose of the squitters. Need to go in the bushes.'

'No one's gonna mind if you do it 'ere. Christ, the wogs do it all the time.'

'I may not be able to walk, but I've still got my pride. I'm not crapping in front of the ladies. Come on, be a pal.'

Wagstaff helped him up, handed him the crutch and supported him on the other side. They weaved a zig-zag course towards the encircling trees; the silence broken by the sound of nearby running water.

'Where the stream is, Waggy. Nice and clean. Have a wash-down after.'

They reached s sharp incline and Fazackerley insisted on going to the top. They found themselves looking down into a ravine where water flowed over rocks in a white frothy cascade.

'This'll do fine. I'll give a shout when I've finished.'

Wagstaff saw him undo his belt and fumble with his buttons on his fly. Fazackerley, upright on his crutch, gazed over his shoulder in a way that suggested he wished to be alone and Wagstaff moved away, respecting his need for privacy. He sat on a rock, lit a cigarette and waited for Fazackerley to call him. He waited for ten minutes before he shouted, 'You all right, Zack?' When there was no reply he hastened to his feet and ran to where he had left his friend, but there was no sign of him. The crutch lying on the ground was the only indication he had ever been there. Beside it was his identity disc and chain.

Wagstaff looked down into the ravine; the swirling water was carrying away large branches and the occasional dead animal, and although he knew that no one, least of all a man with a useless leg, could survive in it, he slithered down and struggled along the bank, clinging to shrubs and rocks to prevent himself from being swept away. He went as far as a waterfall where the sun shining through a curtain of water had made a rainbow, and realised he was wasting his time.

He climbed back up and walked slowly to the camp to break the news to Harris.

'He might have slipped, Sarge.'

'We'll never know.'

Wagstaff handed him the brown identity disc. 'We do though, don't we?'

'The ladies can think it was an accident. No point in burdening them with a sense of guilt. Nothing preys on the mind more than knowing that someone has committed suicide in order to make life easier for you.'

Harris underestimated the perception of the two women and completely misread their reaction, for when he told them that Fazackerley had met with a tragic accident they scoffed at the suggestion.

'It's an insult to his courage,' said Kitty vehemently. 'He sacrificed his life for us, and all you can do is dismiss it as an accident. You know damn well he knew we couldn't make it with him on a stretcher, so he relieved us of the burden.'

Avril broke in, 'Are you saying it was an accident to salve your own conscience? If so, that's a pretty shabby thing to do. I can't remember the name of the man who walked out of Captain Scott's tent ...'

'Oates,' said Harris flatly.

'Whatever it was doesn't matter. What does is that Scott didn't write in his diary that he had met with an accident. He wanted to acknowledge his courage.'

Harris held up his hands in a gesture of defeat, then wearily wiped them across his eyes. He had simply been trying to spare their feelings, thinking, quite wrongly, that they would be consumed with a feeling of guilt. Instead, like him, they were grateful for the nobility of Fazackerley's decision, and he was the one who felt ashamed. To make amends he said, 'Don't worry. At the first opportunity I'll report it officially and suggest it deserves some form of recognition.'

'That's the least you can do,' said Kitty coldly. 'It's not asking a lot. After all, he's given us a sporting chance.'

Harris said lamely, 'So I made a mistake. Wagstaff and I knew what he'd done, we just wanted to spare you.'

'You didn't think we'd believe he'd committed suicide — what's the phrase — because the balance of his mind was disturbed?'

'For God's sake, Kitty, we didn't exactly sit down and mull it over. We decided on the spur of the moment that it was the best thing to say. When you write to someone's next of kin you don't say he died slowly and in agony. You try to spare their feelings. That's all I intended. He meant a heck of a lot to us, don't forget that.'

Avril squeezed his arm. 'You thought you were doing the right thing.'

Somehow her sympathy made him feel worse than Kitty's angry condemnation, and he lost his temper.

'Right, let's get cracking. We don't want Zack's sacrifice to have been in vain, do we?' He knew it was a cheap jibe, but he could not help himself because he felt he had betrayed someone who was very dear to him.

He led them at a brisk pace which left them breathless, and although he could hear them panting and struggling to keep up with him, he pressed on relentlessly, silent and brooding and quite forgetting the strict routine he had imposed in order to conserve their strength. Two hours passed and he gave no sign of calling a halt, and when Kitty drew alongside and suggested it was time for one, he rounded on her and snapped, 'If the pace is too hot, you can always drop out and catch us up later.'

'I'll cope,' she said evenly. 'It just struck me that this is rather self-defeating.'

He knew she was right and he was being mule-stubborn, but he could not bring himself to admit it and continued to stride on, although he was aware that Wagstaff's tuneless whistling was an admonition and a request for him to stop being so 'bleedin' 'alf-baked'. He longed for an excuse to call a halt without having to admit defeat, and it was thankfully provided by Wagstaff who looked as if he could have continued all day without a break.

'Sorry, Sarge, but I gotta 'ave a break. Stone in my boot as big as a football.'

Harris glanced at his watch. 'Time for a brew-up. You deserve it.'

Wagstaff made an ostentatious display of unlacing a boot and shaking it vigorously, and if Harris noticed that nothing fell out he did not say so.

When they resumed, Harris set a pace that was markedly less punishing and the tension that had built up gradually dissipated. He found himself calling out words of encouragement as they struggled on, resuming the old routine of an hour's walking followed by an hour's rest.

The jettisoning of food to make space for Fazackerley on the stretcher meant that their rations and water had to be reduced to an absolute minimum, and soon they were tortured by thirst and their tongues became so dry and swollen they feared they would choke. Hunger gnawed at them and they were only able to keep going by thinking of the meagre meal that awaited them at the end of the day. Incongruously, they also found relief in thinking and talking about food and drink, and when they rested they spoke of the meals they would have when they reached India: underdone steaks oozing blood, surrounded by mounds of roast potatoes and green vegetables, followed by ice cream and strawberries, all washed down with ice cold wine. At the same time they found themselves wishing against their will that Fazackerley had made his decision earlier, then they would not have had to abandon so much food.

They tried eating various roots which Nellie said were edible – bamboo shoots, berries, and a gruel made from the sap of a banana-like tree – but they only gave them griping stomach cramps. Someone suggested that a pebble under the tongue helped to ward off the craving for water, but they found it had the opposite effect. They found too that the nightly doses of quinine and salt also added to their craving for water.

In the half world between sleeping and waking, Avril and Kitty imagined they were staggering down a timeless tunnel. A weary fatalism overtook them and they had an overwhelming desire to let perpetual sleep envelop them, but Harris jerked them back to reality, sometimes using the toe of his battered boots to rouse them. They might feel like giving up but he was determined they would not. They hated him, but were grateful once they began dragging one leaden-weighted foot after another.

Only Wagstaff seemed immune to the agonising routine. When someone stumbled he was near at hand to steady them, and when they fell he hauled them upright. When they marvelled at his stamina he said, 'Where there's no sense there ain't no feelin'.'

One morning they observed a party of Chinese kill a python and make it into a soup, and Harris and Wagstaff organised a hunt, beating from shrub to shrub until they raised a sleeping python which had recently eaten and clubbed it to death with the butts of their weapons. They boiled it and found it quite tasty.

A few days later they came across a rapid flowing stream and Nellie hacked some branches from a tree and crushed the bark into a pulp which she tossed into a small pool. A few minutes later a dead or stunned fish floated to the surface and Nellie grabbed it, rubbing her tummy, saying, 'Good.' She grilled it, and although it was extremely boney and hardly lived up to her promise, it made a welcome change.

When it rained water filled their boots, and dripped from the rim of their topees so that they were unable to see ahead. The track was turned into a porridgy morass into which they sank up to their thighs, and the effort of dragging each other clear left them totally exhausted. They felt like convicts on a treadmill as they slithered and slipped, sometimes falling flat on their backs, other times face downwards so that their eyes and nostrils became clogged with the foul-smelling mud. Some hills left them gasping for breath and with a sword-like pain thrusting through their chests, while others could only be descended by sliding down on their backsides.

Then when the rain stopped and the sun came out, the mud dried on them in thick heavy layers which weighed them down like suits of armour, and when they slapped themselves it fell off in crumbling chunks. Soon afterwards they were forming an arm-linked chain to wade across chaungs of tumbling breast-high water which froze them to the marrow, and they longed for the heat they had so recently been cursing.

At dusk Harris and Wagstaff had the additional tasks of dismantling their weapons and cleaning them, unloading the magazines and wiping each bullet, then reassembling them and reloading. With their lacerated fingers it took them well over an hour, but they were grateful for the sessions, which they had thought meaningless at the time, when they had been made to strip the weapons while blindfolded.

They lay in a huddle in a hollow beside the track. Overhead the sun shone with an incandescent intensity, burning through their topees until they felt dizzy. Hardly a word was exchanged. Talking required too much effort. They feebly brushed away the flies that gathered round their eyes and on the sores which had broken out on their arms and legs, but it was only a momentary respite; the flies immediately returned.

Ten days had passed since they entered the valley and they were all suffering from dysentery, but they no longer bothered to go far from the track to relieve themselves. They felt filthy and humiliated, but there was nothing they could do about it. Their skin was drawn tight over their faces and their ribs were as prominent as a pi-dog's. Their clothing hung in shreds.

Then, twenty-one days after leaving Kalemyo, they reached Tamu where they managed to bribe with biscuits, a compass, a dah and Harris's watch, the owner of a bullock cart to take them some of the way to Palel.

One morning they observed what appeared to be a sandstorm in the distance that seemed to be approaching them at great speed. Then they heard the unmistakable sound of an engine, and through the red dust a truck emerged, dark green with the upright figures of helmeted soldiers waving over the top of the driver's cabin. It ground to a halt beside the bullock cart and a British sergeant vaulted over the tailboard.

'Fancy a lift to Palel? You look as if you could do with it,' he said, casting his eyes over the emaciated party.

Kitty Bradshaw threw her arms around him. 'You'll never know what a welcome sight you are, Sergeant.'

The others embraced each other and literally jumped for joy.

'We made it,' shouted Avril. 'We bloody well made it.'

Wagstaff said, 'You wouldn' 'ave a fag on you by any chance, Sarge? I smoked me last way back.'

The Sergeant produced a round tin of fifty Players. 'Fill your boots, chum.'

He looked at the smiling group. 'Better get you to the sawbones as quick as we can. Lucky for you we've got one at the camp.'

They clambered into the back of the truck and burst into impromptu song with Harris wielding the encased Colours like a baton:

Roll out the barrel
We'll have a barrel of fun,
Roll our the barrel
We've got those blues on the run ...

The Sergeant scratched his head and said, 'When you see Palel you mightn't be so ruddy cheerful. Not exactly Butlin's.'

It was no more than a collection of tents pitched on the outskirts of the town and established as a forward post to assist the retreating army when it arrived. They were taken before an officer who said, 'We can't offer you much in the

302

way of comfort, but we'll do what we can. First you'd better see the quack.'

He took them to a longish hut with a red cross painted on the roof and there a medical officer sounded their hearts and examined their bodies.

'Considering what you've been through you're in pretty good shape. A few days' rest and you'll be ready to move on.'

Two medical orderlies bathed their sores and blisters in a strong disinfectant, dressed them and gave them several tablets to swallow. 'A vitamin cocktail,' said one. 'Have you running round like Sidney Wooderson.'

When they had finished the MO said, 'I'll see what can be done to rustle up some clean clothes and footwear. Then we'll give you a decent meal. Not too much, although I expect you feel like eating a horse, but you mustn't overtax your stomachs which have been empty so long. Quality is more important than quantity at this stage.'

Harris and the three women sat in a large mess tent replete after a meal to which more attention had been given to nutritional content than culinary delights, and revelling in the forgotten pleasures of clean clothes and comfortable boots.

Wagstaff had obeyed doctor's orders so far as the food was concerned but was unable to refuse an invitation to the wet canteen where he abandoned all caution and advice and sank glass after glass of cold beer while regaling his attentive audience with the story of the nine-hundred-mile trek. Although it needed no embellishment, he managed to add several fictional episodes. He was not, he conceded, going to feel like a route march in the morning, but that did not bother him; if the MO was to be taken at his word a nice long rest awaited him.

Later they slept on comfortable charpoys with clean blankets covering them and encased in a mosquito net that really worked.

They remained in the camp for a week, during which time they did nothing but eat and sleep, slowly regaining their strength and watching their sores responding to treatment. Then the MO examined them and pronounced they were

303

fit enough to carry on to Imphal, and they left early next morning in a lorry.

The reception they received there was in marked contrast to that which had greeted them in Palel.

Imphal was Palel on a much grander scale. Rows of regimented tents and ramshackle bashas dotted the plain outside the town, the former housing troops, the latter the hundreds of coolies who had been recruited to work on the road that was being built to ease the lot of the retreating army. The untimely influx of thousands of refugees was an added problem which was viewed with a marked lack of sympathy.

While the rest of his party was escorted to a tent that served as a guard room, Harris was taken to another to be interviewed by the officer in charge. He found himself standing before an immaculately uniformed major who was sitting behind a desk which was devoid of any papers; his peaked cap and swagger stick placed carefully on it side by side, seemed the sole excuse for the desk's existence.

The major, a sandy-haired man with a clipped moustache, asked in crisp tones who Harris was and what on earth he was up to, appearing out of nowhere with one private, two white women and a coloured girl. It was obvious he considered them all to be a confounded nuisance.

Harris gave his name, rank and number and the regiment to which he was attached.

The major drummed the desk with the silver top of his cane. 'To the best of my knowledge, the Rocks are part of the rearguard. How is it that you've managed to dodge that?'

Harris, standing rigidly to attention, told him about the Silver and explained how the women came to be in the party.

'You don't look as if you've travelled the whole length of Burma. Just look at yourself! Spanking new uniform ... It's a tall story to swallow.'

Harris explained that he had been issued with new clothing at Palel.

'My instincts tell me you could well be a deserter. Your story's too damn pat. No Silver, because you had to bury it? No covering letter from your colonel?'

304

'I resent that, sir.'

'Damned sure you do. But I've too much on my plate to consider putting you under close arrest until your story is confirmed. Better to be shot of the lot of you. Let someone else sort it out.'

The major believed that his show of bad temper was perfectly justified. He had been enjoying a comfortable unruffled existence in Calcutta which had been rudely interrupted by the plight of the withdrawing army. A plight, he thought bitterly, for which they had only themselves to blame. They had bolted like rabbits when a ferret invades the warren, scared witless by a raggle-taggle outfit of myopic pygmy-sized yellow men. The idea of wet nursing them was bad enough, but to be lumbered with an influx of disease-ridden Indians was enough to test the patience of a saint.

'I think you're being extremely unfair, sir. You've jumped to totally unjustified conclusions ...'

The major silenced him with a brusque wave of his hand. 'The fact that you allowed yourself to become tied up with these filthy refugees is ample indication of your irresponsibility, so don't add insubordination to incompetence. And don't ask me to treat you any differently.'

'I didn't come here to ask for any favours, sir. I was told to report to you.'

'You think I'm a callous bastard?'

'I've expressed no opinion, sir.'

'Well, just try and see my side of the picture. I'm told to prepare to receive an army that's been routed, and what do I find? Thousands of natives who would have been better off staying in Burma instead of panicking. Where on earth am I expected to put them? Even if I had enough canvas I couldn't risk accommodating them. No ruddy respect for anything. Like animals, crap where they stand. So they're all huddled together wallowing in their own filth and expecting me to wave a magic wand. Are you telling me that you aren't asking favours?'

'We're ready to move off as soon as you permit, sir.'

'That can't be soon enough as far as I'm concerned. Therefore I propose to provide transport to take you and your party to the railhead at Manipur where you can pick

305

up a train to Calcutta. Let some bloody desk wallah there sort it out.'

'Is there any possibility of getting an advance of pay so that Private Wagstaff and I can purchase a few essentials for ourselves and the ladies, sir?'

'I'm sure that can best be sorted out in Manipur. Your story's unlikely enough as it is without my authorising cash handouts.Transport will be standing by at o-six-double-o. Make sure you're on it. That's all.'

Harris saluted, turned on his heel and strode out. He had endured too much to be upset by an officious bastard who was resentful at having to leave Calcutta in order to attend to the needs of wretched refugees and an army he considered had let the side down.

They reached Calcutta after a long and tiring journey only to find they were as unwanted there as they had been at Imphal. The city already had more European refugees than it could cope with, refugees who had flown in with nothing and yet expected everything. They were also a painful reminder that the war was getting closer.

Harris and his party were each given twenty rupees for which they had to sign in triplicate, and handed rail warrants to Delhi where they were told things were a little less chaotic and their problems would be sorted out in double quick time. They felt like discarded bones, to be kicked around until lost.

They stood in an awkward group on a platform at Delhi's main railway station, knowing they were about to part but lost for words to express their feelings.

Eventually Harris broke the silence. 'As no one seems to know what to do with us, we've been told to report to Clive Barracks. What are your plans?'

Kitty said, 'I'm going to look up an old chum who's in the QAs. I'm hoping she can find me a job. If you want to contact me, try their HQ.'

Avril said, 'I'm going to the Willingdon Hotel in the old part of the city. The only place I've heard of. Come and see me as soon as you get sorted out. Remember we have a dinner date?'

306

'I've not forgotten, but it may be some days before they let me out on the town.'

Wagstaff solemnly shook hands with Avril and Kitty, saying, 'Lookin' back on it, it wasn't so bad. An' it's been a proper pleasure knowin' you both.'

He took Nellie's hands in his and kissed her swiftly on the mouth. 'I'll be in touch, an' don't worry – I ain't forgot wot I promised Simmo. We'll get aroun' to that, though it may take a bitta time.'

Harris kissed Kitty on the cheek. 'Look after yourself. You've been a tower of strength to us all.' Then he embraced Avril. 'I'll ring you at the hotel.'

He turned and walked away, the covered Colours resting like a rifle on his right shoulder, his Lee-Enfield at the trail in his left hand.

At Clive Barracks no one seemed at all interested in their existence. The adjutant passed them on to the RMS who passed them on to the duty sergeant who said, 'I'll find you both a billet, show you where you can eat, shit, shave and shampoo. After that you're on your jack jones. You'll have to leave your weapons in the armoury. You'll get them back when, and if, you're drafted.' He winked. 'You may think you've come back from the forgotten army, but wait till you've been kicking your heels here for a few weeks.'

'Any chance of collecting any pay?' asked Harris. 'Neither of us has had any for a long time, so we're very much in credit.'

'You can try the paymaster, and I shouldn't think you'll have much trouble as long as you've got your paybooks.'

'We have,' said Harris.

'See him first thing in the morning.' He winked again. 'He's all for the quiet life. Won't raise any problems in case it reminds anyone of his existence. Just remember, keep your heads down and enjoy a good long skive. Delhi still doesn't know there's a war on so no one's going to come looking for you. All red tape and bullshit here. The brass hats are far too occupied worrying about the next cocktail party and dance to bother about two squaddies who can't wait to get back into action. That's a dirty word in these parts. Any fighting they do is with knives and forks. Don't call them the gaberdine swine for nothing.'

Avril took a taxi to the Willingdon Hotel close to the Mutiny Memorial where the receptionist took one look at her, then at Nellie, and noting the absence of any luggage said, 'I'm afraid we're fully booked.'

'You will find two adjoining rooms,' said Avril in her most imperious tone. 'Or I shall telephone Lord Linlithgow and tell him how awkward you are being. I am attached to the personal staff of Sir Reginald Dorman-Smith, and we have just walked the entire length of Burma.'

The mere mention of the Viceroy's name coupled to that of the Governor of Burma was enough to make the receptionist fearful for his job. 'I'll get the manager, madam.' He wondered why the memsahib should arrive unannounced without any luggage and say she had walked all that way. It was most confusing. In Delhi a memsahib would not walk as far as St James's Church, and that was just across the way.

When the manager arrived at the desk, Avril insisted on talking to him in the privacy of his office and there she explained her circumstances, embellishing the story with a little casual name dropping which included the Viceroy's, Sir Reginald's and her father's.

The subdued manager said, 'I recall your father staying here, and I'm more than delighted for you to stay the night, but after that I must have some ... financial guarantee.'

'If I can have the use of a telephone, I will quickly sort that out.'

The manager coughed. 'I'm afraid there is one other thing I must mention. The native lady will have to go to the servants' quarters.'

'What absolute nonsense! Obviously you do not recognise her. If you had you would not be so thick-headed. She stays in the room next to mine. Now get the boy to show us the way.'

The manager wilted. He had made a mistake; clearly they were not two ladies who wanted rooms in which to entertain casual friends. They were obviously well connected. Baggage or no baggage they knew the Viceroy. They also knew Mr

Carfax, and if his memory was not playing him tricks anyone who knew the awful Scotsman was not to be trifled with. Apart from that, it had been a trying day: a cocktail party followed by a tiffin lunch, and even worse was to come – a whist drive, and in the evening a dinner and dance thrown by a victorious polo team which would be attended by several high-ranking officers and most of Delhi's eligible English spinsters. There would be the inevitable display of stupid horseplay, a lot of glasses would be broken, a lot of complaints registered, and no one willing to accept responsibility for the damage. He wondered why everyone had to make so much effort to enjoy themselves. Admittedly there was a war on, but it had not reached Delhi. The last thing he needed was a row about two women who might turn out to be who they claimed they were.

He walked back to the reception desk with her and brusquely demanded the register, his tone implying that the receptionist had made a ghastly error that would be looked into later.

'Would you please sign?' he said. 'There was no need, no need at all, for your word to have been questioned.' He clicked his fingers and demanded two keys. 'Fourteen and fifteen.' He looked at the receptionist. 'We will discuss this later. I shall require a full explanation.' He smiled at Avril; whatever the outcome he had covered his stumps.

He clicked his fingers and a small boy wearing a pill box hat appeared as if from nowhere. The manager handed him the keys. 'Take them to their rooms,' and to Avril, 'You will find a telephone there.' He bowed. 'Do not hesitate to ask for anything.' He glared at the receptionist. 'Did you hear that?'

Avril fingered her way through the bedside directory until she found a number for Army Headquarters, and when she got through asked to be put in touch with someone who was dealing with European refugees from Burma. A female with a cold plummy voice said, 'Can I help you?'

'I've just arrived from Burma, and I'm most anxious to contact my mother, Mrs Carfax, who left Rangoon by ship some time ago.'

The remote voice said, 'Hold the line, please.'

Avril, flushed with what she considered a victory over the rather offensive behaviour of the hotel manager, said. 'Certainly, but I haven't got all day.' She was rather disconcerted when the distant voice said, 'In that case, perhaps you'd better call at a more convenient time.'

'I'll hang on,' she said, somewhat deflated.

She heard the rustling of papers, and had to wait ten minutes before the voice spoke again. 'I have no such name on my list here, but that doesn't mean much. The whole system is somewhat anus upwards. If she arrived in Calcutta, I suggest you try this number.'

Avril jotted it down and then booked a call through the switchboard. She had to wait three-quarters of an hour before an equally indifferent voice said, 'Can I help you?'

Again Avril related her story, and again there was a lengthy pause followed by more rustling papers.

'I think you will find Mrs Carfax at the Great Eastern. Would you like the number?'

Avril said she would, and when she got it put another call through the switchboard.

She had an even longer wait before a voice, Indian this time, said, 'Great Eastern Hotel. How can I help you?'

'I would like to speak to Mrs Carfax please.'

'One moment,' Another prolonged pause. 'She has left instructions saying that she will not be back until six o'clock this evening. Can I take a message?'

'Will you ask her to call this number? It is very important. Tell her Avril phoned.'

'I will personally attend to ensuring she receives your most important message. I am at your service.'

Avril thought there was a lot to be said in favour of someone who was paid a wage to do a job and very little for someone who was a volunteer.

She bathed, dressed, ordered some tea and sat on the edge of the bed waiting for her mother to call.

The telephone rang shrilly, and in her haste to answer she dropped the receiver. She heard the familiar voice of her mother, irritable and demanding, 'Avril, what on earth is going on? Did you drop the receiver?'

'Yes, Mummy, I was so excited.'

'Just compose yourself and tell me how you are. Why haven't you kept in touch? I've been so worried. Where are you?'

'I'm in Delhi.'

'Delhi! What on earth are you doing there?'

'Mummy, I've just travelled the entire length of Burma! I could hardly give you a progress report.'

'I'm sorry, darling. How thoughtless of me. I had no idea. How are you?'

'As well as can be expected in the circumstances. It was no picnic.'

'I'm sure it wasn't, darling. I've heard the most harrowing stories since I arrived. I'm afraid we've suffered a terrible loss of face ...'

'I couldn't care less. I'm just grateful to have got out in one piece. Anyway, that's all water under the bridge as they say. How are you?'

'Bearing up, darling. Kicking my heels until I hear from Daddy. He's as bad as you for keeping in touch.'

'I'm afraid you aren't going to, Mummy. Hear from him. I've some awful news − Daddy is dead.'

'Are you sure?'

Avril could detect the note of disbelief. 'As sure as I can be,' she said hesitantly, before going on to relate what she knew. 'If he'd got through you'd have heard from him by now.'

She heard her mother sobbing and imagined, unkindly, her dabbing her nose with a small handkerchief. It was a gesture she used for all crises, big or small, a barometer to indicate that she was not an uncaring person.

Avril had to wait some time before her mother was composed enough to resume the conversation. Then she told her what she knew, and heard her say, 'He was a good husband to me, and a good father to you, and we must never forget that.'

'I did not intend to, Mummy. I don't know what prompted you to say such a thing.'

She heard a loud sniff. 'When you've lived as long as I have, you get to know how callous and short-memoried people can be.'

'Mummy! I am not *some* people.'

'I know. Forgive me. I'm letting my feelings get the better of me. Is there anything I can do for you?'

'Can you arrange for some money to be sent to me here?' The bluntness of her request seemed to surprise her mother.

'It's hardly the time to talk about money,' said her mother querulously.

'I wouldn't if it were not so important.'

'Are you short, darling?' Her mother sounded surprised that such a situation could ever arise.

'I have exactly five rupees, and what I'm standing in. I need you to talk to the hotel manager and assure him I can pay for my accommodation. If I can't, I'm out on my ear. He's sceptical that I can get hold of some cash.'

'How dare he entertain such thoughts!' The mere idea of her daughter being turfed out on to the street made Mrs Carfax forget her own bereavement. The suggestion that anyone could treat a memsahib in such a churlish fashion enraged her. 'How much would you like?'

'As much as you can spare, Mummy. I need to get clothes and a lot of other things. I'm wearing army issue slacks and shirt. I hate to sound so mercenary.'

'You're wearing what? It all sounds very confusing. I won't ask why you're wearing such humiliating attire because I'm sure you must have a good reason. Thank God your dear father was a man of considerable foresight and made arrangements to ensure I would have ample funds when I arrived here, and of course he was anxious to make sure he wasn't a burden on anyone when he turned up himself.'

'Are you sure you'll be able to manage?'

'No problems in that quarter. He transferred a large sum of money to Calcutta. But I will certainly have to see a solicitor tomorrow to get him to look into his other business interests. I suppose there's some way of finding out what they were.' A note of concern entered her voice. 'You don't think there'll be any problem getting anyone to accept he's dead?'

'I shouldn't think so. I can provide a statement. That should be good enough.'

'You are a darling. Now if you'll transfer me to the manager, I'll sort out this more immediate problem.'

'I can't transfer you from here without risking cutting you off. I'll send Nellie down to get him.'

'You mean that silly chit of a girl is still with you?'

'I won't have you talking about her like that ...'

'Let's not quarrel, Avril. I'm sure you have your reasons, but do remember that undue familiarity can create a bad impression. Now while we're waiting for the manager we might as well sort out a few things. When can you come to Calcutta?'

'Not for some time, Mummy, but I'll ring you every day. I'm really too tired just now to make definite arrangements. I need a long, long rest.' She felt herself flushing with guilt, aware that she wanted to be where Harris was.

'You'll *love* Calcutta. One mad social whirl, for which I'm extremely grateful. It's helped to take my mind off you and Daddy. Without the distractions I'd have worried myself sick. Now with the sad news it will be even more indispensable. And, Avril, there are so many eligible young officers here ...'

Avril halted her. 'I have a boy friend. I'm hoping to marry him.'

It took some time for Mrs Carfax to absorb the shock. 'Who is he? Has he promising prospects?'

Avril said wearily, 'No more than any other soldier. But I really don't want to discuss it just now. I've just arrived and I'm absolutely whacked. Just promise to send the money.'

'First thing in the morning. Now tell me about this young man, you can't leave me on tenterhooks. I also want to hear about your journey.'

But Avril was saved from saying any more by the arrival of the manager. She handed the telephone to him. 'My mother is waiting to speak to you.'

It was obvious to Avril that the manager was having trouble for his conversation consisted entirely of 'Yes, madam', and 'No, madam'.

He passed the receiver back to her, mopped his brow and said, 'Everything is settled. Your mother wishes to say a few words.'

Avril listened to the strident voice reminding her of her

313

responsibilities now that her mother was a widow and in need of all the comfort she could get.

'I'll try and get to Calcutta, but I've a lot of things I must do first. I have to report to whoever's responsible and then I want to find a job. I can't just hang around here kicking my heels.'

'Surely you don't intend staying in Delhi? That would be very cruel.'

'I must be near him. He may be shunted off somewhere at very short notice.'

She heard her mother sniff. 'In that case I'd better make arrangements to visit *you* and meet this young man who clearly means more to you than I do.'

'All right, Mummy, you do that. I'll be here some time, but I don't know when you can meet him because I don't know what his movements are. He's promised to get in touch.'

'It sounds a very odd arrangement. Can you send me a snapshot of him in uniform? What is his rank, darling? Captain, major, or above?'

'I'll call you in the morning. And I'm sorry about having to break the sad news about Daddy. I know you'll miss him dreadfully.'

She could hear the sobs and hastily hung up, but was left with the lingering feeling that her mother would cope quite ably. Uncharitably Avril felt she might even enjoy the role of the heartbroken widow.

'I'll have some food sent up, Nellie, then we'll have a good sleep. Tomorrow we'll go to the bank, then do some shopping.' She picked up the telephone and asked for the laundry. 'Can you send someone up to collect a dress, please? I want it dry cleaned and pressed.'

Avril was awakened early next morning by the sound of the telephone, and when she answered it a voice said, 'This is the Deputy Manager of the Standard Bank. Your mother's manager in Calcutta has been on to inform us she is transferring some money here for you. It may take a little time, but I wanted to let you know that we are perfectly willing to advance a loan in the meantime. How are you placed just now? Financially, I mean.'

'I'm penniless.'

314

'Would five thousand rupees be satisfactory?'

'It certainly would.'

'When can I expect you?'

'I'll take a taxi as soon as I've bathed, and thank you very much. Whereabouts are you?'

'The driver will know. I look forward to meeting you, Miss Carfax.'

She laughed. 'Not as much as I'm looking forward to meeting you.'

She went through the connecting door and shook Nellie. 'No time for breakfast. We'll grab a bite to eat later.'

As she left the hotel she paused at the reception desk to say that if there were any callers could they be asked to leave a message.

When she had signed for and collected the money, she turned to Nellie and said, 'First a handbag, then tiffin. I can't walk around with all this cash in my hand.'

With a handbag stuffed full of rupee notes of various denominations, she looked around for a suitable place to eat and found one off Connaught Place that was clean, air conditioned, and where Nellie was not looked at with hostility. They ate a light vegetable curry, followed by ice cream and fresh fruit, then set off on a shopping spree.

'I'll have to get you some suitable clothes, Nellie. Can't have you going around looking such a mess. Some stockings too, and a pair of decent shoes. But no thanaka. Lipstick and face powder from now on.'

They arrived back at the Willingdon laden down with boxes containing dresses, underwear, shoes, silk stockings, and all the other necessary accessories. Avril had also bought a crimson wide-brimmed hat of the kind favoured by matadors. 'That topee can go into the dustbin. I've seen the last of it.'

A uniformed Sikh opened the taxi door and waved a white-gloved hand to summon a porter to carry the shopping. Avril stopped at the reception desk and asked if there had been any messages.

'A Sergeant Harris telephoned to say he would call around at six o'clock. If it was not convenient and you had other arrangements, he would understand.'

315

'Call me when he arrives.'

When she reached her room she remembered her promise to call her mother. It took an hour to get through, and when she did she steeled herself for the grilling she knew was coming.

'Thank you for the money, Mummy. I've just got back from shopping.'

'Forget about that. I want to hear about this young man, and no evasions, please. I have a right to know.'

'He's a sergeant in the regular army, the Rocks. You remember them?'

There was such a prolonged pause Avril was afraid they had been disconnected. 'Are you still there, Mummy?'

'Of course.' Her voice sounded faint and distant. 'The shock and horror was so great I had to fetch my sal volatile.' Her tone turned strident. 'Do you know what you're doing to yourself and me?'

'What on earth are you talking about?'

'You know very well. I couldn't possibly approve of such a union. It's totally out of the question.'

'I thought you'd be delighted.'

'Delighted! That you want to marry a sergeant? If you'd told me you wished to marry one of your father's junior assistants I could not be more appalled.'

'I'm sorry you feel like this, but there is nothing you can do to alter things.'

'We'll just have to wait and see about that Avril. I'll not sit back and watch you ruin your life.' Her voice was menacing.

'You make that sound like a threat, Mummy. It won't work. My mind's made up.'

Mrs Carfax became conciliatory. 'I'm only concerned with your happiness.'

'It doesn't sound like it.'

'Believe me, darling, I've seen common soldiers at close quarters; they have no place in decent society.'

'So you've always led me to believe, but you're wrong.'

It was as if Mrs Carfax had not heard. 'That's not to say they cannot appear attractive to impressionable young girls – they can. I've seen it happen before in Rangoon. Girls get swept away when they see them strutting around like

316

bantam cocks or putting on a colourful show at a durbar. I'm just surprised that someone with your upbringing could have been so misled. But it's not too late to sort things out.'

Avril detected an 'I understand' note in her mother's voice which over the years she had learned to mistrust.

'If he has compromised you in any way, don't worry, darling. There are discreet ways of dealing with such mishaps.'

'If you mean am I pregnant, the answer is no,' said Avril tersely. 'And I didn't meet him in Rangoon. I'd never set eyes on him until I was leaving. He was driving some valuable things to Mandalay and Daddy arranged for me to have a lift. We didn't get to Mandalay, but that's too long a story to try and tell over the phone. It'll have to wait until we meet.'

'He gave you a *lift*, and you fell in love? Just like *that*?' Mrs Carfax could hardly suppress her bewilderment. 'Love at first sight, you'll be telling me next!'

'We were together a long time. And in circumstances which enabled us to get to know each other extremely well.'

Mrs Carfax's voice became stridently maternal. 'Darling, promise you won't rush into anything. I'm sure you can do much better for yourself. It's not your money he's after?'

'He doesn't know I've got any. He knew Daddy was a bigwig, but he also found out he'd been killed, and was hardly in a position to know he'd got most of his money out of the country.'

Mrs Carfax said cautiously, 'The final amount has yet to be assessed, but we shan't be in need. Perhaps we could purchase him a commission. Such things were once possible. Maybe they still are. It'd make him so much more acceptable to our friends.'

'Mummy, I've changed a lot since we last saw each other. I don't think much of the suggestion, and I'm sure David wouldn't.'

'At least now I know his first name, which is something.' she said huffily.

'Don't be so bitchy. I'm not withholding anything.'

'I'd like to think so. You must come to Calcutta without delay. We must thrash this out together and we can't do that over the phone. I must make you listen to reason.'

Avril was determined to keep as much distance between herself and her mother as possible, and put herself beyond the reach of any planning and plotting.

'Someone knocking on the door,' she lied. 'I'll ring again first thing in the morning. Lots of love, Mummy.'

She replaced the receiver and heaved a sigh of relief. Her mother could be so tiresome. She hoped that when she did meet David she would like him and not adopt an attitude of open rivalry before he had been given a chance to prove his worth. Not that it mattered, she would not change her mind. Even so, she nursed a nagging fear that even though they were separated by half the length of India, her mother was still capable of carrying out her implied threat.

She bathed and called through the open door: 'You don't mind if Sergeant Harris and I go out to dinner, do you, Nellie?'

'First I want to speak with him,' Nellie replied. 'He may know where Private Wagstaff can be.'

Avril showered and as she dried herself glanced at the newly purchased watch and wondered what she would do with herself until six. It was still an hour away.

She put on new underwear, but left the new dresses unpacked; she knew exactly what she would wear. There was only one dress for their first evening out together.

She went down to the lounge and ordered a gin and tonic. She thought it might calm her nerves. A boy came in and announced that her visitor had arrived.

'Send him in, please.'

Harris walked in looking extremely smart in his new uniform.

'Would you like a drink, darling?'

'I wouldn't mind a cold beer. That's if they'll serve a non-commissioned officer.'

'I've got them eating out of my hand.'

Nellie came in wearing a bright blue dress, white silk stockings and a pair of matching shoes with heels that made her totter as she walked.

'Perhaps we ought to let you stick to sandals, Nellie,' said Avril laughingly.

318

Nellie said, 'I would like to see Private Wagstaff.'

Harris said, 'He thought you might.' He gave her the address of the barracks. 'Ask for him at the guard house. He'll be waiting.'

Avril handed her several rupee notes. 'Take a taxi, and treat him to a real blow out.'

When she had gone, Harris refrained from asking Avril about the source of the newfound wealth; she would tell him in her own good time.

'I like the dress,' he said.

'I thought you would. Do you feel like eating yet? The restaurant is very good.'

'If you don't mind I'd rather go elsewhere. I gather from the noticeboard in the foyer that there's some kind of shindig on this evening, and I don't relish the idea of some drunk objecting to my presence. Let's find somewhere in town. Have to be reasonable though. They were very stingy with an advance of pay.'

She opened her bag and produced a wad of notes. 'Money no object. It'll be my treat.'

His eyes widened with astonishment. 'First Nellie all togged up, now you flashing enough money to choke a mule. You haven't robbed a bank?'

She laughed. 'No, my mother sent some money from Calcutta.'

'I'm glad to hear she made it. Did you tell her about your father?'

'Yes, and she took it amazingly well.'

'I suppose you'll be joining her?'

'Not just yet. I told her I wanted to be with you.'

'I'm glad. No one here seems to want to acknowledge my existence, so I could be here some time. Free as a bird on the wing,' he said sourly.

'You don't seem overjoyed at the prospect?'

'I love the idea of spending some time with you, but I know I should be doing my utmost to rejoin the Battalion. Trouble is getting anyone to listen.'

She nodded understandingly. 'I know how you feel, but you're surely entitled to a spot of leave? Long enough to get married.'

'Let me meet your mother first. I'd rather have her approval.'

'So would I, but it won't make any difference. Let's get married and present her with a fait accompli.' She laughed gaily. 'Even if she doesn't like you, I don't think she'll miss the opportunity of playing the martyr. You know, "I'll never let my personal feelings stand in the way of my daughter's happiness." '

'That's a bit catty.'

'Wait till you meet her. I've changed, she hasn't. I only wish she could have travelled with us. Then she might see things in a different light,' Avril said wistfully.

They found an attractive restaurant which served superb Italian food, good wine, and had an illuminated glass circle in the floor which was so small they could hold each other close while dancing without attracting ribald comments.

It was well past midnight when they returned to the hotel, slightly tipsy and immensely happy.

'Come in for a nightcap? You can see my room.'

Harris could hear the sound of boisterous enjoyment flooding from the chandeliered ballroom and he imagined the drink-flushed officers cavorting with the pick of Delhi's young ladies. He had enjoyed himself too much to risk spoiling it by providing the opportunity for someone to ask him what he was doing trying to slink up the stairs with a young woman.

'I'll give it a miss, darling. We've plenty of time to be able to pick a night when half of Headquarters' staff isn't here. I'll ring in the morning.'

'Not too early. I need to catch up on my beauty sleep.'

Harris held her at arm's length and studied her face in the glow of the porch lantern. 'I'd never have believed anyone could recover so quickly. You're very beautiful.'

'So are you.' She drew herself close to him and kissed him firmly and passionately. 'And I'm very happy.'

'See you tomorrow.'

'Promise?'

'Promise.'

It was a promise he would be unable to fulfil.

Chapter 19

The bugle was still sounding reveille when Harris was shaken awake by a private bringing him a cup of tea.

'Soon as you've got that down, Sarge, and had a bite of breakfast, you're to report to the company office.'

Harris sat on the edge of his cot sipping the over-sweet tea which had been liberally dosed with sugar in addition to a dollop of syrupy condensed milk, and was so thick the spoon almost stood upright in it. 'Know why?'

The private tapped his sun-tanned forearm and winked. 'I've got three good conduct stripes, Sarge, and I've never heard a shot fired in anger. I've accomplished it all by not asking why. With me it's always been, "Yes, sir, yes, *sir*, three bags full." That made me in their eyes' (he did not qualify who they were) 'a first-class soldier, and one who should be kept in barracks as an example to newcomers, whereas those who questioned an order were bolshie sods to be got rid of as quickly as possible, preferably to where the fighting was the hottest.'

Harris had met too many old sweats to be critical of the man's approach to army life; the ranks were full of skivers who were solely concerned with getting a soft number and clinging to it, in barrack room parlance, 'like shit to a blanket'.

When he had finished breakfast Harris went into the lounge where he browsed through a copy of an English language newspaper. Much of the front page was filled with news of the Congress Party's campaign to whip up anti-Allied feeling and its appeal to all Indians, even those

321

in the army, not to co-operate with the war effort. Gandhi was also advocating a resurgence of passive resistance in the apparent belief that the Japanese, once they had entered India, would gracefully withdraw and let Congress govern the country.

Harris knew that the army could be relied upon to be 'true to their salt', but he feared that the civilian population might easily be inflamed into indulging in an orgy of violence which would seriously hamper the defence of the country if the Japanese did invade.

He hoped that the depressing news would shake Delhi out of its deplorable complacency and encourage the authorities, military and civilian, into thinking it was time to start convincing the Indians they had just as much to lose as the British. There were ample examples to cite, showing the Japanese would be far from benevolent conquerors.

The news of the gathering unrest was continued on the inside pages and on one of them Harris was surprised to see a picture of his father alongside a story headlined 'General Appeals for Unity'.

Lieutenant General Sir Laidlaw Renshaw, one of India's most distinguished soldiers, yesterday appealed to all loyal Indians to boycott the Congress Party's campaign of non-co-operation.

In a blunt address to Delhi's business community, he said that it was a fallacy to think that Indians were being asked to fight for the survival of the Raj.

'We, the British, are only the caretakers: Indians will be fighting for India. It is absolute folly to be misled into thinking that their genuine aspirations for Independence will be furthered by a Japanese victory. Great progress has already been made towards self-government and even more momentous steps will be taken once the common enemy is defeated ...'

The story went on to say that British and Indians were not mere comrades in arms, they were brothers who together would pave the way for a new and enlightened future.

Harris thought the newspaper must have used a very old

322

picture, for his father did not appear to have aged much although his views had certainly mellowed. The army was no longer a threatening Sword of Damocles, propping up an unwanted British presence ever ready to castrate political aspiration, but the custodian of Indian nationalism.

He had certainly shifted ground since the days he told me that India was and would always remain the jewel in the crown, Harris mused.

He did not doubt his father's sincerity, although he could not help thinking of his own disgrace which Sir Laidlaw had described as political expediency. He wondered if his father might not again change his views when Japan was defeated. Would he renege on his words and fall back on the age old excuse, 'India is not yet ready for self-government'? He recalled him saying at the time of his own trouble, 'It would be criminally irresponsible of us to hand them Independence in one big helping. It must be handed out slice by slice. You must remember, they are children who should be taught to walk before they can run. You are one of the slices, for your disciplining will restore their faith in British justice. In times like these there always has to be a scapegoat.' And he had winked. 'You know what I mean. Sometimes when tempers get a trifle frayed on the field, the umpire gives you caught out behind when he knows darned well you didn't even get a snick. Cools things down.'

The cricketing analogy had been lost on him at the time because he had been unable to equate widespread and violent unrest to a game, but now he was inclined to be more charitable towards his father. Maybe he was less blinkered than he had been and was prepared to give him the benefit of the doubt. He hoped that the General's appeal would not fall on deaf ears for if it did he had no doubt at all that the British would do what they always had in the past – arrest the ringleaders and throw them into prison.

Harris walked across the parade ground to the office where a sergeant said, 'Adjutant wants to see you and Private Wagstaff.'

'Any idea why?'

'Haven't a clue, but you'll find out soon enough. Told me to take you in as soon as Wagstaff surfaces.'

When Wagstaff appeared they were marched in to see the Adjutant who was sitting behind a large desk, the surface of which was almost obscured by In and Out trays and others marked 'For Immediate Attention', 'Transport' and 'Tewts', 'Routine Orders'.

They saluted and the Adjutant stood them at ease. He was an affable-looking man who gave the impression that the desk had been built around him and he was incapable of leaving it.

'Sorry to be the one to break the bad news.' (He did not look at all sorry.) 'But your sojourn in the flesh pits of Delhi has come to an abrupt end. You are to rejoin your unit.'

Harris said, 'Does that mean they've got through, sir?'

'Not exactly. You'll be joining a newly arrived shipment of replacements from the UK. From the little we know, your Battalion is very much depleted.'

'What's the latest news, sir?'

The Adjutant chewed the end of his pencil. 'Not too bright, I'm afraid. The army in Burma has crossed the Chindwin, but they had to destroy most of their transport and armour at Shwegyin. They're now marching towards Imphal. That's where you'll wait for them.'

'I ain't complainin', sir, 'cos there ain't nuffink I'd like better than joinin' up with the lads again, but we ain't been 'ere five minutes,' said Wagstaff.

'Sorry, out of my hands. You should consider yourselves honoured. They need veterans like you to stiffen the rather raw recruits who'll be replacing the dead, wounded and sick.'

'Crikey, sir, surely they ain't thinkin' the army'll be in any fit state to turn right roun' and march back into Burma?' said Wagstaff anxiously.

'No. You'll regroup and undergo a lengthy period of re-training, especially in jungle warfare. Seems the lack of it was the main reason why the Nippos walked all over you.'

Harris bridled. 'With all due respect, sir, it was official policy not to allow us to train in the jungle on the grounds that it would be injurious to our health.'

'Well, we all have to learn from our mistakes, Sergeant.' He smiled bleakly. 'You're not going to deny a few were

324

made? A shambles from start to finish. Not much fun for us in Delhi seeing the native language newspapers crowing over our humiliation. Got to put the ship back on course again.'

Harris thought it would take a long, long time if the task was left in the hands of men like the pompous ass sitting in front of him.

'When do we leave?'

'First thing in the morning. You'll travel with the replacements to Calcutta and from there on to Imphal.' He handed them an envelope each. 'Here are your travel documents, and you can collect any equipment you need from the quartermaster. Oh, and don't forget to pick up your weapons from the armoury. That's all, I think, except to wish you good luck.'

'With your permission, sir, can Wagstaff and I nip in to town? There are some people we ought to let know we're leaving.'

'Sorry, Sergeant, but you're confined to barracks until you leave. Not my orders, came from higher up. With the present agitation that's going on, troop movements are a closely kept secret. Too many wagging tongues around. The Japs think they have us on our knees and we can't risk word reaching them that we're determined to hold India and reinforcements are flooding in.'

'I would have thought that was the last thing the Japs would want to hear, sir. So a deliberate leak might be to our advantage.'

The Adjutant tapped the side of his nose with his pencil. 'Then you'd lose the element of surprise, Sergeant. Case of "Come into my parlour said the spider to the fly".'

'Is a telephone call in order, sir?'

'Fraid not, but you can write a letter and I'll see it's passed on.'

Harris and Wagstaff saluted and left.

Outside Wagstaff said, 'I'd be much obliged, Sarge, if you put in your letter that I'm sorry I couldn't meet Nellie. Not much of a 'and when it comes to scribblin' an' I don't want 'er thinkin' I've done a bolt. Say I ain't forgot my promise to Simmo.'

Harris returned to his quarters and wrote a long letter to Avril care of the Willingdon Hotel, in which he explained that owing to unforeseen circumstances he would be leaving Delhi at very short notice but would write as soon as he had reached his destination. Wagstaff, who was going with him, sent his love to Nellie as he did to her.

He left it unsealed and handed it in at the guard room asking for it to be passed on to the Adjutant.

The Adjutant read the letter very carefully, his brow creased in concentration. He felt sorry for the sergeant who was surely entitled to a longer spell of leave considering what he had been through, but with the best will in the world there was no way he could allow the letter to be posted. Anyone with half a brain reading it would know he had been drafted. It was none of his business to enquire how a sergeant was on such intimate terms with a young lady residing at the Willingdon, the city's oldest and most prestigious hotel, but he did know enough about Delhi's flibbertigibbet memsahibs to appreciate what inveterate gossips they were. Once she let slip at a dance or cocktail party that her soldier boyfriend had left Delhi in a hurry, people would begin to deduce things, and before anyone knew it the city would abound with rumours of massive troop movements. God, he ought to know, he had been to enough parties and heard the tongues wag. He reluctantly tore up the letter and dropped the small pieces into his wastepaper basket, comforting himself with the knowledge that he was only doing his duty. Harris could write again when he got to Imphal.

In the morning when it was still dark, Harris and Wagstaff joined the pink-faced draft on the parade ground. The soldiers were laden down with equipment which included greatcoats, gas capes and gas masks, and Harris wondered who in their senses had considered those items necessary for warfare in Burma. What he did approve of though were the steel helmets they had been issued with; at last someone had realised that the topee was a thing of the past.

Harris was also introduced to three new officers; two of them were freshly commissioned subalterns who looked lost and bewildered, the third was a Dunkirk veteran who had been promoted from sergeant.

326

He took Harris aside and whispered, 'I've told the young gentlemen to lean on you as much as they can — by that I don't mean be heavy-handed, but as a prop till they feel their feet. They are very raw and, thank God, they know it. The troops aren't any better. Basic training and a few exercises on Salisbury Plain, a bit of bayonet practice and a magazine of live ammo on the rifle range, just about sums up their experience. As for myself, I'm as ready to learn as the next man. The nearest I've been to the jungle is Kew Gardens.'

Harris said, 'We've all had to learn, but they couldn't be joining a finer outfit than the Rocks. They might come in for some heavy leg-pulling from the old sweats, but they really couldn't be in better hands. They'll mother them like a hen with chicks.'

'You must be well and truly pissed off at having to go back so soon,' said the officer.

'Not really. It has been Wagstaff's and my intention to link up as soon as possible. Apart from that, we'd like an opportunity to collect something we had to bury on our way out. Must do it because that was the sole reason for us leaving the Battalion in the first place.'

The replacements piled into a convoy of trucks and were driven to the station where a train was waiting to take them to Calcutta.

Avril did not leave the hotel for three days in case she missed a telephone call from Harris, and she persistently pestered the reception desk asking if they were *sure* there had been no calls they had forgotten to pass on. Eventually she decided that he must have been taken ill, but she quickly abandoned that idea because Wagstaff would surely have contacted her. She told Nellie to wait in her room in case there was a telephone call while she took a taxi to the barracks.

She presented herself to the sentry on the gate saying she wished to see Sergeant Harris. The sentry made a slight gesture with his head. 'Report to the guard room. The building on the right. Don't let on I told you, supposed to be no visitors unless they got a pass.'

She reported to the duty sergeant and asked if she could see Sergeant Harris.

'No one of that name here,' he said briskly.

'There must be,' she insisted.

'There's no "must" about it at all. I'm telling you, there's no Sergeant Harris here, and I should know, madam,' he said cagily.

'Well, he *was* here.'

The sergeant inclined his head. 'That's a completely different question. He *may* have been, but he isn't now.'

'Can you tell me where he is, *please*?'

'I'd like to help, but it's more than my life's worth. Troop movements are strictly secret. Walls have ears, so they keep drumming into us, although anyone with any loaf who wanted to know what's going on has only to nip down to the station, but that's not the point. It's pretty obvious that Sergeant Harris had orders that he wasn't to mention to anyone that he was moving.'

'Isn't there any way of finding out?'

'Not that I know of. You'll just have to wait until he's allowed to write.'

'Can you tell me if Private Wagstaff is here?'

'The same answer applies, madam.'

He watched her walk dejectedly back to the waiting taxi, thinking to himself that it was not the first time a soldier had moved off without telling a young lady about it. Although speaking personally he would think twice before giving such a nice bit of crumpet the old heave-ho.

He appeased his conscience by reminding himself that he couldn't have helped her in any case, because all he knew was that a large number of bods had been moved out under cover of darkness and there had not even been a buzz in the Sergeants' Mess as to their destination. From a personal point of view he was of the opinion that all the cloak and dagger stuff was a sheer waste of time because he was ruddy certain the Japs had agents all over the place logging the arrival of troopships and the movements of men in transit. But no doubt it made a lot of desk wallahs like the Adjutant feel they were pulling their weight, and as long as they looked busy there was no danger of them being posted to an active service outfit.

328

Although Delhi was considered a plum posting, he personally was sick to death of the dump and he would have given a month's pay to be in Harris's boots.

When Avril got back to the hotel, she was surprised to find Kitty Bradshaw waiting for her in the lounge. They embraced like long lost friends and Avril said, 'This is a pleasant surprise, Kitty. I thought you'd forgotten I still existed.'

Kitty was wearing a smart new khaki uniform with the insignia of the Indian Military Nursing Service. 'I've come to say goodbye. Thought it would be a nice idea to take you out to lunch.'

'Where're you off to?'

'I'll tell you over lunch.'

They went to one of Delhi's finest restaurants where Kitty had booked a table for two. 'Wanted to be alone with you so that we could have a real heart-to-heart,' she said.

She explained that when she arrived in Delhi she had been unable to find accommodation in an hotel, being told they were fully booked, although she suspected it was because she had no baggage and very little money. .

'So I went to see a sister I know in one of the hospitals and she had an extra bed put in her room. It was fun for a while: endless invitations to parties and dances, and no shortage of attractive dates, but it was all too reminiscent of Rangoon. If anyone asked me about Burma and I tried to tell them, they quickly got bored. I thought of joining the QAs but after meeting some of the nurses in it I cried off. They spoke so arrogantly of coloured girls and what they called the "chilli-crackers". It was all so bloody patronising! They were nice enough girls and no doubt dedicated to their work, but they were fresh out of the UK and had not met anyone other than Delhi's tight social circle and so assumed that that was how they were expected to talk. I knew I wouldn't fit in. My friend then offered to get me a post in her own hospital, but I didn't fancy treating VD cases — there's quite an epidemic in Delhi — plus a lot of lead swingers. I needed something that was more rewarding, so I joined this recently formed outfit. I'm going to Ranchi to treat what remains of the Burma army. Then if all goes well I'll go back into

329

Burma when they set off to recapture it. Field hospitals are going to be established close to the front line. Right in the thick of things.'

Well fed and slightly fuddled with wine, they returned to the Willingdon where they carried on drinking. 'Might as well have my last fling because there won't be much social life where I'm going,' said Kitty.

Avril said, 'I really must find something useful to do. I just can't stay here twiddling my thumbs.'

Kitty nudged her jovially. 'With Sergeant Harris on your doorstep, I can't imagine you doing that.'

'He's gone, Kitty, and no one will tell me where.'

'Between you, me and the gatepost, I've heard on the grapevine that large numbers of troops have been arriving in India to reinforce the army. Supposed to be very hush-hush, but you only need a few to end up in hospital for the news to get around. If you ask me, David and Wagstaff have been attached to one of the batch of replacements.'

Kitty remained until it was almost dark. 'Time I hit the road. Don't like going around Delhi in the dark on my own. But first I must say goodbye to Nellie.'

She found the Burmese girl sitting dejectedly in her room, brooding over the sudden and unexplained departure of Private Wagstaff.

'You've only yourself to blame, Nellie,' said Kitty heartily. 'You want to be a soldier's wife – well, now you know what it's all about. Here today, gone tomorrow.'

'What happens if he don't come back?'

Kitty hugged her tightly. 'If he survives, he'll come back. He doesn't want to be haunted by Private Simmonds. Anyway he promised, and Mr Wagstaff won't go back on his word. You could sue him for breach of promise. You've got enough witnesses.' Nellie did not reply. She could never tell when the sister was being serious or when she was joking.

When Kitty had gone, Avril decided that first thing in the morning she would set about finding a job and an apartment she could rent. Hotel life with its non-stop whirl of social events did not appeal to her because she had no intention of burying her head in the sand as long as Harris was on his way to the real war. Watching young officers and young memsahibs dancing and drinking the days and nights away would only remind her of her own silly approach to the war before Burma was invaded, and she had not travelled all this way to slip back into the same old routine.

She found a pleasant and comfortable small bungalow in the British Civil Lines whose owner had enlisted in the army. It had two bedrooms, a verandahed lounge, bathroom, kitchen, and postage stamp garden. Not included in the rent were a mali, cook, two house servants and the services of a local laundry known as the 'flying dhobi'.

Having signed an agreement with the agent acting for the absent owner and paid a deposit, she then set off in search of a job. She was offered one, which she accepted, at a stall at Delhi station serving tea and snacks to troops in transit, although it meant joining the WVS. The hours, she was informed, were rather elastic because the army did not keep office hours; sometimes she would have to work early in the morning, or very late at night. She willingly accepted, happy in the knowledge that she would be doing something worthwhile and quite rewarding physically if not mentally.

She returned to the hotel, settled her account and impressed upon the manager that any letters should be forwarded to her new address and any telephone callers given her new number.

Only when she and Nellie had packed all their belongings and seen them taken to the foyer did she telephone her mother to tell her she was moving because David had been posted to an unknown destination and she saw no point in wasting money on an expensive hotel where the noise of rowdy parties made sleep almost impossible.

She had a sneaking feeling that her mother was rather pleased with David's unexpected departure.

'I know how miserable you must feel, darling, but it may turn out for the better. If a romance can survive a long separation you'll know it's the real thing. If it doesn't, you'll realise you've made a mistake.' said Mrs Carfax. Avril got the impression that her mother hoped the latter suggestion would prove to be prophetically accurate.

'Mummy, have you a pen or pencil handy? I want you

to write down my new address. You can take a taxi from the station, it isn't very far. When do you think you'll be coming?'

'Well, darling, I've already made enquiries about trains, but the news about David has rather taken the urgency out of the situation. It's not that I'm not dying to see *you*, I really am, but I'd rather like to postpone it for a while. I've so much on my hands here I have no time to call my own. I'm on a committee for comforts for the forces, running whist drives to raise money for a Spitfire, and trying desperately hard to sort out Daddy's affairs. It's not as simple as I'd imagined, and some aspects of his business affairs may have to wait until the war's over. Some piffle about War Compensation – I think that's the phrase that was used. Don't bother your little head about that, leave the worrying to me.'

From the martyred tone her mother adopted Avril thought she would thoroughly enjoy it. 'And don't worry about finances, Avril. I've transferred some more money to your account, and when I do visit you we'll come to some more permanent arrangement – unless of course you'd prefer to join me here? It may be a trifle sticky, but it's far less starched and stuffy than Delhi. They certainly aren't letting the war get on top of them. A splendid thing too, if you ask me; bad for morale if everyone goes round with a long face looking like a wet week in Manchester. Mustn't let the Japs think they've got us down. Got to set an example and show the horrible little monsters in no uncertain fashion that life goes on as usual. Just like London, where the people have thumbed their noses at the Blitz by still going to the theatre and the cinema and attending dances. Got to show the Nippos we're made of the same stuff.'

'I'm glad to hear that, Mummy, and you'll be pleased to hear that Calcutta's example is being copied here,' she said sourly.

'Darling, you sound as if you thoroughly disapprove.'

'Do I? I didn't mean to. Maybe I'd be a little more enthusiastic if I knew that David and his comrades were also having a whale of a time.'

'Now, now, darling. For all you know he may be.'

'I must dash, Mummy, I've just been told the car has arrived to collect our bits and pieces. You know where to find us?'

'Us?'

'Yes, Nellie's coming with me.'

'Is that wise? Indians may not take too kindly to someone doing them out of a job. We'd never have dreamed of employing anyone other than Burmese over there.'

'There'll be no problem. She's coming as my guest.'

Mrs Carfax's voice was strident with indignation. 'Have you lost your senses, Avril? What on earth will your neighbours . . .'

Avril said, 'Bye, bye, Mummy,' and hung up.

Frankly she did not care what her new neighbours might think. If eyebrows were raised she would simply introduce Nellie as the daughter of a Burmese prince. After all, there were enough of them in existence to stifle any questioning. It would be tantamount to saying she was the daughter of a rajah for all barriers, racial and social, would automatically be lowered when there was a hint of nobility.

Chapter 20

The journey to Calcutta was five days of unrelenting torture. At Delhi Station thousands of troops milled around the platforms, while equal numbers of Indians huddled around flickering fires along the tracks outside, waiting with infinite patience for the soldiers to be cleared so that they could board trains to take them to their various destinations because the army had been given top priority. A few crack expresses were still running to time, but they were mainly reserved for government officials and European VIPs.

The replacements for the Rocks were herded into wagons which, judging from the stench, had recently been used to transport mules. They were packed in so tightly there was no room for them to stretch out their legs and they were forced to sit in a hunched position, burdened down by equipment they were unable to remove. The wagons were hot and airless and during the heat of the day the stench of animal manure mingled with the sickly sweet odour of human sweat. At night they sat in pitch darkness because no lights were allowed, and by mutual consent no smoking was done after sunset because the fug in the poorly ventilated trucks was intolerable, and the incessant coughing of puffing men who could not sleep made it impossible for those who wanted to. Often without explanation they were shunted off into sidings where they remained for hours, sometimes an entire night, before moving off again, the clatter of wheels over the lines inducing a stupefying languor. Hardly anyone spoke because there was nothing to talk about.

There were no sanitary facilities and the men had to put

up with bursting bladders and griping bowel pains until the train stopped and they were able to stumble out and relieve themselves by the side of the track. No toilet paper had been provided and they were reduced to groping around for a leaf or some other suitable substitute. Some preferred to use a handkerchief which they kept for future use; others wasted precious water or used packs of cigarette papers. A few did not bother with anything. When they had finished relieving themselves, they stamped up and down, flapping their arms and massaging their legs in an attempt to restore some feeling to their cramp-ridden limbs.

Each man started with two full waterbottles having been assured they were sufficient for their needs, the journey would take less than two days. The contents of the bottles were consumed by the end of the second night and they suffered agonising pangs of thirst which were only relieved when one of the officers managed to get a water container attached to the rear of the train, although he was unable to procure any sizeable urns into which water could be transferred and conveyed to the thirsty men, so they had to line up with their mess tins for a meagre ration which had to meet all their needs, including shaving. In addition to being thirsty, the men were also ravenously hungry because the mobile kitchens which should have been provided at the numerous halts failed to materialise.

When one of the subalterns summoned up enough courage to seek out a transport officer to protest that his men were being made to travel in conditions that would have raised howls of protest among animal lovers, he was blithely assured that everything possible was being done to remedy the situation but owing to the great increase in troop movements every type of rolling stock had to be utilised and it was the luck of the draw that his men had ended up in wagons normally reserved for the transportation of army mules.

'When you get to Calcutta you'll see a vast improvement. There you'll find it all tickety-boo. Meantime just soldier on, there's a good chap.' The transport officer strode away. He had no idea what conditions were like in Calcutta, but he had to say something to cheer the poor beggars up. He had worn himself out asking for trackside kitchens to be established, along with rows of Elsan closets and other basic requirements, and the answer was always, 'Will do,' but nobody did.

Wagstaff, who was sharing the same wagon as Harris, said, 'These poor little sods are gonna end up in a worse state than those wot 'ave been in the retreat, Sarge. Whoever's in charge a movements couldn' organise a piss up in a brewery.'

Harris replied, 'If we were only allowed to light a ruddy fire we could have a brew-up. This obsession with black-out is laughable.'

'Know wot we did years ago when we got stuck in a train on the way to Peshawar? We took water outa the engin'.'

At the next halt Harris got the men in his wagon to form a queue alongside the engine where he persuaded the driver to fill each man's dixie with boiling water, but the news spread so quickly that a file as long as the train itself quickly assembled and the driver abruptly ceased his services as a tea-wallah because he feared losing too much steam.

It was then that Harris suggested to the officers that the black-out precautions should be ignored because there was no possible danger of an air raid, and fires could be lit for a brew-up. 'Every town and village we've passed through has been twinkling away like a Christmas tree,' he pointed out.

They arrived in Calcutta in the middle of the night amidst scenes of organised chaos. RTOs with megaphones were trying to make themselves heard above the cacophony of sound that filled the station and meeting with little success. The platforms were packed with sweaty soldiers wondering if the incredible muddle would ever be sorted out. The replacements for the Rocks disembarked and the officers were told that they would have to wait three hours for a replacement train that would take them to their next destination. The three hours turned out to be twenty-four, but no one was particularly dispirited for at 9 am sharp there was the rattle of wheels, the tinkle of cutlery and the clink of china as several trolleys manned by women from various voluntary organisations were wheeled along the platforms and they were served, free of charge, with hot drinks, sandwiches, homemade cakes and water for shaving.

336

Harris tagged on to a queue being served by portly middle-aged ladies dressed in very smart and very clean linen dresses with shoulder flashes and matching hats. They held big metal tea pots and milk jugs over regimented rows of cups, and intoned, 'Tea? Milk? Help yourselves to sugar and something to eat.' They had meticulously refined accents as if they feared they might be mistaken for railway employees. As Harris's turn approached he heard one of the women say to another, 'We shall need some more hot water soon, Mrs Carfax.'

'It's being attended to,' said the other woman.

Harris wondered if by one of those lucky thousand-to-one chances that occasionally popped up he was about to confront Avril's mother, and when he eventually paused in front of her, said,' Excuse me, Mrs Carfax, I couldn't help overhearing your name and I wondered ...'

She interrupted him, saying brusquely, 'You're holding up the queue, Sergeant. What is it – tea with or without?'

'With, please,' and as his cup was being filled he said, 'I wondered if by any chance you have a daughter named Avril.'

Mrs Carfax began to feel flustered; she really did not want to be asked questions about her family in front of friends she would be confronting over the bridge table later in the day. 'Move along, please. There are others waiting to be served.'

'I would like an answer, please, Mrs Carfax,' he said stubbornly.

She took her eyes off the cup and glanced at him. She thought he looked rather scruffy, ignoring the fact that he had been incarcerated in a train for several days. And she certainly did not like the look of that scar on his face – clearly a memento from a bar-room brawl.

'I do have a daughter named Avril, but I fail to see how it can be of interest to you.'

He said, 'My name is David Harris. I thought she might have mentioned it.'

Mrs Carfax felt her heart jump in her rib cage like a small frightened animal, and wished her husband was at her side; he would have known how to deal with this unexpected crisis. 'I can't recall her doing so.'

'It is of tremendous interest to me, Mrs Carfax.'

The men standing behind him began shouting in mock anger, 'Get a move on, Sarge,' and, 'Stop chatting up the grannies,' and 'Let's get at the char,' and other ribald and unflattering comments.

Mrs Carfax felt her cheeks burning. What must the other ladies be thinking? She couldn't just stand there. What if he blurted out something terribly indiscreet? She wiped her hands on her apron and boomed over her shoulder, 'Mrs Colquhon, could you please relieve me for a moment? This young man has a problem,' and to Harris in a much lower voice, 'I am very busy as you can see, so please make it quick.'

He followed her to a vacant seat by the side of the buffet room. 'Now how do you think I can help you?' she said, rapidly regaining her composure. She had already decided that she would not raise a finger to help him. She was thinking only of Avril, and could see nothing but disaster ahead if she countenanced such an ill-matched relationship.

'Mrs Carfax, I had arranged to meet Avril when I was suddenly drafted without being able even to telephone her. I did drop a line, but in case it went astray I'd be grateful if you'd pass on a message saying that I'm all right and will be in touch.'

Mrs Carfax chewed her lip and took the plunge. 'I spoke to Avril the day before yesterday and she told me she was leaving for home as there was nothing to keep her in India.'

'That seems a rather abrupt decision, Mrs Carfax. Our friendship was not a casual thing. We're hoping to marry.'

Mrs Carfax felt as if the bird that had been fluttering in her chest had suddenly been released and she knew she had done the right and proper thing. She affected what she hoped was a sympathetic laugh. 'How typical of Avril! I'm afraid she can be rather irresponsible at times.' Mrs Carfax fanned her throat. 'She had – how can I put it kindly? – led more than one young man up the garden path.'

Harris felt his temper beginning to rise. 'Mrs Carfax, I don't think that is the case here. We came out of Burma together. She hasn't had a chance to speak to another man.'

'I'm not suggesting she has. I'm talking of Rangoon, and old habits die hard.' She patted his hand to convey her sympathy. 'Don't think too harshly of her, Sergeant, she is still very young.'

'I don't believe you, Mrs Carfax,' he said bluntly.

'You must believe what you wish, but I ought to know my own child. You don't seriously imagine I'd deliberately stand in the way of my daughter's happiness? Now, if you'll excuse me, I think we've squeezed this particular lemon quite dry. My heart bleeds for you, but if you choose not to believe me there's little I can do about it.'

'Will you please telephone her and pass on my message?' pleaded Harris.

'I'll do that. I only hope that I manage to catch her before she leaves. I know she was offered a berth on a ship which brought some soldiers out, and I doubt if she would have cancelled it. They are like gold dust.'

'Do you know where she's going to in the UK?'

'Goodness me, no. She has a list of addresses to call on. It depends entirely who has the space to put her up.'

Harris thought of Wagstaff. 'Did she mention Nellie?'

'Nellie?'

'The Burmese girl who came out in our party?'

'Oh, *that* Nellie,' she said, sounding as if there were dozens of them. 'I'm afraid she did not. She'd hardly be taking her to England, the cold would kill the poor thing, but knowing Avril I'm sure she'd see her settled in a respectable household.'

Harris rose, accepting that Mrs Carfax was lying for reasons he was unable to comprehend, and equally convinced that she would not pass on any message. He would write to the Willingdon marking the envelope 'awaiting collection'; there was nothing else he could do. 'Thank you, Mrs Carfax, for being so considerate,' he said sarcastically.

'Not at all, Sergeant. I'm just sorry I had to be so cruel, but one often has to be cruel in order to be kind. And do look after yourself, wherever you're going. Now I must get back to the trolley.'

Harris rejoined Wagstaff who said, 'You look like you've lost a quid and found a tanner, Sarge.'

339

'I've been speaking to Miss Carfax's mother. She tells me Avril is going to the UK.'

'Sounds a bit of a rum do to me. You believe 'er?'

'No, Waggy, but she's stymied me. Said if she managed to catch her in time she'd pass on a message, but that's a load of bilge. If she can lie about Avril going to England she won't bother to mention our meeting next time they chat on the phone.'

'She mention Nellie?'

'Not in a way that helps you. Said something about her being found a job.'

The two soldiers sat on the platform with their backs resting against a wall and waited for the replacement train.

Wagstaff looked up the platform to where Mrs Carfax was busily dispensing tea. 'Bleedin' odd way to carry on, Sarge. Woulda thought the old trout'd be 'appy at the idea of her daughter marryin' a man like you. They don' come any better.'

'She clearly thinks otherwise, Waggy.'

'An' all that cobblers about Nellie. That don' make much sense neither. They was gettin' to be like two peas in a pod.'

They closed their eyes and dozed off, a capacity which had only been acquired over years of experience, until they were awakened by the mournful toot of a whistle announcing the approach of their relief train. The long wait was worth it for this train had proper carriages, and attached was one with a stove and tea urns.

Two days later they arrived at a railhead from which all signs of identification had been removed, a pointless precaution because porters were dashing around announcing the destination at the top of their voices, and there they boarded a convoy of trucks which would convey them along the new road which had been excavated through the high hills leading to Imphal.

They careered round hairpin bends, over saw-toothed ridges, zig-zagged their way up escarpments and roller-coasted through deep valleys.

Imphal was a sprawling mass of mosquito-infested, fraying tents and dilapidated bashas with thatched roofs, all of which

340

leaked and were water-logged with monsoon rain. Crowded into them were the fever-ridden decimated remnants of the army which had marched out of Burma. There were English, Indian, Gurkha, Scots, Irish and Welsh. Most were in rags and bootless, but they still bore their arms and were full of fight. They may not have looked it, but they were still soldiers.

The more seriously sick and wounded had been transferred to hospitals in India, and those who remained had been entrusted with the task of halting the advancing Japanese army, mercifully slowed down by the monsoon which, ironically, had enabled the Burma army to reach safety.

The replacement Rocks piled out of the trucks, formed into orderly lines, were stood at ease and given permission to light up. One of the new officers called Harris aside. 'As you know the CO it might be a good idea if you found him and let him know we've arrived. Seems a bit disorganised here.'

Harris looked around until he spotted Wagstaff. 'Better come with me. Nothing like a double surprise.'

They found the Rocks in a collection of tents and bashas, and were directed by a corporal whose only comment on seeing them was 'Jesus, talk about bad pennies!' to the tent occupied by Colonel Selthorpe. The corporal lifted the flap and bellowed, 'Visitors, sir.'

The Colonel was sitting on a wooden crate and working over another that served as a desk. The muddy floor was covered with crude duck-boards made from lengths of bamboo.

'Escort and Colours ready for inspection, sir,' boomed Harris.

Selthorpe looked up, and a broad smile illuminated his face.

'By God, what a sight for sore eyes – and they are bloody sore.' He rose, and casting military etiquette to the winds, embraced them. 'Sergeant Harris and Private Wagstaff! You made it!'

Harris handed him the Colours, still encased in their dark shiny cover. 'We got these through all right, sir, but we had to bury the Silver. But the spot is clearly marked.'

Selthorpe barked, 'Orderly,' and when he appeared told

341

him, 'Bring three mugs, there's a fine fellow.' To the two soldiers he said, 'This calls for a toast. Managed to scrounge a bottle of Dimple from the man responsible for setting this camp up. Useless sod who's been sent packing to Delhi. Seemed to think the men should be punished for losing, and he had to run a bloody prison camp.'

When the mugs arrive he filled them, poured in water and raised his own to toast: 'The Colours.'

Harris looked at him and thought: The old devil hasn't changed much. He had never been a big man and what weight he had lost was hardly noticeable. His face had a jaundiced look, and his shorts and shirt were darned and patched, but he still managed to look dignified. He reminded Harris of a gentleman who has fallen on hard times but is still determined to maintain appearances.

'Wagstaff, when you've finished your drink nip off and tell one of the new officers that the new arrivals can be fed and settled in as I won't be seeing them till the morning. Give them a chance to sleep and freshen up. I'll send someone to show them their quarters. Meanwhile, Sergeant Harris can tell me your story. Want to hear it all, nothing left out.'

Harris related in detail all that happened from the moment they left Rangoon until the time they reached Imphal. How Simmonds was buried with the Silver, and Fazackerley had died.

Selthorpe said softly, 'We left a lot of men in similar graves to Simmonds' and there were several who died as nobly as Fazackerley. Asked to be left with something to smoke and a couple of full magazines so they could deal with any Japs hot on our tails. I just hope the replacements will make as good Rocks as those we left behind, and those who managed to get through. But that's entirely up to us. At the moment they're green as grass youngsters: tomorrow they'll be Rocks.'

Harris asked him what the retreat had been like, and Selthorpe gave him a graphic account. When he had finished he said, 'So you can see, it wasn't the débacle Delhi likes to make out it was. We fought every inch of the way, and you have my permission to punch the head of anyone who says otherwise.'

'What will happen next, sir?'

342

'For the time being our role is to stop the Japs entering India, but I don't think that is an immediate threat. They've had a bellyful and need to regroup just as much as we do. But the respite mustn't be frittered away.' He banged the top of his makeshift desk. 'We must not become the forgotten army. We want vast amounts of equipment, modern up to date stuff, not the cast-offs that nobody else wants: tanks, artillery, transport, weapons, ammunition, wireless sets that work, ambulances and field hospitals. Decent accommodation, not these bloody hovels they've dumped us in, and new clothing and boots, not to mention steel bowlers. And we need someone at the top who's prepared to kick a few backsides to get what he needs. Now off you trot, Sergeant Harris. I'm sure there are a lot of old friends you'll be wanting to meet, and who'll be wanting to meet you. And thank you very much.'

Harris saluted and left the tent, feeling that as long as men like Colonel Selthorpe were around there was not a lot to worry about.

In the morning the newly arrived replacements were inspected by the Colonel who stood them at ease and gave them a pep talk.

'You don't look like Rocks, but you soon will. Life is going to be very hard from now on because you're going to learn to be fighting soldiers. You're going to be taught how to take on the Japs on their own terms, and there's no shortage of men in the Battalion who can do just that. You'll train in the heat and in the pouring rain, in the jungle and in the hills, and you'll curse me for it. But at the end of the day you'll be grateful because that's the only way to survive, and I'm sure that thought is uppermost in your minds. It certainly is in mine. If you ever want anything don't be afraid of asking your officers or senior NCOs, that is what they're there for. They'll be relying on you, and so you're perfectly entitled to lean on them. And I shan't be backward in asking for and seeing I get every item of equipment a first-class fighting outfit is entitled to.'

When the men were dismissed he invited the new officers to meet their colleagues in the mess he had had constructed by coolie labour. Nearby a gang of native labourers were busy building a large basha that would serve as a canteen for the men. Selthorpe wanted them to know he put their interests before everything else.

Kitty Bradshaw had not been expecting a comfortable time in Ranchi, but she was appalled by what greeted her there on arrival. The town, which was situated on a wide plateau, had been chosen by General Slim, the man who had been given the task of reconquering Burma, because it provided an ideal setting for the training of a new army. Within reach were jungles, open country, and numerous rivers and streams. It had also become one vast hospital for the sick and wounded who had arrived from Burma.

In addition to the already established hospital there were others which had been set up in requisitioned buildings and under canvas.

The sick greatly outnumbered the wounded, and there were thousands of men suffering from malaria, dysentery, skin diseases, malnutrition, mite and jungle typhus, and the number was increasing daily.

Immediately she stepped off the train she was whisked away to a tented hospital, shown the small tent she would be sharing with three other nurses, given time to unpack, then introduced to the matron who designated her to a ward to start work straight away.

There was a chronic shortage of nurses — one to every fifty beds — doctors, equipment and medical supplies, a position Kitty was assured was no worse yet no better than any other hospital's. The only item that did not seem to be in short supply was officers who seemed to have all the time in the world but nothing to fill it with.

But within days there was a remarkable transformation. Slim, with the full co-operation of General Auchinleck, Commander-in-Chief of India, began clearing out the dead-wood like a berserk lumberjack. Men who could not provide what he demanded were removed, and bad officers weeded out and replaced by men of energy and ability. Those officers who had run the transit camps as if they were adjuncts of Calcutta's famous slums were jolted out of their complacency or dispatched to some place where they could do no harm.

344

Kitty had met General Slim only once – when he visited the sick at her hospital – and was impressed by his compassion and linguistic ability; he was capable of talking to British, Indians and Gurkhas in their own language and jargon. He promised them he would get things done, and she believed him. He struck her as being a human dynamo, a man of pugnacious and determined appearance whose deeds matched his looks.

'We've been last in the queue far too long because the defeat of Germany has been top priority, something I wholeheartedly endorse, but I'm going to make sure we get a fair share of the cake now.'

He had a hard time living up to his words for soon afterwards the Cripps Mission to India failed, and Gandhi called for a nationwide campaign of civil disobedience. Although he and Congress chiefs were imprisoned, organised and widespread rioting broke out in Bengal and Bihar. In Calcutta trams were burned and government transport wrecked, while wires were stretched across the roads to decapitate army despatch riders. In Bihar and many other places, armed gangs went on the rampage, disrupting the railways by tearing up lines, destroying signalling equipment and stations, and dragging European passengers from carriages before hacking them to death.

Their actions played havoc with the movement of essential supplies and manpower but these continued to trickle through until the army restored order and the stream became a flood. Skilled surgeons and doctors arrived, along with more nurses, who, although still raw, were willing and ready to learn.

Kitty, who had previously found she had to rely on her own personal skills and tender care for the treatment of her patients, could now call upon many drugs she did not know existed: sulphanamodes, DDT compounds, mepacrine for malaria, penicillin and blood plasma. The death rate, which had been alarming, was drastically reduced. She tumbled into her canvas camp bed at night totally exhausted but content. Some mornings before going on duty she scribbled a hasty letter to Avril, passing on any news she felt would safely escape the censor's blue pencil or scissors.

Then as the weeks passed Malaria Forward Treatment

Units were established not far from the front lines which meant that sick men no longer had to be sent back to India; a five month or longer absence from their unit need now only be three weeks. The burden on Kitty's hospital was considerably lessened; so much so that the staff had time for some social life in which the Indian nurses too were encouraged to take part. She received the occasional reply from Avril who described the voluntary work she was doing and her dismay and bewilderment at not having heard from David.

In Imphal there were also marked improvements. Tanks, artillery, ambulances, field hospitals, ammunition, mortars, plus Tommy-guns, Brens, wireless sets, stubborn mules and nippy four-wheel drive American jeeps which were capable of operating in the most rugged country, and every other appurtenance of modern warfare, continued to arrive in a steady stream along the newly built roads. The men who had survived the retreat were issued with new uniforms and footwear. Shorts were now strictly taboo, and every man had to wear slacks and roll his sleeves down at sunset.

Food, however, remained a problem and weeks went by without the Rocks tasting fresh meat and vegetables. There were no cold storage facilities or insulated wagons, and vegetables quickly rotted in transit. They had to exist on bully beef which in the hot weather poured out of the tins like a thin stew. Local cattle could not be purchased because goats and sheep were a scarcity, and what bullocks there were were needed for agriculture. To have slaughtered them would simply have caused starvation among the native population. Occasionally their diet was varied with a consignment of tinned herrings, but there were no dehydrated foods or tinned fruit.

If the British troops fared badly, the lot of the Indians was even worse; mainly vegetarian, or only able to eat ritually slaughtered meat, they had to rely on a mainly rice diet and chappatis made from atta flour, but there was an acute shortage of both.

Despite the shortcomings and hardships, the Rocks continued to train hard. They exercised in the jungle, learned how to cross rivers, carried out attacks with tanks and artillery, mastered the art of patrol work and how to gather information and not be totally reliant on motorised transport. In short, they were being taught how to beat the Japanese at their own game.

General Slim had drawn up a list of essentials which he put under three headings: spiritual, intellectual and physical. In this last section he had stated:

The man must feel he will get a square deal from his commanders and from the army generally;

He must, as far as humanly possible, be given the best weapon and equipment for his task;

His living and working conditions must be made as good as they can be.

As the weeks passed, the Rocks admitted that Slim's demands had certainly been met as far as they were concerned, especially when it came to accommodation. The old and rotting tents and bashas had been replaced by new ones which were waterproof, and the floors covered with duck boards and coconut matting. The food was still awful, but the canteen had plentiful stocks of beer.

Soon after his arrival at Imphal Harris wrote to Avril c/o the Willingdon Hotel, and continued to write even though his letters went unanswered. Then, as the weeks passed, he grudgingly accepted that perhaps Mrs Carfax had been telling the truth. He hated the thought, but could think of no other reason to account for Avril's silence. He wondered if she believed his failure to keep the promised appointment had been a deliberate act on his part to indicate he wished their association to end. But he dismissed that from his mind; he had written from Clive Barracks explaining he would be unable to turn up. Whatever the reason, there was nothing he could do about it, stuck as he was in the middle of nowhere.

If he had known what had happened to his first letter he would have been driven to a fit of uncontrollable fury which would have been inflamed even more if he had been aware of

347

the fate of his subsequent letters. But the explanations would have done a lot to lift the dark cloud of depression that threatened to engulf him when he lay down on his charpoy at the end of a gruelling day.

The manager of the Willingdon had gone to a more lucrative position at another hotel and had taken the receptionist and his assistant with him. Considering his responsibilities to the hotel ended with his departure, he had not bothered to pass on to his replacement the need to hold on to any letters for Miss Carfax until she called to collect them. And so the letters piled up in a pigeon hole until the replacement receptionist decided it was safe enough to consign them to the wastepaper basket. Clearly, he reasoned, the young lady attached no great importance to them.

Then when, out of the blue, Miss Carfax turned up to claim her letters, he did not have the courage to admit his folly but assured her there had been no mail.

He felt extremely ashamed when she explained that she had just returned from Simla where she had been sent to convalesce after a spell in hospital with a severe bout of malaria and dysentery, and a broken arm incurred when she collapsed on duty with the onset of the illness and had fallen heavily against a heavy steel trunk left unattended on the platform.

The young man assured her that he would contact her immediately if any letters did arrive, but mercifully they ceased.

Harris resigned himself to the fact that, whatever the reason, he had lost contact with Avril, but life had intensified to such a degree he had little time to brood over it. Like most men about to go into battle he became totally engrossed in learning how to take life while preserving his own, and like a condemned man his mind became concentrated on the present rather than the future.

Now their encounters were no longer exercises but the real thing. Intelligence gathering patrols regularly penetrated the enemy lines, killed a few Japanese, collected maps, signals, took out forward observation posts with grenades and mortars, and picked up the odd trophy. Wagstaff returned from one brandishing an officer's sword, but was outdone by

348

a Gurkha patrol who brought back several severed heads.

Shortly after one successful patrol Harris, who was the acknowledged master of the hit-and-run patrol, sought an interview with Colonel Selthorpe where he suggested something that put a spring in the CO's heels.

'We penetrated far enough, sir, for me to be convinced we could, with two jeeps, retrieve the Silver and be back before the Japs even know we've been there. The jeeps with a couple of trailers behind can get up the valley like steeplechasers. The Japs have nothing to touch them, and as long as we've got enough concentrated fire power, sir, I don't think they'll even try to stop us.'

'I'd be for the high jump if it leaked out to army command,' said the Colonel doubtfully. 'If it failed, General Slim would have me put against a wall.'

'If it didn't, sir, imagine the headlines it would make in SEAC, not to mention the London papers.' Harris spread his hands indicating an imaginary headline. 'Daring raid to rescue regimental Silver. Wonderful boost to morale.'

'General Slim stressed the importance of morale in his new army,' said Selthorpe musingly. 'He's been reported as saying, "It is that intangible force which will move a whole group of men to give their last ounce to achieve something, without counting the cost to themselves; that makes them feel they are part of something greater than themselves." So impressed me, I memorised it. Well, as we both know the regimental Silver can instil that feeling in men. I'm half convinced, so convince me more.'

'If you could get the workshop to mount two twin-Vickers to each vehicle — one next to the driver, the other in the rear — and load them with HE, armour-piercing, and tracer ammo, they'd be like battleships on wheels and capable of taking on any armoured stuff if we came across it.'

'Personnel?'

'Four men to each vehicle, sir, each with a Thompson and several grenades. We could leave here in daylight, get there in darkness, recover the Silver, hole up for a while and come back in the dark. We've been doing similar trips for some time now.'

'It will have to be a volunteers only job.'

'You've got two already, sir. Wagstaff and me. Six more will be no problem.'

'I'll leave it to you, Sergeant Harris. I'll attend to the jeeps.'

A week elapsed before Colonel Selthorpe summoned Harris to his tent. 'The jeeps are ready. Better come and see if you approve. Took so long because the engineers had a spot of bother with the swivels on the Vickers' mountings. Wanted to give you a wide field of fire. They've also fitted rather nifty blinkers on the headlights.'

As they walked to the workshop, Selthorpe asked, 'Got your crew?'

'The first time of asking, sir. The commissioned sergeant who came with the new draft, sir, three long service men, and two newcomers.'

'Fine mixture,' nodded Selthorpe approvingly. 'Like the hymn book, a blend of ancient and modern.'

Harris was impressed with what he saw; the two jeeps looked lethal.

'Let's try one out,' said Selthorpe.

'He took the wheel of one and Harris sat beside him, and they drove off down the plain. When they were well clear of the camp Harris fired a series of short bursts on the front Vickers, testing its field of fire. It was about 180 degrees: beyond that it automatically locked to rule out the possibility of shooting anyone in the back of the vehicle. He then tested the rear gun and expressed total satisfaction.

'Take the crew on a few practice sorties, and then report to me when you're ready for the off,' said the Colonel.

Harris carried out a series of high speed exercises during which he devised a simple but effective system of hand signals so that the Jeeps could be deployed with maximum fire power without running the risk of shooting each other up, then reported back. 'I've checked with the Met Office, sir, and there'll be a full moon in five days time. If we set off tomorrow we'll have some light at night, but not too much. I've loaded the jeeps and trailers. Plenty of food and ammo, and enough rations and water to see us through comfortably.'

350

'Well done. I won't see you off, not physically at least, but I'll be with you in thought and prayer. Come and have a drink before I go and see the padre and solicit His help.'

Harris set off next day behind the wheel of the leading jeep. An uneven but clearly visible track had been worn along the Kabaw Valley by the feet of countless refugees and the retreating army and they made excellent progress, sometimes achieving speeds in excess of thirty miles an hour. He had timed the departure so they would have the maximum hours of daylight before they were in danger of encountering any enemy patrols, but as soon as sunset came their speed was reduced considerably as they had only the visored headlamps to light the way ahead. Towards dawn Harris called a halt and the jeeps were driven to the cover of some nearby trees and hidden beneath cut down branches and foliage. Then he and Wagstaff set off to find Simmonds' grave. They quickly located it and were delighted to find it had not been disturbed; the small cross was still in position with the topee on top of it. They returned to the jeeps and drove cautiously to the grave. Spades were unloaded and the soldiers began to dig. It took the strong able-bodied men far less time to uncover the canvas shroud and then the Silver than it had taken Harris and Wagstaff to excavate the hole. No words were exchanged, they were unnecessary, it had all been explained in minute detail in advance. Two hours later the Silver was in the tarpaulin-covered trailers and Private Simmonds' body had been reinterred.

'Shouldn' we 'ave taken 'im back, Sarge?' whispered Wagstaff anxiously.

'No, Waggy, we'll collect Simmo with all the others. When it's over and finished with. They'll be buried in proper cemeteries.'

They returned to the spot where they had hidden before and Harris said, 'We'll hole up for the rest of the day. An hour before sunset we'll start back. Everyone get their head down, I'll keep watch.' But none of the volunteers felt like sleeping; extra ears and eyes might pick up some slight sound Harris's had missed.

They sat hunched under a canopy of foliage, their Tommy-guns at the ready. They heard many faint rustlings in the jungle and undergrowth, but could never be sure whether they were caused by animals or humans. The sweat poured off their faces, and the tension was unbearable. Their eyes kept turning towards Sergeant Harris who sat motionless as a carved Indian outside a cigar store, his expressionless face giving nothing away. The clank of a water bottle being raised to parched lips sounded like a waterfall, and the crushing of a biscuit like a cement mixer at full blast.

Harris looked at his watch. 'Get ready. We leave in half an hour.'

The thirty minutes passed with agonising slowness and the soldiers began yawning to disguise their threadbare nerves.

'Right. Mount up.'

The camouflage was hurled aside and the men piled into the jeeps. The engines revved and the wheels churned up clouds of dust as they broke cover and headed for open ground.

They heard the shrill blast of whistles and the air became bright with flares and the sound of rapid gunfire was heard. A Japanese light machine gun opened up with the staccato chatter sound which had led to it being christened the 'woodpecker' by men who had survived the retreat.

Harris put his foot down, churning up the dust like a smokescreen as he saw Japanese soldiers, identifiable by their baggy trousers, puttees and weird little caps, bursting out of the forest firing as they came towards him. 'Give them a burst, Waggy,' he yelled.

Beside him Wagstaff stood up, held secure by a belt harness, and opened fire with the twin-Vickers and was quickly supported by the Thompson. He used the harness for purchase, swinging the blazing barrels in wide sweeps. He did not need to use the sights, the tracers told him when he was shooting high or low. The mixed ammunition created havoc among the screaming Japanese as they advanced at the double. Harris gave a signal with his right arm and the rear jeep pulled out of line and veered to the right to bring its own front machine gun into action.

The concentrated fire cut through the Japanese and they

fell like corn under the scythe. As the two jeeps passed them the rear guns took over. They turned and headed back, this time the front guns hammering in unison.

As they passed through the Japanese soldiers grenades were lobbed and what had been battle cries became agonised screams as razor sharp fragments of metal tore into flesh. Under the combined onslaught of shrapnel, high explosive and armour piercing bullets, men were cut in two, decapitated, disembowelled. Several of the enemy turned and ran for cover, leaving a solitary officer standing waving a long curved samurai sword above his head. Wagstaff fired a short burst and the officer literally disintegrated. He then turned on the fleeing soldiers and mowed them down like skittles in a bowling alley. 'They died for the Emperor, but they didn't seem too bloody keen about it,' he shouted above the din.

Harris waved his hand high above his head, signalling the withdrawal, and the two jeeps roared off. When they were clear the second jeep resumed station astern.

The Silver in the trailers clinked and clattered, and Harris bellowed, 'Hope we don't have too many dents and scratches, Waggy. The Colonel will blow his top.'

A veteran of the retreat sitting in the back said, 'That was a sight for sore eyes, Sergeant. When we were fighting our way out we didn't see one of the yellow baskets turn tail and bolt. It was an honour to die. Wouldn't be taken prisoner either. Bastards used to walk towards us with their hands in the air and a grenade under their tunics. We learned to shoot them before they reached us. Don't know whether it was true or not, but we were told they always left a bit of fingernail or a lock of hair behind at home so there was something to bury with their ancestors. I hope these poor bastards we've left out there took that precaution because there isn't much left of them.' He sounded quite pleased.

Harris felt the gorge rise in his throat. It had been a sickening spectacle, but he realised it was only a foretaste of what was yet to come; the Japs would give no quarter and would expect none in return. The armchair pundits would no doubt argue about the rules of war, but those about to fight it in Burma would have to tear the book up.

Colonel Selthorpe was waiting on the perimeter of the

camp, and judging from his agitation had been there some time. When the jeeps braked to a halt he said, 'Everything go according to plan, Sergeant Harris?'

'Like clockwork, sir. We had to sort out a few Japs though. Must have wondered where we sprang from, but we left them in no doubt that we'd been there.'

'What took you so damned long?' said Selthorpe. 'Been kicking my heels waiting to get in touch with the SEAC chappie. When you've stowed the Silver in the armoury and I've looked it over, get yourselves to the canteen and tell the bar steward to put it all down to me.'

When the Silver had been safely stowed away in crates, Colonel Selthorpe called Harris aside. 'Want you to come to my tent. Have a chotta peg together. Want to make a proposition.'

They sat on real chairs, and when Selthorpe had poured drinks he said, 'Thought of changing your mind about a commission, Harris? Could get you commissioned in the field.'

'I might have considered it a short while ago, sir, when I was thinking of getting married. Would have pleased the young lady, and certainly made my life easier with her mother, but that's collapsed like a pack of cards so I don't think I'll bother, sir. But thanks all the same.'

'You'd make a damn fine officer, Harris, but I respect your wishes. What was it Kipling said — man had a phrase for every damn thing — "the colonel's lady and Kitty O'Grady are sisters under the skin". Well that applies just as much to officers and sergeants. Your health, Harris, and my sincere and heartfelt thanks. Won't pry into what's none of my business, but if I could wangle you a spot of leave and you thought that might help, I'll do all I can.'

'Thanks very much, sir. That would be appreciated.'

Chapter 21

Training continued without respite, and as the year drew
to a close General Slim's dynamism began to reap results.
The railway system was extended and made more efficient,
a network of roads was bulldozed through what the pessimists had predicted was impenetrable territory. Mammoth
American-built earthmoving machines were brought in to
confound the cynics, and if not actually *moving* mountains
heaved great paths through them, while thousands of coolies
with pickaxes and rock-breaking hammers hewed ribbon-like
tracks through terrain which had defeated the efforts of the
most sophisticated equipment.

With the improved transport system, the much needed
supplies poured into the front line and into the build-up areas
until the men of the 14th Army no longer felt they were forgotten. Food which animals would have spurned was replaced
by carefully balanced rations which were nourishing and far
less monotonous. Plans were also drawn up for a large-scale
air, land and sea reconquest of Burma. Deep behind the
enemy lines Wingate's Special Forces were creating havoc
and proving that, man for man, the British and Empire
troops were more than a match for the dedicated armies
of Hirohito. But even more important than the damage they
inflicted was the experience they acquired and passed on.

If the men preparing to go into battle had a grouse it was
over the curtailment of leave to Calcutta, a decision General
Slim had made with considerable reluctance, for although
the city boasted numerous cinemas, restaurants and clubs, it
offered little to the poorly paid and not too welcome fighting

soldiers who were constantly attracted to the dubious dance halls and foul, disease-ridden brothels. As a result, the VD rate rose alarmingly, while too many men with memories of deplorable leadership in their minds, had yet to realise a new broom had arrived and went AWOL. In addition there were frequent and often violent brawls between American and British troops, usually started by the Tommies who resented the GIs money-to-burn attitude and envied the fact that they were not so restricted by social mores. Slim therefore decided that Calcutta would remain out of bounds until abundant and more wholesome entertainment was provided.

Aware of this, Harris was understandably surprised when Colonel Selthorpe took him aside one morning and asked him how he felt about a short spell in Calcutta.

'Not leave, I hasten to add, official army business. I've got to attend a forward planning conference along with other commanding officers. General Slim is going to put us in the picture.'

'Where do I fit in, sir?'

'You don't. We're being flown in from here, and I've obtained permission from General Slim to transfer the Silver to some bank vaults in Calcutta. Apparently he was delighted with our little enterprise, and the subsequent publicity it attracted, especially in England. He attaches as much importance to tradition as I do. So you'll act as custodian of the Silver until it's safely underground.'

'Thank you, sir. I'm honoured.'

'Didn't intend honouring you, Harris. I could have sent any useless bod. Nothing risky about it. I just wanted to give you an opportunity of sorting out your domestic problems. It'll only be for three days, so make the most of the time.'

'There's someone I can look up there. I'm grateful for the chance.'

'How are you off for money, Sergeant?'

'Haven't drawn any for weeks, sir.' He grinned. 'Not a lot to spend it on here.'

'Well, draw some. Might as well enjoy yourself at the same time.'

Harris flew out four days later in a Dakota which carried several commanding officers and the crated Silver. On arrival the Silver was transferred to army trucks with an armed escort and driven to a bank where Harris saw it safely deposited in the vaults. He was then driven to a new rest camp run by the civilian community at the racecourse whose conscience had been pricked by mounting criticism of their outspoken dislike of the men who were standing by in readiness to preserve their cherished way of life. It was superbly managed with supper bars, clubs and regular dances, and a comforting reminder that Calcutta was slowly emerging from its carapace of indifference. Not so long ago the people now running it had considered it witty to repeat Lady Curzon's remark that the two ugliest things in India were the water buffalo and the British soldier; now the seats in the concert hall had printed song sheets on them containing such barrack room favourites as 'Bless 'Em All'.

Harris telephoned the WVS and was told that Mrs Carfax could be contacted most evenings at the Great Eastern Hotel. He had his khaki laundered and pressed, and polished his boots until they shone and worked on his webbing as if he was about to mount guard at the Viceregal Lodge in Delhi. Memories of her expression of disdain when she had looked him up and down on the railway station were still fresh in his mind.

He introduced himself to the receptionist and asked for Mrs Carfax. The receptionist rang through, and Harris was surprised to be told that she was prepared to see him.

A houseboy knocked discreetly on her door, and she called out, 'Please enter.'

Mrs Carfax was sitting beside an open window with a small table in front of her bearing an assortment of bottles, ice and soda water. Overhead a fan rotated slowly, churning up the sultry air. Dotted around the room were open bowls filled with the dried petals of flowers and sachets containing sprigs of lavender. Mrs Carfax, who exuded the smell of cologne, was wearing a floral patterned dress and cooling herself with an ivory-fingered fan decorated with Chinese figures crossing bridges and being swooped upon by swallows. When she lifted the fan he could see damp patches under her armpits.

She was not an unattractive woman; her figure, although

357

tending towards what was unkindly called middle-aged spread, was still shapely, and her hair showed no traces of grey. Only the hairline wrinkles below her eyes and on her neck gave any indication of her many years in the tropics.

She gestured with a beringed hand to the chair opposite. 'No need to introduce yourself, Sergeant, I have a good memory for names and faces. May I offer you a drink?'

He hitched up his carefully pressed slacks, sat down and said, 'A cold gin would go down very well, Mrs Carfax.'

She poured him a generous measure, added tonic water and some ice. 'Lime or lemon?'

'Lime, please.'

She studied him with amazingly blue eyes and thought he looked far less disreputable than he had at the railway station.

'Are you enjoying your leave? We're really working our hands and feet off trying to make Calcutta more attractive to our soldiers.' She pointed a finger at the ceiling. '*They* have told us we have been rather remiss. It seems we've got to remember Queen Victoria is no longer with us.' (He assumed that this meant they had been told to keep abreast of the times.) She snorted belligerently. 'We needed no reminders. You have only got to look around to realise that times have changed, more's the pity.'

'I'm not really on leave. Here on official business.'

She nodded and vigorously fanned herself. 'Well, let's not beat about the bush in that case. You must be very busy. Why have you called on me?'

'I'd have thought you knew the answer. I want to talk about Avril.'

She spread her arms in a gesture that suggested any number of things: bewilderment, impotence, a desire to help, an inability to do so, sympathy.

'I though I'd explained the situation when we spoke on the railway platform. She's gone to England. More I cannot add.'

He leaned forward, flicking an imaginary speck of dust off his slacks, and spoke slowly, trying desperately hard to control his mounting anger, anxious not to antagonise her. 'Mrs Carfax, Avril and I are in love.' (She tut-tutted,

358

but he could not make out if it was from approval or disapproval.) 'Therefore it seems odd that she should go off without leaving any kind of message.'

'Sergeant, I'm not answerable for Avril's foibles. Perhaps she had a good reason.' She sighed. 'As you've no doubt discovered, she's a headstrong young lady. A thought occurs to her and she acts.' She clicked her fingers. 'Like that. She didn't discuss her intentions during our little têtes-à-têtes over the telephone. Maybe her departure was abrupt because it was a case of accept or miss a passage. I simply don't know.'

'What I can't understand is why she should want to go to England.'

'There's little to hold her here in India.'

'That's not very flattering.'

'I had no intention of being offensive, Sergeant.' (Harris realised that, despite her memory for names, she had no intention of using either of his.) 'What I meant was that her roots were in Burma, not here, whereas England is and always has been home.'

Harris knew it was all verbal fencing, but he was in a cleft stick; if he adopted a conciliatory approach so as not to alienate Mrs Carfax who, whether he liked it or not, might one day become his mother-in-law, she would interpret it as a sign of weakness. If he became aggressive she would take that as an opportunity to be deeply offended and ask him to leave. He decided on a middle of the road course. 'I haven't much time left before I return to my unit, so you'll pardon me if I'm frank. Do you dislike the thought of us marrying?'

He immediately realised it had been the wrong choice.

'My likes and dislikes do not enter into it,' she said disarmingly. 'As I have said, Avril will make her own decision.'

'That really isn't an answer.'

She stiffened in her chair but replenished his glass to cushion the blow she was about to deliver. 'If you persist in pressing me, then the answer is yes. I have nothing against you personally, Sergeant. How could I? I know nothing about you. But you must realise that Avril has been accustomed to the very best in life. What can you offer in

359

exchange? Very little, I'm afraid. Letters from some remote battle area? Possibly a letter of condolence from the War Office, and a widow's pension?'

'That has always been the lot of women who marry soldiers.'

'Precisely. That is why you do not have my blessing.'

'Aren't you being unduly pessimistic? More men return from the battlefield than do not.'

Her eyebrows rose until they almost formed a straight line. 'And then? The life of a non-commissioned officer's wife? Moving from one garrison to another, never settling to a stable, rewarding existence. A brutal, coarse life, lacking comfort or the prospects of advancement. Accept it, Sergeant, the lot of the peacetime soldier is not enviable. I've observed it.'

'I've *experienced* it, and it isn't as bad as you make out. You should try asking some of the wives.'

'I've no wish to sound disparaging, but the average soldier's wife is hardly in a position to know what a dismal existence it is. What she has never had she can never miss. With Avril it's quite the opposite.'

'Believe it or not, I've seen the other side of the coin, and I've no regrets.'

Mrs Carfax showed not the slightest inclination to pursue this hint of a more distinguished past but carried on as if he had not spoken. 'And what of any children? A sparse neglected education with little or no continuity? A life dictated by the sound of hobnailed boots and brass bands, and where the best doors must remain closed to them. Avril deserves something better. She is a woman of refinement and breeding. Time, as they say, heals all wounds, and I'm sure she can do much better for herself.'

'I don't intend remaining in the army when the war is over.'

'And what will await you? A position in the Corps of Commissionaires? Really, Sergeant, you stretch my tolerance to its limits.'

Harris rose, leaving his drink untouched. 'There's not a lot left for me to say.'

'Nothing, I would have thought.'

She rose and extended her hand. 'I wish you all the best of luck, Sergeant, and do take care of yourself. You may have a very low opinion of me, but you must realise that I am concerned solely with Avril's happiness. It would never work out. Take my advice and find a nice young lady more suitable to your status.'

He picked up his hat and walked towards the door, pausing before he let himself out to say, 'I'm not sure Avril will appreciate what you're doing for her.'

'Not at the moment, possibly, but later, yes. You can never make a silk purse out of a sow's ear, but you can quite easily reverse the process and I'm determined to see that doesn't happen to my child.'

He slammed the door and heard her call after him, 'Sergeant, you haven't finished your drink.' Her voice registered genuine surprise and he realised that she really was offended with him for rejecting her hospitality.

Harris walked back to the leave centre where he drank himself into a semi-comatose state, and when he tumbled into bed he reflected wryly that if Mrs Carfax had been able to see him she would have claimed that his condition justified her misgivings. It would not occur to her to ask why.

Shortly after the Dakota became airborne for the return flight to Imphal, Colonel Selthorpe came and sat beside Harris in one of the hard bucket seats that lined each side of the fuselage. 'Manage to sort anything out, Sergeant?'

'Afraid not, sir. I met her mother, but she's violently opposed to her daughter marrying an NCO and wouldn't help me get in touch.'

'Silly bitch. You should have told her General Slim started as a private.'

'Maybe I should become a little more career conscious, sir.'

Selthorpe slapped him on the back. 'That's the ticket. Not only more money, but a little more comfort. If you're serious nothing would please me more. I need a few more officers with your experience.' He lowered his voice in a conspiratorial whisper. 'Big things are afoot. General Slim has had to amend his plans a little. Intelligence reports the Japanese 15th Army is preparing to attack Imphal and

Kohima. We're going to establish fortified positions and dig in. The Imphal Plain is an ideal setting for a set piece battle. We're going to destroy them in a place of our own choosing. Then we'll take the rest of Burma.'

When Selthorpe returned to his own seat forward, Harris dozed off and thought about the future. Three pips on his shoulders might make Mrs Carfax view him in a more acceptable light, but that he knew was the easy and cowardly way out. If he did that it would make a mockery of the decision he had taken so many years ago. Apart from that, despite the Colonel's belief, it was unlikely he would be allowed to remain with the Rocks. A man commissioned from the ranks was invariably moved to another regiment because it was considered unfair to him and the men under him if he was allowed to remain. He wondered why he had given it a second thought: Avril loved him for what he was, and that was good enough for him if not for Mrs Carfax.

Chapter 22

On 6th March 1944, the Japanese launched their long awaited offensive when one hundred thousand men crossed the Chindwin and drove into India in a five-pronged attack. Kohima, Imphal, Dinapur and Tamu were the main targets.

In a rousing Order of the Day, General Mutaguchi announced, 'This operation will engage the attention of the whole world, and is eagerly awaited by a hundred million of our countrymen. Its success will have a profound effect on the course of the war, and may even lead to its conclusion. We must therefore expend every ounce of energy and talent to achieve our purpose.'

The army responded magnificently, and very soon afterwards the Rising Sun was flying for the first time above Indian soil.

In Delhi the speed of the advance shocked everyone, and a sense of fatalism seized the civilian population. Avril suffered an oppressive bout of déjà vu. It reminded her so much of Rangoon when Burma was invaded. Far from diminishing, the social whirl seemed to increase. It was as if most people believed they had little time remaining for a last fling.

She followed the progress of the war as best she could from the unreliable reports which appeared in the newspapers, but she suspected they were gilding the lily as far as British resistance went. Then, as in Rangoon, rumour began to take the place of fact: the British army was being routed, the way to Delhi was wide open, Imphal was starving, and Kohima had fallen.

To allay mounting fears General Sir Claude Auchinleck,

speaking in his capacity as Defence Member, told an anxious Assembly in the capital: 'Imphal is still in our hands and is strongly held. Penetrations by small parties of the enemy are always possible but are not likely to be of major importance. Our commanders do not intend to let Imphal fall into enemy hands.'

Some believed him, most did not. Many preferred to listen to and accept the day and night broadcasts the Japanese made in atrocious English proclaiming their successes. They also heard with mounting dismay that many captured Indian troops had joined the Indian National Army and were now fighting alongside the Japanese.

Avril listened to one or two of them in a similar frame of mind to those people in England who listened to Lord Haw Haw, but she soon found them too depressing and too demoralising; whereas the people in England could laugh at the boasts of the nasal-toned traitor, she felt the claims of the Japanese had the ring of truth. She also stopped reading the newspapers because individual units were never mentioned; there were only references to 'British and Commonwealth troops', and such a blanket term did not interest her. She was solely concerned with hearing news of the Rocks.

She found herself ceaselessly worrying about Harris and often thinking the worst, so in order to obtain some peace of mind she threw herself wholeheartedly into her work with a passion that left her completely exhausted and with no desire to do anything except fall into bed and sleep until her next spell of duty. She likened herself to a nun who endlessly polishes the perfectly clean flagstones in her cell in order to shut out the outside world. In her case, however, the flagstones were the thousands of cups of tea she poured, and the countless sandwiches and hot samosas she handed out to the young soldiers in transit.

Her mother visited her twice in Delhi, and had been coldly indifferent when Avril voiced her concern for Harris. 'If he cares as much as you say he does, he'd surely have got in touch,' she had said, and strongly advised Avril to forget about him and start life afresh. 'He isn't the only pebble on the beach. Delhi is full of young men with excellent prospects who are too valuable to be sent

364

to the front. If you can't find anyone here, then come to Calcutta.'

Avril had been glad to see the back of her, and after a time she no longer bothered to telephone her in Calcutta, and when her mother rang *her* it was as much as she could do to listen for five minutes without hanging up.

Meanwhile at Imphal the British and Indian troops dug in on the six hundred square mile plain and waited for the Japanese onslaught. Among the defenders were the Rocks.

Harris and Wagstaff were manning a Bren-gun post on the outskirts of the town itself, listening to the sound of the approaching gunfire.

'What's the latest gen, Sarge?' asked Wagstaff.

'If Intelligence can be relied upon the Japs propose throwing three divisions at us in their main thrust, at the same time cutting off our lads further down the plain. I expect they'll employ the usual roadblock tactics. Judging from reports they aren't short of tanks and artillery. They'll do their utmost to stop any of our withdrawing troops from reaching us intact and staging a set battle piece.'

There was a steadfastness among the defenders which would have surprised the defeatists in Delhi. None of them was in the slightest doubt as to the importance of Imphal, standing three thousand feet high in the heart of the Manipur mountains, which acted as a wall between Burma and India. If it fell the road to India was wide open, but they were determined to hold it. The Imphal Plain would become the killing fields on which Japanese aspirations would die.

On the Eve of St Patrick's Day the enemy began their advance on Imphal and Kohima. The speed of their advance was phenomenal, and within five days they had closed in upon Imphal. But they paid a high price for the incursion into India, and more than a thousand corpses littered the ground.

At Imphal supplies and reinforcements continued to pour in by land and air until it more resembled an offensive springboard than a defensive fortress.

The Japanese swept up the plain and were greeted with a barrage from guns, tanks, machine guns, rifles and grenades,

and for the first time in the war in Burma the British had
air superiority: Spitfires, Hurribombers, and Blenheims shot
the enemy out of the sky, pulverised their lines of transport,
strafed bunkers, foxholes, gun positions and ammunition
dumps. But the Japanese continued to fight on, indifferent
to their mounting casualties, spurred by a desire for glorifi-
cation in death.

At Imphal Harris and Wagstaff fired so many rounds the
barrels of their Bren-guns needed frequent changing. The
ground outside their post was piled high with corpses, and
during the rare lulls in the fighting they were cremated with
flame throwers.

It was only when the wounded from Kohima were flown
into Imphal's airstrip that the Rocks heard of the desperate
plight of the garrison where 3,500 men were being besieged
by 15,000 Japanese.

During a break in the fighting Harris had been sent with
a small detachment of men to help with the unloading of
the wounded, and as the stretchers were carried from the
aircraft, asked a wounded sergeant how things were going
in Kohima.

'We were told to hold it to the last and we're doing just
that,' he answered proudly. 'If there's such a place as hell
it can't be any worse than Kohima. The Japs have set up
guns on the heights overlooking it and they've blown every
basha, bungalow and tree off the map. Water's so scarce the
RAF are dropping inner tubes filled with the stuff. Christ,
they're even fighting in the garden and tennis court of the
Deputy Commissioner's bungalow. Instead of tennis balls
they're lobbing grenades at each other and shooting over
open sights. You should have seen us! When the Japs held
the bungalow one of our tanks drove up to the front door
and pumped shells inside. Soon shifted the sods. But if
reinforcements don't arrive soon, they'll be wiped out.'

Harris returned to his own position and related what he
had heard to Wagstaff.

'Our turn next, Sarge. Well, we gotta put up as good
a show.'

The next day the Rocks were lined up to listen to Colonel
Selthorpe read aloud an Order of the Day by General

Mutaguchi which had been picked up on the battlefield and was addressed to the crack 33rd Division, the heroes of Sittang.

Colonel Selthorpe said, 'Thought you'd like to know just how lucky you are to be in the British army.' He cleared his throat and read the order: "The coming battle will decide the success or failure of the war in Asia. Regard death as something lighter than a feather, you soldiers must seize Imphal. You must expect that the division will be annihilated. Rewards and incentives must be given on the spot. A soldier who puts up a good show must be decorated, a man guilty of misconduct must be punished. In order to keep bright the honour of his Unit a Commander may have to use his sword as a weapon of execution, shameful though it may be to shed the blood of one's own soldiers on the battlefield and though the shirker may be worth no more than a horse's backside."

'All I can say is you'd better make sure they become more shit-scared of you than their own officers.'

He looked at the sea of grinning faces and added, 'I've no objection to the Japs killing each other, but I want you to promise me one thing: the General's expectation of total annihilation is granted.'

The men cheered themselves hoarse and prepared to do just that. The battle raged for week after week with neither side having any clear idea of who was gaining the upper hand.

Then came the welcome news that Kohima's valiant garrison which had held out for more than three weeks had been relieved, although the battle continued unabated.

At Imphal the men who had fought their way out of Burma eagerly awaited the men who had humiliated them. Revenge was about to be exacted.

The 33rd Division attacked with incredible ferocity, but as they emerged from the foothills they were greeted with a withering hail of tank and artillery fire which forced them to withdraw into deeply dug bunkers. Not a man remained above ground on the Imphal Plain. Dive bombers and artillery pounded them mercilessly until the time came for the infantry to move in for the kill.

367

The Rocks were always to the forefront with Selthorpe leading, a pistol in one hand, a cane in the other, as they fixed bayonets and stormed bunkers and foxholes. They matched the fanaticism of the enemy, losing many men but killing far more, spurred on not by the threat of execution from a samurai sword but the Colonel's swagger stick.

Harris and Wagstaff knocked out three 'woodpecker' nests with twenty-five pound charges attached to six-foot-long bamboo poles and were recommended for gallantry awards.

For days the battle raged, shrouded in what the militarists call 'the fog of war'. There were advances, withdrawals, successes and setbacks, and Imphal became known as the 'bloody plain'. Then the monsoon started and for every two steps forward the British and Empire infantry slipped one step backwards. Roads became muddy quagmires, streams swollen torrents, bomb and artillery craters treacherous water-filled death traps.

Although driven onto the defensive, the enemy asked and gave no quarter. Suicide squads volunteered for impossible tasks and died with oaths of loyalty on their lips.

The Rocks manhandled guns up precipitous ridges, forded flooded nullahs, and hacked their way through rain-drenched jungle, and when manpower failed they used captured elephants to free the tanks and transport from the mud.

In Delhi voices clamoured for the enemy to be driven from Indian soil, but Slim ignored them; he was more concerned with destroying the enemy and paving the way for the reconquest of Burma. It became a war of attrition in which lives meant more than territorial gains.

The Rocks fought through a landscape that resembled Flanders in 1918; the trees were leafless, charred skeletons or mutilated stumps, and the ground was strewn with the bodies of fifty thousand Japanese soldiers.

In December the drums boomed, the bugles blared and the flag of the 14th Army was proudly hoisted above the Imphal Plain.

Harris sensed that the end of the war in Burma was not far off, and it was this awareness that gave him and his comrades the tenacity and purpose to fight on in the appalling conditions. And as the British advanced he became aware that the number of Japanese they killed was far outweighed by the number who had died from disease. The roadsides were littered with wrecked transport all with skeletons inside, and even more on the ground outside, the flesh eaten away by white ants. Ironically many had perished with small ration bags of rice dangling from their necks; they had been so weakened by acute beri-beri they were unable to eat. But those who remained continued to fight with suicidal zest. It seemed as though the Japanese would have to be totally annihilated before victory was achieved.

Harris, together with a Naga tracker, was leading a group of men along a narrow path through a stretch of jungle he had been warned was mined and booby trapped. The headhunting Naga, clad only in a blanket and armed with an ancient shotgun, was one of the many hillmen who had volunteered to help the army. Despite floggings, torture, execution and the destruction of their villages, they refused to help the Japanese and remained steadfastly loyal to the British.

They collected information about enemy movements, laid ambushes and brought in the wounded, and they could read signs that were invisible to anyone else.

The tracker, who had no name and spoke no English, froze in his tracks and gestured to Harris to take cover.

Although he could see nothing suspicious, Harris signalled to his men and they melted into the undergrowth while the tracker slipped off his blanket and wriggled snakelike into the jungle on the lower side of the path.

He reappeared without sound or warning at Harris's side, and with a series of animated gestures and a violent pecking motion with his head and proddings at one of the Brens, he conveyed the message that there was a machine gun emplacement just ahead.

Harris signalled to his men to remain where they were and provide covering fire while he and Wagstaff followed the Naga. The three men made a circuitous route approach to the dug-out which was so well concealed Harris still could not see it when they were only ten yards away. The Naga pointed and Harris was just able to make out the entrance hole, no bigger than a manhole cover. They waited, hardly daring to breath, for fifteen minutes, but there was no sign of life.

'Just to make sure, Waggy, lob a grenade in.'

Wagstaff removed the pin from a grenade and tossed it underhand through the entrance. There was a muffled explosion and clouds of dust and smoke emerged from the emplacement, then three men appeared with their hands above their heads. Their heads were shaven, and they wore only loin cloths, exposing their emaciated bodies which were covered with fly-infested jungle sores.

Harris fired a short burst of Tommy-gun fire above their heads, then motioned to them to sit down with their hands folded on their heads. They sat there expressionless, like the legendary three monkeys.

'Take a look inside, Waggy.'

Wagstaff moved cautiously towards the entrance, his Thompson held hip high. There was a short report and he staggered, spun round, then fell as a rifle bullet tore through his shoulder. Harris reached for a grenade, ran forward and dropped it into the dug out, and as he did so he saw from the corner of his eye one of the seated men draw a grenade from his loin cloth. The Naga blew his chest out with the shotgun, but by some superhuman effort the man removed the pin and rolled the grenade along the ground.

The blast hurled Harris several feet into the air and he was vaguely aware of a fusillade of shots and the bodies of the two remaining soldiers sprouting blood as the bullets thudded into them.

He heard himself call out, 'You all right, Waggy?' before he lost consciousness.

The army surgeon looked down at the naked man lying on the operating theatre in the field hospital. 'He's lucky to be alive; missed everything vital. Must have half a pound of shrapnel in him. Whoever he is, the war's over for him.'

The blast from the grenade had torn off Harris's clothing

370

and identity disc, and as far as the surgeon was concerned he was about to operate on an unknown soldier.

The Sister holding the blood plasma said, 'He's Sergeant David Harris. The one outside waiting his turn is Private Wagstaff. They're good friends of mine.'

'In that case, Sister Bradshaw, we'll have to take doubly good care of them.'

The hospital was only four miles from the front line and the sound of battle was clearly audible.

It took the surgeon four hours to remove the bigger splinters; the smaller ones he left to be dealt with in a better equipped hospital or to work themselves out.

Wagstaff had also lost a lot of blood and needed a transfusion of several pints, but his wound, although bad, was only a flesh one; no bones had been shattered.

Stretcher bearers carried them to a large tent occupied by about twenty men, and there they were placed on adjoining camp beds. When they came to from the anaesthetic Kitty Bradshaw called to see them.

'You'll be flown out tomorrow,' she said cheerfully. 'If you ever meet General Slim, don't forget to thank him; but for him you wouldn't be here. He's the one who insisted on forward surgical teams being allowed into the battle zones.'

Harris croaked, 'How did you manage to join them?'

'Volunteered. It's the only way I could get to Rangoon and pick up where I left off. Now you'd better get some sleep. You could double for the invisible man with all those bandages.'

'How do I look?' he asked anxiously.

'A bit lumpy and bumpy all over, but what do you expect? You look like a poacher who's been peppered by the gamekeeper.'

'Is it permanent?'

'They're all tiny bits the surgeon didn't have time to take out. Most will work themselves out. You might end up with some small blue patches, but you can tell people you've worked down the pits. Thank your lucky stars you've still got your sight.'

'Maybe we can have a longer chat when I feel more up to it,' he said.

'Sorry, won't have a chance. We're working round the clock trying to cope with the casualties. Getting through forty ops a day and still not catching up. What time I have off I need for sleep. You'll be gone first thing in the morning.' She felt in one of her pockets and produced a sheet of paper. 'You'll be needing this.'

'What is it?'

'Avril's address in Delhi. We've kept in touch and she's driven me potty writing and saying how worried sick she is wondering where you are and what might have happened to you. Now you can tell her yourself.'

Harris said, 'Her mother told me she'd gone back to England. The wicked old bitch.'

'I think I can guess why, but it'll all have been in vain. She may have thought she was acting in Avril's best interest, but now I should imagine she's lost her for good.'

Harris said, 'I don't know how to thank you, Kitty. If I hadn't met you I'd never have known.'

'You can thank me by sending a slice of the cake. I'll put it under my pillow. Oh, I forget to mention it – Nellie is still with her, so take Wagstaff with you when you go to Delhi.'

The private who had been listening in silence, said, 'I dunno that I wanna get 'itched till the war's over. Wouldn' be fair to 'er.'

'The war *is* over as far as you two are concerned. You'll both need a spell of convalescence by which time the good old Union Jack will be flying over Government House in Rangoon.'

She kissed them gently, squeezed their hands and said, 'It really has been wonderful knowing you both. I'll never forget our trip together. Pity about the Silver though.'

'It's safely in a vault in Calcutta,' said Harris.

'Simmo and Zack can sleep peacefully after all then.'

Early next morning they were driven in a jeep to an airstrip which had been cut through the jungle, and there they were put aboard an Auster aircraft and flown to Imphal. Then they were transferred to a Dakota and flown to a general hospital in Ranchi.

Two weeks later they were sent on extended leave.

372

The senior medical officer said, 'Anywhere in particular you fancy? There are several splendid rest camps in the hills. The one in Bangalore takes a lot of beating.'

Harris said, 'Is Delhi included? My fiancée is there, sir.'

'Perfectly all right. Just see to it you pop in and see the MO from time to time. And be careful when you're drying after a bath. You'll find you'll keep pulling bits of shrapnel out.'

It required a great effort of will for Harris not to write to Avril, but he had convinced himself that she had gone so long without news that another couple of weeks would make no difference.

He and Wagstaff flew into Delhi in a Dakota returning empty from a supply run, and from the airport were driven to the rest camp. Their reception was in marked contrast to their last visit. They were welcomed and treated royally; their distinctive slouch hats and dagger insignia of the 14th Army, along with the medal ribbons on their tunics, were an open sesame to everything.

Three days later they were allowed into town and took a rickshaw taxi to the address Kitty had provided.

Harris pressed hard on the doorbell, but there was no answer. A white woman appeared at the door of the adjoining bungalow. 'I'm afraid you'll hang around all day before you get an answer. Miss Carfax and the princess are at the station. There's a war on, you know. All hands to the pumps. Main line platform. Can't miss them.'

They shouldered their way along the crowded platform, muttering 'pardon' and 'excuse me' until they caught sight of Avril and Nellie standing beside a refreshment trolley surrounded by soldiers in transit.

Harris bent low and moved slowly until he stood beside her. 'One tea, milk and lots of sugar,' he said.

The two couples were married by special licence at St James's Church, not far from the Willingdon. It was the nearest they could get to a soldier's church and its origin was in keeping with their own deeply held feelings. When James Skinner, born of a Scottish father and Rajput mother, lay gravely wounded on the battlefield, he promised that if his life was spared he would build a church in thanksgiving. Skinner, who raised the famous cavalry regiment that bore his name, kept his word.

There, surrounded by faded battle honours and below the cross and orb which still bore the bullet marks of the 1857 Mutiny, Avril became Mrs Harris and Nellie Mrs Wagstaff. They wore rings the two soldiers had purchased from a roadside goldsmith in Chandi Chowk, the busiest and most bustling street in the city.

Mrs Carfax travelled up from Calcutta, and although she still strongly disapproved of her daughter's choice knew when she was beaten and put on as bold a face as possible in the circumstances.

Her late husband's estate had been settled, as much as it could be, and Avril had been well looked after, another factor that made Mrs Carfax realise she would get nowhere by bullying or threatening in a last desperate attempt to make Avril realise the folly of her ways. But she did not stay long at the private lunch at the Willingdon. She still felt ill at ease sitting at the same table as Nellie who, she could never forget, had been a former servant. But she had the good grace to give Avril a beautiful ruby bracelet, 'for both of you', and present Wagstaff with a Dunhill pipe in a velvet-lined leather case, confusing his smoking habits with those of her son-in-law.

She could not wait to get back to Calcutta where she had become entrenched in a way of life that was much like the one she had enjoyed in Burma.

Postscript

When Rangoon was liberated, Kitty Bradshaw asked for permission to leave the Indian Military Nursing Service and return to her old job. She met and married a doctor who had spent the war years in a Rangoon POW camp and resigned to help him run a clinic for the war orphaned native children of the city.

Mrs Carfax also returned to sort out the question of compensation for the goods and property her husband had lost. Balmoral, she was delighted to find, was virtually untouched and much as it was when last she saw it. A fair amount of renovation and refurnishing was needed, but there was little to show that it had ever served as a brothel for high-ranking Japanese officers. Even more astonishing, the old servants who had survived appeared as if from nowhere to offer their services. But far more gratifying than their loyalty was their ability to pinpoint the exact spot where burra sahib Carfax had buried so many valuable things. Her contact with Avril was limited to Christmas and birthday cards.

Nellie's dream of being a soldier's missus was shortlived. Soon after her marriage, Wagstaff was invalided out with a disability and long service pension, as was Harris.

Three months after the atom bombs devastated Nagasaki and Hiroshima, bringing the war in the Far East to an end, the four of them travelled home to England on a P & O liner, hastily restored to peacetime comfort after many years of trooping.

Wagstaff visited his parents who now lived in a splendid

detached house in Burgess Hill. The war had been very kind to Wagstaff senior. The 'black market' had enabled him to demonstrate an enterprise and initiative which peacetime had denied him. His ill-gotten gains from forged clothing coupons and ration books, and under-the-counter luxury goods, had enabled him to invest wisely in further shops – more up-market than the original oil shop – and a garage purchased with the cash obtained from petrol coupons and fuel siphoned from the tanks of army vehicles by men who needed to supplement their pay.

Wagstaff was not in the least offended by his father's new-found wealth, and happily agreed to share and help enlarge it. It was a far more acceptable way of life than the one he had so happily deserted when still in his teens.

Nellie let it be known to their neighbours that she much preferred being addressed as Princess rather than Mrs Wagstaff.

Harris and Avril bought the tenancy of a wisteria-covered coaching inn with six bedrooms, a real skittle alley and three acres of land in the heart of Dorset's Hardy country. It had the appealing name 'The Last Order'. There Avril milked two cows, fed the chickens, renewed her interest in golf and tennis, and bore the first of her four children. Harris served behind the bar of the public house, explaining away the blue marks that pitted his face as the after effects of a kiss from his mother-in-law.

He became a mainstay of the local British Legion, was elected to the Parish Council, and devoted much of his spare time to the needs of ex-servicemen and war widows. Once a year he went to the Albert Hall for the Burma reunion, where he teamed up with Wagstaff and joined Vera Lynn in singing old favourites before enjoying a monumental binge during which he and Wagstaff toasted the Rocks and old comrades here and departed.

The body of Private Simmonds was exhumed and reburied in the war cemetery at Kohima where a monument was erected to the 'forgotten army' bearing the words:

For your tomorrow they gave their today

Colonel Selthorpe died of wounds received in a jungle ambush and was buried in a grave that, like so many others in Burma, was quickly reclaimed by the jungle and never traced. But, like Simmonds, he was in good company.

At the last stroke of midnight on 14th August 1947, the Union Jack was lowered on the ramparts of the Red Fort in Delhi and the flag of independent India hoisted. At the same time, Pakistan came into being. In the Hindu-Muslim-Sikh feuds that followed, more died in the mass pilgrimages to the land of their choice than had on the battlefields of the Middle East and Burma. A year later Gandhi, the architect of Independence, was assassinated by a Hindu fanatic.

At Port Said where East meets West, the British returning 'home' covered the sea with a bobbing, wave-lapped sargasso of topees, a token gesture marking the end of a hundred and sixty-three years of the Raj.

The Silver was transferred to the home garrison where it remained until defence cuts were introduced and the Rocks ceased to exist as a regiment of the British army. Some of it was auctioned and purchased by freshly formed regiments and collectors of military memorabilia, other items ended up in the silver vaults in Chancery Lane or in the country mansions of a new breed of squire the war had spawned.

Japan rose Phoenix-like from the ashes of the A-bombs to become the most properous nation in the world, the yen achieving what the sword had failed to do.

377

You have been reading a novel published by Piatkus Books. We hope you have enjoyed it and that you would like to read more of our titles. Please ask for them in your local library or bookshop.

If you would like to be put on our mailing list to receive details of new publications, please send a large stamped addressed envelope (UK only) to:

Piatkus Books, 5 Windmill Street
London W1P 1HF

PIATKUS

The sign of a good book